DEREK LANDY

UNTIL THE END

HarperCollins *Children's Books*

First published in the United Kingdom by
HarperCollins *Children's Books* in 2022
HarperCollins *Children's Books* is a division of HarperCollins*Publishers* Ltd
1 London Bridge Street
London SE1 9GF

www.harpercollins.co.uk

HarperCollins*Publishers*
1st Floor, Watermarque Building, Ringsend Road
Dublin 4, Ireland

1

HB ISBN 978–0–00–838635–1
LIMITED EDITION HB ISBN 978–0–00–853317–5
ANZ TPB ISBN 978-0-00-838637-5
EXP TPB ISBN 978-0-00-838636-8

Derek Landy asserts the moral right to be
identified as the author of the work.

A CIP catalogue record for this title is
available from the British Library.

Typeset in Baskerville MT 11/13.5 pt by
Palimpsest Book Production Ltd, Falkirk, Stirlingshire

Printed and bound in the UK using 100% renewable electricity at
CPI Group (UK) Ltd

MIX
Paper from
responsible sources
FSC™ C007454
FSC
www.fsc.org

This book is produced from independently certified FSC™ paper
to ensure responsible forest management.

For more information visit: www.harpercollins.co.uk/green

UNTIL THE END

*This book is dedicated to Iron Man.
Tony Stark stopped Thanos and saved us all and I,
for one, will never forget the sacrifice he made.
Also to Natasha Romanoff for yeeting herself off that cliff.*

"Welcome," she said.

The Faceless Ones were in her soul.

She felt them, an entire race of them. Hundreds of thousands? Millions? Billions? More? She had no way of knowing. The only thing she knew without question was that there were multitudes squirming and writhing within the essence of who she was. They flitted to her light, to her aura, like moths, and when they were ready they left her soul and emerged, intangible to the touch, invisible to the mortal eye. They stood on the horizons and they waited until it was time to become solid.

They were her children, and they were going to reshape the world.

1

Getting punched through a building at sixteen was new and fun and actually pretty cool. Getting punched through a building at twenty-six was annoying, frustrating, and, when she really thought about it, kind of rude.

Valkyrie picked herself up, bits of broken masonry falling from her shoulders, clouds of dust blossoming and swirling on the breeze that came through the ruined structure. She pulled the skull mask off her face and it flowed into the hood, and she pulled that down and shook out her hair. The sorcerer hovered in the night sky above her, his arms folded, waiting for her to look up. Instead, she walked over to a piece of the collapsed roof, and sat.

She crossed her legs. Took out her phone.

The sorcerer drifted down a little, trying to catch her eye without making it look obvious. Finally, he said, "What's happening?"

"I'm not fighting you," Valkyrie said.

"So you surrender?"

"Nope. Just not fighting you."

"Why not?" he asked.

Her thumbs danced over the screen, replying to a message. "Because fighting is dumb," she said, and sent it off.

He drifted down lower. "What do you mean?"

She looked at him now. His hair was long and brown and he had a little beard, and he wore colourful robes with intricate designs. His name was Mansel, or Mantle, or Barney or something.

"Is this really the best way to resolve a problem? By punching the person you're arguing with? Being powerful doesn't make you right."

"Being powerful means you don't have to be right," Barney said, smiling with evil intent. Or just regular intent. Valkyrie couldn't be sure. She had a lot going on these days.

Headlights swooped in as a car approached. Most people would run from a battle that had already demolished two houses in this construction site. It took a certain kind of person to drive towards it – a certain kind of person driving a certain kind of car. The 1924 Rolls Royce Phantom 1 pulled up to the kerb, and Skulduggery Pleasant got out.

His three-piece suit was dark blue tonight, with matching hat, and his skull reflected the orange streetlamp. It was October but Dublin was still warm. Ignoring the front door, which had miraculously survived the battle, Skulduggery stepped through a massive hole in the wall and made his way over.

"Have you surrendered yet?" he asked Barney, checking the time on his pocket watch. His head tilted in annoyance, and he started winding the crown.

"I'm not the one surrendering," Barney said. "I'm winning this."

"You're not, though," said Valkyrie.

"You're really not," said Skulduggery.

"I've thrown her through two buildings," Barney said with a hint, a smidge, a *soupçon* of exasperation in his voice.

"No," Valkyrie corrected. "You've only thrown me through *one* building. I bounced off the second."

"My point is," Barney continued, "I am too powerful to be stopped by the likes of you."

Valkyrie raised an eyebrow.

Skulduggery lifted off the ground slowly, the dust whirling beneath him. "You're too powerful for us?" he said. "Too powerful

6

for me? A man who was murdered and came back to something resembling life? A man who has saved the world from gods and monsters and the wickedest of the wicked? Too powerful for her? The woman who has gone toe to toe with Mevolent himself? The woman whose bad mood turned into a god that was a moment away from killing everyone on the face of the planet? The woman who, as we speak, commands thousands of Faceless Ones that stand – invisible to mortals – over every major city in every major country? *You* are too powerful for *us*?"

Barney hovered in the air. "She doesn't command them," he said quietly.

"What? What was that?"

"She doesn't command the Faceless Ones," he said, louder this time. "She brought them here, yeah, fair enough, but she's not, like, in charge of them or anything."

Valkyrie swiped through her social-media feed. "I'm the Child and the Mother," she muttered.

She felt Barney's gaze swing back to her. "What?"

"It's what they call me," she said. "I'm the Child of the Faceless Ones because I'm descended from them, but I'm also their Mother because I'm the conduit through which they must travel to this dimension." She put her phone away and looked up. "The Child and the Mother. See? Which means they do what I tell them."

Barney licked his lips. "Why are you doing this? Why did you come after me? I didn't do anything to you."

"You tried to steal some very powerful weapons for your own destructive purposes, and you killed three mortals doing it."

"So?" Barney responded. "I thought you were, you know..."

"What?"

"I thought you were on our side," Barney said. "I know you were a what-do'ye-call-it detective, an Arbiter, but haven't you changed? Like you said, you're working with the Faceless Ones now. You're a bad guy. What do you care if the rest of us kill a few people?"

Valkyrie sighed. "I'm not a bad guy, you idiot. My horizons

may have been broadened recently, but I'm still me. I'm still an Arbiter, and part of our job is to bring in murderers like you."

"Why, though?"

"Because murder is, like, totally wrong," she said. Sarcastically.

"But you brought the Faceless Ones back!" Barney exclaimed, really not getting it. "The mortals don't know they're here right now, but sooner or later they'll be able to see them and then..." Barney looked like he was running out of words, so he waved his arms around. "They'll kill them! The Faceless Ones will kill them! So, if they're going to die anyway, why amn't I allowed to start off by killing a few myself?"

"Barney, I don't think you're grasping the fundamentals here."

"Who the hell is Barney?"

"The Faceless Ones are love and light and peace and happiness, and, if they have to kill some people, it'll be for a very good reason, and those deaths will have meaning. But you're just a dude with a little beard who got a power boost along with the rest of the sorcerers and now thinks he's a big deal. You're not a big deal, Barney."

"Seriously, who is this Barney person?"

"Are you going to come quietly," Valkyrie said, "or will I have to continue beating you up?"

Barney sneered. "You'll need an army to stop me."

Skulduggery had drifted in behind him by that point, and snaked an arm round his throat. He applied the choke before Barney knew what was happening. Barney struggled and flailed. He tried using magic, but he was panicking too much. He went red, then purple, and finally went unconscious. He fell, but Skulduggery used the air to catch him and hold him upside down. All the change fell out of his pockets.

"I'll find him a nice cell in Roarhaven," Skulduggery said. "You may as well go home and feed your dog."

"Yeah," said Valkyrie, letting that go without comment. "See you tomorrow."

She flew to her bike, put on her helmet, and eased out on to the road. She would have loved to go home and be greeted by her dog, by the excited patter of doggy feet and that dopey grin, but Xena didn't live with her any more. That was one of the side effects of her new status as the Child and the Mother: animals didn't like being in her presence. Not even Xena, the most loyal German shepherd to ever stride this Earth. Valkyrie missed her terribly, of course, and her heart physically ached whenever she thought about what she'd had to give up – so she tried not to think about it. Besides, Xena seemed happy enough to be with Militsa.

Valkyrie found herself on familiar streets. Glad of the distraction, she pulled up outside the site that used to house the old Waxworks Museum and, below that, the Sanctuary. It was a hotel now. She thought of the museum itself and the dark halls of musty, cobwebbed celebrities. She thought of the wax figure of Phil Lynott that stood at the secret entrance, given a kind of life through magic, and for the first time wondered if that had been sacrilege, of a sort. This had been a real person, a talented man beset by his own demons, and they'd used his likeness to check passwords and open doors.

It was odd the things that occurred to her now that they had passed. Despite what she had insisted at the time, despite what Skulduggery had said, perhaps plunging into danger at twelve years old had, in fact, been astonishingly reckless and incredibly stupid.

Valkyrie sat on her bike and thought of the Elders, of Meritorious and Crow and even Tome. She thought of Nefarian Serpine finding the Sceptre of the Ancients, charging it with his magic, then accidentally using it to destroy the Book of Names. She thought of how the Sceptre had exploded when Skulduggery used it. She remembered Serpine trying to keep himself together when the black lightning struck him. She remembered how he crumbled to dust.

Something flashed into her head, a memory or a thought, and it seemed hugely important in that instant, but it moved too quickly for her to latch on to. The more she tried to pin it down, the further it scrambled, until Valkyrie couldn't even be certain it had been there in the first place. She shrugged. If it was important, it'd come back to her. Probably.

She put her helmet back on, started the bike, and joined the easy flow of traffic.

A few years after Serpine's death, Valkyrie herself had replaced the broken crystal – hirranian, the scientists now called it, or katahedral, to use its traditional name, capable of absorbing the souls of those it destroyed to add to its strength – and used it to kill two of the Faceless Ones who'd come through at Aranmore Farm.

She shook her head as she rode. She hated remembering this. Now that she understood what they truly were, she hated remembering the fact that she'd been responsible for the deaths of some of them. To get her mind off the oncoming wave of guilt and shame, Valkyrie focused on the last time she'd seen that black lightning, when the new Sceptre had exploded in her hand just five months ago. She'd been lucky it hadn't killed Skulduggery. She'd been lucky it hadn't killed *her*, come to that. The only explanation she could come up with as to how she'd survived was that the universe, in all its wisdom, had needed her alive.

But of course it needed her alive. Within an hour of the new Sceptre exploding, she had thrown herself into the path of Creed's Activation Wave and had become the Child and the Mother of the Faceless Ones.

Proof, Valkyrie reckoned, that this was always meant to be.

She stopped at the traffic lights in Drumcondra and put her foot on the road, the engine idling. She was alone here, at the lights. No cars around. Someone was out walking their dog. The dog barked its little head off at something its owner couldn't see, but Valkyrie could. At first, Valkyrie had been the only human

10

who could see the Faceless Ones standing over the cities of the world, but now all sorcerers had acclimatised to their presence – and soon the mortals would be able to see them, too. And there were plenty more to come, plenty more to emerge from Valkyrie's soul and take their place in the world. She knew each of their names, or at least a pronounceable, shortened version. Cyarrnaroh's full name was over eight hundred letters long, and Dhahun'garun's name involved half an alphabet that no one with ears had ever heard. This one, the one towering over Dublin like a mountain of flesh and claws, folds and tentacles, bore the name Khrthauk, and it was beautiful.

Valkyrie smiled up at it, and then the lights changed, and she rode on, towards home.

2

China woke from another bad dream and someone was standing over her.

A twist, a roll, throwing sheets aside, and China dived on the intruder and passed straight through, clutching nothing but air. She turned, the sigils on her palms burning and ready to release twin streams of energy, and the image of the old woman chuckled in the dark.

"Oh, Mother," said Solace, "you do amuse me."

Heart rate lowering, adrenaline calming, China straightened.

"Solace, my dear," she said, "it is so good to see you again. One of these days, we simply must do this in person."

"So you can kill me?" Solace asked. "Or, more likely, have me killed? I know how you loathe to get your hands dirty."

"Oh, I think you'll find I'm not averse to spilling a little blood if the situation calls for it." China passed through her daughter's psychic projection, picked the jug off the bedside table and poured herself a tumbler of water. "What can I do for you tonight?" she asked, before taking a sip.

"I'm here with a warning."

"Oh, good, I do so adore those."

Solace smiled. "I understand how busy you are in the resistance, struggling against Damocles Creed and all those people who so rudely helped usurp you as Supreme Mage, and it is

12

endlessly entertaining watching you and your friends flail under the unstoppable Wheel of Fate, but I'm afraid all things must come to an end – you, especially."

"Pray continue."

Solace's smile hardened. "I don't like this attitude of yours, Mother. It is almost disrespectful. Do I really have to hurt you again? Is that what it's come to?"

China took another sip and placed the tumbler back on the bedside table. "Aren't you bored of that by now?"

"Ah, but I will never get bored of hurting you. Just as I will never get bored of tormenting you with knowledge of the horrors to come. Your world, such as it is, is soon to come crashing down. Tell me, Mother – what do you remember of the Shalgoth from your days as a worshipper of the Faceless Ones?"

"Monsters," said China, "sent by the Faceless Ones to hunt down the Ancients when they first rebelled. The Shalgoth themselves staged a rebellion and the Faceless Ones imprisoned them deep within the Earth."

"Where they have been stirring for millennia," Solace said, "only too anxious to atone for their sins."

"And you are here to tell me that the Faceless Ones are about to give them that chance?"

"They're waiting for the signal to attack. I can feel it. Their thoughts are unfathomable, alien to me, but I can sense their intention as clearly as I can see you before me. You and your little resistance friends think that Creed is the problem, or Obsidian, but things are far worse than you can possibly... You're smiling, Mother. Why are you smiling when you know I'll hurt you for it?"

"Because, my darling daughter, you seem to have forgotten who it is you're dealing with," said China, and tapped the wall. Sigils lit up all around them and Solace gasped, hands going to her head.

"Pay attention, dear," China said. "Next time you want to draw somebody's attention away from your true goals, try not to be so obvious about it."

13

"The Shalgoth will rip you apart," Solace snarled.

"Oh, come now. You said it yourself: you don't care about the Faceless Ones or the monsters beneath our feet. You're here to deliver a warning, are you? Since when do you deliver warnings? Threats, promises of pain, absolutely – but warnings? No. You just want to distract me from investigating the Hosts, don't you? So the rumours must be true. I have to admit, I only half believed them, but now that I know that's what you're scared of, well... my interest is piqued."

Solace glared at her until the sigils pulsed again and the pain became too much. Her image blinked out.

3

"You're going to be late for breakfast," said Gerontius, and left the room still fiddling with his tie. Omen turned over in bed to lie on his stomach. He tried settling down, then flipped the pillow to the cool side and tried again. His eyes stung, and he was so tired after a night plagued by bad dreams, but he knew he wasn't going to get back to sleep. Groaning to the empty room, he turned over again, and his thoughts drifted into nonsense for a moment before he checked the time, and jackknifed out of bed.

He'd fallen asleep. How the hell had he fallen asleep? He'd had his eyes closed for a moment, just a tiny little moment, but that moment had gone on for half an hour and now he was late for morning assembly and he was still struggling to put his trousers on.

Omen brushed his teeth, did his best to tame his hair, checked his face for spots (there were some new ones – yay), pulled on his shirt and blazer, stuffed his feet into his shoes, grabbed his tie and his phone and ran. As he ran, he put his tie on. It was not done well.

Footsteps echoing in the corridor, he sprinted to his locker, grabbed his bag, wheeled round to run on, and froze. Principal Duenna was looking at him.

"Hmm," she said.

Omen didn't know what to do. "I'm late," he said.

"Quite," said Duenna. "Mr Darkly, we haven't had a chance

to chat since the new term started. How are you coping with the loss of your brother?"

Omen blinked at her. "He's not lost."

Duenna smiled and inclined her head. "I'm sorry?"

He cleared the croakiness from his throat. "My brother isn't lost," he said.

"I see. Do you know where he is?"

"No," Omen admitted.

"Do your parents know where he is? Do the authorities?"

"No."

"Then that would appear to be the very definition of the word lost, would it not?"

"Not really, miss. Not so long as he knows where he is."

Duenna observed him. "Yes," she said. "I've given the teaching staff strict instructions regarding you, Mr Darkly. You have obviously been through a great deal, and your teachers will be looking out for you. We can't let your studies lapse, now can we?"

"I suppose not."

Duenna took a small step forward. "We're keeping an eye on you, Omen. We all are. Everyone's very concerned. Your behaviour last term was far from exemplary. Why, there were even calls to have you arrested. Arrested! A Corrival student arrested." She shivered. "Perish the very thought!"

Omen nodded, but said nothing.

"Some of the parents are worried," Duenna continued. "They've requested that you be removed from your classes. They worry that you invite trouble. That you're a bad influence."

Omen said, "I'm not trying to—" but Duenna held up a finger.

"Don't interrupt me, Mr Darkly."

"Right," he said. "Sorry."

"They've been saying awful, disparaging things about you and your parents, and your upbringing – and especially about your brother." She shook her head. "Terrible, what's happened to him. Just terrible. To go from being the Chosen One to being...

16

that thing. Obsidian. It must be awful. Some people are calling him a monster, you know. In some respects, it's almost a kindness that he no longer comprehends what's happening to him. To go from hero to villain is something I doubt he could handle."

"He's not a villain," Omen said before he could stop himself. "And we don't know what he can or cannot comprehend. We don't know *anything* about his condition."

"You sound angry, Omen. I understand that this is a difficult time, and that you're under a lot of pressure, but I'm afraid I can't allow you to take that tone with a member of staff."

He swallowed. "I'm sorry."

Duenna looked at him, and thought for a moment. "There are some members of our faculty who didn't believe you should have been let back into the Academy," she said. "You and your friends were, of course, involved in violence on school grounds. It was all very disturbing. Teachers, Omen – *teachers* – were calling me, demanding that you be expelled, demanding that the City Guard arrest you. The crimes they accused you of... Terrible things. They said you were guilty of blasphemy, Omen – of working against the Faceless Ones. There were some who accused you of treason against Roarhaven – but, of course, that wasn't an actual crime when you committed it. Luckily for you. But our Supreme Mage decided in his mercy and benevolence that you should not be punished for your many, many transgressions. It was his decision that we keep you safe, and keep you close. And who are we to argue with Arch-Canon Creed?"

Omen kept his mouth firmly shut.

"But you are a challenge, Mr Darkly. You present, to me, a problem. Perspicacious Rubic, my predecessor in this role of principal, left to become Ireland's Grand Mage, and he now sits on the Council of Advisors to the Supreme Mage himself. What higher calling could there be than to advise as great a man as the Supreme Mage? Once I have turned Corrival Academy into the beacon of enlightenment I know it can be, who knows the heights to which I could ascend? My point, Mr Darkly, is that I am fully invested in the education and well-being of each and every one of my students because their success is my success. We all share the glory. Isn't that a wonderful thing? The inverse is, of course, also true. Their failures are my failures. Decisions you make and actions you take that reflect poorly on you also reflect poorly on me. My track record is exemplary. I plan on maintaining that."

She looked him in the eyes and he held her gaze until it became awkward, and he looked away. "What do you know about how this school was built?"

"I know a bit," he said. "Erskine Ravel got Creyfon Signate to design the whole city so that it could be superimposed over the old town of Roarhaven."

"So you have been paying attention in class," said Duenna. "What you won't have been taught is how Supreme Mage Creed got involved."

"He got Mr Signate to alter his designs," Omen said, and enjoyed seeing the surprise on Duenna's face. "He made him use the streets and buildings to form sigils so that he could send out his Activation Wave."

Duenna's eyebrow rose a fraction. "Of course. Of course you know that. How silly of me. Yes, the Supreme Mage explained to Creyfon Signate what he needed him to do."

"He threatened him."

"The Supreme Mage doesn't threaten people, Mr Darkly."

"He threatened Mr Signate," Omen said. "Threatened his wife."

"Don't be absurd."

"It's not absurd. Mr Signate told me himself."

"Creyfon Signate told you himself, did he?"

"Yes. Right before he was murdered."

"This is no time for dramatics, Mr Darkly."

"I'm not—"

"Be quiet!" Duenna snapped.

Omen shut up.

18

The principal composed herself, and continued with a slight smile as if nothing had happened. "The Supreme Mage added his own details to various buildings in Roarhaven – this school being one. He foresaw obstacles to his great work. He foresaw people like the so-called resistance, the terrorists. He foresaw attacks, assassinations, attempted coups – and he planned accordingly. There is a level below ground, Mr Darkly, that contains what can be charitably described as 'holding spaces'."

Omen frowned. "Cells?"

"This is just a warning," said Duenna. "For a student with your family history, not to mention your own history of associating with known killers and criminals, the utmost care must be taken. Any detention you get will, therefore, be spent in a holding space. Do you understand?"

"Yes, Principal Duenna."

She smiled. "Good. If there is anything I can do for you, Omen, any way that I could possibly help you with your current circumstances, do not hesitate to contact my secretary. Now run along – assembly has already begun."

Omen turned, walked quickly into the assembly hall, ignoring the glare from Vice-Principal Noble. Filament Sclavi stepped into his path, holding out a smooth black bracelet.

"Here you go," he said, all smiles.

Omen frowned, noting that everyone else seemed to be wearing them. "What's it for?"

"You," Filament said unhelpfully. "You have to put it on before you can line up, I'm afraid."

The bracelet was a black circle of what looked like cheap plastic. Omen slipped it on and it hung loosely from his wrist, and Filament stood aside, allowing Omen to take his usual place beside Never. Never was not looking impressed at having to wear an accessory they had not personally picked out.

Duenna walked onstage, gave three quick claps and the assembly hall went quiet. "Do you all have them on?" she said,

19

her voice loud in the silence. "Everyone? Raise your hands so the prefects can check."

Hands went up. Omen and Never shared a look, and reluctantly did likewise. The prefects marched up each row, and when they got to the top they called out, "Aye!"

"Excellent," said Duenna, and took a slim piece of that same black plastic from her jacket. She tapped it twice and the students' bracelets tightened and clicked. Omen didn't like that: it felt way too much like handcuffs.

"You may be wondering why you have each been given a stylish piece of school-approved jewellery," Duenna said, briefly wearing something that resembled a smile. "You may also be wondering if this means our uniform policy has been relaxed. It has not. The bracelets you now all wear round your wrists cannot be removed, and they are for your own protection."

Omen frowned amid the mumblings and mutterings, and tried to open the bracelet. He couldn't even detect a seam.

"In these uncertain times, precautions need to be taken. There have always been limits on the types of magic students are allowed to wield on school grounds, but to that list we are adding Teleportation."

Omen glanced at Never, saw them stiffen.

"Teleportation without supervision is simply too dangerous and too unpredictable – as such, these bracelets have been fitted with Restriction Sigils."

Duenna pressed the remote control in her hand, and every bracelet chirped lightly as a sigil flashed up on its surface.

"You can't do that," someone said, and the hall echoed with shouts of outrage.

Duenna clapped three times again, but the outrage continued. Another three claps, accompanied now by a look of absolute fury, and the shouting gradually reduced to mere mutterings.

"We can indeed do exactly '*that*'," Duenna said. "Your parents or guardians were each contacted by a member of the Committee of Well-being, set up as a joint venture between Corrival Academy and the Church of the Faceless. Each of them acquiesced. I understand that some of you may have bought into the idea of teenage rebellion so I shall overlook that outburst this one and only time – but believe me when I say that the grown-ups know what's best for you. Any further disruption will result in immediate detention. Does anyone want to test me on that?"

She watched them all, alert for any further signs of discontent.

"Binding another sorcerer's magic is illegal," one of Omen's fellow Sixth Years said, unable to help herself. "It's written into the Roarhaven Constitution!"

Duenna pointed. "Detention," she said. Two prefects marched forward, grabbed the Sixth Year's arms, and escorted her out of the hall.

When the doors had swung shut behind them, Duenna continued. "The Restriction Sigils do not bind your magic," she said. "They merely scramble the signals that go to your brain."

The atmosphere in the hall grew heavy with words unsaid.

"It's all very non-invasive," Duenna continued. "Let me assure you, your well-being is our top priority. We live in a dangerous world where not everyone can agree on the wisest course of action. But the staff here at Corrival Academy, and the High Sanctuary of the City of Roarhaven, have faith on our side, and the knowledge that what we are doing is good and just and right. Trust in us, children, and we will guide you to the new world." She smiled.

"This," Never whispered, "can only end badly."

4

Valkyrie didn't need to sleep that much lately, so she lay in bed, looking at the ceiling. Whenever a flutter of anxiety rose from her belly to her chest, she glanced through the open curtains, towards Dublin. Even at this distance, thirty kilometres away, she was unable to see Khrthauk's head, though in the moonlight she could see the tendrils that swayed from the underside of his jaw. Every time she saw him, she relaxed, and smiled, and felt herself flooded with love.

She watched the lights of a distant plane disappear behind his immense mass, and wondered if those passengers could feel, in some way, that they were passing through the incorporeal body of a god. Were the hairs standing up on the backs of their necks? Did they suddenly feel as if they were being watched? Were they suddenly nauseous, or paranoid, or were they struck with migraines or thoughts of violence and chaos? Were arguments breaking out on that plane, even now? Were old grievances reigniting?

The effects the Faceless Ones had on mortals were known to be unsettling, and that was deeply, deeply unfortunate, but once the truth came out the world would be a better place. Valkyrie believed that with every single part of who she was.

When morning came, she took the M50 past Dublin, overtook a few tractors on quiet country roads, and rode by half a dozen signs advising her to turn round and try another route. The old man in the tired old shack nodded to her as she navigated the potholes on the dirt road that seemed to lead to nowhere. Beyond him, she rode through the cloaking bubble and the city of Roarhaven appeared before her like a flower opening its petals. The Cleavers standing at Shudder's Gate watched her as they watched everyone, and she continued on, through Oldtown and into the Circle Zone, where she took the ramp down to the car park underneath the High Sanctuary.

Her phone beeped as she hung her helmet off the bike's handlebars. She read the message, activated the necronaut suit to protect her clothes while she flew, and took off. Leaving a trail of energy behind her, she followed the ramp back outside and blazed across the city, meeting Skulduggery at the crime scene.

The apartment was open and airy. Lots of light. The armchair was turned over on its side and there were pieces of broken sculptures across the floor. A framed painting – a summer's evening, on the docks – had been dislodged. It slumped against the wall at an angle, like an old man needing a rest.

"This is where Mr Accrue died?" Valkyrie asked.

The woman, a large woman with magnificent bone structure and red shoes, nodded. "Right where you're standing," she said.

"Where I'm standing right now? Literally where I'm standing?"

"Literally."

Valkyrie reached out with her thoughts, but couldn't find any hint of trauma in the space around her. There was, however, an absence of trauma – or the absence of anything, really, as if the space had been scrubbed clean before her arrival.

"Tell me about him," Valkyrie said.

The woman took a breath and let it out with a shrug. "He was a nice man, I suppose. He paid his rent on time. He didn't make any trouble. He never bothered the other tenants. Don't you want to know about the thing that killed him?"

"We know about the thing that killed him," Skulduggery said, emerging from the room behind her. He had a book in his hands, leatherbound and thick, that he placed on the side table as he passed. "Approximately six foot tall, by all appearances male, with pitch-black, rock-hard skin."

"Obsidian," said the woman. "They're calling him Obsidian. They worship him, you know."

Valkyrie frowned. "Who does?"

"The fanatics. I've seen them at night, going around in groups, telling people that the end is nigh, all that kind of malarkey. I mean, people have been saying that the end is nigh for centuries, so I don't put much stock in it myself, but even so..."

"When you heard the victim shouting," Valkyrie said, "what did you do?"

"I grabbed my keys and ran up the stairs and let myself in."

"You ran towards the sound of danger?"

"I... I suppose I did."

"That's very brave of you," said Valkyrie.

The woman shrugged.

"And when you entered the apartment," said Skulduggery, "what did you see?"

"I saw Mr Accrue backing away from him. From Obsidian. Mr Accrue was knocking things over, throwing things..."

"What was Obsidian doing?"

"He just walked towards him. One of the pieces of art there, the sculpture, it hit him, hit Obsidian, right in the face and he didn't even flinch. Then he reached out, just with a fingertip, and touched Mr Accrue's chest, and he... I don't know how to describe it. I've seen people disappear before – my husband, rest his soul, was a Teleporter – but this wasn't like that. Mr Accrue kind of..." She frowned, searching for the words. "The space swallowed him."

"The books in his bedroom," Skulduggery said, not giving the woman time to lapse into the numbing shock she was clearly circling, "indicate that Mr Accrue was a worshipper of the Faceless Ones."

The woman nodded. "Yes, indeed."

"Would you say he was devout?"

"Oh, I would, I would. He was a good man." She smiled nervously at Valkyrie. "A good, kind-hearted, devout man."

Valkyrie smiled back. "That's good to hear. So at least, in his dying moments, he was comforted by his faith."

"Did he pray?" Skulduggery asked, pulling the woman's attention back to him.

"Pray? Yes. Of course."

"Did he pray much? Did he pray loudly?"

"Not... not loudly," said the woman. "He didn't chant or anything like that. He didn't sing the hymns. But he prayed. I know he prayed."

"How do you know he prayed?"

She frowned. "I... I'm not sure. He seemed the type."

Skulduggery looked at her, his head tilted to one side. Then he nodded. "I'd agree with you. He did seem the type. But he didn't pray loudly, you say. That's interesting. What about you? Do you pray?"

"Yes," the woman said immediately.

"And are you devout?"

"I am."

"Have you always been devout?"

She went pale. She kept her eyes on Skulduggery. Didn't even glance at Valkyrie. "I have become more devout in my later years."

"And in your earlier years?" he asked. He took his hat off, placed it on the back of an armchair, and looked at himself in the mirror above the fireplace.

"I worshipped in my own way."

Skulduggery brushed imaginary dust from the top of his skull. "So you weren't a member of the Church of the Faceless?"

"Not an official member, no."

"Were you a member of the Legion of Judgement?"

"No. Dear me, no. Terrible people."

"Yet they share the majority of your beliefs, do they not?" Skulduggery pressed.

"Our beliefs," Valkyrie corrected.

"The Legion of Judgement share the majority of *our* beliefs," said Skulduggery. "They believe that the Faceless Ones are the true gods of humankind, who bore witness to the fire of creation as recounted in the Book of Tears."

The woman nodded quickly.

"But the Legion of Judgement followed Mevolent's teachings," Skulduggery continued, "while the Church of the Faceless has been guided by Damocles Creed."

"Supreme Mage Damocles Creed," Valkyrie said. "Arch-Canon Damocles Creed."

"Our boss," Skulduggery said, his tone curiously gentle. "And this is the church you belong to, yes?"

"Yes," said the woman.

"But only as of recently."

The woman swallowed. "Yes."

Valkyrie smiled. "You don't have to worry."

The woman's gaze flickered to her and Valkyrie saw genuine terror in those eyes.

Valkyrie hurried towards her and held her hands. "Oh, no. No! I don't mean to scare you! You really do have nothing to fear from me. As the Child of the Faceless, I'm just the conduit through which they're entering our world. It's a wonderful thing, actually, although I totally understand why it'd be intimidating. But they're not here to punish you, and I'm not here to hurt you. The Faceless Ones are... love. They're love and forgiveness and acceptance. They're here to guide us out of the muck. That's why I've been chosen. I'm the Child of the Faceless Ones, but also their Mother, and I could never, ever hurt anyone who loves them like I do."

"Valkyrie," Skulduggery said.

She looked back at him, smiling. "Yes?"

He nodded to her hands and she looked down, realised she had taken hold of the woman's wrists and had crushed them in her grip. She released them at once and the woman gasped, staggered back, tears already running down her face.

"I'm sorry," Valkyrie said, appalled. "I am so sorry. Are you OK? I am so dreadfully sorry. I can fix these. I can. I just need to be around a healer and then I'll be able to—"

"I'll take care of this," said Skulduggery, coming forward. "Reverie's clinic is nearby."

"I can take her there faster."

"But with me, her journey will be less jarring." He guided the crying woman to the window. "Stay here, keep looking around. I won't be a minute."

The window opened and Skulduggery lifted off the ground, taking the woman with him, and they floated through and rose up, out of sight.

Valkyrie looked at her hands. She hadn't even been aware of the force she'd been exerting.

She frowned. Or had she? There had been a sound, a crack, and even a sudden sharp inhalation as the woman drew in the breath she'd need to scream, then stopped herself, preferring to suffer in silence than risk antagonising someone she was clearly petrified of. All this was clear in Valkyrie's memory, and yet in the moment she had happily ignored it all. That was odd. That was odd and unsettling.

She had changed. She knew that. Ever since she'd intercepted the Activation Wave before it could reach her sister, ever since she had become the Child of the Faceless Ones in Alice's place, the old Valkyrie had disappeared. The Valkyrie who doubted and fretted and feared, the Valkyrie who obsessed over her own failings and flaws, who had allowed her regret for past actions to permeate everything she was – that person had been swept away by the light and the love of the Dark Gods. Her old self, the person she used to be, had been a sliver of who she was now.

A facet. Valkyrie Cain, detective and Arbiter, had been the tip of the iceberg that rose above sea level. Valkyrie Cain, Child and Mother of the Faceless Ones, was the whole thing, the mountain of ice that lay heavy and solid beneath the freezing waters.

But Valkyrie was still Valkyrie. She still loved and cared and wanted to help. She didn't want to hurt anyone – at least not anyone who didn't deserve it. The woman hadn't deserved the hurt. She hadn't deserved to have her wrists broken.

She probably hadn't anyway.

There were thousands of sorcerers, tens of thousands around the world, who had only recently become converts – and only then because Damocles Creed had made the worship of the Faceless Ones mandatory for citizenship of Roarhaven. That's not how Valkyrie would have done it – she believed each sorcerer, and eventually the mortals, too, should find their own way to the truth and the light – but then she wasn't in charge. She was the Child and the Mother, and had no interest in leading a world. Let Creed shoulder that burden.

The air whispered and Skulduggery glided back through the window.

"How is she?" Valkyrie asked. "Is she OK? She understands, right, that I didn't mean to do it?"

Skulduggery walked by. "Do you care?"

"What? Of course I care."

"She's not a believer."

"She prays. She worships."

"Not by choice. Not because she wants to."

Valkyrie hesitated. "You're sure?"

Skulduggery picked up his hat. "Mason Accrue was a believer. Like the five others that Obsidian has, for want of a better term, killed, he worshipped the Faceless Ones. He wasn't anyone special."

"Everyone is special in the eyes of the Faceless Ones," Valkyrie reminded him.

"Of course," Skulduggery said, after an almost unnoticeable hesitation. "I mean he held no great office or title. He worshipped, but he wasn't one of the Dark Cathedral's priests. He was just an ordinary sorcerer who happened to love and worship the Faceless Ones – and that's why Obsidian killed him. Due to the random nature of these attacks, I think it's probably that Obsidian was literally in the neighbourhood when he picked up on Accrue's prayers."

"But he didn't pray out loud."

Skulduggery put his hat on, tilting it lower over his left eye socket. "Which would suggest Obsidian has a highly developed psychic ability. He sensed the thoughts of a worshipper and he came to wipe him from reality."

"That's why you think the landlady was lying about being a devout worshipper," Valkyrie said. "Obsidian didn't go for her because he read her mind – he knew she was faking it."

"Indeed."

Valkyrie sighed. "Well, at least now I don't have to feel bad about hurting her wrists."

"Why is that?"

"She's a liar."

"So that means it's OK for you to break her bones?"

"Of course not. It's just..."

"It's just what?"

"Ah, no. We're not doing this. We're not having another argument about this."

"What do you think I'm going to say?"

"I don't know, Skulduggery – probably something about how I only care about the people who worship, when we both know that isn't true. I care about everyone. I care about all sorcerers and all mortals. I'm the Child and the Mother of the Faceless Ones – I have to love everyone."

"But you love the sorcerers who pray to your children more, yes?"

29

"Are you intentionally picking a fight?"

"We're not fighting."

"It sounds like we are."

"If we were fighting," Skulduggery said, "then we'd be on opposing sides – but we're not. I'm beside you, like I've always been. You became the Child of the Faceless Ones and I could have walked away, but I didn't."

"You've just stayed because you love me."

"Yes."

"Not because you love the Faceless Ones."

"Are you so sure about that? Can you reach into my thoughts and see my truth?"

Valkyrie smiled. "I would if I could."

"But you can't. So you're just going to have to take my word that I've opened myself up to the possibility that the Faceless Ones will not bring death and destruction to innocent people."

She looked at him, and laughed. "Creed would love to turn your bones to dust."

"Yes, he would," said Skulduggery, lifting off the ground. "But, while I've got you by my side, he won't touch me, will he?"

"No, he won't. But he will hunt down the others. I mean, you realise that, yeah? China and Tanith and Temper and every other member of the resistance? He'll find them eventually and he'll have one public execution after another."

"I'm well aware of what he'll do if he catches them."

"And you're OK with that? You'll just stand by and let it happen?"

"That's not the question, though, is it?" Skulduggery asked, drifting out through the open window. "The question is: will *you*?"

5

The Dark Cathedral stood like some evil wizard's palace in an old Disney movie, the kind that should have been perched on the edge of a forbidding cliff, its black stones lit up by the hands of forked lightning reaching down out of the clouds. Instead, it stood in the bright sunshine, occupying the eastern edge of the Circle Zone in the middle of Roarhaven, a sulking, spiked counterpart to the taller, more handsome High Sanctuary.

Looks, as ever, were deceptive, as the cold darkness of the Cathedral had been infiltrating the High Sanctuary for months, corrupting it from the inside out. The Sanctuary agents and operatives who didn't share a deep and abiding love for the Faceless Ones were quitting, one by one, leaving every institution of authority under the control of either the Church of the Faceless or the City Guard – which amounted to much the same thing.

It was a Tuesday, mid-morning, and there was a long line of people waiting to worship in the Cathedral. They stared at Valkyrie as she walked by. She was used to it. People in Roarhaven had always stared at her – whether it was because of Darquesse and Devastation Day, or whether it was because of her new status as the mother of their gods, it all resulted in wide eyes, terrified whispers, and some actual crying.

She was so done with it all, she didn't even smile at them any more. She entered the Cathedral and walked to the desk. "He in?" she asked.

Valkyrie had been the Child and the Mother for five months now and the Cathedral staff – the true believers who really should have known better – still had a tendency to drop to their knees when she neared. The public's reaction was bad enough. This was ridiculous.

"The Arch-Canon is in his office," someone squeaked from the floor.

"Cheers," she said, and flew upwards, leaving a trail of crackling white energy as she zipped past floor after floor, coming to the top and dropping down on to the walkway.

The guards opened the doors for her and she strode in.

Creed's office used to be a shrine to minimalism. The floor-to-ceiling windows didn't have curtains, the walls were decorated with nothing but heavy, rusted chains, and the only pieces of furniture in the room were the desk and the straight-backed chair behind it.

But now the office was dominated by a large table littered with machine parts, wires, coils and casings. Cables covered the floor, lying across each other like dead snakes, hooked up to various lights and tools and computers that whirred and beeped and hummed. Valkyrie could put a car engine back together, build a motorbike from scratch, and knew how to rewire a house and defuse all but the most complicated of bombs, but she hadn't a clue what most of this junk was and cared not one bit. All she knew was that Creed was obsessed with building what he called a "Nexus Helmet" – a means of communicating personally with the Dark Gods.

At first, she'd thought he was merely jealous. Yes, the Faceless Ones had been reaching people through their dreams for the last few months, driving dozens mad and encouraging dozens more to hunt down and murder random people in their neighbourhoods for various acts of blasphemy, but the only person they could talk to, who could talk back, was Valkyrie. For the

Arch-Canon of the Church of the Faceless, she'd thought, this was unacceptable. Creed, it seemed, had a desperate fear of missing out.

But she'd changed her mind in the last week or so. Now she didn't think it was merely jealousy that drove him – she suspected it might be something deeper. She was the Child and the Mother, the Faceless Ones' favourite human, but she couldn't help but feel that Damocles Creed didn't quite trust her.

This thought amused Valkyrie no end.

"How's it coming along?" she asked, more out of politeness than any real interest. Creed put down the goggles and the blow-torch, sweat shining on his bald head, drenching his cotton shirt. The air stank of burning metal.

"It proceeds," he said, wiping his face with a towel. There was a man helping him, a Sensitive called Robert Scure – Bob to his friends – who gazed at Valkyrie like a lovesick idiot. The Nexus Helmet was a bizarre device with copper and brass towers. It was upended, and she could see all the wires and circuitry on the inside. It looked complicated and uncomfortable, but she didn't want to say that. Didn't want to be rude.

"Looks rubbish," she said instead.

"Thank you, Mr Scure," Creed said, doing his usual wonderful job of ignoring her taunts. "That will be all." He wasn't any fun, was Damocles Creed. Not like Skulduggery.

Scure nodded quickly, smiled at Valkyrie and blushed, then hurried out of the room. What an odd little man.

"Obsidian has killed someone else," she said, picking up a piece of something and examining it. "Or, you know, wiped him from reality."

"Who was it this time?"

"Some dude."

Creed took his shirt off, bunched it up and used it to wipe beneath his armpits. "Your daily briefings have become less detail-oriented as the months have passed."

She sighed. "Some dude named Mason Accrue. He's a member of the church."

"Another one."

"Looks like Obsidian's targeting worshippers. You are going to put that back on, are you? Your shirt?"

He ignored her question and asked one of his own. "How is he choosing his victims?"

"We haven't confirmed it, but Skulduggery thinks Obsidian might be psychic. He passes by, he hears particularly loud thoughts, and he pops in to erase someone's existence."

"So long as those thoughts are in favour of the Faceless Ones."

"Looks like it. We might have a prejudiced serial killer on our hands. Like serial killers aren't bad enough already, right?"

"And Detective Pleasant, once again, chose not to deliver this report alongside you? I worry."

"Do you now?"

"I think he might be a subversive."

She laughed. "Of course he's a subversive. It's Skulduggery Pleasant we're talking about."

"Subversives are to be put to death. That is the law."

"That law doesn't apply to Skulduggery."

"Your fondness for him is admirable, the way fondness for an unruly dog is, but are you entirely sure he's worth the effort?"

"You're not killing him."

"Because you believe you share a bond, yes? With everything you've been through, with your friendship, you believe this bond is unbreakable. Valkyrie, you're young, and so take it from me when I tell you that nothing is unbreakable. Maybe once, years ago, Skulduggery would have sacrificed the world for you – but do you really think that's true any more?"

"He wouldn't hurt me."

"I believe he would because the Valkyrie Cain he knows would never forgive him if he chose her over others."

"I am the Valkyrie Cain he knows."

"No. You're not."

She went to the window, gazing up Khrthauk as it stood over Dublin city.

"You're not killing him," she repeated.

"I may have to," said Creed.

"Then I'll kill you."

"You don't believe in killing people."

Valkyrie looked at him. "Get me mad enough, Damocles, and you'll see what I believe."

He returned her gaze for a long moment, and then nodded. "Of course. Whatever the Child and Mother of the Faceless Ones wants."

"So glad we agree. Now then – seeing as how Obsidian seems to have a thing for killing the members of your congregation, maybe it'd be an idea to pause with the worshipping and stuff. Maybe tell them to think about other things until we find a way to stop them from getting erased."

"I don't think that will be necessary. The faithful are willing to die for their beliefs."

"I notice you haven't asked their opinion on that."

"Because I don't have to."

"You're putting the whole of Roarhaven in danger."

"The dangers of the flesh pale in comparison to the dangers of the soul, Valkyrie. Besides, I have every confidence that you and your pet skeleton will stop Obsidian before many more lives are lost. If you can't, after all, then who can?"

6

"It's not easy," said Bennet Troth, "worshipping someone who's probably going to kill you."

He kept his voice down because the others were sleeping, but it really didn't make any difference. There was always someone talking or shouting or begging or crying down here, down in the dungeons beneath the City Guard headquarters. In the cell across from them, there was a man who screamed himself hoarse every morning.

"I don't know why we do it," Bennet continued. "Sometimes I think we're all quite mad. Maybe we've been mad for years, you know? Since Devastation Day, when Darquesse levelled half the city and we got our first real glimpse of an actual god."

Sebastian lay on his bunk, eyes focused on the end of the beak of his plague doctor's mask, and grunted a response. He'd had this conversation before. It was one of Bennet's favourites. When he had nothing left to talk about, he would always start wondering about his own sanity. Sebastian couldn't blame him. They'd been down here since June, and the only charge levelled at them so far was of being "members of an illegal organisation". Sebastian doubted that the Darquesse Society *was* illegal: it had a grand total of six living members, and no one else even knew it existed.

He knew why they were down here, though, and it wasn't

because they posed a threat to anyone. They were insurance, or maybe a human shield, in case Darquesse escaped wherever they were keeping her.

Sebastian had found, as the weeks had turned into months, that he cared less for his own circumstances – which were, to be honest, too dreary and mundane to bother fretting over – and more for the current well-being of Darquesse, whom Commander Hoc had dragged away, bound and unconscious. He worried about her constantly. A concrete ball had formed in his stomach like a tiny, heavy planet with its own gravitational pull, and it caught every other thought in his head and dragged it down so that he was incapable of thinking about anything else.

Darquesse was not his biological daughter, and due to her rapid ageing until she hit twenty-six, he'd only had to take care of her for a matter of weeks. But there was still some part of him that demanded that she be protected from harm at all costs – and that part had been tortured every single day since they'd been captured.

Bennet started praying, his mutterings like the faint dripping of water. The other members of the Darquesse Society also spent a good portion of their day praying to Darquesse. Sebastian didn't pray – he just worried.

Bennet finally fell asleep and Sebastian dozed. Midway through the night, he turned over to gaze upon the brickwork of the wall next to him and jerked back so suddenly he fell off his bunk.

Instead of a patch of empty ground between Sebastian and the wall, there was now a blanket, and upon that blanket lay a figure, stirred now by Sebastian's reaction. An old man with long grey hair as straggly as his long grey beard sat up and blinked at Sebastian through the gloom.

"You look like a bird," the old man said in a thick Kerry accent. "Do you sound like a bird? Say something to me and try not to squawk. What kind of bird are you? Do you lay eggs? I'd quite like some eggs. I haven't had eggs in a long, long time."

Sebastian checked behind him as he stood. None of the others had woken. "Who are you?" he asked, keeping his voice down.

The old man got to his feet. He was dressed in rags, and his coat looked as old as he was. "Name's Flibbertigibbet Bedfellow, though you can call me Nuncle if you want. Everyone does. Everyone who knows me – and everyone does know me, even if they don't know they know. I would digress, but I'd never be able to find my way back. You're a curious-looking thing. Were you born with that face?"

"It's a mask," said Sebastian, tapping the nose.

Nuncle laughed. "I know that, lad. You're wearing a mask; I'm wearing a mask; we're all wearing our masks. But were you born with yours?"

"Uh, no."

"You have quite a beak."

"Yeah. I didn't hear them bring you in."

"Didn't hear who?"

"The guards. I didn't hear them chain you up."

Nuncle nodded. "They must have been very quiet."

"You don't remember?"

"I was a million miles away," Nuncle said, putting his fingertips to his temple and fluttering his hand in the air. "Can I ask you a question, boy?"

"Sure."

"Good," said Nuncle. "You should never be afraid of questions. That's what my mother used to tell me, whenever I got chased home by a pack of them. Course, back when I was a lad, questions were a different sort. They had teeth, and they snatched little children and ate them up like crunchy apples."

"Right," Sebastian said slowly. "What did you do? To get thrown in here, I mean. What did you do wrong?"

The old man frowned. "I don't rightly know. I'm not sure I did anything. Or maybe I did everything. Ah, sure, how are you meant to know these days? Time makes a fool of us all, does it not?"

"I suppose."

"Are we going to be friends, then?"

"Uh... I suppose."

"Well, that's good news," said Nuncle, smiling. "You can never have too many friends." He lay back, and before Sebastian could ask him anything else, he went to sleep.

7

A torn piece of paper skittered by on the breeze and Omen curled his fingers and the breeze diverted the paper into his hand. Feeling pretty good about managing that move without blasting himself with a gust of wind, he scrunched the paper up and tossed it into the recycling bin next to the bench. Feeling absolutely astonished that he had managed that without missing, the promise of an amazing day where everything went right was shredded by Filament Sclavi appearing before him, his prefect badge shining.

"You can't help it, can you?" Filament asked with a smile that was not technically unkind, but which was loaded with an as yet unknown agenda.

"Sorry?" Omen said, looking up at him, but making no move to stand.

"Do you even realise it when you do it, I wonder?" Filament said. "Or is it unconscious? Is it such a part of you that you have no idea it's even there?"

"Well, I have no idea what we're talking about, if that's any use to you."

"Are you trying to make up for what's happening with Auger? Everyone knows that the Chosen One brand is very important to your family. Is that what it is? Are you trying to be the hero now that Auger's the bad guy?"

Omen's chest tightened, but he said nothing.

Filament pointed to a First Year picking up rubbish across the courtyard. "Cleaning up the litter is what he's doing. It is a punishment. You know this concept? The definition of *punishment* is the infliction of a penalty as retribution for an offence. It is meant to be a burden on the transgressor of this offence, and nobody else. Do you understand this?"

"I'm still dealing with the fact that you went to the trouble of looking up and memorising the definition of the word *punishment*, to be honest."

"If you help someone with their punishment, it is no longer their punishment."

"What'd he do?"

"That is no concern of yours."

"Are you even allowed to punish First Years? You're not a teacher."

"Under the new Code of Conduct for Prefects, introduced by Principal Duenna, I am allowed to punish any student for certain transgressions."

"Like what?"

Filament folded his arms. "Disrespect for one. Authority must be maintained – that is one of Principal Duenna's guiding rules. If the students don't respect the prefects, order crumbles and chaos reigns."

"Order's on pretty shaky grounds already if a little cheekiness could topple it."

"Principal Duenna gave instructions to send you to her office if you disrespected us, did you know that?"

"Really? You're going to send me to the Principal's Office?"

"Not yet," Filament said. He started walking. "Come with me."

Omen watched him without moving. When it became obvious that Omen was staying where he was, Filament stopped, sighed and turned.

"Mr Darkly," he repeated, like he was calling a dog to heel.

Omen just smiled and waved and walked the other way.

Hurrying footsteps, and then Filament was standing in front of him.

"Filament," Omen said, "what's up?"

"I told you to follow."

"You did, yeah."

"Then follow, Mr Darkly."

"We don't have to be so formal, Filament. You can call me Omen."

Another theatrical sigh. "Omen, follow."

"Why?"

"Because I told you to."

"Getting someone to follow you isn't one of your prefect powers, though, is it?"

"I never said that it was."

"Then I'm not going to follow you."

"I have something to show you."

"What is it?"

"Come with me and you'll see."

"You sound like you're going to take me on a tour of your chocolate factory."

Filament frowned. "I don't understand."

"You sound like you're going to break into song and take me on a tour of your – never mind. What do you want to show me, Filament?"

"You'll have to see for yourself."

"I think I'll wait and see it later."

"But you need to see it."

"I don't really, though, do I?"

"Omen," said Filament, taking a deep breath, "I'm asking you to come with me. I have something to show you. I don't want to tell you what it is because I want it to be a surprise. You're not going to like it, but believe me when I tell you that you need to see it." He bristled. "Please."

"Will it take long?"

"No."

"I have somewhere to be."

"It'll only be a few minutes."

"OK."

They made their way towards the stairs.

"I was lying," Omen said. "I don't have anywhere to be."

They went outside, walked up to the school gates, and Filament checked his watch.

"Gonna tell me what the big surprise is?" Omen asked.

"No," said Filament. "But it should be here any second."

"Can I ask a question? Now that we're alone and everything. Do you like being a prefect?"

"Of course."

"Why, though? Everyone hates the prefects."

"They hate us because they fear us."

"You're thinking of the X-Men. Everyone hates prefects because you're a bunch of narks."

Filament frowned. "What's a nark?"

"Oh, it's someone who turns you in to the authorities whenever you do the slightest thing wrong."

"Yes," said Filament. "Because we're like the secret police."

"That's really not it. It's way less cool."

"I like being a prefect because it means I can serve my school and my city," said Filament. "It means I can serve the Faceless Ones, even in small ways."

"Like giving detention to little kids who don't know the rules? Yeah, that's really helping the Faceless Ones. That's really proving your worth there."

Filament looked at him. "You think you're on the right side, but you're not. You think you're one of the heroes, but you're not. The funny thing is, it's too late for you to change, and it wouldn't do you any good anyway."

Omen patted him on the shoulder. "I'm going to head off now, dude. Have a nice time standing here."

"Wait," said Filament, eyes on a car that was pulling up outside the gate. "He's here!"

Omen had to admit he was curious as to who it was who'd got Filament so excited, so he stayed still while the car idled. It was a nice car, big and expensive with tinted windows. Finally, a door opened and Jenan Ispolin got out.

Omen's insides went cold and plummeted.

"They let him out," Filament informed him gleefully. "Jenan's father, he's the Bulgarian Grand Mage – you know that, right? He's been trying to get Jenan released from prison, but China Sorrows kept saying no – she probably thought Jenan was too much of a threat and that you, personally, would be in danger. I don't think Supreme Mage Creed cares about that a whole lot."

Jenan saw them, his eyes fixing on Omen, and he came over.

"Hello, Jenan," Filament said brightly.

Jenan ignored him and kept his eyes on Omen. He leaned in and Omen resisted the urge to lean away.

"I'm going to kill you," Jenan said into Omen's ear, and then looked at him again, before walking away.

Filament laughed and clapped. "This," he said, "has been so much fun."

8

Leaving a trail of crackling white energy behind her, Valkyrie touched down at the gates of Corrival Academy and smiled as the passers-by broke out into a spontaneous round of applause. Cars driving by honked their horns to show their support for the Child and the Mother, and there were even a few cheers. It was a nice change from the accusatory whispers and not-so-subtle glances she used to get.

The students in the school stared as she walked by, like she was a movie star they'd never expected to see in real life. Yes, there was some fear in the air, but the students here were young – they had plenty of time to realise they were all on the same side.

Fletcher Renn nodded to her from the staffroom, but the look on his face was decidedly unfriendly. The City Guard were keeping close tabs on him: as the only experienced Teleporter in Roarhaven, he was extremely valuable, but his ties to various members of the resistance marked him as a high-risk individual.

Principal Duenna and an assistant rushed to meet Valkyrie. "Detective Cain!" Duenna said quite breathlessly. "If I had known you were coming, I'd have prepared a suitable reception!"

"Don't worry about it," Valkyrie said as her necronaut suit flowed into the black skull amulet on her belt. Her smile was polite and she genuinely appreciated being welcomed into the school as opposed to being banned from setting foot in the place, but the inescapable fact was that she just didn't like Duenna. She was a manipulative opportunist, and had proven all too eager to impose harsher and more stringent rules on her students. It had been eight years since Valkyrie had been a student herself – in a regular mortal school – and she hadn't much liked obeying the rules back then. She liked it even less now.

"I just have a bit of business with Militsa – is she around?"

"I'll send for Miss Gnosis immediately," Duenna responded, ushering her assistant away. "Can I get you anything while you wait? Tea or coffee? Would you like a quick tour of the chapel?"

"There's a chapel? In the school?"

"We renovated some space. Quite a large amount of space, actually. I find it's important to lead by example, so the full teaching staff prays to the Faceless Ones twice a day and, of course, all of the pupils join us. Would you like to see it? The carvings are quite exquisite."

"I'm sure they are," said Valkyrie, "but this is just a flying visit."

Through the sea of gawping faces, she spotted Omen Darkly, wandering around like he was trying to figure out what the fuss was about.

"Nice seeing you," she said, and left Duenna standing there as the bell rang.

The students fled the corridor like they were scared of something, leaving only Omen behind. He had changed so much since the first time Valkyrie had seen him. He was taller, less awkward, less unsure of himself. He watched her approach.

Valkyrie smiled. "Hi."

"Is there news?" he said back. "About Auger?"

"None that I can share," she told him. "None that would be helpful anyway."

"But he's been seen? Recently, like?"

She nodded. "Obsidian is still active, yes."

"His name's Auger."

46

There was a defiance in his voice and anger in his eyes so Valkyrie just nodded again. "Yes. Sorry. Auger is still active."

"Has he... has he hurt anyone?"

"I'm afraid so."

Omen's gaze faltered and he looked away and Valkyrie put a hand on his shoulder.

"How are things?" she asked as gently as she could. "How are the parents?"

"They're handling the situation with their usual warmth and understanding."

Valkyrie had met Omen's parents, so she let that go without comment. "There's a lot going on," she said. "If you ever need to talk to someone about it, I'm a pretty good listener."

"Yeah," he said, and something about the way he said it made it clear she was going to be the last person he'd talk to. "Thanks."

"I'm not the bad guy, Omen."

He looked at her. "I'd better get to class. Duenna has the teachers handing out detentions all over the place."

Valkyrie tried a grin. "If you get one, just let me know and I'll give her a call. I don't know if you've noticed, but I'm a pretty big deal around here these days."

"Yeah," said Omen, not responding to her good humour. "I noticed."

He went into a classroom and shut the door, leaving Valkyrie without any ointment for that particular burn. The shadows drew in ahead of her, gathered and coiled, and Militsa lunged out, eyes wide with alarm. Those eyes narrowed when she saw who was waiting for her.

"Hi," Valkyrie said brightly, butterflies in her belly.

Militsa walked closer. "You're the emergency? I was told to come here without delay because there was an emergency and it's you? Seriously?"

"In my defence, I didn't ask anyone to use the word emergency."

"Why are you here, Valkyrie?"

47

"I thought Xena might be missing home," Valkyrie said, pulling a small toy squirrel from her back pocket. "I brought this in case she's disturbing you too much. It'll help calm her down if she's fretting."

"Right," Militsa said, taking the squirrel. "She's fine, though. She's not fretting. And she's got plenty of toys already."

"Yeah, but one more can't hurt, right?"

"I suppose." Militsa's red hair fell across her face but she didn't flick it out of her eyes or tuck it behind her ear, the way she used to when she was flirting. She just left it there.

"How have you been?" Valkyrie asked. "Haven't heard from you in a while."

Militsa nodded. "That's what happens when you break up."

"Have we, though? Broken up? Like, really broken up? I don't know if we have. I feel there's still a load of stuff we need to talk about."

"No, we have," said Militsa. "Remember? I told you we're breaking up and then we broke up."

"But I didn't want to."

"Wasn't a requirement, though. I did want to break up, and so we broke up. You can't really have a relationship when there's only one of you in it."

Valkyrie tried smiling. "But I was hoping that you'd reconsider your position, like, now that some time has passed. We were really good together."

"We were."

"And I think that, maybe, we broke up because of the Faceless Ones thing."

"That's exactly why we broke up. I told you that."

"I know, I know, but, see, what you've got to understand is that nothing's changed. The Faceless Ones thing is happening, and that's still going on, but nothing has actually changed about me. I'm still the same person, you know? It's just that you might think it's changed me, but it hasn't."

"Valkyrie, I really don't want to talk about this. We've broken up, so the best thing for both of us to do is move on."

"I don't want to move on. Militsa, I love you."

"You'll stop loving me eventually."

Valkyrie looked away, her eyes stinging. "Wow."

Militsa said, "Sorry," but didn't sound it.

They stood there for a few seconds.

"Right," said Valkyrie, and walked away. She hoped that Militsa would call her back or come running after her, but that didn't happen.

Duenna was waiting for her when she stepped outside, but Valkyrie wasn't in the mood so she took off, shot straight up into the air. She tapped the black skull on her belt and the necronaut suit flowed over her clothes, protecting them from the scorching fingers of that crackling energy. She raised her hood and then pulled down the stark white skull mask, feeling it harden around her face as the suit sealed itself. She veered up, into the clouds, water droplets splattering across the mask's eyeholes.

She flew over Dublin, and Khrthauk made a sound as she passed, a sound only she could hear, like it was calling to her. That made her feel better, and she couldn't help but smile as she circled its head, dodging between its swinging tentacles with her arms by her sides. It threw some images into her mind, taking it easy because it was aware of how easily a human mind could be overwhelmed by the thoughts of an ancient god. She caught glimpses of its intent and responded as best as she was able, and then she blew it a kiss and flew on. Being in the presence of a Faceless One made her miss her other family, so she left the city behind, skimmed beneath a passenger plane on its way to the airport, and flew over the motorway, over roads and lanes and housing estates and farms and fields of different colours. The sea grew closer and in moments she was passing over Haggard, the small town on the coast.

Then she cut off her power and fell.

Plummeting was an exhilarating feeling, the world tipping over as she tumbled out of the clouds. She let loose with a blast of magic every now and then, to prevent her from reaching terminal velocity and to adjust her course. As the ground hurtled to greet her, she found that she was grinning.

She closed her eyes, listening to the wind rushing by her mask, rustling her hood. How easy it would be to keep her eyes closed.

She snapped them open and veered up, away from the ground, landing outside her parents' house. A neighbour she'd never seen before, out walking his dog, stared at her in frozen astonishment.

Valkyrie pulled up her mask and walked over. "Hi," she said. "What's your name?"

The neighbour shook his head. He'd gone quite pale and his dog was barking.

"Your name," Valkyrie repeated. "What is it?"

"Mikey Coghlan," he said.

"Michael Coghlan, forget what you just saw, cool?"

"Cool," said Mikey Coghlan, and walked on, wondering why his dog was going nuts.

Valkyrie chewed the inside of her cheek as she walked up to the house. She'd thought her self-destructive impulses were behind her, especially now that her soul was churning with a race of gods counting on her to bring them into this reality with the utmost care.

Obviously, she'd been wrong. She'd have to watch that.

A tap of the amulet and her suit flowed away from the clothes she wore underneath. "Hi," she called, walking through the front door. "Anyone home?"

Her mother came down the stairs. "I wasn't expecting you."

Valkyrie shrugged. "I was passing, more or less. Thought I might drop by, see how everything is. Dad at work?"

"They're busy again. Suddenly every building project is going ahead so he's up and gone by seven every morning and not back till late. You want a cup of tea? I was just about to make myself one."

"Sure," Valkyrie said, following Melissa into the kitchen. She sat while her mum filled the kettle. "Is Alice back from school yet?"

"She's in her room."

Valkyrie raised an eyebrow. "And she hasn't come running down to hug me?"

"She's in a mood."

"Sulking?"

"She wanted to play over at her friend's house this afternoon."

"Ah," Valkyrie said, grinning. "And why couldn't she?"

Melissa frowned slightly. "You said it wasn't safe."

"I didn't say that."

"You said we shouldn't let Alice stray beyond the routine."

"Well, yes, but I didn't mean, like..." Valkyrie laughed. "I didn't mean that she couldn't go play at a friend's house – just that her security detail would need to be updated."

"But it's safer for her here, right?"

"Yeah. I suppose."

"Then that's that. She knows full well that she's allowed to go to school and football practice and self-defence, but apart from that, she stays home."

"Her friends can play with her here," said Valkyrie.

"She says they won't. She had three friends over last week and they saw one of the Cleavers. The next day, they went into school and told everyone about the scary man watching the house, so now nobody wants to visit."

"I'll have a word with the detail, tell them to be more discreet."

The water boiled, and Melissa made two mugs of tea. "Do you have any idea how much longer we'll need them?"

"I'm afraid not. You're not scared, are you?"

Melissa handed Valkyrie her mug. "Of course I'm scared. There are people out there who want to hurt us."

"Mum, the chances of the resistance targeting anyone here are practically non-existent. These people were my friends, and they still are, in a way. They're just misguided."

"If you didn't think it was likely, you wouldn't have organised all these invisible sorcerers to be watching us every minute of every day."

"It's better to be safe," Valkyrie said, "and I genuinely can't see Tanith coming after any of you to get at me... but yeah. The tiniest possibility is still too much of a risk."

Melissa sat. "And are you going to tell me why this is happening yet?"

"I told you why."

"You said you're on opposite sides, that your friends are now the bad guys. But opposite sides of what argument?"

"It's magic stuff, Mum."

"I'd still like to know why our lives are in danger. You said it was about the Faceless Ones, how they aren't the big evil monsters everyone thought they were."

Valkyrie blew on her tea, and took a sip. "They're not. Think of them like, I don't know, bears or something. If you provoke a bear, it's going to attack you, right?"

"I don't know. Your father's the bear expert."

"Not a bear, then. A shark or something. A wild animal. If you provoke a wild animal and the wild animal attacks you, is that really the wild animal's fault – or is it your fault, for not understanding how to approach it?"

"So the Faceless Ones are wild animals," Melissa said, "and the only reason everyone thought they were monsters was because no one understood how to interact with them?"

"Exactly," said Valkyrie.

"And now you're the Faceless Ones' ambassador? Their spokesperson? But Tanith and the rest of your friends don't understand this, and now they're fighting against you."

"Except for Skulduggery."

"And you're sure that your friends are wrong?"

"Absolutely positive," Valkyrie said, smiling.

Melissa tapped her mug and thought about it for a moment. "And what about Militsa?"

Valkyrie hesitated. "What about her?"

"Is she on your side, or their side?"

"Mine. She's still working at Corrival Academy."

"But she's not your girlfriend any more?"

"She's just really busy," Valkyrie said, "and I've got all these new responsibilities. I just don't have time for a relationship right now."

"I don't know, Steph. I have to be honest with you: this is worrying."

Valkyrie tried a reassuring smile. "We'll get back together, I know we will. Militsa's great, and there's no way I'm going to let her go. A lot of things are happening and a lot of things are changing, and she still doesn't know how she feels about the Faceless Ones, but once that's all cleared up we'll be fine. We'll be good."

"You're sure?"

"I am."

Her mum's phone rang and, as she answered it, Valkyrie pointed at the ceiling. Melissa gave her a nod and Valkyrie went upstairs. She stepped into her old room. Alice lay sprawled across her bed, head in a tablet. When Valkyrie was nine her head would have been stuck in one of her uncle's books. Times change.

"Hey," said Valkyrie.

"Hey," said Alice, not looking up.

"How you doing?"

A tiny little shrug.

"Mum says you're mad at her for not letting you go over to your friend's house. It isn't her fault, sweetie – it's mine."

"I know," said Alice. "I'm mad at you, too."

"Oh. Can I come in?"

Alice put down the tablet and sat up. "Are you going to give me a talk?"

"What do you mean by a talk?"

"You know," Alice said, "you come in and you say nice things and make me laugh so that I won't be in a bad mood any more."

"Ah, the talk. I was planning on it, to be honest, but I don't think it'll work if you know it's coming." Valkyrie walked in, sat beside her sister. "So what if we just chat about stuff?"

"What kind of stuff?"

"Anything you want."

"Are we in danger?"

"No. That's why all those Cleavers and sorcerers are around. They're here to protect you."

"I don't like them. I don't want them here. Why can't you protect us?"

"I am protecting you. I'm just doing it from further away."

It looked like Alice was going to argue, but then she shrugged and her mood changed, like a shaft of sunlight breaking through grey clouds. "Will you teach me some more Brazilian Jiu-Jitsu before my next class?" she asked.

Valkyrie smiled. "Sure thing."

9

Once they were confident that the building they were comman-
deering was secure, Temper and Kierre of the Unveiled joined
Tanith Low and her boyfriend, Oberon Guile, and entered
the conference room. The table was expensive and there were
three wooden bowls of artfully arranged fruit placed at stra-
tegic points down its length. There was also a cloaking sphere
ticking quietly away on the cabinet in the corner, ensuring
that anyone trying to spy on them from the outside would see
only empty chairs.

It was early morning, on a Wednesday, with dawn bursting
across the Melbourne sky in an indulgent display of luxurious
splendour. Technically, they were safe here – but that safety was
fragile at best. The Sanctuaries in Africa were about to fall to
Creed's manipulations, according to trusted sources on the inside,
which would leave Australia as the last independent Cradle of
Magic – but where there were sorcerers there were spies, and
where there were spies no one was safe.

The Monster Hunters walked in a few minutes later, wearing
smiles brighter than their tropical shirts. Donegan Bane had
bananas on his. Gracious O'Callahan had tiny X-wings. Temper
watched Tanith immediately relax in their company. She knew
them from way back, and she trusted them. This was good. Trust
was hard to come by.

The door opened and Dexter Vex stood there, eyes flicking around the room before he committed to stepping inside. He'd had a haircut and a shave since Temper had seen him last. He looked well – fit and strong – and though he smiled like he already trusted everyone here, there was caution there, too. Temper couldn't blame him. You didn't get to be one of the two surviving members of the original Dead Men – and the only one actually alive – without developing a heathy sense of paranoia.

Kierre nudged Temper's leg with her foot and when he looked at her she raised an eyebrow that asked how he was doing. He gave her a smile back. She seemed satisfied with that.

When the small talk died down – which translated to when Gracious stopped asking people how they were doing – Temper tapped a message into his phone, and a few seconds later China Sorrows walked in. The gentle quiet in the room turned to silence – cold and stony. China chose the chair at the very top of the table. She sat and crossed her legs, entirely at ease.

"What the hell is she doing here?" Tanith asked.

"I've joined the resistance," China answered.

"But you're the bad guy."

"I was the bad guy," China corrected. "But, after I was ousted by an even worse bad guy, I'm now on your side."

"No," Tanith said. "Just no. Who invited her? She was the Supreme Mage. She set up the power structures we're trying to dismantle."

"Which would make me invaluable in their dismantling, would it not?" China asked.

Tanith leaned forward. "China bloody Sorrows is responsible for more crimes than I can list, not least a whole slew of murders and assassinations."

"Regrettable," said China, "but necessary."

"Necessary for what?"

"Necessary to establish order between the Sanctuaries. After Erskine Ravel's failed takeover bid, some of the most prominent

Sanctuaries on the planet were being run by nothing more than political opportunists and puppet Grand Mages. Was blood shed during my own takeover? Yes. Was it vital that this blood be shed? Absolutely. Did I like issuing those orders? No. But somebody had to make the hard choices because no one else seemed interested in taking responsibility for an entire world. So you may continue to despise me, Tanith Low, and for very good reason, but your name wasn't in the hat, was it? You took the easier route: you joined Black Sand, and you directed terrorist attacks against the system you walked away from. I had no such luxury."

Tanith sneered. "And I suppose your own personal ambitions, your sheer thirst for power and influence, played no part in any of this?"

"Of course they played a part," China answered. "I wouldn't have been able to accomplish half of what I did without that thirst driving me onwards. But it doesn't detract from the truth of what I've said."

Tanith glared and China appeared disinterested, and Temper realised that was as close to a resolution as they were likely to get.

"Uh," said Oberon, before the silence dragged on too long, "can I ask a question? Who's in charge here?"

No one said anything for a couple of moments.

"Well," Gracious said, sitting forward slightly, "Donegan and I don't really do the whole 'in charge' thing. The Monster Hunters are a team, an equal partnership. We make decisions by consensus. So I think if you all vote for me to be leader it might cause some friction within that dynamic."

"Why would they vote for you over me?" Donegan asked, looking genuinely puzzled.

"Because of my natural leadership qualities."

"Do your natural leadership qualities include sleeping in? Because we would have missed this meeting entirely if it wasn't for me."

"And this is why you are an essential part of my team."

"Your team?"

Gracious smiled his apologies at the group. "It is for this reason that I am withdrawing my name from contention."

"That's OK," said Tanith, reluctantly drawing her eyes away from China. "We weren't going to vote for you anyway."

Gracious laughed. "That's hurtful."

"Tanith," said Donegan, "what about you? You've led us before. You were pretty good at it, too."

Tanith shook her head. "I'm more use to the resistance in the field than issuing orders behind the scenes. Dexter?"

"Not interested," Dexter said.

"I think I should withdraw my name, too," said China, "for obvious reasons. Also, I'm far too busy with a Host problem, so I'm sure that will take up a lot of my time in the foreseeable future."

Dexter frowned. "The Hosts are real?"

"Quite real."

"Who are the Hosts?" Oberon asked. "I don't think I've ever heard of them."

"Few have," China told him. "Suffice it to say, there may be a possible threat on the horizon to civilisation as we know it, and it simply must be seen to."

"Yeah, well," Tanith muttered, "it can get in line behind all the *other* threats to civilisation."

"Indeed," said China. "If anyone at this table should lead this last-ditch effort against the Faceless Ones and their fanatics, however, I say it should be Temper Fray. He's done rather a good job of it up to this point, so why not let him continue?"

"I can think of a few reasons," Temper said.

"I agree with the witch," said Tanith.

"You have my steel," said Gracious.

"And my bow," said Donegan. "Metaphorically speaking."

"Before we all get carried away," Temper said, "what about Skulduggery?"

"Skulduggery's no use to us right now," Tanith responded. "He has to stick by Valkyrie's side – he's the only chance she has of remembering who she is."

"Do you think he'll be able to get her back?"

"If anyone can, it's him."

"But do you think he'll be able to do it?"

Tanith didn't answer, and Temper looked around the room. "We're on the losing side of this thing. You all understand that, don't you? The resistance consists of a few dozen mages, and we're up against everybody else."

"We're not alone, though," said Oberon. "The vast majority of sorcerers will rise up given the opportunity."

"But if we can't generate that opportunity, with what little support we have, they'll stay quiet, and do what Creed tells them to. This little enterprise we've got going here is pretty much doomed to failure – unless we make some drastic moves."

China's eyebrow moved a fraction. "Such as?"

Temper slumped in his chair. "We're going to have to start considering the possibility of killing Valkyrie."

"No," said Tanith.

"No chance," said Donegan.

"She's the number-one threat," Temper said. "The Faceless Ones are here, yes, but we can't even hurt them. Taking Valkyrie out of the equation would upset their plans, whatever those plans are. I'm not saying I want to do it because obviously I don't – but it has to be on the table. It has to be an option."

"I agree," said China.

"You're supposed to be her friend," Tanith responded. "That was your one redeeming factor, and now you're voting to kill her?"

"Hard choices," China replied simply, and Tanith fell silent.

"Even if we all agreed to kill Valkyrie," Dexter said, "it's not nearly as easy as that, is it? We'd be going up against her and we'd also be going up against Skulduggery, who would not look kindly on this course of action. It's possible, yeah, but we'd suffer incredible losses. Do we have any other plans?"

"Yes," said Temper. "We hope things get better."

Gracious nodded cautiously. "I'm not saying I don't like that plan, as it sounds like a lot less work than a plan involving actually doing something, but maybe we should, I don't know, actually do something?"

"Right now," said Temper, "Creed is controlling practically every Sanctuary around the world and every sorcerer is frowning disapprovingly, but not actually doing anything about it because no one is leading the way. We're the resistance. That part's down to us. So we give them hope by showing them this thing can still be won. China, you've described how all the Sanctuaries under Creed's control are propped up by what sounds like delicate power structures. I'm assuming you know how to dismantle them?"

"I know which pillars to knock so the whole thing comes crashing down, yes."

Temper nodded. "There's no way of telling what will happen next – how Creed will react, or even if the mages of the world respond how we'd like them to. But this is the one thing we can do to destabilise the Creed regime, so that's what we're going to do. This is our Plan A. If it doesn't work, only then will we consider the alternative."

10

It was good to get out of the house.

Tyler's folks had been arguing lately, mostly about the upcoming election. His dad – he was a Flanery man – had the bumper sticker on the back of his pickup and a sign on the front lawn that he refused to pull up. His mom hated that sign, hated the bumper sticker, and even hated the pickup. She drove a hybrid to the hospital where she worked as a nurse, and she didn't like the direction America had been going these last few years. Tyler had been a kid when Martin Flanery became president. Now he was fourteen, and he couldn't even remember what life under the previous guy had been like. His mom was going to vote for Paul Donovan.

None of his friends cared about politics, but it had scared Tyler ever since he'd started to take notice. His sister, Mila – she was seventeen – had told him that politicians all over the world had been shown what they needed to do to prevent ecological catastrophe, but there were too many rich people and powerful corporations standing in the way. Mila got real upset about it, too, which tended to upset Tyler, so he tried to avoid politics whenever he could. He had a ball of anxiety in his belly whenever he thought about it, and every day it was getting just that little bit bigger.

Tyler skipped the woods – it was already dark, and the woods were creepy enough in the daytime – and rode his bike round the better-lit neighbourhoods till he ran out of neighbourhoods. He really should have planned this better, but he was almost home. He just had to put his head down and pump his legs.

It was a long, straight road, with the woods on the right side and farmland to his left, and he plunged into pockets of darkness before exploding out into the electric light of the streetlamps. Into darkness and out into light. Into darkness and out. It occurred to him that the light was actually working against him, preventing his eyes from adjusting to the gloom. It occurred to him, also, that there could be anything waiting for him in those patches of darkness. Any kind of murderer. Any kind of monster.

He shook his head as he cycled. There it was again, that imagination that was starting to get him in trouble at school. Morbid, his teachers called it. He'd had a few letters sent home that his mom had rolled her eyes at.

There was a flash of purple light and Tyler slowed, coming to a stop about halfway down the road. Another flash, off to his left, behind the farmhouse that used to belong to Mr Madison before he died last year. Since then, the place had stood empty, the land rented out to other farmers. There was no one living there now, Tyler was sure of that.

He started moving, slowly following the trail in the darkness leading to the narrow road that skimmed the Madison land. When he was a kid, a power line had come down and electrocuted a bunch of cattle near his cousin's. If that's what had happened here, he didn't want any animals hurt.

He veered off the narrow road, bike bumping through the long grass, and he came up beside one of the smaller sheds and took it carefully now. He didn't want to ride over a power line. He freewheeled gently as he passed the corner, then jabbed one foot into the dirt to bring him to a sudden, jarring stop.

Three men were fighting behind the farmhouse, two white guys against a Black guy, and one of the white guys was holding something that glowed with the same purple light that Tyler had seen. He went tumbling, the white guy, and Tyler realised the purple light was coming from his hand, and then there was a flash and a stream of that purple light sizzled into the Black guy's shoulder, spinning him in place. He went down.

There was a moment of quiet as the two white guys got their breath back, like they were expecting the other man to pop up again. When he didn't, they exchanged a few words and the other white guy picked a gun up off the ground.

And then, all of a sudden, they were looking at Tyler, and the guy raised the gun and fired.

The bullet missed – Tyler had no idea how close it came to hitting him – but he hopped back into the saddle, yanking the handlebars round and speeding back behind the cover of the shed.

The white guys shouted at each other and Tyler got to the road and pedalled like crazy. He was glad of the darkness now, thankful for the way it drank him in.

A car started up behind him and cold terror spread through his gut. A few seconds later, headlights swooped, then swung back and latched on. The car roared as it gave chase.

Tyler reached the long road and crossed it, going for the woods. The car was almost upon him and he dropped the bike, sprinting through the trees. The car braked, he heard it slide on the grass, and doors opened and the men cursed and shadows moved through the headlights that Tyler was leaving behind.

Another gunshot. It missed.

In the dark now, Tyler stayed low and tried to stay quiet as he ran. He didn't look back at the lights, didn't want his vision ruined. A stream of purple energy cut through a half-dozen trees way to his left. They didn't know where he was. They were firing and hoping.

Tyler tripped and sprawled, banged his knees painfully, scrambled up behind a tree and took a deep breath and held it. The men crashed through the undergrowth after him.

"Stop," one of them said. "Stop, for God's sake!"

"What?" the other one responded. "You see him? Where is he?"

"Just stop moving and listen."

Tyler blew out his breath as quietly as he could and sucked in more.

"He's around here," said the first guy. "He's hiding."

"Hey, kid!" the second guy shouted. "It's OK! Come on out! We're not going to hurt you!"

"He knows we're going to hurt him."

"How's he know that?"

"We've been shooting at him!"

"Oh, yeah."

"Hey, kid! We're real sorry. You saw something you shouldn't have. We can't take the chance of you telling anyone so, yeah, we gotta kill you. But you step forward now, we'll make it quick and painless. You hear?"

They were moving up on either side of him, taking slow steps.

"There he is!" the first guy shouted, and Tyler closed his eyes and prepared for the gunshot.

"Where? Where is he?"

"Ah, never mind," the first guy said. "Thought that might scare him into running. OK, we need a strategy. You go back and finish off Jones. I'll keep looking for the kid." He waited for a reply. "You listening? Hey, you hear me? Where are you? Where you gone, you—"

Something hit the first guy and he went down and there was suddenly a whole lot of grunting and cursing. Tyler peered out. He saw two men rolling around in the dirt and the twigs. The white guy's hand lit up purple and the Black guy, the one they'd called Jones, he held the white guy's wrist at bay. A stream of purple light barely missed Jones's face.

Jones hit him, and hit him again, and then a blazing energy burst out of his eyes and the darkness swallowed what it did to the white guy's head. Jones stayed where he was for a few seconds, breathing fast. He tried to get up, then toppled, and fell.

Tyler ran over.

11

Waking in an empty house was still taking some getting used to. She missed the excited trot as she came to the bottom of the stairs, where she would normally sit and cuddle a very appreciative Xena before starting the day. This morning, Valkyrie came downstairs without incident, without greeting. She made herself a shake and worked out for a bit without enthusiasm, then showered and dressed. It was raining so she took the car.

As she drove, she switched on the radio to a news report about the American president saying something oafish, and she changed the station to one playing music. She wasn't in the mood for Martin Flanery's bewildering stupidity right now.

She got to Roarhaven and parked, then took a tile up into the High Sanctuary.

"Detective Cain," the Administrator said, glancing over, "if I'd known you were coming, I'd have planned a parade."

Valkyrie took a moment to appreciate the sarcasm, especially in light of how much it could potentially cost. Cerise had been brought in by China Sorrows to co-ordinate the day-to-day running of the High Sanctuary, and she would have been the first for the manacles were it not for proving herself utterly indispensable. As it was, Creed had eyes and ears on her constantly, so that little jibe was unlikely to have passed unnoticed.

"Detective Pleasant is in your office," Cerise continued.

Valkyrie frowned slightly. "Skulduggery's here?"

Cerise nodded. "And in your office. Please have a great day."

Valkyrie watched her walk off, and when she turned a man with his head buried in a book walked into her, rebounding off her shoulder.

"Oh dear!" he said, looking around like he'd just woken up.

Valkyrie smiled. "Hey there, Destrier. Been a while."

"Detective Cain," Destrier responded, and went quiet for a moment before speaking again. "Yes. Hello. How are you? You look well. Lovely weather for this time of year, isn't it?"

She held up a hand. "It's OK," she said, "you don't have to run through all of your small-talk options with me. You can just be your weird self when I'm around, remember?"

"Oh, that's right," said Destrier. "Yes. Thank you."

"How's work? They treating you well?"

"Everyone here is very nice – although I don't think they understand many of the things I say, probably because it's mostly about temporal manipulation and, really, in order to remotely understand temporal manipulation you have to be *capable* of temporal manipulation, and no one is. No one apart from me. I have a joke about time, if you'd like to hear it?"

"Sure. I love jokes."

"It's not very good."

"That's OK."

"You won't find it funny."

"Try me."

"What time is it when an elephant sits on your watch? Time to get a new watch."

"Yeah," said Valkyrie. "That's not funny."

"I'm not a very funny person," Destrier said sadly, and wandered off.

Valkyrie took the elevator up to the security floor. Her office, kindly supplied by the Supreme Mage himself, was a lavish room with a wonderful view over Roarhaven and somewhere Valkyrie herself had visited a grand total of three times: once to check it out, again to leave her coat, and the third time to pick up said coat.

Skulduggery was sitting behind her desk, reading from a monitor. "Hey," she said. "Want to hear a joke about time?"

"No," he responded, still reading. "The Obsidian worshippers are becoming a nuisance. The City Guard's reports are full of minor incidents involving scuffles and public intimidation. People are calling them the Nulls."

"Are they a problem that we need to sort out?"

"Not yet."

"Cool. That's cool. Skulduggery, what are you doing here?"

"Appraising myself of the latest reports surrounding Obsidian," he said, finally looking up at her.

"And I'm assuming this is because you've had a thought?"

"I always have thoughts. I'm full of them."

"Thoughts about how to deal with him?"

"Possibly," Skulduggery replied. "What do we know of the Obsidian Blade?"

"It's a knife. Or it was a knife, and then Auger broke it while stabbing the King of the Darklands."

"Before that."

"How long before that? A few hundred years ago, Mevolent used it to—"

"Before that."

Valkyrie sighed. She just wasn't in the right frame of mind for this. Not today.

Skulduggery seemed to recognise her mood, and continued. "When the Big Bang occurred and the universe began to spread outwards, existence snagged, forming a minuscule gap in the fabric of reality. A sliver of nothingness. A hole in the sock of what is."

"Sometimes your words are like poetry."

"Over time, this piece of nothing drew the detritus of the

universe towards it – particles of matter, sprinklings of dust – until it attained a weight of its own. This speck of nothingness, entombed in rock, drifted through the cosmos until it fell to Earth as a meteorite where the Faceless Ones found it, discovered its obsidian centre, and forged it into a knife."

"No," said Valkyrie.

His head tilted. "No?"

She shook her head. "They didn't need to. I'm... with all the Faceless Ones inside me, I can kind of look into their memories, you know? So much of it is overwhelming – like, the human brain isn't capable of storing even a fraction of their experience. But I can pick up impressions."

"So what are you seeing?"

"They didn't need a knife. Why would they? A knife is a weapon for humans – or humanoids, at least. It has a handle to grip, and a blade to cut. But this was a weapon they didn't need to hold – once the obsidian was exposed, they basically threw the meteorite at each other with their minds. They killed... God, they killed so many of their own kind. The images... It's incredibly sad."

"Incredibly."

"I know you don't like them, Skulduggery, but that's no reason to be mean."

"On the contrary, it's every reason to be mean."

"The Faceless Ones are still living beings who deserve compassion."

"They're murderous monsters."

"And how are they any different from humans?"

"Humanity is young and stupid. The Faceless Ones should know better."

"So, anyway," said Valkyrie, trying not to get too annoyed at him, "the Faceless Ones stopped fighting among themselves and decided to put the meteorite out of reach, so they dumped it on a parallel Earth in another universe."

"Where the mere presence of the unrefined obsidian meant that everything on that planet slowly became infected over eons, and was wiped away," said Skulduggery. "That Earth is what we know as the Void World."

"And then the Darkly Prophecy warned the Unnamed that one day he would battle Auger Darkly," Valkyrie said, "and, since the only weapon that could kill him was the Obsidian Blade, he sent Mevolent to find the meteorite so that Auger wouldn't be able to use it against him. Which, ironically, meant that Auger had it to actually use against him a thousand years later."

"And do you know how Mevolent found it?" Skulduggery asked.

"Not a clue. Do you?"

"Mevolent and his team shunted from one dimension to another. They spoke to, or tortured, any Shunter they found on their travels in order to build up a better picture of the dimensional network. This is how they first heard of the Dire Dimension."

Valkyrie raised an eyebrow. "Sounds like a positively charming place."

"In the Dire Dimension, the Earth was, essentially, a prison planet that, back then, was ruled by a man called Quietus."

"Quietus is a nice name."

"He was also known as the Tyrant of Gaunt, a genocidal warlord who was responsible for the deaths of billions."

"He sounds pretty bad, all right."

"When the sorcerers of that Earth found out that there were other realities, they renamed their planet Gaunt and ensured that their whole reality be called the Dire Dimension, in order to intimidate visitors from other universes."

"They really take first impressions seriously," Valkyrie muttered.

"The Dire Dimension has some unusual properties, one of which means that travel in or out of it is on an exchange basis. In order for someone from here to shunt over there, someone from there has to be shunted over here."

"That's inconvenient."

"Undoubtedly," said Skulduggery, "although it's also the only thing that has stopped a Dire army from invading other realities, so, all in all, probably for the best."

"So Mevolent found the Dire Dimension."

"Yes, he did," Skulduggery said. "And in 1546 he paid them a visit. Quietus granted him an audience and confirmed that he did, in fact, know where the Void World was located. Quietus met with the Unnamed and passed on the information."

"In exchange for?"

Skulduggery tilted his head. "How do you know he received anything in exchange?"

"He held all the cards, right?" Valkyrie said, shrugging. "The Unnamed had gone to him. He had the location. He was a tyrant and a mass murderer. Stands to reason he'd want something pretty major in return."

"And I'm assuming he got it," Skulduggery responded, "but the Unnamed never told anyone what it was. Quietus held up his part of the deal, and the Unnamed sent Mevolent to the Void World, where he found the so-called Void meteorite with the obsidian core. Mevolent extracted the obsidian and used some of the meteorite to form a handle."

"Then Mevolent came back home and stabbed the Unnamed with it."

"Yes, he did. Approximately sixty years later, one of Mevolent's subordinates stole the Obsidian Blade, planning to kill Mevolent himself and take over. He died – in an accident, apparently – and the blade was lost until 1865 when it was used to kill a sorcerer in Turkey. From there, it made its way through the underworld, bought and sold on the black market, until it came into the possession of Assail Devon, and then Omen Darkly, and then Auger – at which point it transformed him into Obsidian and seems to have destroyed itself in the process."

"And not once during all of that," said Valkyrie, "did you

actually answer my question and tell me how you plan to stop Obsidian."

"On the contrary—"

"Right," Valkyrie interrupted. "So you have told me, then. Somewhere in all that, you told me how we're going to do it. Has it ever occurred to you to just tell me what I want to know instead of, like, talking for an hour and hiding it in all those words? Fine, let me think. Hold on." She closed her eyes and replayed the conversation in her head.

"Do you want a clue?" he asked.

"Shut up." She opened her eyes. "The meteorite," she said. "Mevolent made the handle out of the meteorite because the one thing the obsidian hadn't wiped from existence was the rock that had formed round it. So that's the only substance in the universe, or in any universe, that can stand up to it."

"Precisely."

"So we find the Void meteorite and we... what? Make a pair of shackles?"

"If we can. It all depends on how much we can find."

This was brightening Valkyrie's day considerably.

"Where is it?" she asked. "Please tell me that Mevolent brought the meteorite back to our universe with him."

"He did not."

"Please tell me it's not still on the Void World."

"It is."

"Please tell me we don't have to go to the Void World ourselves."

"We don't."

"Oh, thank God."

"We do, actually. I lied about that part."

"Dammit, Skulduggery. Do we even know where the Void World is? We don't, do we? Of course we don't. So we've got to ask this Quietus guy?"

"We might not have to. I'm hoping his son, Ragner, will be able to tell us. He's far nicer."

"Far nicer than a mass-murdering tyrant isn't that difficult, though, is it? So is he actually nice, or is he just nicer in comparison to his dad?"

"Ragner is actually nice, I promise."

"And where do we find him? Some strange, unsettling, bizarre world populated by freaks and weirdos?"

"Los Angeles."

Valkyrie looked at him. "So yes, then."

12

"I hate this," Never said, rattling the black bracelet on their wrist, the noise adding to the cacophony of the cafeteria. "Look at it. It's stupid and cheap-looking and horrible. It's also oppressive. This hideous thing is oppressing me right now, even as we sit here, eating lunch. You know those little pastry things I like to have for breakfast?"

Omen nodded. "They're lovely. Why didn't you have one this morning?"

"Because I buy them from a tiny bakery in Italy and then teleport back before anyone notices I'm gone. I haven't been able to do that today, Omen."

"They were delicious."

"They were," Never moaned, dropping their head into their folded arms on the table. "And they will be again, on this I swear."

A nearby table of Second Years laughed uproariously at something, and Never managed a scowl. "No one understands my pain," they muttered.

Omen's phone buzzed with a message from Gretchen. He was aware of a smile forming as he sent a reply.

"So is it serious?" Never asked.

"Very serious," Omen said. "This oppression will not stand."

"I'm not talking about me now, doofus. I'm talking about you and this lovely American girl you're always chatting with."

Omen gave a small laugh. "She's too old for me."

"Only by a few years."

"Still too old. She's giving me advice about getting into art college, though."

"Ah, college. Have you talked to your folks about it?"

Omen hesitated.

"That's what I thought," said Never.

"I don't think they're ready to discuss any of that while Auger is still missing."

"He's not missing," Never said, their voice gentle. "He's gone."

"You know what I mean. They're worried about him. Once we get him back, once he's Auger again, I'll tell them about art college and that I'm preparing my portfolio, and I'm sure they'll be cool with it."

"Yeah," said Never. "Because your parents are the epitome of chill."

The day stuttered by. Some classes seemed to drag and others passed before Omen could figure out what he was meant to be doing. The teachers were subdued and the students upset. The last few classes blurred by when Omen wanted them to take their time: he was having dinner with his parents that evening.

On his way back to his dorm room, he noted how Jenan's old followers were avoiding him in the corridors, even going so far as to walk the other way when they saw him approach. Ever since they'd returned to school, after Abyssinia had tried to have them killed and framed for the massacre that never happened at Whitley naval base, they'd slunk their way back into their old lives. They'd walked with their heads down, eyes averted, so far from the arrogant swagger they'd adopted as Arcanum's Scholars. Especially with their leader gone, locked up for murder, attempted murder and terrorist activities, they'd pretty much retreated from view, and the world had carried on, happily leaving them behind.

With Jenan now stalking the corridors of Corrival Academy once more, Omen thought they might emerge from the shadows, hold their heads a little higher, and try to regain some of that cockiness they'd lost. But it seemed as though the Jenan Ispolin brand was now so irretrievably tarnished that not even his former lackeys wanted to be associated with him.

Omen changed out of his school uniform into neat trousers and a good shirt. He stood in front of the mirror and frowned at his ankles. He was pretty sure that they shouldn't be on show, but apparently his legs had stretched since he'd last worn this outfit. He looked like a child.

The door opened and Byron Grace slipped into the room.

Omen blinked at him. "Hey," he said.

He'd once had to knock Byron out to stop him from killing him, but Byron had been corrupted by a man called Smoke at the time so Omen didn't think it counted as a personal attack. He really hoped it didn't anyway. He quite liked Byron. He'd been one of the Arcanum's Scholars, so he wasn't great, but he abandoned them before Abyssinia turned them into First Wave, so he wasn't the worst.

"I'm leaving," said Byron, who looked pale and nervous, "and I think you should, too."

"What do you mean? You're leaving the school grounds or you're leaving school?"

"I'm leaving this place and I'm not coming back. Jenan's been here one day and already no one will talk to me. You know why they won't talk to me? Because they know it's only a matter of time before he comes to exact his revenge."

"You might be overreacting here..."

Byron started pacing. "He tried to kill you, Omen. He almost killed Auger. How can you, of all people, think that I'm over-reacting?"

It was, admittedly, pretty hard to argue with that.

"Just because we're all back at school doesn't mean we're safe.

It just means that now he knows exactly where to find us any time he wants."

"Byron, if you're feeling threatened, you should tell someone."

"Like who?" Byron said, laughing. "Miss Gnosis? Mr Peccant? And what are they going to do – go to Duenna? She's the one who let Jenan back in. She's not going to protect us. She'll just look the other way. Omen, please tell me that you understand this."

"I mean—"

"Omen."

"Yes," he said, "I understand. I can't tell you you're wrong about any of it. Jenan's a psychopath and it's completely in keeping with who he is that he'd take his revenge. He reckons you betrayed the lot of them and he hates me for, well, obvious reasons."

"Then why are you sticking around? Is it for the exams? We've been taught how to forge anything, Omen. We can certainly cobble together some exam results."

"It's not the exams," Omen said. "It's *really* not the exams. When I'm here, I'm in the middle of things. Nothing can happen to Auger without me knowing about it. If I run, I'm cutting myself off from everyone I want to help. I was actually hoping that you'd be here to..."

"To what?" Byron asked. "To lend a hand? Sorry, I can't do it. I'm not a hero, and I have no interest in pretending to be one. I don't like it when people want to kill me."

"You think I do?"

"No, but I think you're getting used to it. I never want to get used to it. I don't want to be special. I don't want people coming after me. I want to have a life where I have money and hot boyfriends and I do a job I love and I get to play video games and hang out with actual friends. This stuff? It's not for me, man. And it shouldn't be for you, either. I'm leaving – now. This evening. I just needed to tell you to do the same."

"Thank you, but... I can't."

Byron nodded. "Good luck, Omen."

"Same to you."

They shook hands, and Byron left, and Omen noticed the time and winced.

The restaurant was fancy and the Darklys were taken to a good table and everyone fussed round them like they were royalty, but when the staff went away Caddock glowered.

"You see this?" he muttered. "You believe it?"

Emmeline moved her folded napkin a fraction to the side. "Don't let it get to you," she said. "People are watching."

Omen tried figuring out what their problem was, but he was lost. His mother was right, though: people were watching. Most of their fellow diners had the good grace to try to be sneaky about it, but others just out-and-out gawped, shocked that the family of Obsidian would dare show their faces in public.

The *maître d'* escorted a small group to another table, and Emmeline smiled at them in recognition as they passed. The moment they were gone, her smile turned decidedly frosty.

"*They* get our table?" Caddock whispered, his face reddening. "We're booted off to the back of the bloody restaurant and they get the best table in the house? Those social-climbing sycophants?"

"Caddock," Emmeline said tightly. "Control yourself."

Omen looked at his napkin. He didn't see anything wrong with their table. It was a nice one, and it was near the toilets, so that was handy.

"Omen," Emmeline said in an obvious effort to improve the mood, "how is school?"

"Fine."

"Maybe some more detail, if you please? One-word answers are not acceptable, as it leaves the responsibility for the conversation entirely in the other person's lap."

"Show some damn consideration," Caddock said as a member of the serving staff came over to pour the wine.

Omen waited until they were left alone, then gave another answer. "I don't feel safe there," he said.

"Don't feel safe where?" Caddock asked, irritation flickering across his face.

"In school."

"What? What are you going on about? Why wouldn't you be safe? It's a school."

"Creed's running it."

"Principal Duenna is running it. Omen, you're lucky they even allowed you back into that place. Do you know the strings we had to pull for them not to expel you? Never mind expel you, they wanted to imprison you for what you did!"

"Creed was going to—"

"Enough about the Supreme Mage," said Emmeline, her voice sharp. "We don't want to hear about more accusations, conspiracy theories, plans or plots or schemes or anything like that. We have enough to deal with right now without you adding to our burden. Tell me you understand that, Omen. Tell me that you at least understand that much."

The heat rose into Omen's cheeks, and he looked down. "I understand."

Caddock reached out, patted his wife's hand. "Your mother has a very important meeting at the High Sanctuary in the morning. We need it to go smoothly, Omen – so none of your silly adventures tonight. You stay in your bed and you don't leave your dorm room until breakfast, are we clear?"

"What's the meeting about?"

"Are we clear?"

"Yes, we're clear. What's the meeting about?"

Emmeline squared her shoulders a little. "The High Sanctuary is looking to establish a department devoted entirely to Chosen Ones," she said. "A team dedicated to uncovering, collecting and cataloguing prophecies from around the world, collating them into a database, and then deciding on the best course of action. There are some who want me to lead this department."

"It's a great honour," said Caddock, "and it could put the Darkly name back where it belongs."

Omen frowned. "What about Auger?"

"Meaning?"

"Like, what about finding Auger? I thought that was your number-one priority – finding and helping Auger. That's what you said. Last time we were out for dinner, you said the only thing you cared about was—"

"I know what we said," Caddock interrupted, "and obviously our first priority is to help him. Of course it is. Your mother didn't go looking for the opportunity at the High Sanctuary – they came to her."

"It can only be to our advantage," said Emmeline. "If I get to lead an entire department dedicated to Chosen Ones, just think of the resources I'll have at my disposal."

"I suppose," Omen mumbled. He knew his dad was glaring at him, but he kept his eyes on his plate.

"This is a big opportunity for us," said Emmeline. "For all of us, do you understand? We used to be the singularly most important family in the world. Grand Mages took our calls without question. Everything we said was acted upon. Everyone knew who we were and understood the power we wielded. Our son was the Chosen One. All our hopes rested on his shoulders."

"And now he's the villain," Caddock said.

Omen glared. "Auger is not the villain."

"Look around. See everyone staring at us? They don't share that opinion. They've already forgotten about the sacrifices and the heroism and the leadership that we've demonstrated over the years. All they care about is what's happening right now, in front of their stupid faces, and right now Obsidian is a threat. Our power and influence have crumbled, but this is a chance to claw some of it back."

"Omen," said Emmeline, reaching out to pat his hand, "we're all after one thing. We all want Auger back. This is our strategy to do that. Until we have reclaimed some of our standing, we can't afford any distractions, and we can't risk any scandals. For the time being, you are our only son, and we need you to not embarrass us. Can we trust you to do that?"

Rage boiled away any words he could use, so Omen just sat there and nodded and didn't meet their eyes. He didn't hate anyone. He never had, and he'd never wanted to. But there, right in that moment, he was pretty sure he hated his parents.

13

"Hello, Nefarian."

Nefarian Serpine, looking casual all in black, put away his phone as Valkyrie sat at his table. He signalled to a passing member of the bar staff, and when they came over he said, "A coffee for my guest, please. Americano?"

"Thank you kindly," said Valkyrie. When they were alone, she nodded to the full glass in front of him. "Something's put you off your wine?"

"I'm savouring the anticipation," he said. "You have no idea what it's like to spend hundreds of years drinking ale brewed by mortal peasants and then to arrive in a universe that has perfected a thing called Chardonnay. One must prepare accordingly." He smiled. "So how is the pet skeleton?"

"You're the second person to call him that in the last twenty-four hours. I don't think he'd appreciate the nickname."

"His own fault for following you around like a lost puppy."

Valkyrie let that go. "He's good. I'm meeting him tonight. We're heading to LA later."

"Ah," said Nefarian, "Los Angeles. Yes, I have seen it in films. Very sunny. Do tell him I said hello."

She grinned. "I'm sure he'll ask me to return the greeting. How's the hand?"

Nefarian wriggled the perfectly normal, skin-wrapped fingers of his right hand. "Oh, this one, you mean? The one you gave me in place of the one Skulduggery Pleasant allowed to be chopped off? It's fine, thank you for your concern."

"Still no pain? No loss of feeling?"

Nefarian sighed, allowing his irritation to drift away. "No. It's working perfectly."

"You said last time your fingertips were getting numb."

"That stopped. In the last two weeks, it's been like I was born with this hand."

"I'm glad. Do you miss the one without the skin?"

"I do, actually," Nefarian said. "I miss the power that came with it."

"The power, or the fear it instilled in others?"

His smile was slight but genuine. "I miss the look in people's eyes, this is true. I miss the respect that terror brings."

"But now you're treated just like an ordinary Roarhaven citizen."

That amused him. "Not quite, no. When people realise it's me, and realise I don't have my Necromancer ability, they make their displeasure at my presence known and, indeed, felt."

"People don't like you?"

"I was as shocked as you are."

"But it's not like you're defenceless. You're still an Energy Thrower."

"Sadly, it's just not the same."

"And, once you explain to them that you're not this reality's Serpine, surely they accept this and move on?"

"Amazingly, they don't seem to care."

"I'm stunned."

"I thought you might be."

"Maybe you shouldn't have been such a bad guy, though, in whatever universe you happened to be in."

"That's what I was thinking." He sipped his wine, his green eyes fluttering closed.

She grinned again. "Enjoying that?"

"There are many things in this world for me to grow fond of, Valkyrie. The chance to leave my past behind. The chance to start over. And the chance to sample the simple delights of a mortal world unencumbered by the rule of sorcerers."

"Cheers to that," she said, and had a little more of her Americano.

"Does Skulduggery know?" Nefarian asked, his gaze settling on her once more.

"About our chats?" she said, her cup tinkling slightly against the saucer. "Nope."

"Why haven't you told him?"

Valkyrie shrugged. "It'd put him in a bad mood. He's OK with you being here, and he's cool with you remaining, you know, *alive*. He understands that you're not the same Nefarian Serpine who killed his family—"

"—but I *am* a Nefarian Serpine who killed *another* Skulduggery's family."

"Yes. So he's never going to like you."

"But you're OK spending time with me, knowing the things I've done?"

"Skulduggery's done bad things, too, and so have I," Valkyrie said. "When it comes to sins and mistakes and forgiveness, I reckon I'd be quite the hypocrite if I didn't at least give you the chance to redeem yourself."

He watched her, and nodded. "Redemption is important, isn't it?"

"Yup."

"It gives one hope."

"That it does."

"It gives one comfort."

"Why do I get the feeling you're trying to tell me something, Nefarian?"

He didn't have to look away to gather his thoughts. That's what she liked about him. Centuries of being the villain had made him unflinchingly honest. "You're lost," he said.

"I'm what?"

"You've got no friends and you're lost. That's why you're here."

"I have loads of friends. What are you talking about?"

"You *had* loads of friends," said Nefarian. "Then this happened. You became the Child and the Mother. Now you're struggling to find people who want to spend time with you who aren't Faceless Ones fanatics, who don't worship you as much as they worship the Dark Gods. It's why we meet up every few weeks – simply so you have someone to talk to."

That was the problem with unflinchingly honest people. They were annoying.

"Has it ever occurred to you that I might meet up with you every few weeks because I like you and I think you're actually an OK person?"

"Undoubtedly," said Nefarian, reaching out to tap her hand, "but it's also because you have no other friends."

She pulled her hand back and looked away, and when she went to argue some more Nefarian had grown quite pale. "You OK?"

"Excuse me for just a moment," Nefarian said, getting up and walking quickly to the Gents.

When he was gone, a man approached. It took Valkyrie a moment to place him as Robert Scure, the Sensitive who'd been helping Creed with his Nexus Helmet.

"Miss Cain," Scure said, almost bowing. "It is an honour to see you again."

"Hi."

Scure licked his lips. "I just wanted to... Every time we've met, I've always been somewhat overwhelmed by your presence, if that doesn't sound too off-putting."

"It certainly sounds a little off-putting."

"It's just, as the Child and the Mother of the Faceless Ones, as someone whose very blood runs with their power, with their purity of purpose, it is beyond an honour to be around you. To be, dare I say, close to you."

"Apparently, you dare."

"You are as close to divinity-made-flesh as any human being alive, Miss Cain. I might be doing what I can to assist the Supreme Mage, to allow him to converse with the Faceless Ones, and that will surely be a marvel of magic and technology, but you... you were born with that power in your very veins. I hope I'm not being too forward when I say that I love you."

"Jeepers."

"It's not just the kind of love one of the faithful would feel towards their messiah, either. I assure you that this is a real and genuine—"

"I'm going to stop you right there, Robert," Valkyrie said. "It crossed over into creepy territory a while ago and I let it continue simply out of curiosity, but my friend's on his way back and I think we should say goodbye."

Tears sprang to Scure's eyes. "Yes. Of course."

Nefarian arrived back at the table, noticed Scure and glared at him like he was something he'd trodden in.

Scure, for his part, tightened like a slug sprinkled with salt. "Nefarian," he said.

Valkyrie raised an eyebrow. "You two know each other?"

"Scure here used to do some work for Mevolent, back in the old days," said Nefarian. "How've you been, Bob?"

Scure went to answer, then frowned, then hesitated.

"That's unfortunate," said Nefarian, pulling a gun from his jacket and shooting Valkyrie before she could react. She fell sideways, cursing even as Nefarian shot Scure three times in the chest. She hit the floor, her hands clutching her wound. She was aware of Nefarian running out of the bar and a load of people rushing forward, completely ignoring Scure's dead body in order to fuss over her.

"Dammit," she muttered, and then slipped out of consciousness.

14

Valkyrie woke to find Damocles Creed leaning over her.

"Ew," she said.

He hadn't shaved and he was all sweaty like he'd just been working out, and he needed a shower.

"Valkyrie," he said. "How are you? How do you feel? Are you OK?"

"I'm grand," she muttered. "Stand back, would you? You stink. Is bathing against your religion, or something? As someone who is actually a part of your religion, I feel I should be told these things."

"There's nothing wrong with the smells of the human body," he said, doing as she'd asked. "I came right over when I heard what happened. Rest assured, the City Guard are searching for Nefarian Serpine as we speak. It's only a matter of time before we have him."

She shifted slightly, and moaned. "Who the hell fixed me?"

"I did, Miss Cain," said a doctor, hurrying forward. "The bullet perforated your lung, but we were able to—"

She waved a hand weakly to shut him up, then reached out, put that same hand to his face and drank in his knowledge. The doctor gasped, his entire body stiffening. Valkyrie absorbed his expertise, searched for the trauma in her own body. He'd done a pretty good job, all things considered, and had already set her up for a quick recovery. She treated herself to an immediate recovery, though, and when she took her hand away he collapsed.

Creed didn't even glance at him, and Valkyrie sat up, feeling back to normal. "How long was I out?" she asked.

"Five hours," said Creed. "I insisted the medical staff proceed slowly, to minimise the potential for mistakes."

She looked around. "Where's Skulduggery?"

"We can send for him if you'd like."

"You mean you haven't already? I was shot. When I get shot, Skulduggery gets told."

"I apologise," said Creed. "I didn't appreciate how important he remains to you."

"He's my partner."

"Absolutely – though I confess I do not know why."

Valkyrie got out of bed. "Right. I've heard this before so you can save what's coming next."

Her clothes had been cleaned, and were now folded on a table against the wall. She picked up her T-shirt. The blood was gone, but the bullet hole was there. She sighed. It had been one of her favourite tops.

"We'll step outside," said Creed. He took hold of the doctor's collar and dragged him out of the room like he was pulling a wheelie bin to the end of the driveway.

Valkyrie dressed. She checked her phone. No missed calls. No messages. She put it away and clipped the black metal skull to her belt. As if he knew exactly what she was doing, Creed spoke through the not-quite-closed door.

"After this assassination attempt, I feel I have to insist that you wear your necronaut suit at all times. You are the most important person on the face of the planet – which means you're a target."

"This wasn't an assassination attempt," Valkyrie said, pulling on her boots and lacing them up. "Nefarian wasn't interested in killing me – he just wanted to make sure I wouldn't stop him from killing Scure. I'm assuming Scure's dead?"

"Yes. A sad loss. Fortunately, he'd already completed most of the work he'd been doing for us."

"That is *very* fortunate," Valkyrie said, sure that he'd miss the sarcasm. He did.

"Rest assured, the project is still on track for completion within an acceptable timeframe."

"Happy days," she said, back on her feet and walking to the window. "Any idea why he'd want to kill Scure in the first place?"

"Undoubtedly, he wished to stall, if not derail, the project. Perhaps out of jealousy. Perhaps he feared what the Faceless Ones would tell me. He did fail them on multiple occasions in his dimension, after all."

Valkyrie opened the window. "I suppose that's true," she said, climbing out, the lights of Roarhaven swimming below her. "But then why..."

She let herself fall, mid-sentence. The wind tore at her hair and clothes and filled her cheeks and made her eyes water, and she turned the fall into a swoop, veering up before she hit the ground, and a few pedestrians cheered and waved and she grinned and waved back.

She gave Skulduggery a call, arranged to meet him outside Fletcher's place. She got there first and waited. It was late. Fletcher had agreed to teleport them to LA at nine sharp, and that was hours ago.

Skulduggery landed beside her, and tilted his head. "What happened?" he asked.

"What do you mean?"

"Your clothes have been cleaned and you have glue residue on your hand where the IV drip was attached," he said. "Your jacket's closed and you like to keep your jacket open unless it's markedly colder than it is now, which means that you're hiding something – damage to your clothes. Not from a stab wound –

you wouldn't let anyone get close enough with a knife. A bullet wound, then – or the work of an Energy Thrower."

"Bullet."

"And Creed didn't think to tell me."

"He still views you as the enemy."

"How do you view me?"

"As my partner. But also the enemy."

"What a tightrope you walk."

"Isn't it, though? I was talking to Nefarian Serpine, just passing the time, and Robert Scure walked in. You know him?"

"I do. One of Mevolent's Sensitives."

"Nefarian shot me, then killed Scure and left. They're searching for him now."

"And when was this?"

"Around six."

Skulduggery nodded. "I see. And why were you meeting with Serpine?"

Valkyrie shrugged. "I check in on him from time to time."

"That's nice of you. What were you talking about?"

"This and that. Then Scure came in, said some creepy things, was pretty weird towards Nefarian, and Nefarian pulls a gun."

"Do you think it was premeditated?"

"Like, did he wake up this morning, planning to kill Scure? I doubt it. He was in the toilet when Scure arrived, and when he came back to the table his mood was different. I think he saw an opportunity to kill him and just took it. I don't think he was carrying the gun to kill Scure in particular."

Skulduggery nodded. "A man like Serpine would have been carrying it for an added layer of protection."

"So the mystery we have to solve," said Valkyrie, "is why did he want to kill Scure?"

"That's only part of the mystery," Skulduggery said.

"Oh?"

"This happened at six? You're absolutely positive?"

"Around six, yeah. I got to the bar at a quarter to, and not more than fifteen minutes had passed. Why?"

"Because at six o'clock I was across town," Skulduggery said, "and Serpine was trying to kill me."

15

"I see," said Valkyrie. "Any chance you're wrong about that? I have witnesses. Do you have witnesses?"

"I don't need witnesses – I have me."

"Good point."

They looked at each other.

"So what happened with you?" Valkyrie asked.

"Right before six, Serpine approached, complained about the time I allowed his hand to be cut off—"

"Such a baby."

"—and proceeded to attack me. When his initial attack failed, he sat by the side of the road and started telling me about life back in the Leibniz Universe."

"You talked?"

"He complained. The conversation was mostly him complaining. But yes, we talked – for almost an hour. Then he got up, apologised for attacking me and walked away. He was wearing a grey suit with a dark blue shirt."

"In the bar," said Valkyrie, "he was wearing black trousers and a black shirt, untucked. You're sure it was Nefarian? It wasn't, like, someone with a Nefarian façade or some kind of reflection or, I don't know, a shapechanger?"

"Shapechanger?"

"We have those, don't we?"

"Not really."

"I could have sworn we had shapechangers. What am I thinking of?"

"I have no idea."

"We have sort-of shapechangers, though, right?"

"This wasn't a shapechanger. This was Nefarian Serpine."

"So how can there be two of them? Oh! Of course. He's an alternate-reality Nefarian."

"A possibility," Skulduggery said, "but the Serpine I spoke to was definitely the Serpine who accompanied us on our mission to kill Mevolent."

She frowned. "But the Nefarian I spoke to was definitely that one, too."

"So we return again to the essential conundrum: how can there be two Serpines?"

Valkyrie sighed. "Another case to solve, because we don't have enough things to do already. Can we just focus on maybe stopping Obsidian before we get sidetracked into doing something else?"

"I think that's a wonderful idea. Have you woken Fletcher?"

The door opened and Fletcher glared at them. "You both woke me when you decided to have a conversation beneath my bedroom window. We were supposed to do this hours ago. I do have work tomorrow, you know."

He was in Daffy Duck pyjama shorts, T-shirt and slippers, and his hair was a flattened mess.

"You look grumpy," said Valkyrie.

"I feel grumpy. Maybe he used a Teleporter."

"Sorry?"

"Serpine," Fletcher said. "I heard every word because you two talk so bloody loudly."

Valkyrie was a little insulted by that. "I have to talk loudly because he talks so much I have to shout to be heard."

"And I have to talk loudly because I always say the most

interesting things and as many people as possible deserve to hear me," Skulduggery added.

"Right," Fletcher said, scratching the sleep from his eyes. "But like I was saying, maybe you got your times slightly wrong and Serpine used a Teleporter to take him across town in an effort to confuse you."

"I cannot be confused," Skulduggery responded.

"That's the logic you're using?"

Skulduggery watched Fletcher. "You were more fun before you became a teacher."

"I've heard."

"But Serpine having a Teleporter ready to go," Valkyrie said, "forgetting for a moment that Teleporters are still quite rare commodities, would mean that he planned to kill Scure – and I really don't think he did."

Fletcher shrugged. "It's just a suggestion. To be honest, I don't know this dead guy, but seeing as how he used to be one of Mevolent's henchmen, I can't say I'm too cut up about his death. Now can I please take you to LA and then get back to bed? I'm a responsible adult these days and I need my sleep."

Skulduggery looked at Valkyrie. "He is very grumpy."

"See?"

Fletcher rolled his eyes, put his hands on their shoulders, and before Valkyrie could blink they were standing in the foyer of the Firehand Club, the premier nightspot for mages in North America.

"Hi, Fletcher," said a woman in black leather as she passed, her voice a purr. "Nice jammies."

Fletcher scowled at Valkyrie and Skulduggery, and vanished.

The music was loud, but the club wasn't as busy as when Valkyrie had been there last, so they had no trouble making their way to the VIP section. Skulduggery got a few nods and Valkyrie got more than her share of sidelong glances. The party-going side of magical society wasn't big on the Faceless Ones, it seemed. She did her best to smile politely as the security staff let them through to the cordoned-off area. Here, the music dimmed a little, allowing for conversation.

The man who came forward was a giant. He loomed over Skulduggery as he shook his hand, a broad smile on his broad face, his long hair a dark blond. He carried a few extra pounds to soften the sheer amount of muscle on his frame.

"My friend, Skulduggery!" he said in an accent that was a mix of Californian and something way more exotic. "It has been far too long since last I gazed upon your bony head!" He turned to Valkyrie, his huge hand completely enveloping her own as they shook. "And this, of course, is the Valkyrie Cain! I have heard tales of your exploits, and they are as magnificent as they are terrifying. But, now that I gaze upon you, I see that while you have the soul of a warrior, you have the face of an enchantress."

"I've always said so," Valkyrie replied.

"I could gaze into your eyeballs for hours, if not more."

"You've got very pretty green eyeballs yourself."

"My eyeballs? No. My eyeballs are unhealthy foliage growing as weeds along the banks of a boring river compared to the deep walnut splendours of your own. Walnut with hints of mahogany, I see now, and flecks of startling gold."

"You have a way with words."

"Thank you. I enjoy forming them with my mouth. Would you enjoy very much a drink, fair warrior?"

"That's quite enough of that," Skulduggery said, stepping forward to separate their hands. "We're here on business, Ragner."

Ragner looked surprised. "Cannot business be also a pleasure, my friend? For instance and example, I would quite immensely enjoy discussing very serious matters while becoming romantically entangled with Miss Valkyrie Cain."

"Sadly," said Valkyrie, "I am already romantically entangled with somebody else. Or I want to be, at the very least."

"Then I shall not complicate matters," Ragner said solemnly, "for matters of entanglements are already complicated enough, are they not?"

"So glad we managed to get that sorted out," said Skulduggery. "The reason we're here, Ragner – the Void World. We need to get to it."

The good humour on Ragner's face fell away. "And why would you want to do a silly thing such as that, my bony friend?"

"Matters of importance."

"I dislike those."

"I'm aware."

"I came here to escape such matters."

"I'm also aware of that."

Ragner shook his head. "And I'm afraid I can't help you, for the location of the Void World is knowledge in my brain that I lack and also do not have. There is only one I know of who possesses this knowledge, and that person is my father who is also my dad."

"I was afraid of that."

"So what's wrong with that?" Valkyrie said. "If he knows, why don't we just ask him?"

"We cannot," said Ragner. "We cannot even speak of why we cannot ask him. That is the agreement. That is the vow. That is the oath. Isn't that right and correct, Skulduggery?"

Skulduggery sighed.

"Wait," said Valkyrie. "You've both taken this vow?"

"Yes," Skulduggery said. "We can't ask Ragner's father. Or tell you why."

Valkyrie raised an eyebrow at Skulduggery. "You're seriously not going to tell me?"

"Not while you're like this."

"Like what?"

He tilted his head. "Compromised."

She looked at him and said nothing for a while, then shrugged. "So we've come all this way for nothing, it looks like. That's a shame. Do we have any other way of finding the Void World?"

"I can't think of one," Skulduggery replied.

Ragner's phone beeped and he glanced at the screen. "Excuse me for a moment of time," he said, smiling at them both and then walking off.

They found an empty table, and when they were seated Valkyrie leaned in. "So the only way to find the Void World would be to ask this Quietus guy, and we can't do that because of reasons. That's awkward, it really is, because that's the only way we know of to stop Obsidian. Unless, of course, you don't want to stop Obsidian."

"Why wouldn't I want to stop him?" he asked.

"Because he's going after disciples of the Faceless Ones. You want him to continue, don't you?"

"Actually, no, I don't."

"But you're not overly concerned about his actions, right?"

"No, I'm not."

"But I am, see," she said. "I do actually care. Right now, Obsidian's going after the followers – but what happens next? Does he go after the Faceless Ones themselves? Could he? Is he capable of wiping a Faceless One out of existence just as easily as wiping away one of their worshippers?"

"I suppose we'll find out," Skulduggery said, "if it happens."

"And that's where we have our problem, because I can't allow that."

"Sure you can."

"The Faceless Ones are my children."

"You're not thinking clearly."

Valkyrie laughed. "You have no idea how I'm thinking. You have no idea what this is like. Believe me when I say that they're my children, OK? Believe me when I say that I love them, that they're a part of me, that I'm a part of them. And believe me when I tell you that anyone who tries to hurt my children will have to go through me to get anywhere close to them."

Skulduggery didn't say anything.

"Do you believe me?" she asked.

"I believe you."

"So now you understand why I've got to get to the Void World, and you understand why I'm going to have to insist that we speak to Quietus."

"We'll find another way."

"There is no other way – you said it yourself."

Ragner came back to their table before Skulduggery could respond, another man in tow.

"Allow me to introduce to you a friend of mine that I have," said Ragner. "This is he who has the name Eraddin Tomb."

Tomb was slender, dressed in tight black jeans and black boots and a baggy black T-shirt with a skull on it. His face was sharp, his hair black and kind of punky. He wore black nail polish and eyeliner.

"Skulduggery Pleasant, as I live and breathe. So good to see you again."

Skulduggery tilted his head. "I don't believe we've met."

"Oh, we have," Tomb replied. "I wasn't wearing this face, though, so maybe that's what's throwing you. And Valkyrie! How have you been?"

"Good," she answered cautiously. "Have we met, too?"

"Oh, yes."

"I don't remember."

"You had other things on your mind."

"And when was this?"

"A few years ago. You'd just died."

"I'm sorry?"

"Maybe Ragner should have used my other name when introducing me," said Tomb, his smile widening. "Hi. My name's Eraddin Tomb. I'm the God of Death."

16

"The God of Death," Skulduggery repeated.

"Yes," said Tomb.

Valkyrie frowned. "Are you one of the Viddu De?"

"No, no. They're dead gods. I'm the God of Death. Huge difference."

"And in what way are you the God of Death?"

"In every way there could possibly be, I should imagine," Tomb answered. "All the ways."

"But in what ways," Skulduggery said, "specifically?"

"I'm not sure I understand the question."

"They don't have the belief that you are who you say you are," said Ragner. "They are disbelieving."

"Oh," said Tomb. "Well, I can understand why. It's quite something to claim that you're the god of anything. You have a right to be suspicious, Skulduggery. As do you, Valkyrie – don't try to hide it."

"I wasn't."

"So Death has a god, does it?" Skulduggery asked.

Tomb nodded. "Most things have gods. Or they did anyway. Or they would have had, at least. I don't think there was ever a God of Microwave Ovens, but if the Faceless Ones hadn't slaughtered most of us, there may well have been one at some stage."

"I have a question," said Valkyrie. "If there had been a God of

Microwave Ovens, and he died, what would happen to microwave ovens? Would they stop existing?"

"No, no, not at all," said Tomb. "But they might stop working properly. I knew the God of Stars. The universe was still expanding and she took over until her untimely death, so, if you travel far enough in a particular direction, you will eventually come to a region of the cosmos that is remarkably precise, very structured and well-thought-out. Then she was killed and it all went higgledy-piggledy again."

"So you're not actually Death," Skulduggery said.

"Correct."

"You're just the God of Death."

"Indeed. Think of me as the curator, or the janitor, even. I make sure that death proceeds along its usual routes."

"In this universe alone?"

He shook his head. "Multiple universes. As many as will have me, in fact. But not all. Some universes have their own Gods of Death, some have no need for death at all, and, of course, there are the Viddu De." He fixed his eyes on Skulduggery. "I would be very interested to hear about your interaction with them. You visited, didn't you? To persuade them not to breach this universe?"

"We chatted," Skulduggery said.

"You must have been very convincing."

"I simply delayed them for an opportune amount of time."

"Ah, yes," said Tomb. "Long enough for Damocles Creed to seal them away again. What did you talk about?"

"This and that," said Skulduggery.

Tomb chuckled, and Ragner poked him in the ribs.

"Tell them," he said.

"Tell us what?" Valkyrie asked.

"Nothing," said Tomb. "It's nothing. It doesn't matter."

"Tell them," Ragner insisted.

"There really is nothing to tell."

"They might be able to help."

99

"Ragner, you're a good friend, but I don't need any help. I'm a god."

"And what are the words you tell me often? Gods are people, too."

"What appears to be the problem, Mr Tomb?" Skulduggery asked. "Maybe we can help, if it's within our power."

Tomb hesitated. "I wouldn't want to trouble you. I know how busy you two get."

"Mr Tomb," said Valkyrie.

He sighed. "Very well, very well. I think – and I preface this with the assurance that it really is no big deal – but I think someone is trying to kill me. But, again, it's no big deal."

Valkyrie frowned. "Can someone kill you?"

"No. Well, yes, but really no."

"He has died before," said Ragner. "Many, many times this has happened. He dies, and somebody new becomes the God of Death. It's him, but it's not him but it's him."

"It's a title that's passed on from person to person," Tomb explained, "along with the power and a bit of the personality. The fun bit."

"And who do you think is trying to kill you?" Skulduggery asked.

"I have no idea."

"Why would anyone want to?" Valkyrie asked. "What would they gain?"

"Not a whole lot," said Tomb. "They'd kill me, but there'd instantly be another God of Death to continue doing what I'm doing."

"Do you have any enemies?"

"Not really."

"He's very well liked," said Ragner.

"I have friends," Tomb said modestly.

"So why do you think someone's trying to kill you?"

"Little signs. Subtle hints. A growing sense of unease. Also a note that read 'I'm going to kill you'."

Ragner nodded. "That is what we are calling our first clue," he said.

"Do you still have this note?"

Ragner looked sheepish. "I ate it."

"Why?" Skulduggery asked.

"I thought it might be poisoned."

"So why did you eat it?"

"To find out if it was poisoned."

"And was it?"

"I don't know. I'm immune to poison."

"Have you eaten any more clues?"

"I don't think so. Maybe, if they were disguised as food."

"When did this note arrive?"

"A few weeks ago," said Tomb.

"Had you upset anyone? Met anyone new? Run into any old faces?"

"Not that I can remember."

"It might be a prank," Valkyrie said. "A bad joke. Someone messing with you."

Tomb snapped his fingers and pointed at her. "See? Yes, exactly. That's what I said, too. I said this is probably nothing. People get death threats all the time. Everyone does."

"Not everyone."

"Almost everyone. It's a part of life."

"Not *really* a part of life."

"I said the smartest thing I could possibly do was ignore it."

"Not sure I agree with that one."

"Tell them about the bomb," said Ragner.

Skulduggery said, "What bomb?"

"It's nothing," said Tomb. "A bomb I found in my apartment. It barely went off."

"It destroyed his apartment," said Ragner.

"Barely destroyed it," corrected Tomb. "I'd completely forgotten about it until now."

"When did it happen?"

"This morning."

"Mr Tomb," said Skulduggery, "it would appear to me that your life is currently in danger."

Tomb laughed. "I hardly think danger is the right word here. Under slight threat, maybe."

"Perhaps you should contact the Sanctuary," Valkyrie said. "They could put you in protective custody, or at the very least assign you a security team. I'll ask them, if you'd like. Sanctuary people tend to do what I tell them."

"That's very sweet of you, but I doubt it's necessary."

"Someone is trying to kill you."

"But they're not trying very convincingly."

"Aren't you curious, though? Don't you want to find out who it is?"

Tomb gave the slightest of shrugs. "Mildly curious, I suppose."

"And wouldn't you like to stop them before anyone else is hurt? Like maybe they try to kill you and they get Ragner instead?"

"Ragner's pretty hardy."

"Hardy and hearty is Ragner," said Ragner, and chuckled.

"But are you immortal?" Valkyrie asked him.

"Not in a way that is real, no," said Ragner.

"And you're not a god of anything, are you?"

"I'm the God of Fun Times!" Ragner bellowed, laughing again, then became serious. "But not really, no."

"So death, for you, is quite a serious proposition?"

"One of the most serious."

Valkyrie raised an eyebrow at Tomb. "You wouldn't want to see your friend hurt, would you? You wouldn't want to see him killed?"

"I would not," said Tomb, suddenly sombre.

"Then the best way to ensure his safety is to get the Sanctuary to investigate this."

Tomb sighed. "I guess."

"Maybe even take you into protective custody."

"Now that is where I draw the line," Tomb said firmly. "Any Sanctuary operatives assigned to protect me are Sanctuary operatives who are not out there helping people who need it the most. I will not be responsible for that."

"Where are you going to be living now that your apartment has been destroyed?" Valkyrie asked.

Ragner grinned. "Sleepovers we will be having, at Ragner's house!"

"And is your house secure?"

"Very secure probably."

"Does it have an alarm system?"

"Alarm systems are so impersonal. I prefer guard dogs."

"So you have guard dogs?"

"Unfortunately, I am allergic."

"So no guard dogs?"

"I have sturdy locks and many games consoles. My sleepovers are legendary."

"Then how about we accompany you both back to Ragner's house?" Skulduggery said. "We'll check out how secure it is, make some suggestions, and talk further about what to do concerning the location of the Void World. Does that sound agreeable?"

"Immensely!" Ragner boomed.

The valet brought Ragner's SUV around and they left the club through the rear exit. A moment before getting in, something whipped by Valkyrie's ear and she heard a shot, then two more, and Eraddin Tomb fell back, blood blossoming across his T-shirt. Skulduggery caught him and Valkyrie left them to it and flung herself into the sky, tapping the amulet on her belt. As the suit flowed over her, she scanned the buildings in front, catching a glimpse of an aura through a top-floor window.

She pulled her mask down and smashed through the glass, turning in mid-air as she cut the power, hitting the wall with her feet and rebounding. The man inside threw down his rifle – it was too long to use in such close quarters – and took a knife from his belt. He wore black, and a mask that covered his whole head. Just like she did.

The blade skimmed harmlessly across her chest and she lunged, wrapping both arms around him, pinning his knife hand to his side. She heaved him off his feet, allowed herself to fall backwards, slamming his head on to the ground. He immediately broke free and rolled off and Valkyrie got up, swerved the punch that came next and grabbed his arm. She stepped in with a stomp that should have broken his foot, and an elbow that should have shattered his jaw, and he responded with a punch that should have flattened her nose and a kick that should have destroyed her knee. They broke apart. His suit and his mask – they were armoured, just like Valkyrie's.

Well, that was just unfair.

His magic swirled and he raised his hand to do something, but she got there first, blasted him off his feet with her lightning. He flew all the way across the room, hit the wall and stumbled to his knees. He looked up, his eyes locking on to hers, and then he took a small glass tube from his pocket, no longer than a matchstick, half filled with a blue liquid, and broke it. The liquid flashed when it came into contact with the air, filled the room with a light so powerful it actually hurt Valkyrie's eyes, and when the flash faded a moment later, he was gone.

Still seeing bright spots and feeling remarkably unsteady, Valkyrie took the stairs down in case the assassin was doing something stupid like hiding nearby. He wasn't. She got back to where Skulduggery and Ragner were kneeling by Eraddin Tomb's side.

"Is he dead?" she asked, finding no delicate way to broach the subject.

"No," said Tomb, raising a hand weakly. "But I am hurt. Have you ever been shot?"

"Yes."

"Then you know what it's like."

Skulduggery looked up at her. "He's been shot in the heart," he said. "Three times."

Valkyrie absorbed the information. "That's usually enough to kill someone."

"Usually."

"I am quite resilient," said Tomb. "I just need another moment."

"The shooter?" Skulduggery asked.

"Got away," she told him. "He was masked, and armoured, and pretty good." She raised an eyebrow at Tomb. "What do you think, Eraddin? Now that you've been shot in the heart, do you reckon it's time to take these threats on your life seriously?"

Tomb managed to sit up. "I guess so. That being said, so long as I have friends around me, I can think of worse ways to go."

"Friends forever," said Ragner, grasping his hand and pulling him to his feet.

"Friends forever," said Tomb.

"Why is my life so weird?" Valkyrie muttered.

17

Martin Flanery was well acquainted with glitz and glamour.

As a self-made billionaire who'd built up his company from practically nothing to a world-conquering brand of high-end real estate, he knew full well that good things came in gold and anything less was for losers. He had brought this sensibility with him when he became president, and made a point of being singularly unimpressed by whatever the White House offered.

Air Force One? He'd owned private jets that had golden faucets. The Executive Residence? He could count seven houses that left it in the shade without even trying. The Oval Office?

Fair enough, that one was pretty hard to beat.

But White House shindigs were a different affair. His own parties were a lot more fun and had a younger and hipper type of guest, but the bashes that the White House threw were, admittedly, pretty damn classy. There was the occasional movie star wandering around – the kind who talked about political issues and did charity work – but mostly the guest list comprised ambassadors, CEOs and world leaders. The difference wasn't so much about fame, and not even about money – it was about power.

But there was more than one kind of power in the world.

Flanery greeted an Arab prince like an old friend, ignored the president of a news network that was intent on spreading nothing but scurrilous rumours and lies, and shook hands with the British prime minister. They talked about golf, and Flanery insulted the game of cricket, something he knew the prime minister was a big fan of. Instead of defending his beloved sport, the man laughed along and agreed it was dumb, and Flanery felt that familiar warmth spreading. Offending someone weaker, to their face, and having them suck it up... that's what true power was.

Flanery left the prime minister to flounder for conversation with somebody else, and turned to see a tall man with neat blond hair standing on the other side of the room.

Flanery didn't know how to react. His brain just wouldn't form the necessary thoughts. He gaped, and suddenly became aware that any angry response whatsoever would attract the attention of everyone at this party and he really, really didn't want any attention attracted to this man.

Flanery walked straight over, ignoring the hopeful faces that turned to him as he passed.

"Terrific party," Perfidious Withering droned in that ridiculous English accent. "All the big nobs are here, swanning around, looking important. How much do you think you'll raise for your campaign tonight alone? I suppose the sky's the limit with this lot, eh?"

"What are you doing?" Flanery managed to say, keeping his voice down. "What are you doing here? You're not supposed to be here."

"You haven't been returning my calls, Mr President. I understand that you are a frightfully busy man and you must be getting exceedingly worried that Paul Donovan is outstripping you in the polls—"

"You can't trust those polls," Flannery said automatically.

"—but you didn't turn up to our appointment yesterday. It would seem, to any outside observer, that you were avoiding me."

"You can't be here," Flanery said, keeping his voice down. "There are press here. Photographers!"

"Oh, worry not, Mr President – I'm not afraid to have my picture taken. The dinner jacket I'm wearing was made by the finest tailor in London."

"You don't have the credentials to be here."

Perfidious smiled. "Of course I do. I have all the credentials I need to go anywhere in the White House. I am nothing if not prepared. Preparation is key, as dear Nanny used to say."

An aide approached, leading some smiling foreign dignitary. Flanery glared, and the aide redirected the dignitary to the Chief of Staff.

Flanery stepped closer to Perfidious, hoping to intimidate with his sheer size. "Why are you here?"

"I am concerned, Mr President," said Perfidious as he failed to appear intimidated. "We had an arrangement. Crepuscular Vies issues a directive, I relay that directive to you, and you carry out said directive. It was as simple as it was effective. And yet you are thus far failing to comply with the directives you are given."

"You don't issue orders to me," Flanery sneered.

"On the contrary," Perfidious said, "that is exactly what I do."

Flanery took a moment, then tilted his chin. "You're uninvited to this party. Get out."

He went to move away, but Perfidious gripped his wrist and squeezed and Flanery had to stop himself both from crying out and falling to his knees.

"Listen to me very carefully, you outrageous buffoon," Perfidious said, leaning closer. "Crepuscular sent me because he felt his personal relationship with you had grown too adversarial. He felt that you might disobey him out of sheer spite – not to mention stupidity. But with me, you had the opportunity to start again. We had the opportunity to be jolly good friends. And yet here we are, with me about to break your wrist in a room full of important people, surrounded by the Secret Service. You don't want me to break your wrist, do you, old boy?"

"No," Flanery whimpered.

"You were given instructions on how to proceed with Doctor Nye, were you not?"

"Yes. Yes, I was."

"And what were these instructions?"

Beads of sweat were forming along Flanery's forehead. He wasn't used to sweating. He didn't like it. "Report back to you on every decision I make."

"No," said Perfidious, his grip tightening so much Flanery thought he was going to wet himself. "You were to report back to me after every stage is complete. You are not allowed to make decisions, Martin. Do you remember why?"

He remembered, but refused to say.

"Do you remember why, Martin?"

Flanery caved. "Because I'm a moron," he whispered.

"Precisely. The work we are doing with Doctor Nye is delicate. It requires patience and timing. According to the schedule Crepuscular set out, the next stage of the operation wasn't due to be undertaken for another two weeks. And yet what have we heard, from Doctor Nye itself? You ordered the next stage to be implemented *yesterday*."

"Please..." said Flanery. "My wrist..."

"You have placed the lives of the servicemen and women under your command in the greatest jeopardy. These are your own soldiers, for goodness' sake."

"Nye... Nye said it'd be OK."

"Doctor Nye is a sadistic psychopath whose only concern is reaching the next stage of its experimentations. It doesn't care one jot about the lives lost or ruined if something goes awry. You, Martin, are supposed to. You're supposed to care."

"I do. I do care!"

"You are an impatient child throwing temper tantrums whenever something doesn't immediately go his way."

Perfidious looked down as if he'd just remembered that he was crushing Flanery's wrist. He let go, and Flanery actually sobbed in relief.

"I have spoken to the good doctor," Perfidious said, helping Flanery straighten up. "It will now be making its reports to me, and me alone. I thought I could trust you, Martin, to be sensible. To shoulder some of this responsibility. Obviously, I was wrong. In future, I will be informing you of what I decide you need to know. Do you understand these new terms?"

"Yes," Flanery whispered.

"I wish it could have been different. I so would have liked it if we could have been friends. Have a good evening, Mr President, and maybe put some ice on that wrist."

Perfidious smiled politely and walked away, and Flanery stalked for the exit, blinking back tears and ignoring anyone who called out for his attention. There were different types of power in the world, all right, and he had just been given a taste of the oldest and most primal.

And that was never going to happen to him again.

18

Due to the drastic reduction in Cleaver numbers around the world in the last ten years, Sanctuary security had become a primarily mage-centric endeavour – something Temper Fray was very much appreciative of. Outwitting a team of bored, listless sorcerers was merely a matter of patience, as opposed to a mind-numbingly stupid suicide run. While he waited in the car park across from the restaurant, Tanith opened the door and slid in beside him.

"Any sign?" she asked.

Temper nodded. "He's in there, at his usual table."

"Bodyguards?"

"Five in there with him, three more outside. So far, he's sticking to his schedule."

She nodded. It was a warm night in New York, and quiet. "Did you hear what happened to Valkyrie?" she asked.

"You mean Serpine?" Temper said. "Yeah, I heard."

"Did you have anything to do with that?"

He raised an eyebrow at her. "You think I tried to have her killed?"

"Last time we were chatting, you were talking about doing just that."

"And we all agreed that we wouldn't make a move without everyone's consent. I didn't know about it. I'm not in contact with

Serpine and I don't know why he did what he did. Last I heard, Valkyrie was the only friend he had in Roarhaven."

Tanith shrugged. "I'm just checking."

"She was rushed to the High Sanctuary Medical Wing after he shot her, did you know that?"

"I did."

"She was in there for ten hours."

"I heard five."

"She was in there for a while," Temper said. "You know what that means, yeah?"

"Valkyrie didn't heal herself."

Temper nodded. "It means she can be killed. A mortal wound probably won't do it – we'd be running the risk of her finding a way to repair the damage herself – but if we attacked her like Serpine did, to either kill her instantly or at the very least leave her unconscious so that we could move in closer to finish the job... It can be done."

"I still don't think we'll need to."

"You reckon she's going to come back on her own, do you?"

"The Valkyrie we know is still in there," Tanith said.

"You hope."

"Don't write her off, Temper."

"Given enough time, I'd agree with you. But things are moving way too fast for my liking. We might still be waiting for the old Valkyrie to re-emerge and miss the only opportunity we have to save what's left of the world."

Tanith sighed, and looked away.

"How are your friends?" Temper asked, changing the subject.

"You're going to have to be more specific," she said. "I have loads of friends. I'm very popular."

"Your Black Sand friends. I heard Africa's Sanctuaries are now under Creed's control."

"I heard that, too. They said they'll join with us if we need them, but I don't know what state they'll be in if we do have to call on them. Their best sorcerers are being taken down every time I look round."

"Is it true? Was Frightening Jones captured?"

"We don't know. He was on assignment in Michigan, but he's dropped off the radar. We don't even know if he's still alive. Black Sand are fighting a losing battle, but what the hell else are they going to do? Quit? Go home?"

Temper was searching for an answer when their target came out of the restaurant. Elder Pericles Boon said farewell to his dinner companion, then got in the car that pulled up in front of him. His security detail arranged itself and a small convoy drove off.

"Like clockwork," said Temper.

Tanith got out and Temper pulled on to the road and followed the convoy at a respectable distance. The security detail had grown lazy due to overfamiliarity with the routine and the route. They probably hadn't even noticed him behind them.

Even so, Temper turned down a side street as Tanith took over, driving a delivery van. He swapped cars and worked his way back to the convoy, allowing Tanith to drop back before anyone got suspicious. Tailing someone was a lot easier when you knew exactly where they were going.

The convoy turned into the gated compound, and Temper drove by and pulled in at a safe distance. He got out and Tanith joined him.

"They make any stops?" she asked.

He shook his head. "No stops, no doubling back, no nothing. He has no idea we're coming for him."

"Well, OK then."

They hurried across the road and Tanith walked up the wall, helping Temper up after her. Once they'd dropped down the other side, she slipped into the shadows and he lost sight of her. Temper stayed where he was, in the bushes. Listening.

After seven minutes, he heard a chirp, and crept forward, past the deactivated security cameras, stepping over the unconscious forms of Boon's security detail. Boon's house was big, and the patio door was open, and Temper walked straight in. Tanith was sitting on the couch, watching the news on the huge TV on the wall. From elsewhere, a toilet flushed, and moments later Pericles Boon walked in, his shirt undone.

"Pericles," Temper said, smiling, "could we have a word?"

Boon wheeled round, but Tanith was already leaping backwards over the couch to block his exit.

"This doesn't have to get ugly," Temper said.

Boon clicked his fingers and summoned flame, and Hansel shot out of Temper's palm and bit Boon's thumb. It was barely more than a nip, but came close to severing the digit, and Boon reeled away, howling at the blood and the pain, the fireball extinguised before it got going.

Tanith took hold of Boon and steered him to the couch, letting him collapse back on to it while they stood over him.

"We're not going to hurt you," Tanith said.

"My thumb's hanging off!" Boon cried.

"That's a bit of an exaggeration," said Temper, feeling Hansel curl up contentedly in his forearm. "We just want to have a quick chat with you."

Boon shook his head. "I can't. I can't speak to either of you. The Supreme Mage will find out."

"Nonsense," said Tanith. "He's way too busy to take notice of what happens to some random Elder. We're fine."

Boon glared. The pain was making him sweat. "You can threaten me all you want, I'm not going to betray the Faceless Ones."

"This isn't about betraying the Faceless Ones," said Temper, "this is about the people who've betrayed you."

"What? What are you talking about?"

"I'm talking about Uziah Kudos."

"You mean *Grand Mage* Uziah Kudos."

"That's right. Your boss. When China Sorrows made him Grand

Mage, he made you an Elder, right? He got you into this position of power. Finally, after hundreds of years, you achieved your dream."

"You don't know anything about me."

"We know a bit," Tanith said. "We know you and Kudos were friends once. Partners. Then rivals. You'd get the upper hand, then he would, then you'd pass him by, then he'd overtake you, all the way up through the ranks, both of you with your eyes on the Grand Mage position."

"But then China made him Grand Mage," said Temper, "which must have been a kick in the teeth, right? Still, at least Kudos turned round and appointed you as one of his Elders. That's a nice consolation prize, isn't it? A nice runner's-up medal?"

"I know what you're trying to do. You're trying to drive a wedge between us. It won't work. Yes, we were rivals, but Uziah didn't have to make me an Elder. He did so out of respect, and I owe him a debt I can never repay."

Tanith hunkered down. "China was going to make you Grand Mage," she said.

Boon blinked at her. "I'm sorry, what?"

"You were her number-one candidate. But Kudos heard about this and told her of an incident involving you begging a witch for your life, back in 1610, or thereabouts?"

It might have been the blood loss, but Boon went deathly pale. "He didn't."

"I'm afraid he did. All those secrets you divulged? Those compromises you made? I mean, you betrayed a whole lot of people back then—"

"I didn't betray anyone!" Boon snarled. "I wasn't even conscious! It was Kudos who begged! Kudos who told her everything she wanted to know! Afterwards, he made me swear to never tell a soul what he'd done and I kept it to myself for all these years—"

"A lot of people died because of that witch," said Temper. "Everyone knew someone had betrayed them, but no one ever found out who. Uziah Kudos told China it had been you."

"He's a liar. He's a liar and a coward."

"And he's Grand Mage," said Tanith, "when really you should be Grand Mage and he should be just getting out of prison."

Boon cradled his bleeding thumb.

Tanith stood. "You were right when you said we came here to drive a wedge between you and your Grand Mage. That's exactly why we're here. We have secrets like this about every Council of Elders around the world, and we're driving wedges left, right and centre."

"But that doesn't mean that Kudos didn't stab you in the back to get to where he is today," Temper said. "So the question, Pericles, is what are you going to do about it?"

And they left him there.

19

At precisely 9.43 am, Commander Silvano Hoc left the Vault – the ugly, functionally squat concrete headquarters of the City Guard – and strode to the Dark Cathedral. He could have taken a car, but he preferred to walk. It was important, he felt, to be seen out and about on the streets of the city he was responsible for protecting. It was also important that the people see him walk into the Dark Cathedral, knowing he had business with the Supreme Mage himself.

He ignored the Cathedral Guards who bowed to him as he passed, and gave a curt nod to the priests on their way to deliver the sermon in the nave. He took the elevator to the very top floor, his heels clicking pleasingly on his way from the elevator to the doors of Damocles Creed's office.

"You may enter," said the man at the desk outside. "The Supreme Mage will be with you shortly."

Hoc entered.

It was always a thrill stepping into this office. No matter the temperature outside, Damocles Creed's room was always cold, never comfortable. Upon the massive desk was a small box made of black wood mixed with black metal. Hoc picked it up, examined it. Each side was carved with sigils in a language he didn't recognise.

"You've found her prison," said the Supreme Mage, walking in.

Hoc replaced the box on the desk and turned, standing to attention. "Sir?"

"I call it the Cage," said Damocles Creed. "It will be enough, I think, to hold her. To hold her many times over, I should imagine."

"To hold who, sir?"

The Supreme Mage didn't say anything. Hoc knew why. It was because Damocles Creed didn't answer questions he viewed as stupid. So the answer must have been obvious, and in a way it was, though Hoc still didn't understand.

"Would an Eternity Gate not suffice, sir? We have Mevolent in one. Surely one could be fashioned for Darquesse?"

"Eternity Gates slow time," said the Supreme Mage, "so it takes a thousand years to form a single thought. What do we do when a single thought from Darquesse could destroy the world, Commander? No, no – a new prison is required."

Hoc nodded. He had so many questions, not least a very practical one. Darquesse was a six-foot woman with broad shoulders, and this box was barely as long as Hoc's hand.

The Supreme Mage, as usual, seemed to have anticipated Hoc's confusion. "I want you to push her past her breaking point. I have taken note of your readings, and I want you to increase the output another one hundred and twenty-five per cent."

Hoc paled. "Sir?"

"I want Darquesse's physical form destroyed. I want her reduced to mere energy. That energy you will trap in the Cage. Do you understand?"

"Yes, sir."

The Supreme Mage sat behind his desk. "Report, Commander."

"Sir, we have found and arrested Nefarian Serpine. He was hiding out in the Humdrums, hoping to evade our Sense Wardens. He is now in our custody, and I can promise you that justice will be swift."

"Valkyrie Cain wants to handle the investigation," said the Supreme Mage.

Hoc faltered. "Sir? We... He's in custody, sir, and we—"

"If Valkyrie Cain wants to assert jurisdiction, Commander, then you acquiesce. Are we clear?"

"Sir, yes, sir."

"Any updates on our search for Obsidian?"

Hoc hesitated. "That is a most difficult operation, Supreme Mage. I'm afraid I am unable to make any sort of estimation as to when that threat will be neutralised."

"Then it's a good thing Valkyrie Cain and Skulduggery Pleasant are on this case, too, wouldn't you say?"

Hoc bristled. "Yes, Supreme Mage."

"What about these Obsidian obsessives I keep hearing about?"

"The Nulls, sir, yes. They are increasingly a worry, I'm afraid. Largely made up of disaffected citizens, known troublemakers and anti-Faceless Ones activists, their numbers, thankfully, remain low – we estimate there are no more than thirty Nulls at present."

"But they are dangerous."

"They are responsible for several attacks throughout the city, yes."

The Supreme Mage sighed, squeezing the bridge of his nose with the thumb and forefinger of his right hand. "Leave me," he said. "I must pray on this."

Hoc's salute was as keen as his fervour.

20

China watched the normal people in their normal world, jogging and walking and sitting in the park, and felt overdressed.

It wasn't what she was wearing – a skirt and sensible heels, a simple off-white blouse and an elegant yet understated jacket – and it certainly wasn't her make-up because she wasn't wearing any. It was, as it always was, her face.

People stared. People had been staring for most of her life. Sometimes she welcomed it, sometimes she enjoyed it – but most of the time she endured it. Even now, sitting on this bench, her hair down, the biggest sunglasses she owned failing to disguise her cheekbones, they stood around, sneaking glimpses, pretending to talk on their phones, some of them just openly gaping. It was why she didn't go out in public an awful lot any more. Well, that and she was a wanted fugitive.

A man walked up, sat beside her. He didn't profess his love for her, his devotion, he didn't offer to leave his partner for her – not like four other men and three other women had done so far today.

"Hello, Grantham," she said.

Grantham Arrant sat back, crossed his legs, eyes flicking to each of her admirers as they stood there and glared. "I thought we were meant to be keeping a low profile. Isn't that what you said?"

"Sometimes that's harder than it sounds," she responded. "You're looking well."

"I'd return the compliment, but we both know how redundant that would be. You're taking quite a risk, aren't you? I could have gone straight to Creed when you got in touch."

"You could have."

He smiled at her. "I'm assuming there are at least two snipers who have me in their sights even as we're sitting here?"

"Grantham," China said, "you wound me, you really do. I've known you for centuries and I trust you as much as I trust anyone."

He grunted, amused. "What can I do for you, China? If you're about to ask me to join your resistance, I'm afraid I'm going to have to be one of those strange, foolish people over the years who have said no to you. I have dedicated my life to working within the Sanctuary system, but I do not involve myself in Sanctuary politics."

"A fact of which I am well aware, fret not. No, Grantham, I'm not here to recruit you – I'm merely here to chat."

"About what?"

"I've heard rumours, and then I have had those rumours confirmed, that you and your fellow Hosts are searching for ways to sabotage your own Doomsday Protocol."

That amused half-smile of Grantham's slipped from his face, and he took a moment. "Would I be wasting my time if I were to ask how you heard all this?"

"Indeed you would."

"I can't talk about it, China. You know I can't."

"And, of course, I would never dream of prying."

"Thank you."

"But pry I must. This is quite an alarming turn of events, and would indicate that something has gone quite drastically wrong. There's a powerful Sensitive, named Solace, who has already attempted to distract me from whatever the Hosts are up to. She is obviously invested in the Doomsday Protocol – though whether she wants it to go ahead or she's seeking to disrupt it, I do not yet know. It's entirely possible that your

121

group is being influenced without you realising it. Where are the Twenty, Grantham?"

"In a secret location."

"And where is the vessel?"

He hesitated.

"Grantham? The last I heard of this ever-so-mysterious person or object, it had been lost, possibly destroyed."

"It has since been recovered," he replied unhappily.

"I see. And would I be right in assuming that the recovery has directly led to this somewhat undignified scramble to abort the Protocol before it can be activated?"

Grantham stood. "I'm... I'm sorry, China. I can't talk about this."

"What is the Doomsday Protocol, Grantham?"

"It's always good to see you," he said, already walking away.

21

The Vault was an ugly building. The cops glared at Skulduggery, but failed to meet Valkyrie's eye as they made their way down to the interrogation room. Nefarian Serpine was already sitting at the small, notched table when they walked in. He was wearing prisoner orange and sporting brand-new bruises.

They sat down opposite.

"Really?" Nefarian said. "That's what this is about? You try to kill one measly Arbiter and suddenly that's an arrestable offence? If I had known that, I probably wouldn't have done it. It's just not worth the hassle."

Skulduggery put his hat on the table. "Why don't you tell us what you were doing at six o'clock yesterday evening?"

Nefarian frowned. "What? You know what I was doing."

"We need you to tell us," said Valkyrie.

"You're seeking a confession? Since when are confessions necessary? The terribly unfair Sanctuary justice system means that a detective has to do little more than believe a suspect is guilty – for Arbiters, it's even more weighted in their favour. Why would you need a confession? You know what I did."

"Where were you?" Skulduggery asked.

A moment passed in which Nefarian glared, and then he shrugged and sat back in his chair. "At six? Oh, I remember – I was attacking you."

"Attacking which one of us?" asked Valkyrie.

An arched eyebrow. "The thinner one."

"So at six pm yesterday," Skulduggery said, "you were attacking me?"

"Half-heartedly," said Nefarian. "Let's make that clear, all right? If I wanted to actually kill you, I would have succeeded. As it was, I saw you, I grew irate at the memory of that time you allowed a group of Necromancers to cut off my hand, and I let my temper get the better of me. Then we spoke, exchanged insults, you intimated that you wouldn't be seeking retribution for the attack, and we parted ways. Obviously, you changed your mind, and sent those delightful City Guard officers after me." He folded his arms.

"And what about me?" Valkyrie asked.

"What about you?"

"You didn't attack me?"

"Of course not. You weren't there. Even if you were, why would I have attacked you? You gave me a new hand. I'm on the verge of actually liking you as a person."

Skulduggery tilted his head. "And what are your feelings towards Robert Scure?"

Nefarian blinked a few times. "The Sensitive? What does he have to do with anything?"

"Please answer the question."

"My feelings towards Robert Scure border on the indifferent. He worked on some projects for Mevolent and one or two for me during the war, but always as part of a larger team. I wouldn't particularly rate him as a genius scientist. He worked well with others, though, which I suppose could be seen as a strength."

"So you harboured no animosity towards him? No ill will?"

"No will of any kind. Why?"

"He's dead," said Valkyrie.

"And?"

"And you murdered him."

"I most assuredly did not."

"You shot him three times yesterday at six pm."

Nefarian watched her, then watched Skulduggery, and smiled. "Ah," he said.

"Ah what?"

"You have a mystery to solve," he said. "Someone has done their very best to frame me for a murder I didn't commit – but Skulduggery Pleasant himself is my actual alibi, so you know I couldn't have done it. Oh, this is wonderful! An attempt at framing me and I just happen to be around a witness whose account cannot be faulted! I couldn't have timed this better if I'd tried! So who is claiming I did it?"

"Among others," said Valkyrie, "I am."

Nefarian's smile faded. "I don't understand."

"I was with you when you killed him."

"You...? You saw me do it?"

"I did."

"You're mistaken. Or you were fooled. It happens to the best of us."

"I'm not mistaken, Nefarian. We'd been talking for fifteen minutes up to the moment you pulled out your gun, shot me, and then killed Scure."

Nefarian looked at her and didn't say anything.

"When was the last time, according to you, that we spoke?" she asked.

"Two weeks ago," Nefarian answered. "You wanted to check up on me, see how my hand was doing."

"And how did we end that conversation?"

"You said we'd meet again soon."

"And then I sent you a message on Wednesday morning, arranging to meet you at the bar."

"I didn't get a message from you on Wednesday. You can check my phone. They took it off me when they arrested me, but you can—"

125

"Phone records can be altered," Skulduggery said.

Nefarian looked straight at Valkyrie. "The last time I spoke to you was two weeks ago. I didn't get a message from you, we didn't arrange to meet, and I didn't spend fifteen minutes talking to you. I'm being set up."

"We talked, Nefarian."

"I swear to you, we didn't."

"You killed Scure right in front of me."

"You can't believe that." He switched his gaze to Skulduggery. "If they think I killed Scure, one of the High Sanctuary's top Sensitives, they'll execute me. You know I didn't do it. You know I was with you."

"I do know that," Skulduggery said.

"But I know that you were with me," said Valkyrie.

"Someone is framing me," Nefarian snarled. "I understand that you're probably very busy saving the world from evil-doers, but if you had a spare moment or two to sort this out and save my life I'd be ever so grateful." He waved his hand in Skulduggery's face. "I think you owe me that, don't you?"

They left the building and got into the Phantom.

"This is intriguing," Skulduggery said, pulling out into light traffic.

They drove in silence for a few minutes.

"OK," Valkyrie said, nodding behind them, "so that, back there, is the Nefarian that you were talking to on Wednesday night."

"Yes."

"So what happened to the Nefarian that I was talking to?"

"You mean the imposter."

"He wasn't an imposter, for God's sake – I'd know the difference. I'm pretty sure I'd know the difference. Wouldn't I?"

Skulduggery shrugged.

"Well," she muttered, "that's helpful."

"It's a mystery," he said. "Mysteries are good. They make you think in unusual directions. When you start thinking in unusual directions, you can solve all kinds of problems – and 'all kinds' is precisely the type of problem we are beset with right now."

"So you're saying that this extra workload might actually be to our advantage?"

"That's exactly what I'm saying."

"Or it might distract us from a threat that could end civilisation as we know it."

"Or that," he said, nodding. "But what is life, Valkyrie, if not a journey of discovery?"

"I'll take your word for it." Her phone buzzed. She tapped the screen and read the message. "Eraddin Tomb has received another death threat."

"Please tell me that Ragner hasn't eaten it."

She showed him the photograph of the note on her screen. "It's in one piece, don't worry. It accuses Eraddin of being a demon. There's some stuff about the Bible and God, most of it spelled wrong... Huh, that's interesting. It says, 'The assassin may have failed, but I will not.'"

"So the gunman in the armoured clothes was hired," Skulduggery said. "He's not the one sending the threats."

Valkyrie swiped the screen. "You're kidding," she breathed.

"What is it?"

"The person who threatened Eraddin sent him a photo along with the note," said Valkyrie. She waited until they'd stopped at a set of traffic lights and passed him the phone.

The photograph was badly lit, and showed a man's arm and hand brandishing a pistol. His face wasn't visible. He was wearing a blue T-shirt tucked into jeans. On the table beside him was a stack of unopened mail. Skulduggery tapped the screen and zoomed in on the address.

"Walter Egmont," he read, "of Brentwood, Los Angeles."

"Are bad guys getting stupider," Valkyrie asked, "or are we getting smarter?"

"A little bit of both," Skulduggery said, passing back the phone and taking the next right. "We'll have a chat with Walter once we're done here."

Valkyrie frowned. "Wait, where are we going? Are we headed for Corrival?"

"We need to talk to Omen," Skulduggery said. "We need to ask him to do us a small favour regarding Obsidian."

"You're going to ask him to lead his brother into a trap, aren't you?"

"I am."

"He won't do it."

"He might."

"Would you?"

"No."

"Me neither, and Omen's more like us than you realise. He won't do it."

"Probably not," Skulduggery said. "But we have to try, don't we?"

22

"Mr Darkly," Skulduggery said, adopting a friendly tone as Omen stepped out of the classroom into the corridor, "have you been staying out of trouble?"

"Hey, Omen," Valkyrie said, smiling.

Omen ignored her, focusing his gaze on Skulduggery. "Have you found Auger? Is he OK?"

"As far as we know, he's fine, yes."

"Then why are you here? You didn't call me out of maths just to ask how I'm doing." Omen frowned. "You need me to do something. You wouldn't be here unless you needed me to do something. It's the only reason you ever talk to me."

"That's not true," said Valkyrie. "Omen? Omen, please look at me. Why won't you—?"

"Because you're the Child of the Faceless Ones," Omen said, failing to keep the hostility out of his voice. "It's because of you they're standing over every city on the planet. You brought them back."

"But I'm still me," Valkyrie said.

"No, you're not. You think you are, but you're not. The real Valkyrie Cain wouldn't let this happen. She wouldn't help the goddamn Faceless Ones take over the world."

"You're saying that because you don't understand."

"What do I need to understand? You're a bad guy. You're co-operating with the enemy."

Valkyrie sighed.

"We do need something from you, you're right," Skulduggery told him. "We have to stop Obsidian. He's hurting people."

"What people?"

"Roarhaven citizens. He's wiping them out of existence."

Omen shook his head. "Auger wouldn't do that. You know him. He's a good guy."

"Auger wouldn't do that, no, but Obsidian would, and is."

"Why haven't I heard about it on the Network?"

"The Network relays information the Sanctuaries want out there. They're not journalists, Omen. They don't investigate. Creed doesn't want panic to spread."

"What citizens, then? Who has he hurt? Who were they?"

Skulduggery hesitated. "Followers of the Faceless Ones."

"Like priests?"

"One priest. The others appear to be a random selection of individuals with only their faith to connect them."

Omen frowned, unable to process what he was being told. "Auger's killing them?"

"Obsidian is killing them. Wiping them out. Erasing them from existence."

"And what do you want me to do about it?"

"We need to stop him, Omen. Once we catch him, we can see if there's a way to help him – maybe even bring Auger back."

"My parents were told that's impossible."

"We don't know enough about what's going on to make any kind of assessment like that."

"And what? You want me to lure him into a trap?"

"Without putting too fine a point on it, yes."

"I'm not going to help you hurt my own brother."

"Obsidian isn't your brother. Obsidian is where your brother should be. He's taken his place in the world. We just want the chance to bring Auger back."

"You don't care about bringing Auger back. You just want Obsidian to stop wiping out more Faceless Ones fanatics. You know why he's doing it, right? It's because he knows who the real bad guys are. He knows who poses the actual threat. I mean, doesn't this prove that it's still Auger in there? He's still the hero. He's still protecting us from the bad guys."

"Omen—" Valkyrie started.

"I'm not helping you, all right? I believe in my brother. I believe in him a hell of a lot more than I believe in you."

He looked at Skulduggery. "Or you. I mean, what are you even doing? Why are you still her partner? Why don't you stop her? The world is ending, Skulduggery! You failed! Do you get that? Do you see? All the times you saved the world in the past? They mean nothing! Nothing! Because here, right here, you failed. You're not fighting them, you're not killing them, you're not destroying them, because of her. Because of Valkyrie. Because you won't move against her. Why? Because you're that close? Because you've saved each other's lives a thousand times and you're not going to abandon her now? You had to abandon her! You had to, because it was the right thing to do, but you didn't, and now it's too late because the Faceless Ones are back and they've won. And all you've done is stand around and watch it happen.

"I used to think I was rubbish compared to you. I used to think I was a stupid, fat little kid who never did anything right. I see it now, though. I'm way better than you. I am so much better. She's evil, but you? You're pathetic."

"Omen..."

"Get lost," Omen said, and stormed to the stairs.

Valkyrie watched him go, and turned to Skulduggery. "You knew that would happen," she said slowly.

"We had to try."

"No. I mean, you knew that would happen. You knew he'd react like that and you knew there was no way we were going to convince him otherwise. So why did you do it? Why did we come here?"

"We don't have an awful lot of options available to—"

"Skulduggery," she said, "stop. Why are we here?"

He looked at her and didn't answer.

Valkyrie nodded. "You wanted me to hear that, didn't you? You wanted me to hear him say all that."

"He has a point," said Skulduggery.

She shook her head. "He's wrong. He doesn't understand the situation. He doesn't understand what the Faceless Ones are going to do. He's still scared of them."

"The Faceless Ones are evil."

"You don't believe that any more."

"Yes, I do."

"Then will you trust me when I tell you how much they love the human race? Will you trust me when I tell of the love I feel inside me?"

"Valkyrie..." He shook his head. "You're compromised."

"Is that so?"

"They're changing how you think."

"Then why are you helping me? Why are we still working together? If you actually believed that the Faceless Ones are going to enslave the human race, then you wouldn't be running around with me, solving crimes and saving lives. You'd be fighting me."

"I know."

"But because you're not fighting me, that means you have a teensy-weensy bit of faith that what I'm saying is the truth."

"No."

"I think you're in denial."

"On that, we agree. But what Omen said was right. I'm by your side because of the bond we share. I haven't abandoned you because of our friendship."

Valkyrie smiled. "Because I love you."

"And I love you."

132

"Until the end."

He didn't say anything.

"Skulduggery?"

"Until the end," he said softly.

23

Commander Hoc watched Darquesse scream.

The experts, the people in the lab coats with the clipboards and tablets, had told him this would happen. At first, the damage they were doing to her – physically – wouldn't register.

The *second* part of the process, the really interesting part, was when the damage being inflicted wasn't to her physical form but rather to her magic. Recent advancements in the Research and Development Department had yielded incredible results and a new way of understanding the Source, that dimension composed entirely of magical energy. The same scientists that had managed to widen the Source portals to allow the Faceless Ones to enter this reality were now using their new-found skills to attack the very essence of who and what Darquesse was.

And this, apparently, progressed past the point where Darquesse was able to simply switch off her pain receptors.

And so she screamed.

They were close, Hoc was assured. Close to breaking down her physical form, close to reducing her to energy. The black box, the Cage, was open on the table beside her, ready to drink her in and trap her forever. Some of the scientists, the ambitious kind, were eager to discover what would happen once this occurred. Would they be able to tap into that energy? Hoc had fantasies about turning up to the Supreme Mage's office with a potent, renewable energy source in his hands. He liked to imagine the smile on Damocles Creed's face as, finally, Hoc was able to repay him for the faith he had shown in appointing him to his position as Commander of the City Guard.

The future was bright.

24

Omen slept angry, and woke up incensed, and ate breakfast irritated. By morning assembly, he was merely annoyed, and incredibly tired. It wasn't easy to sleep angry.

"In these uncertain times," Duenna was saying from the stage, "precautions need to be taken."

Omen frowned, trying to steer his thoughts out of the murk to focus on whatever the hell she was going on about now.

"With the unrest caused by the actions of the so-called resistance," she continued, "with the fear generated by the being known as Obsidian, and now with these so-called Nulls causing trouble on our own streets, Roarhaven has never been less safe."

"What about when Mevolent invaded?" Never muttered. "Idiot."

Omen grinned.

"I have no wish to scare you, children. My role as principal is to guide you, to educate you, and to prepare you. It is also to protect you. Corrival Academy is a refuge from what goes on out there, beyond the school gates. Your safety is our primary concern, and as such your bracelets will now allow us to track your location within school grounds during school hours."

Omen sagged. The bad guys were winning.

*

"What I'm about to say may be controversial," said Never as they walked to class, "but who am I to shy away from controversy? This school – wait for it – is going downhill. There, I said it."

"You're so brave," said Omen.

"I'm just saying what other people are too scared to say. Does that make me brave? By definition, I think it does."

Axelia readjusted the bag on her shoulder. "My parents think I should leave," she said.

Never looked appalled. "You can't leave. You're probably the prettiest person in our year, after me. If you leave, I'll get all the attention, and I can't handle that any more. I just can't."

"You're a sweetie," said Axelia. "But I don't want to go, either. All my friends are here. What do they expect me to do – go back to a mortal school for my final year? No. No way."

"Why do they want you to go?" Omen asked.

She nodded behind them. "Because of that. Stuff like that. Third Years being dragged to detention cells underneath the school. My parents, they don't like Duenna, and they hate Creed, and they don't want me around these people. Roarhaven has gone from being the greatest city in the world to the home of killers and fanatics."

Never flicked their hair out of their eyes. "You wouldn't be able to leave, even if you wanted to. None of us would. Creed needs us here. We're his insurance in case the resistance do anything too crazy." They held up their bracelet. "Duenna says these things only track our movements when we're on school grounds – but how do we know they won't be keeping tabs on us when we head into Roarhaven? I'd say they're even listening to us."

Axelia frowned. "But... they can't spy on their own pupils."

"Legally, they can. China Sorrows had it written into what passes for Roarhaven's constitution. It's the bit that's skipped over in civics class."

Axelia sat forward. "So they could already be listening to us? At all times?"

"Maybe, yeah."

She stared. "Why aren't you more freaked out about this? Omen, why aren't you freaked out? Why aren't you angry?"

"I'm very freaked out," said Omen. "I'm very angry."

"I'm not freaked out because this is not the first time this has occurred to me," Never said. "I've had time to adjust to the startling intrusion upon my privacy. I've been having fun with it, actually. I talk in code to a bush. You know the bush beside the tree shaped like a tree?"

"The tree shaped like a tree?" said Axelia.

Never sighed. "There are trees shaped like hands and trees shaped like old men, all gnarly and bent over, but this is a tree shaped like other trees. You know which one I'm talking about?"

"I think I do," said Omen. "The one near the Science Block?"

"That's the one," Never said, nodding. "Anyway, there's a bush beside it."

"What's the bush shaped like?" Axelia asked.

"What? It's just a bush. It doesn't have to be shaped like anything."

"I'm so confused. I'm still angry, but now I'm also confused."

"I talk to the bush in code," said Never. "I've been doing it since we got the bracelets. I'm totally giving the game away right now if they're listening, but what the hell, right? I've been reporting to this bush every day at the same time, and I stand there and don't look at it, but I whisper codes that I just make up on the spur of the moment – you know, like I'm reporting to my secret resistance contact, or whatever. If I'm wrong, and no one's been listening to us, then I've been wasting my lunch breaks on a prank that wasn't even that funny to begin with. But I try not to think about that."

"You're such an odd person," said Axelia.

They got to class and Omen managed to keep up, but his attention span started to flounder in the second lesson, and by the time the third one swam by he was adrift. He got to lunch-time without making a fool of himself, though, and sat at his usual table. He scrolled through his phone while he waited for his friends to join him.

But then Jenan sat opposite.

The chatter in the dining hall dropped to a low murmur. All eyes swivelled.

"What are you expecting?" Jenan asked, his voice low.

Omen kept his mouth shut. He put his phone down.

"You expecting me to take this plastic knife in my hand and dive on you? Stab you till you're dead? You know, if I was gonna do it with a knife – a real knife, I mean, not school cutlery – I wouldn't stab you in the back, yeah? I'd want to see your face. I'd want to see the look on your stupid face. The fear." Jenan smiled. "But that's way too quick, see? I want it to take a bit longer. I want it to hurt a little bit longer. Besides, I already stabbed you once – you and your brother. I kinda want to try something new." He leaned closer. "You're not saying a whole lot. What's wrong? Do I scare you that much?"

"You don't scare me at all," Omen said.

"Liar," said Jenan, relishing the word.

"We don't have to do this. I've got other things to be worrying about, and I'm sure you do, too. We both have school, for God's sake. This is our final year. We've got exams and then college to think about."

"Exams," Jenan said, laughing. "Like you're going to make it that far. Like you're going to live to sit them. Darkly, I'm going to kill you. You get me? I came back to this place for one thing and one thing only. You know what that is?"

"Maths?"

"No."

"Home economics?"

"Tell one more joke and I'll kill you right now," Jenan said. "Say one more annoying thing and I'll beat you to death in this

139

room. I heard you fancy yourself as a bit of a fighter these days. You think you'd stand a chance against me?"

"I beat you once."

"You and your brother, yeah – but your brother's not here any more. He's out there, showing everyone what a weak, pathetic loser he is."

Omen had a response ready to go, but a message came through on his phone. He tapped the screen, then put the phone away. "Nice talking to you, Jenan, but I have to go."

"You know your problem?" Jenan asked before Omen could stand. "You think you're a good guy, you think you're nice, but you came to visit me in prison. Why did you do that?"

"I wanted to understand."

"No. You wanted to gloat."

"Is that seriously what you think?"

"You wanted to see me in my prison clothes, wanted to see me behind that little bullet-proof screen, and then you wanted me to watch you walk out of there. When you left, you know what I did? I went back to gen pop. That's general population, where you mix with all the other inmates. Did you know that Abyssinia wasn't popular with some people? Did you know that some of those people kept beating me to a pulp before I finally learned that you've got to fight to survive in that place? I went through hell in there, and it was all because of you."

"I didn't gloat, Jenan."

"If you want to tell yourself that, go right ahead, but I know the truth. I know everything you did. And you're gonna pay for it all."

"So you're here for revenge, are you?"

Jenan's smile was unnerving. "That's exactly why I'm here. I want you to know that it's coming. I want you to live with that. I want you to be thinking of it every minute of every day."

Omen couldn't help it: he laughed. "I'm sorry," he said immediately. "I'm so sorry. That was rude. Sorry."

"You won't be laughing when I—"

"Jenan, seriously, dude, you want to kill me, you know what? Get to the back of the queue. People have been trying to kill me every couple of weeks for the last year. You had to fight to survive? Well, so did I."

"Then I guess we'll see who's tougher."

Omen stood up. "I guess we will," he said, and walked away.

He sent a message on his phone and got a reply a few seconds later with a place to meet. He went to the West Tower, stepped out on to the balcony that circled the very top. The man waiting for him was tall and slender, dressed in a checked suit that was either the height of fashion or outrageously, ridiculously awful. The bow tie had little skulls on it and his pork-pie hat matched his purple shirt.

"Let's see it," Crepuscular Vies said.

Omen extended his arm and Crepuscular examined the bracelet. The bottom half of his face was fixed in a permanent rictus grin, his mouth lipless, his gums merging with his skin. It was only the top half of his face – those bulging eyes, those sharp brows – that were capable of any expression. One of his eyebrows arched. "And it's tracking your location now, you say?"

"If I go anywhere I'm not supposed to go, it sets off an alarm and they come looking for me. Duenna says it's tamper-proof."

"Well, she would," Crepuscular replied, "but it's nothing I haven't seen before. I'd say you'd be able to find out how to deactivate it completely if you knew where to look in your magic-science textbooks – but the people who write those textbooks have probably done their very best to hide that information from you. No one in a position of authority wants the people they control to know how to wield their own strength." He took a leather strap from his pocket and wrapped it round Omen's wrist so that it covered the bracelet. "In the meantime, I soaked this in brahmi and then a mixture of feverfew and henbane, so it should block the signal. Do *not* lick it."

"I wasn't planning on it."

Crepuscular tied the strap tight. "If someone's tracking you in particular, then you're in trouble, because right now you've just disappeared from their system. But if they're just using the bracelet to set off alarms if you stray, you'll be fine."

"You're pretty handy to have around."

"It has been said. Are you ready to go?"

Omen hesitated. "Are you sure you want to do this?"

"Not at all," said Crepuscular. "But my very good friend is in danger, Skulduggery Pleasant and Valkyrie Cain are bound to be there, and the truth needs to come out before the world ends."

"You're actually going to tell Skulduggery that you're his long-lost partner?"

"Yes, I am," Crepuscular said, a smile in his voice. "And I cannot wait to see the look on his expressionless skull."

25

They waited inside Walter Egmont's Los Angeles apartment for him to return home. It wasn't a particularly nice apartment and the AC was broken, so it was hot and uncomfortable, even at night.

When Walter returned home, they hung back until he had shut and locked his door and was halfway to the kitchenette before Skulduggery said, "Boo."

Walter screamed, whirled, staggered and fell, then tried to turn the fall into a roll that quickly became a crawl. He was a short man with a moustache and he had wide, buggy eyes – though his eyes might only have been buggy because he was suddenly confronted by a skeleton in a suit.

"Stop!" Walter screamed, clambering to his feet. "Don't take one step closer!"

Skulduggery took plenty of steps closer, forcing Walter to back up against the wall.

"Stop! I'm commanding you to stop!"

"You just tried to have someone murdered," Valkyrie said, sauntering after them. "You don't get to command anyone."

"The Lord God compels you!" Walter shrieked.

"Oh, dear," said Skulduggery.

"You are demons!" Walter cried. "You're just like the other one!"

"You mean Eraddin Tomb," Skulduggery said.

"He is Death," responded Walter, pointing. "The same as you. You are Death, too!"

Skulduggery took hold of Walter's outstretched hand and snapped a cuff on to the wrist, then secured the other one to a pipe on the wall.

"Hey," said Walter.

"Am I Death?" Valkyrie asked.

Walter tried pulling his arm free, then snarled. "You're a demon!"

"No, I'm just a regular person, more or less, doing regular things, more or less – like you, without the attempted-assassination part." She shrugged. "I mean, yeah, we were going to assassinate someone not too long ago – an *attempted* attempted-assassination, if you will – but we decided against it because we're good people."

"I'm a good person!" Walter screeched.

"You say that, but you did hire a guy to kill a guy, so that kind of calls your judgement into question."

"Death," Walter growled. "Eraddin Tomb is Death."

"No, he isn't."

"He is the God of Death!"

"Yes, he is, but he isn't Death itself. We had a whole discussion about it – it involved microwaves – you should have been there."

"Is that why you tried to kill him?" Skulduggery asked.

"I'm not speaking to you. You're Death, too. But yes, that's why I wanted to kill him. To save the world!"

"So by killing the God of Death," Valkyrie said, "you thought you'd be stopping anyone from dying from now on? Who told you all this?"

"I'll never tell you. He's a giant – he would smash you."

"How big a giant? Like as tall as a mountain?"

"Don't be ridiculous," Walter sneered.

"As tall as a lamp post?"

"A small lamp post, maybe, or a tall bus shelter."

"How tall is that? I'm six foot. How tall is he compared to me?"

"I don't know – maybe three foot taller than you. But way wider, like he's built of muscles. He would destroy you."

Valkyrie frowned. "Wait a minute – is it Ragner? Is his name Ragner?"

"I don't know who that is," said Walter, "and I wouldn't tell you even if I did."

"Not Ragner," Skulduggery said. "His brother, then. Was it Jagett?"

Walter clamped his mouth shut, and nodded.

"Jagett told you to kill Eraddin?"

"You won't get anything out of me, demon," Walter said. "He said I'd be saving the world!"

"And he put you in contact with an assassin?"

"None of this matters!" Walter sneered. "The God of Death won't even see his own death coming!"

"You're planning an ambush?" Skulduggery asked.

"No," Walter said, going suddenly pale.

"More than an ambush, then." Skulduggery tilted his head. "A trap – and he's walking into it, isn't he? It can't be at his apartment – that's already been blown up. So Ragner's place. You found where Eraddin is staying, didn't you? Do you have another assassin waiting for him? Maybe not. You tried shooting him, but that didn't work. Another bomb, then. Is that what it is, Walter? Is it a bomb?"

"I'll never tell you!"

"That's a yes," said Valkyrie, and they walked to the door. "Stick around, Walter – someone will be here to pick you up in a few hours."

"I have to use the bathroom!" he shouted after them as they left, but they were already lifting into the air.

26

Tyler brought Mr Jones some toast and a coffee to get his strength back, and Mr Jones sat up in the bed in the spare room and ate the toast and drank the coffee as Tyler's folks talked to him and asked him questions. He answered whatever they asked, but skimmed over the truth. He didn't mention the stream of purple light that had given him that burn that Tyler's mom had bandaged up, and he didn't mention the fact that he could shoot laser beams out of his eyes.

"We got a Sheriff's Department in town," Tyler's dad said. "We know you'd rather stay anonymous, but I really do think that calling them in would be the best bet."

"The police don't like me much," said Mr Jones, smiling regretfully. He had an interesting accent. South African, Tyler's mom had guessed. "I made some bad decisions in my youth, decisions I'm trying to make up for now, and I'm afraid they'll come back to haunt me once you alert the authorities. I understand that you may feel you need to inform them and I respect that, but if it's all the same to you, I'd rather not be here when they arrive."

Tyler's mom, standing in the doorway with her arms crossed, looked conflicted. "Mr Jones, you were injured saving our son from whoever these people were, so you can stay with us until you're healed and we won't call the sheriff if you don't want us to. But you've got to be honest, because if your presence here is putting our children in any danger, we need to know about it."

"Thank you," said Mr Jones. "And your family isn't in any danger. The men who went after Tyler won't be missed for another few days, by which time I'll be long gone and leading the others away from here."

"So there are others?"

"Unfortunately, yes."

Tyler's dad shook his head. "I have to ask – what is it you're messed up in? Is it criminal stuff? You got no reason to feel ashamed if it is – we understand that times are tough. Hell, the bank is threatening to foreclose on the farm even as we speak, so we understand that sometimes good people are forced to do bad things just to keep their heads above water."

"It's criminal stuff," Mr Jones confirmed, "but I, myself, am not a criminal. You have nothing to fear from me."

Tyler's parents glanced at each other and seemed to believe him. They talked a little more and then left Mr Jones to rest, but Tyler didn't follow them out.

Mr Jones looked at him. "You didn't tell them about what you saw."

"No, sir. I don't think they'd believe me."

"That's no reason not to tell them."

"I don't think they'd help you if they did believe me."

Mr Jones nodded. "Those men, the ones I was fighting – they were bad guys. You can believe that."

"How did they do what they did? How did you?"

"It's magic."

"Proper magic?"

Mr Jones smiled. "Proper magic."

"Is Jones your real name?"

"Frightening Jones is my real name, yes. Sorcerers pick our own names when we're old enough."

"Why were you fighting?"

147

"There are good sorcerers and bad sorcerers. They were bad sorcerers. You know, if you hadn't come by when you did, they'd have killed me. I owe you my life, Tyler."

Tyler shrugged, and blushed. "It's OK."

Frightening smiled.

27

They flew to Ragner's house in Malibu and landed on the roof. Valkyrie scanned the building and couldn't detect any auras, but one of the skylights was wide open.

"Booby-trapped," Skulduggery said, taking a look. "Sigils on the west and south walls – see them? – set up to trigger a presumably indecent amount of explosives once someone even touches that floor."

Valkyrie stuck her head in. It took her a while to find the sigils, but they were there, waiting to blow her to pieces.

Skulduggery was already tapping out a message on his phone. "Just making sure Ragner and Eraddin stay away until we've defused the bomb."

"And can you defuse it?" she asked.

"There isn't a bomb that exists today that I can't defuse," he responded, pocketing the phone.

"That's good, that's good," Valkyrie said, nodding. Then, "Wait, is that because all the bombs that you tried to defuse but couldn't have gone off, and that's why they don't exist any more?"

"I have to be honest with you: yes, that's exactly why."

"Then we shouldn't try to defuse this one."

"Valkyrie, show a little faith, will you? I am relatively sure that I can manage this without the bomb exploding. There is definitely a forty-forty chance of success."

149

"That only adds up to eighty per cent."

Skulduggery made a seesawing gesture with his hand. "There's always a twenty per cent chance that something unexpected will happen in any given situation. I'm simply honest enough to be open about the possibility."

"I don't think that's how maths works. We should wait. The Sanctuary here in America has some great bomb-disposal people. They'll take care of this."

"They're all busy."

"Oh, really? Doing what?"

"Disposing of bombs."

"Of which this is one."

"But we don't need them," Skulduggery said. "Not when we have these." He waved his hands in front of her.

"Stop doing that," she said.

"The safest pair of hands in the west, that's what these are."

"Skulduggery, this looks like a lovely house. I'm sure Ragner adores it. Did you see the piano down there? That's a huge piano. If we try to defuse this bomb and we mess up and it doesn't kill us, it will, at the very least, destroy this lovely house and that very nice piano. Ragner will be very upset, won't he?"

"I don't think he'd be *that* upset. It's only a house."

"Would you like it if your house was blown up, with all those spare bones in it? You're building your collection back up, aren't you, after Cadaver stole the best parts to make himself a body? What if you lost them?"

"That would be most unfortunate."

"And what about your suits?"

His head tilted. "My suits?"

"Losing the new ones would be bad enough, but what about all the suits that Ghastly made for you? The exquisite ones? All of them blown up, along with those shirts, those ties... those wonderful hats."

"My hats, too?"

"You wouldn't like to lose all that, would you?"

"I would not."

"Then we should call the bomb-disposal people, shouldn't we?"

There was a moment of silence.

"I don't think Ragner wears hats, though," Skulduggery said, and started for the skylight.

"Um," someone said behind them, and they turned as Omen stepped out from behind one of the large vents that criss-crossed the roof. "Hi."

"What are you doing here?" Valkyrie asked, getting the obvious question out of the way first.

"Ragner's a friend," Omen said. "Well, a friend of a friend. I've met him a few times. He's really nice. We heard he was in trouble, heard all this stuff was happening, and we thought we'd... help."

Valkyrie held up a hand. "Who's we? Omen, what the hell is going on?"

"You're not the only one who's allowed to do stupid stuff, you know," Omen said, a little defensively. "And I don't have to run everything by you. I don't have to run anything by you."

"I never said you did."

"You're not even in a position to tell me to do anything," Omen continued, once again on a roll and barely listening to her. "You're the bad guy, and Skulduggery's working with you, so he's the bad guy, too. So it seems to me that somebody needs to be the good guy, and because my brother has been snatched away from us, it looks like the good guy is me. And I know how ridiculous that sounds. I know how stupid and idiotic it is. I'm nobody's idea of a hero. I don't even want to do this. I used to – or I used to think I did – but I really don't. But I can't see anyone else out there who's helping people, so I have to do it."

"And who's helping you, Omen?" Skulduggery asked.

A man walked up behind Omen. Tall and slender, he was wearing a checked suit with a pocket handkerchief, bow tie and a pork-pie hat. His cheekbones were sharp, his seemingly lidless eyes bulging, and he didn't appear to have any lips.

"I've done this all wrong," Omen said, annoyed. "It wasn't supposed to be this big dramatic moment. I was supposed to just prepare you."

"You did great," the man said, patting Omen's shoulder.

Skulduggery tilted his head. "And who might you be?"

"You know me, actually," the man said, "though I admit that I've changed a lot since the last time we spoke."

"And when was that?"

"Way back in 1954."

Skulduggery paused before responding. "That was an interesting year."

"It was."

"A lot of things happened that year."

"I would agree."

"Some interesting things."

"Very interesting."

"Stop, stop," Valkyrie said. "I'm missing something huge here. What happened in 1954? Is this about the Bentley?"

"The Bentley?" said the man.

"I have a Bentley R-Type Continental," Skulduggery said, then corrected himself. "*Had* a Bentley R-Type Continental. It was built in 1954."

"You don't have it any more?"

"It was involved in one too many high-speed chases."

"Such a shame. You're driving a Phantom now, aren't you? Another beautiful car."

"It is."

"So this isn't about the Bentley," Valkyrie guessed.

"That was the year Skulduggery took on a new partner," Omen said.

"All right," said Valkyrie. "Good. I know about that. Fregoli Cleft. He died horribly. Lots of flailing around. What about it?"

"Actually," said Omen, "he didn't die. There was an explosion and a walkway crumbled and he fell into a vat of chemicals. He was presumed dead, but he was captured and then tortured."

Valkyrie frowned at the man with the unusual face. "So, unless I'm missing something else – you're him? You're Fregoli Cleft?"

"I was."

"I thought you died that day," Skulduggery said.

"I know you did. With all those explosions, all the fire and smoke, all those bullets whizzing... I'm not surprised you dropped me."

"You fell. I couldn't get a good grip. You kept squirming."

"Is that why you didn't come looking for me when it was all over? Is that why you didn't search the vats for my remains? Why you gave up immediately and moved on? You never wanted me as a partner anyway – and who could blame you? I was young and foolhardy, intent on proving myself. Where did that get me, I ask you? A surgical table, with rusted scalpels peeling away my ruined flesh. You tried to warn me, of course. You told me of the danger we would be facing, of the horrors, but I didn't listen because of course I didn't. I was Fregoli Cleft – I was indestructible."

"How long did they have you?"

"Two years."

"I'm sorry."

"Don't be," Fregoli Cleft said with a wave of his hand. "Best thing that ever happened to me. When I got out, I swore to myself that I would never again seek anyone else's approval. I would no longer base my identity on the whims of other people. I would be strong. I would be independent. I would be my own person."

"That's a remarkably healthy outlook to adopt."

"Isn't it?"

"But why didn't you come to me? Let me know you were alive?"

"I'll be honest, Skulduggery – I was annoyed with you. Irritated, even. That irritation stayed with me for a long time. But now I'm over it."

"I'm... glad to hear that."

"But even though you left me for dead, left me to my torture and suffering, you were still the source of my inspiration. The person I am today, I owe to you. I have dedicated my life to helping others – just like you've done. And, like you, I realised that I needed a partner. I needed someone like Valkyrie. When I met Omen, I knew instantly that he was the one I'd been searching for: kind, decent, intelligent and brave. Someone I would be proud to fight beside."

"He's just a boy," said Valkyrie.

Fregoli Cleft turned his head to her. "And you were just a girl. But you quickly grew to be a hero – and that's what Omen has done. You underestimate him at your peril."

"I'm underestimating no one – but I know exactly the kind of dangers that he's faced and I have a serious problem with anyone who would drag a kid into this."

"Including Skulduggery?" Fregoli asked, amused.

"Including Skulduggery."

"Let's not get sidetracked here," Skulduggery said.

Valkyrie pushed down her anger. "Why are you here?"

"To help Ragner." He glanced at Valkyrie. "Back when I was Fregoli Cleft, I was making quite a name for myself in adventuring circles. I joined the fight against Mevolent, helped out the Dead Men a few times, generally made good use of myself. Do you remember how we first met, Skulduggery?"

Skulduggery took off his hat, adjusted the brim, and put it back on. "Jagett found where we'd stashed Quietus. He came to break him out. He actually succeeded in removing him from the prison, but needed time for him to wake up. Fregoli delayed him long enough so that I could get there with my brothers and sisters. Ragner came along, too."

"We subdued Jagett," Fregoli said, "returned him to the Dire Dimension, and put Quietus back in his box before he opened his eyes. And I also made a whole bunch of nifty new friends. When one of them is in trouble, I like to help, if I can."

"So you know what's going on?" Valkyrie asked.

"We know Walter Egmont hired an assassin to kill Eraddin Tomb because he thought he was Death itself," said Omen. "We know Jagett manipulated Walter into doing it so that it'd cover up his own involvement."

"And we know Jagett wanted Tomb dead so that it would give him a straight shot at Ragner," said Fregoli.

"Who he could then torture to uncover the whereabouts of Quietus's new prison," Skulduggery said, nodding his approval.

"Did we know this?" Valkyrie whispered.

"We did," Skulduggery whispered back.

"Oh, good."

"So we're working together again?" Skulduggery asked Fregoli. "We all want the same thing, don't we? To help Ragner, and stop Jagett?"

"That is indeed what we want."

"In the spirit of co-operation, then, I should inform you that the building we're standing on is wired to blow the moment anyone sets foot in the place."

"I'm aware."

Skulduggery tilted his head. "You were here before us?"

"We saw Jagett leave," Omen told them. "We tried to follow, but we lost him."

Skulduggery hesitated. "So he knows you're here?"

Fregoli chuckled. "You sound nervous, Skulduggery. Do I have to remind you that there are more of us than there are of him?"

"We barely beat him last time, and I had plenty of back-up with me."

"And we have the magnificent Valkyrie Cain," Fregoli said, "whom I have heard nothing but great things about. With her on our side, is there anyone we couldn't beat, I ask you?"

"Let us find out," said the huge man who stepped out behind Omen, grabbed him and pressed a knife to his throat.

Fregoli spun and Valkyrie raised her hands to fire lightning.

"I will cut the head from this boy if anyone attempts foolish things," the huge man said in a voice that rumbled. He was as big as Ragner, with long black and grey hair and a wild beard. Jagett, son of Quietus, Valkyrie presumed. He wore a dark uniform – trousers with heavy boots, a shirt that left his massive arms bare – and the knife in his fist was long and sharp and had made Omen go very pale indeed.

"If you hurt him," said Valkyrie, "I'll fry you where you stand."

"That will hardly do the headless boy any good."

Valkyrie pulled her hood up, and set her mask over her face. "Let him go."

"As soon as my father is released," Jagett responded, "the boy shall leave with his head."

"I'm afraid that's not how this works," Skulduggery said. "You're in our dimension. This is our world. We can call in a monumental amount of reinforcements at any moment. You cannot. Frankly, I'm surprised you're back. I thought you were smarter than this, Jagett – though, admittedly, not by much."

"I had forgotten how much you like to use words," Jagett said. "I have returned to this place because your universe has an infestation of Faceless Ones. You maybe did not think I would hear of such things in the Dire Dimension? For years, I have been committing much violence upon the illegitimate government of Gaunt – a government you helped install – and I was quite busy and preoccupied, but news such as this tends to travel. Your universe is coming to an end. I am here to retrieve my father and bring him home to safety before your failures cost him his life."

"This universe isn't ending," Valkyrie said. "It's just beginning."

Jagett watched her. "You are one who has the bright flame of fanaticism burning in her eyes."

"The Faceless Ones aren't going to destroy anything. They're going to create a paradise."

Jagett sighed as he returned his attention to Skulduggery. "I thought you were smarter, skeleton. To align yourself with worshippers of the Dark Gods is a desperate ploy indeed."

Fregoli suddenly lunged, but Jagett was ready for him. Moving faster than someone of his size had any right to, he kicked Fregoli square in the chest and immediately hauled Omen to the nearest skylight where he held him, one-handed, over the glass.

"My mind, it has changed," he said. "I will not cut the boy's head from his body. I will instead hurl him to the ground, where he will set off all those lovely explosives I brought with me. If any of you wish to test my fortitude, I implore you to make another foolish move."

Fregoli groaned, and picked himself up.

"We're not going to make any moves at all," Skulduggery said. "You want us to release your father. We can't do that."

"I believe you can, with the proper incentive."

"The risks are too great, both for your world and mine. Billions of lives could be lost."

"And if you do not," said Jagett, "I guarantee you that this boy's life will end here, tonight. What do you think of that, boy? Are you ready to die?"

Omen seemed to want to say something bravely defiant, but his mouth was apparently too dry to speak.

"Let me take my father home with me, skeleton."

"I can't do that."

"Then I will kill the boy."

"No, Jagett, you won't."

Jagett smiled. "But I have to. You see? If I do not demonstrate to you my resolve, if I do not remind you of my ruthlessness, then I am in a weakened position. My father, the great Quietus, the Ruler of Gaunt, taught me from a young age that to be weak is to be defeated." He shook his head sadly. "And I will not be defeated," he said, then dropped Omen through the skylight.

Valkyrie roared and shot forward, but Jagett blasted her with a fistful of energy. As she went spinning, she saw Skulduggery

157

and Fregoli bolting for the skylight, Skulduggery with his hands out, attempting to use the air to retrieve Omen. But Fregoli just dived straight in.

And then the whole building exploded.

28

The world roared and belched fire and wrenched Valkyrie head over heels in a storm of masonry and glass and twisted metal. She was dimly aware of hitting the ground, dimly aware of rolling. When she came to a stop, she couldn't breathe and everything was black and there was something pressing down on her, pinning her where she lay.

She blinked inside her mask, listening to the roar subside. When she was certain that she was still alive, she raised her head as much as she was able. What once had been a building was lying on top of her. It rumbled and creaked, a ruined structure that was going to collapse at any moment. Her necronaut suit wouldn't do a whole lot of good against the weight of a building.

"Help," she called, barely making a noise.

Stones skittered on to the back of her hood. She had the power to blast her way out of here, she knew she did, but she needed to know which direction to go. When she moved, she had to do so without hesitation. Hesitation meant death.

"Skulduggery," she called.

An answer. That's all she needed. All he had to do was shout, and she'd have a direction.

Her mouth was dry and adrenaline made her fingertips tingle. The building pressed down on top of her. She couldn't raise her head without knocking against something. Couldn't move her arms – they were pressed in from either side. Couldn't move her legs, either. There was a bit of the building lying across the back of her thighs.

She barked out a laugh of burgeoning panic, then squeezed her eyes shut.

Keep calm. She needed to keep calm. Calm and cool. She wasn't going to die down here. She was going to get out.

The ground beneath her trembled and she opened her eyes, frowning. Two gloved hands rose slowly from the cracked pavement beneath, took hold of her, and gently pulled her down into the Earth.

Valkyrie focused on her breathing, allowing Skulduggery to take her with him as he burrowed through the darkness, away from the rubble and then up, cracking the surface and guiding her out of the ground.

She yanked back her mask and hood and sucked in fresh air. Then she forced herself to turn to the ruined building. Jagett was gone, but she searched for living auras through the smoke and flame and debris.

There was nothing. There was no one alive in there.

"Oh, God," she said. "He's dead."

Skulduggery took a moment. "You're sure? Valkyrie, are you sure? There might still be a chance."

"There's nothing left," she told him.

"But surely—"

"Omen's dead," said Valkyrie, louder now.

"You see," Fregoli Cleft said behind them, "this is the problem with you."

They turned. Fregoli was fixing his hair, and Omen was rubbing his arm and looking like he'd just been thrown into an exploding building.

Fregoli put his hat back on. "Always so eager to believe that people are dead so you never have to save them."

Valkyrie cried out and ran over, grabbed Omen in a hug.

"Ow," he said. "Ow, my arm!"

"Sorry!" said Valkyrie, not letting go. "Sorry!"

Skulduggery walked over. "How did you do that?" he asked.

"I made an effort," Fregoli said. "I refused to let my partner die. You should try it."

"You didn't have time to grab Omen and escape."

"And yet that's exactly what I did."

Skulduggery's head tilted. "You're like me. You're magically ambidextrous. When you were my partner, you let me think you were only an Elemental, but you're a Teleporter, too, aren't you? That's how you saved Omen."

"Skulduggery, I merely did what you weren't willing to do."

"You did what I couldn't do. You did what was impossible for me to do."

"And why is that? Do you need me to tell you? It's because you're a dinosaur. You're so old-fashioned it would be laughable if it weren't so tragic. You think being magically ambidextrous means you're special? You're limited to two disciplines of magic – you're barely exceptional. But me? I'm evolution itself."

"You have more than two disciplines?"

"My dear Skulduggery," said Fregoli, "I have them all."

He rose off the ground and hovered there, his eyes crackling with energy.

"Oh, hell," Valkyrie muttered.

Fregoli laughed. "I've experimented with every type of magic there is," he said. "Some are stronger than others, some need more work, and others require more study. But I have them all. I'm closer to Valkyrie's power set than yours, old man – and Valkyrie cheated to get hers, whereas I worked for mine."

Valkyrie frowned. "Screw you, I didn't cheat."

Fregoli raised an eyebrow to Omen. "You see? We're better than they are. I've surpassed Skulduggery in every conceivable way – from intelligence to ability to sheer style – and you have saved the world, Omen, despite the disadvantages life has given you. You're not the Chosen One. You never have been. But Valkyrie? Not only has she been the destroyer of this world, she's also been its saviour! Her face is, quite literally, the face of Armageddon. She's both the hero and the villain, blessed with an ever-changing set of powers. Why do you think that is, Valkyrie? What makes you so special?"

"Dunno," she snarled. "Probably my winning personality."

"We've beaten them," Fregoli said to Omen. "We've proven ourselves their superiors. We've won."

Omen stared at him. "What are you talking about? This was never about proving ourselves. This was about helping people. That's why we didn't tell anyone. All this, we did all this, and for you it was just... it was to beat them? It was to beat *him*?"

Fregoli tilted his head. "Yes."

"So everything you said about not having to prove yourself to other people was a lie."

"Not at all. I don't care about proving myself to him – I have proven myself to me. When it comes to figuring out who you are, Omen, you're the only one who matters."

Omen gave a short, humourless laugh. "I thought I could rely on you. Everyone else let me down. Everyone else put me down. You're the only one who didn't."

"You can rely on me."

"I listened to you," Omen said, anger in his voice. "I actually listened. I thought you were a... a real friend. But you were just using me. You needed a partner to prove you could save me when Skulduggery failed to save you. That's twisted. That's sick. We were... We helped people! That was what we did!"

"The lives we saved," Fregoli said, "remain saved."

"This is so messed up," said Omen. "I've been second-best my entire life and the only thing I was starting to feel good about was this – doing good and not bothering with the credit. After my parents ignoring me and using Auger to build up their own lives, after living with that kind of, that kind of artificial...

whatever... this felt honest. It felt real. And now I don't even have that any more."

"I'm sorry you feel that way, Omen."

"Screw you, Crepuscular."

Valkyrie frowned. She knew that name. "Crepuscular Vies?"

"Yes!" he said, turning back to her. "Finally! Fregoli Cleft died in that vat of chemicals. He died again on that torture table. It's Crepuscular now. Pleased to make your acquaintance."

"You're the guy who had Oberon Guile's son kidnapped."

Omen blinked. "He what?"

She nodded. "He hired some people to kidnap a kid so he could force the kid's mother to help get Martin Flanery elected president."

Omen tried laughing, but the laugh died. "What? That's ridiculous."

"When China was Supreme Mage," Skulduggery said, "she asked us to investigate the disappearance of Bertram Wilkes, Flanery's aide. Wilkes was a mage, a spy sent into the White House by Abyssinia to manipulate the American president into a phony war with the sorcerers that Abyssinia would then easily win. Fregoli – Crepuscular – here was advising Flanery in secret, and warned him that Abyssinia was planning on double-crossing him. Crepuscular was also the head of a team of well-paid mortal mercenaries called Blackbrook. I'm sure you remember most of this, Omen."

Omen stared at Crepuscular. "You were behind the Whitley naval base thing? Auger and I were almost killed there."

"I didn't know you back then," Crepuscular said.

"Are you serious?"

"Why are you listening to them? They're trying to turn you against me."

"You almost got me killed!"

"I made a mistake!" Crepuscular said. "I saw what she was trying to do with Flanery and I couldn't let that happen! She

163

wanted to announce magic to the world with a war, Omen! That's insane! So yeah, I did some things I'm not proud of – things I had to do. I foiled her plan. You have to be able to see that. I saved the damn day!"

"You could have alerted the Sanctuaries," Skulduggery said.

"I wasn't ready to go back to working with people like you," Crepuscular replied. "I'm still not."

"Jesus," Omen said, "is there anyone around here I can actually trust?"

Valkyrie stepped forward. "Omen," she said gently.

"No," he said, walking away, "screw you, too. Everyone just leave me the hell alone."

29

The call came through on Flanery's private phone. The number was blocked, which usually meant there was some magical freak on the other end. Flanery waved away the people around him – the advisors, the assistants, the Secret Service detail – and waited until the door was shut before answering.

A soft voice spoke into his ear. "Mr President," said Doctor Nye.

People like Crepuscular Vies and Perfidious Withering were complete psychopaths and, as such, Flanery was careful of his tone around them. Nye, however, was a creature, a thing, and it was stuck in its lab all the way over in Mexico with no way of getting to him, so Flanery felt emboldened to be a little curter.

"What do you want? I'm about to go onstage in front of hundreds of thousands of people. Can you hear them chanting my name?"

Flanery held his phone up. The voices of his supporters drifted through the walls of the stadium and it was a glorious thing.

"I can, indeed, Mr President," Nye said. "I do not pay attention to mortal business and, by and large, your elections are a mystery to me, but I hope you win, sir."

"Of course I'm going to win," Flanery snapped.

"That must be very reassuring," said Nye. "Now, I believe you had a visitor recently."

Flanery glowered. "I did. The psycho attacked me at my own party. Could've broken my arm."

"How dreadful."

"What do you want, Doctor?"

"First of all, I feel I must apologise. Perfidious called by the laboratory on Wednesday morning to check on how things were going and, well... he noticed that we had progressed beyond the agreed stage."

"You told me he'd be OK with it."

"And I truly believed he would." Flanery could imagine the freak shaking its head sadly. "But some people, Mr President, are not forward-thinking enough to seize opportunities when they arise. Perfidious and, by extension, Crepuscular Vies are two such individuals. I thought they would be different. I was wrong."

"You being wrong almost cost me my arm."

"But you, Mr President," Nye continued as if Flanery hadn't even spoken, "you are exactly the kind of leader I've been waiting for. A leader who makes the tough decisions. A leader who sees the big picture. A leader who leads."

Flanery nodded. He'd always liked those phrases – they were phrases his own father had used in a famous speech back when Flanery had been a boy, and they were things he'd grown up thinking about himself. It was probably ironic that the first person to voice these words about him was an inhuman freak, but Flanery had never cared much for irony.

"What do you want, Doctor?" he asked because he'd always been able to spot a shyster lining up the big pitch.

Nye hesitated. "Perfidious instructed me to report directly to him," it said, "but I'd prefer to continue reporting to the man who makes the real decisions."

It took Flanery a moment to realise Nye was talking about him.

"The test subjects are responding well to the treatment," it continued. "There have been some rejections, but no more than a fifth of the volunteers. The others are showing encouraging signs."

"How encouraging?"

"Every single one of the surviving test subjects has demonstrated magical abilities."

Flanery took a moment. "All of them?"

"All the ones left alive, yes. I have been aided in my work by a recent addition to my team. I feel I should inform you now, as it could get confusing later. We have been joined by Professor Nye."

"Who's that?"

"Professor Nye is me, Mr President."

Flanery waited for it to make sense. "That doesn't make sense," he said.

"Professor Nye is an alternate version of me who travelled here from an alternate version of Earth."

"What's an alternate version?"

"It's a different version, sir. From a different dimension."

Flanery didn't understand, and it annoyed him. "So how many of you are there?"

"Two, Mr President."

"So it's your twin brother? Or twin sister, or whatever it is you are?"

"Not really, sir, but if it helps you to think of it as such, please continue to do so."

"OK, whatever," Flanery said, his confusion making him angrier. "So now that you've got this extra help, when would the super-soldiers be ready to deploy?"

"A more cautious doctor than I would give it another eight months of close observation, followed by a limited, staggered deployment."

"Uh-huh," said Flanery. "And what would you give it, Doctor Nye?"

"I can have your super-soldiers on their feet in a month, sir, if you so wish."

Flanery hesitated. "Crepuscular Vies won't be happy," he said. "He'll send Perfidious Withering after me. He might even come after me himself."

"I understand, Mr President – but do keep in mind that by the time Mr Vies or Mr Withering realise what's going on, your Secret Service details, every one of them, will have magical abilities of their own. You, sir, will be unstoppable."

Flanery smiled.

30

The others treated Nuncle like he wasn't even there. Sebastian had introduced them and they'd all said their hellos and Nuncle kept the scatter-brained chatter to a minimum, and then it was prayer time and everyone got on their knees and faced the wall, apart from Sebastian and Nuncle, who stood on the piece of floor that was Sebastian's favourite place to stand.

"That Darquesse now," said Nuncle, keeping his voice down, "she's a queer one, and that's for definite."

"Is she?" said Sebastian. The old man's ramblings were beginning to grate.

"All the power of a god in a cage of flesh and blood and bone. Gods weren't meant to be contained like that, so they weren't. What do you think, yourself?"

"I think Darquesse is more complicated than you'd imagine."

"Aye, probably. I can only imagine so much before I have to stop and start over. That's the limits, isn't it, of the human form?"

Sebastian gave a curt nod.

A guard came to the bars, a pale young man with tired eyes. He motioned to Sebastian and Sebastian hesitated before stepping closer.

"Why can't they take off your mask?" the guard asked.

"Only I can do that," Sebastian told him. "And I've got to keep it on for health reasons."

"Some of the others, the other guards down here, they're saying there's something wrong with your face. Is there something wrong with your face?"

"No, not really."

"You heard of this guy Tesseract? He was this killer-for-hire – Russian, I think – and he wore a mask because he had a disease that made his flesh rot, and if he took the mask off he'd just waste away to nothing as he stood there. Is that what you have?"

"I don't have a disease."

"So your face wouldn't rot off or something like that?"

"No."

The guard nodded. "Still pretty weird, though. To never take it off. What if you have to scratch your nose?"

"It goes unscratched."

"That's weird."

"Yeah," said Sebastian, wondering when he was going to get to the point.

The guard didn't say anything for a few seconds. "I'm going to help you," he whispered.

"Sorry?"

"They put us guards on a rotating roster. It's to make sure we don't spend too much time in the one place, guarding the same prisoners. They don't want us to start conversations, you see. Don't want us feeling sorry for you."

"Understandable."

"Yeah, it is. So I've been rotating between here and a few other places, and one of those places is the Black Room."

"What's the Black Room?"

The guard licked his lips. "It's the place they're keeping her. Keeping Darquesse."

Sebastian's heart bounced in his chest. "Is she OK? What are they doing to her?"

"They're, um, hurting her."

Sebastian shook his head. "They can't. She can turn off her pain receptors."

"Listen, I don't know about pain receptors, but I know about pain, and she's feeling it, so it seems to me they've found a way round it. They're pumping some kind of energy into her, something I've never seen before. And they're only increasing the voltage."

Sebastian was suddenly very, very cold.

The guard swallowed. "But listen to me... I can help you. I want to help you. What they're doing to her, it's wrong. I know who she is, I know what she's done, but that person in the Black Room, she's... She's not the Darquesse who did those awful things on Devastation Day. She's not that monster any more. I haven't talked to her or nothing, but even I can see that. She's a person, and they're torturing her, and I didn't become an officer in the City Guard to torture people. I wanted to help them."

"So you'll help us?" Sebastian said. "How?"

"I'll set you free."

"Seriously?"

"I'll need a little time to organise it, but yeah, I'll let you out, and then you can go help her, right? Only, and you gotta promise me this, you can't hurt anyone. Like, you can't kill anyone. You can't kill anyone in uniform, OK? I can't let you out if you're going to do that."

"We won't kill anyone, I swear. We don't even want to hurt anyone."

The guard nodded. "Tomorrow morning, then – be ready."

"OK, yes, thank you. Thank you so much. What day is tomorrow, by the way?"

"Sunday."

"Thank you. The days kind of run together when you're in here."

"Oh, my name's Raylan."

"Pleased to meet you, Raylan."

Raylan nodded, then backed off, and quickly walked away.

31

Fletcher teleported them to the Italian Sanctuary, grumbled a bit about being treated like a bus service, and then left them to their investigating.

"What was Crepuscular Vies like," Valkyrie asked, "before he became Crepuscular Vies?"

Skulduggery didn't look up from the cabinet of thick files he was flicking through. "Fregoli Cleft was eager. Enthusiastic. Not unintelligent, but a little naive, perhaps. Or that's what I thought. But, seeing as how he was hiding the true extent of his magic from me, it makes me wonder what else he was hiding."

"Like his true intelligence?"

"Exactly. Crepuscular Vies seems like a very sharp fellow."

"Sharp enough to fool you."

Skulduggery grunted. "Here we are," he said, pulling a file and opening it.

Valkyrie peeked over his shoulder. "You're sure it's her?"

"I met Fregoli's girlfriend twice," he said. "And I never forget a name."

"Yeah, but this was back in the 1950s."

"It's her. And now we have an address." He put the file back and they walked over to the door.

"Crepuscular could be on the level, you know," Valkyrie said.

"I'm aware of that."

"He mightn't pose any kind of threat to Omen whatsoever. It could be a genuine partnership, like you and me."

They took the old stone stairs upwards.

"There are different reasons to keep secrets," Skulduggery said. "Some are benign. Some are understandable. Some are darker. We need to find out what Crepuscular's reasons are before we can ascertain whether or not Omen is in any danger. He's our responsibility, after all – we got him involved when we asked him to spy on the Arcanum's Scholars and he's been unable to extricate himself since."

"Look at you being all responsible and stuff," Valkyrie said with a smile. "When did this happen?"

He glanced back at her. "I've been forced to learn my lesson."

Her smile faded as they emerged into a curving corridor. Cleavers ignored them and mages tried not to stare.

The Italian Administrator fell into step alongside them. "Did you find what you were looking for, Arbiters?"

"We did," said Skulduggery. "Would you happen to have a Teleporter on staff?"

"She is at your disposal. Where do you need to go?"

They sat at a table round a fountain in the walled town of San Gimignano and Valkyrie was thankful she was wearing a short dress. Her sunglasses were large and her hair was tied back off her face and she had a cold glass of lemonade and she felt like a proper everyday tourist, and it was nice. Skulduggery sat beside her, his façade disguising him as a handsome young man. He was wearing sunglasses, too.

"Fregoli?" Anamika said. "I remember Fregoli, sure. Nice guy. Charming, you know? For the most part."

"What does that mean?" Skulduggery asked.

Anamika shrugged. She was an attractive woman with an easy-going air about her – 283 years old, but looking forty. "Just that he was changeable. His moods, I mean. He'd be sweet and charming in the morning and then in the afternoon I'd get the impression that he didn't even like me."

"What can you tell us about him?"

"Not a huge amount, I'm afraid. He talked about himself so seldomly. If you'd come here asking about anyone else I've ever been involved with, I'd be able to give you plenty of details. But with Fregoli... he was a very private person. I do remember him mentioning his brothers and sisters, though."

"What did he say about them?"

"From what he told me, he was the only normal one out of the lot – and that's saying something. There were a whole lot of them, too, but that's not overly surprising. People had dozens of kids in those days. It was an odd number. Twenty-one, I think, including Fregoli."

"Wow," said Valkyrie.

"Like I said, a whole lot." Anamika frowned slightly. "I'm trying to remember exactly why they were so odd, and I think they were part of some cult or something. At least, that's what I gathered. Fregoli would complain every now and then that they were well and truly brainwashed, but he never went any further than that."

"What about his parents?"

"Never mentioned them. I don't think they were in the picture by that stage."

"This cult," said Skulduggery, "do you remember anything about it?"

"I'm not certain. I can't be sure that my memories are as accurate as they once were. Events kind of blend together, you know? And then you start to wonder if you were there when something happened or if you've just heard the story so many times that you start to believe you were. I hate that. But, if it's how I remember it, I think the cult revolved round the Hosts in some way."

"The Hosts," said Valkyrie. "Who are they?"

"A rumour," Skulduggery said. "Apparently, there's a secretive group of mysterious sorcerers who stand ready to trigger the Doomsday Protocol, a last-resort weapon of vague yet devastating power in case the mortals ever move against us."

"I'm sorry?" said Anamika. "Are you saying it's real? And it's happening? The weapon's going to be unleashed? What is it? Do you know? Is it a bomb? Oh, God, it's a bomb, isn't it? Oh, we're all going to die."

"No one's going to die," Skulduggery assured her. Then, after a moment, "I mean, plenty of people are going to die and nothing's going to change that, but not because of the Hosts. There are lots of other things – real things, real and actual threats – that will kill them long before some conspiracy theory manages it."

Anamika paled. "Like what?"

"Well," Skulduggery said, "like that," and pointed to the south, where the Faceless One called Phanaror stood, bigger than the mountains around it.

"Oh, yeah," said Anamika miserably.

The Teleporter who had transported them here hurried across the road and lowered her voice as she spoke to them.

"Arbiters, I'm sorry, we have received an urgent message from the High Sanctuary. Obsidian has been spotted in Roarhaven and your presence is needed."

32

Obsidian's skin was impossible, a black rock that flexed and moved, that swelled and twisted, without cracking. His head was angular, his expression blank, his eyes unblinking.

The Cleaver leaped at him, the scythe slashing downwards, but the blade hit his shoulder and bounced off. The Cleaver immediately spun, his heel connecting with Obsidian's jaw. But Obsidian didn't move, didn't give way one millimetre, and the Cleaver's ankle broke with a sharp crack. He completed the spin without crying out, without losing his fluidity of movement, and he struck again with the scythe and now Obsidian smacked him and the Cleaver crumpled.

Obsidian looked down at him, like he was deciding what he should do next. He crouched, reaching out with his splayed fingers – then stopped. Straightened. Looked round.

Looked right at Valkyrie as she landed.

"Auger," she said, pulling down her hood, "I don't want to fight you. I don't want to hurt you. I just want to talk. Can you talk to me?"

She felt him examining her.

"You're hurting people," she continued. "You've hurt these Cleavers and you've hurt others. You've killed others. This isn't you, Auger. You've never wanted to hurt anyone. I know this."

Skulduggery drifted down beside her, but Obsidian kept his black eyes on Valkyrie.

"Your family is worried about you," she said. "Your parents are worried. Omen wants you to come home. He needs his brother, Auger. Please."

Obsidian raised his hand.

She couldn't see the magic inside him like she could in other sorcerers, but she saw it swirl around his hand and frowned at it, watching it, reached out to understand it. Her senses probed at the very edge of what it was and she saw nothing but emptiness and what it would do to her, what it would do to Skulduggery, how it would wrap around them and scrub them from reality. She knew in an instant that she had no defence against it and no way to survive it – nothing or nobody did – and so she shoved Skulduggery away and unleashed her fear in the form of lightning that struck Obsidian in the exact centre of his chest.

And he absorbed it without staggering.

To stay was to fight and to fight was to lose so Valkyrie twisted and her magic burst from her and she screamed into the sky. Obsidian came after her.

She dodged and reeled over Roarhaven, leaving a writhing trail of lightning in her wake and he kept up effortlessly. She veered towards a tower and banked left at the last moment and he passed straight through it without slowing down in an explosion of bricks and dust, intercepting her as she tried flying past.

His hand closed around her ankle. Valkyrie gasped as he yanked her out of her flight path and flung her, head over heels, into the side of the library building. She hit the edge of the wall and went spinning off, went crashing into the street.

Moaning in pain and clutching her ribs, Valkyrie got up, looked at Obsidian as he stood in the air overhead. He could have continued, could have killed her, but instead he rose higher, then shifted direction and was gone.

Valkyrie lowered herself to the road and tried not to pass out.

33

Word spread, and all of Obsidian's little obsessives came scurrying out from underneath their rocks and congregated in the street where their messiah was last seen. The City Guard rolled in to maintain order, but the Nulls didn't retreat like they'd done in the past. Today they stood their ground. Their numbers were still small, but growing.

"He noticed you," Skulduggery said.

They stood on a nearby rooftop, high enough so that they couldn't hear the Nulls' chants, but close enough to feel the simmering violence in the air.

"Sorry?" Valkyrie said, pressing her fingertips into her left side. The healer had done a good enough job that she hadn't needed to take over.

"Obsidian noticed you. You're on his radar. He knows you exist."

"He's Auger. Of course he knows I exist."

Skulduggery shook his head. "We can't assume the things he does or doesn't know. He used to be Auger. How much of Auger is left is yet to be determined. His personality has, obviously, been altered. Maybe his memories have, too. They could have been wiped entirely, they could still be there but are now ignored, or they could have been pushed off to one corner of his mind and locked away. The only thing we know for certain is that he is now aware of you, Valkyrie. He's aware of the Child of the Faceless Ones."

She watched him. "You think he's going to come for me."

"I do."

"And you don't think we'll be able to stop him."

"Do you?"

"Oh, we don't stand a chance," she said, and his head dipped. "Skulduggery?"

"We need a way to subdue him," he said. "We need the Void meteorite."

"But you don't want to—"

"I know what I don't want to do. We don't, unfortunately, have much of a choice."

"So are you finally going to tell me why you didn't want to ask Quietus how to get to the Void World?"

"Apparently."

She sat on the edge of the roof, her legs kicking gently. "I'm waiting."

Skulduggery didn't say anything for a long time. Then he sat beside her, took off his hat and placed it on his knee. "What have I told you about my family? The family I grew up with?"

"Just about nothing," she said. "Other than once upon a time you had brothers and sisters, but now they're all dead, but somehow you still have a brother."

"I had five sisters and four brothers," Skulduggery said. "I was the second eldest. I come from a long line of unusual people. My aunt was Estrilda Gaut, the notorious serial killer, but my mother was a remarkable woman. Her name was Quinlan Forte. She was frighteningly intelligent, astonishingly brave and remarkably funny. She was also sweet, kind, impatient, impulsive, and when she spoke to you, you felt as if you were the only other person in the whole entire world. She loved her children with an intensity I didn't understand until I had a child of my own."

Valkyrie smiled. "She sounds awesome."

"She was awesome. Very awesome."

"Kinda curious to hear more about your serial-killing auntie, though."

He shrugged. "She's not relevant right now."

"And what about your dad?"

"My father's name was Abrogate Raze."

"And...?"

"To understand my father, you have to understand the god he worshipped. You've read the Book of Tears, haven't you?"

"Creed gave me a copy – said it might do me some good to learn the history of the Faceless Ones. It might help me appreciate them."

"And did it?"

"It was interesting, but I don't need a book in order to appreciate my children. Have you read it?"

"I have," said Skulduggery. "I spent most of my life believing that the stories about the Faceless Ones and other gods were nothing more than fairy tales. When that proved not to be the case, I started reading everything I could about them. The Book of Tears would seem to be inaccurate, to say the least."

"I am shocked and appalled."

"It claims that the Faceless Ones were the First Gods that came into existence. According to the literature, that isn't true. There was another race who were already around when the Big Bang occurred – Those Who Slumber, Whose Names We Dare Not Speak Lest They Rouse to Waking."

"I'm sorry?"

"That's what they're called."

"It's a bit of a mouthful, isn't it? So if we were to use their actual name, they'd wake up and come after us?"

"Presumably."

"And does anyone know their actual name?"

"We'd better hope not."

"There has to be a better name for them than the Sleeping Ones Whose Names We've Forgotten."

"That's not even close to what I said."

"It was basically word for word."

"They're called Those Who Slumber, Whose Names We Dare Not Speak Lest They Rouse to Waking."

"I can't see the difference, to be honest. So, these Sleeping Ones—"

"Not what we call them."

"—they were around, somehow, before the Big Bang. OK, cool. Then the Faceless Ones arrived?"

Skulduggery nodded. "Along with pantheon upon pantheon of other gods – some of whom we've met. Like Eraddin Tomb, apparently."

"And which one did your dad worship?"

"Gog Magog – the God of the Apocalypse."

Valkyrie nodded. "So not one of the nice ones, then?"

"Gog Magog would descend on various civilisations after they'd started worshipping one of the other gods, and, from what I can gather, either instigate or lead them to their own destruction. The other gods got annoyed at this and banded together, stripped him of most of his power, and exiled him from the cosmos."

"Harsh but fair."

"My father read about him, and became obsessed. That's a recurring theme when it comes to Gog Magog – when people hear his story, they run the risk of becoming obsessed with worshipping him."

"Seriously?"

"I've heard him described as a virus. Nothing I've learned would lead me to doubt that description."

"So will I start worshipping him, now that you've told me?"

Skulduggery shook his head. "The information needs to come to you in a certain order, presented in a particular way. Besides, you're too busy worshipping the Faceless Ones, aren't you?"

"I don't worship them," Valkyrie replied sharply. "I don't worship anyone."

He watched her, then shrugged and continued the story. "According to my mother, Abrogate Raze had spent his entire life searching for something to fill the emptiness inside him. He found it when he found Gog Magog."

"I'm assuming your mum wasn't happy at this development."

"By this stage, my mother was already dead. My father had killed her."

Valkyrie covered her mouth with her hand. "Skulduggery, I'm so sorry."

"She recognised the darkness in him too late. When she saw what he was, what he truly was, she left him, and took my five youngest siblings with her. By then, the rest of us were already adults and had left home to forge our own paths. We should have done more to protect the others, but war was coming. Our attention was elsewhere.

"Three years after she left him, Abrogate Raze found my mother and killed her in front of the children. Pursued by the Arbiters and, later on, the Sanctuaries, Abrogate became a member, and then a leader, of various cults around the world until he joined Mevolent's army. When I eventually met him, as Lord Vile, it was the first time I'd seen his face for a hundred and twenty-eight years."

Valkyrie's voice was soft. "That must have been... I have no idea what that must have been like."

"There was a storm inside me," Skulduggery said. "I was already working beside Nefarian Serpine – the man who had murdered my wife and child. And now I discover that lurking in Mevolent's libraries after all this time was the man who had murdered my mother."

"You didn't try to kill him?"

"Despite the storm inside me, I had other priorities. I walked away, and a few years later Abrogate made a deal with the

Sanctuaries and betrayed Mevolent. I was ordered to leave my father alone."

"I'm assuming you ignored that order."

"I found out where he was staying. I didn't have time to gather all of my siblings, but four of us went in."

"And what happened?"

"We fought him."

"Did you win?"

"His magic was... I'd never seen it before. We couldn't beat him. Then he started talking, started telling us about Gog Magog. The others listened. He infected them. He got into their heads."

"Jesus."

"The virus doesn't seem to work on skeletons, however, so I ran. Now that Abrogate had three of my siblings on his side, he was more powerful than ever. It took the rest of us two years to find him again, and that was only because my sister, Confelicity, created an intelligent virus that sought them out."

"A what?"

"Since Gog Magog seemed to be a virus in idea form, she hypothesised that an actual virus might be able to locate him, or his followers, for us. She named it Malady."

"And by actual virus you mean an actual virus? Like the flu?"

"A mild cold, really," said Skulduggery, "but Malady spread round the world, searching for my father's bloodline. It found one of my errant siblings, alerted my sister, and we waited and we watched, and when Abrogate was alone we attacked."

"And you beat him?"

"It was not an easy fight, but against the array of magical disciplines directed against him at the one time, he fell, and we bound him in chains."

"So happy ending?"

"Essentially."

"Your sister was pretty smart, then, to create a virus like that."

"All my siblings are highly intelligent, none more so than Confelicity. Unfortunately, Malady grew sentient soon after."

"Seriously? A virus became self-aware?"

"It was as astonishing as it was disastrous. Malady couldn't rest while we still roamed the Earth, so it decided that our entire bloodline should be eradicated. It developed its own virus, sent that out, and it found all ten of us, and drained our life forces. Because I was the only one with any experience in dealing with my own life force, I managed to return to my body, such as it was. My brothers and sisters were not so experienced."

"They died."

"Yes."

"When was this?"

"In 1958."

"So when you told me your brothers and sisters were dead—"

"At that time, they were."

"And then what happened?"

"Seven years ago, they came back to life."

"How?"

"We don't know."

She stared at him. "That's not a satisfactory answer."

"It's not a satisfactory world."

"And, when they came back, they weren't curious as to why they were suddenly alive?"

"Of course they were. They investigated. The investigation is ongoing."

"Wait – all of them came back? Even—"

"Even the ones who worship Gog Magog, yes. They're out there right now. Waiting. Plotting."

"Well, that's creepy. What about Abrogate Raze? What did you do with him after he was defeated?"

"We exchanged him."

"What does that mean?"

"Exactly that. We swapped him for another prisoner."

"So where is he?"

"Not anywhere close."

Valkyrie's eyes widened. "He's in the Dire Dimension. He's on the prison planet."

"He is."

"So you had him here, all chained up, his powers bound, and then you exchanged him for a prisoner that they had on the other Earth."

"Gaunt."

"Gaunt, right. Why?"

"It was just one more layer of security."

"You couldn't have just stuck him in Coldheart, or one of our other prisons here? I know he's a bad guy, and he infects people with words, but locking him up in another universe seems a little extreme." Her head tilted. "What are you not telling me?"

"He's not an ordinary sorcerer."

"In what way?"

"I used to think he was Gog Magog's herald. He would spread the word, tell people about his god, converting whomever he met. But he's not Gog Magog's herald."

"So who is he?"

"When the other gods banded together, they stripped Gog Magog of the majority of his powers and they exiled him... to Earth. With those powers went his memory. He woke up here, assumed he was an ordinary sorcerer, and took a name for himself."

Valkyrie shook her head. "No."

"Yes."

"No."

"Yes."

"Abrogate Raze is Gog Magog? Gog Magog is your father?"

Skulduggery sighed. "Yes."

34

"But... but..."

Skulduggery watched her struggle to absorb the information.

She got up. Walked in a circle. Stopped. "But that means that your father is the God of the Apocalypse."

"Yes," said Skulduggery.

"So that makes you a god."

"No," he said quickly. "No, it doesn't."

"What does it make you? What's it called when there's a...? Demi-god! That's the thing! You're a demi-god!"

"I'm not a demi-god," Skulduggery said. "I'm not any kind of god. That's not how gods work. Well, it might be how some gods work, but not this god. None of his children inherited any of his power."

"But your dad..."

The air shimmered around him and he rose off the edge of the roof, turning as his feet touched down. "I know."

"The God of the... Skulduggery, this is huge. This is amazing. This is cosmopolitan!"

"Do you mean cosmological?"

"I mean your father is an actual god!"

"Then you mean cosmological. Although, I suppose, you could also mean cosmopolitan."

"And all the time we've known each other, you're only telling me now?"

"We've only known each other for fourteen years."

"That's most of my life!"

"But not most of mine."

"Why didn't you tell me before now?"

"Because I didn't want you to know."

Valkyrie opened her mouth to argue, then stopped. "OK, that's a pretty good reason. Am I ever going to meet any of your brothers or sisters?"

"You already have."

"Really?"

"You've met one of my brothers, yes."

"Who is he? Was it Ghastly?"

"You know it wasn't Ghastly."

"Oh, yeah. Do I know him well? Do I like him? Does he like me? What does he think of me? Does he think I'm nice?"

"I'm sure he thinks you're wonderful."

"That doesn't sound very convincing."

"Valkyrie."

"What?"

"Let's get back to the subject."

"What is the subject? I've completely forgotten how this conversation started. A lot has happened since then, you know? Certain things have come to light." She narrowed her eyes, forced herself to focus. "OK," she said. "So you chained up Abrogate – you chained up Gog Magog – and then you swapped him with a prisoner from the Dire Dimension. I'm assuming this prisoner is a pretty big deal, yeah? Like a serious threat? Oh, God – it's not Quietus, is it?"

"It's Quietus."

"But I thought he was in charge! You said he was the Tyrant of Gaunt, a mass-murdering warlord!"

"And he was finally overthrown and replaced with a more democratic system of government," Skulduggery said. "They didn't want him over there because his loyal followers kept trying to free him, and we didn't want Abrogate over here for the same reason, so we swapped."

"And Quietus knows where the Void World is, but you don't want to ask him because he'll ask for something in return, right? He'll ask to be released."

"Which we won't do."

"Then he'll ask for something else. He'll ask... He'll ask to be returned to the Dire Dimension. Which will mean Abrogate Raze comes back over here."

"Correct."

"I see your dilemma."

"I'm glad."

"We don't have much of a choice, though, do we? We need the Void meteorite, or Obsidian's going to find a way to kill me."

"As you said," Skulduggery replied, "a dilemma."

Creed was working in the gardens behind the Dark Cathedral, pulling weeds from the dirt, when Valkyrie landed beside him. She told him what they needed. When she was done, he kept working, and took a moment to respond.

"We do not have many arrangements in place with the Dire Dimension," he said at last. "Nobody does. The fact that they trusted us to hold the Tyrant of Gaunt in one of our prisons has been an important diplomatic bond between us – one that no other dimension can boast. You are certain this is the only course of action available?"

"Skulduggery reckons this is the one thing that would make Quietus tell us where the Void World is," said Valkyrie.

Creed wiped the sweat from his heavy brow, and looked up. "These are surely desperate times if Skulduggery Pleasant is willing to accept Abrogate Raze back into our reality. Very well. At noon tomorrow, Quietus of Gaunt will be transferred to your custody, Valkyrie, to be sent home. Make sure you get what we need."

35

Sebastian ran.

Behind him, there were cries and shouts and curses. He heard Raylan pleading with the other guards to let the prisoners go, and then a sharp yelp and no more from Raylan. Sebastian fought the urge to turn back and help, knowing it would do no good. The escape was a bust, ruined by three City Guard officers stumbling across them at the worst possible moment.

The other members of the Darquesse Society, not a seasoned fighter among them, had launched themselves at the cops to give Sebastian a chance to flee.

There was more at stake than their freedom, they knew. Sebastian had a mission to complete, and time was slipping away.

The door ahead, the one Raylan had told them to run to, the one he'd said would lead to the outside, opened before Sebastian got halfway there. A muscle-bound City Guard officer ambled through, eyes widening when he realised he wasn't alone. Sebastian's stomach flipped. Everything that could go wrong had gone wrong. Bloody typical.

Running footsteps behind and Sebastian prepared himself to be tackled, but then Nuncle was sprinting past and charging into the cop. They went down in a tangle.

"Run, boy!" Nuncle shouted, his face sweaty with exertion. "Get away!"

Sebastian hesitated, then leaped over the tussling figures and ran out into the morning sun.

36

Alice snapped out two jabs and then spun, the heel of her foot coming up to smack into the exact centre of the pad. She continued the spin, settling back into the fighting stance, hands up and elbows in.

"Nice," said Valkyrie, moving round. "Again."

Valkyrie held up the pads and the jabs came in and then the spinning kick, with even more power than before.

"Again."

Jabs. Spinning kick.

"Go nuts."

Valkyrie started throwing the pads up at different heights and angles and Alice caught them perfectly each time, rattling out a combination of jabs and crosses and hooks and uppercuts, mixing it with straight and roundhouse kicks, spinning when necessary, and introducing elbows, knees and headbutts when the pads came close enough.

They moved all the way across the back garden and back again, and then Valkyrie broke away, laughing. "Oh my goodness."

Alice grinned. "That was good?"

"That was brilliant. How are the Jiu-Jitsu classes going?"

She soured. "There's a boy in the class and he always goes really tough on me. He's way bigger and heavier and he never lets me try anything."

191

"There'll always be people like that," Valkyrie told her, taking off the pads. "The best training partners are the kind who don't punish you for attempting something new."

"Dad says he probably likes me. He says all nine-year-old boys are like that."

"What do you think?"

"I think that's a stupid way of showing how much you like someone."

"I'd agree. Do you like him back?"

"Ew, no. I don't like anyone." Alice frowned, then corrected herself. "I don't like anyone in a boyfriend or girlfriend way. I like people in a friend way. But I don't even like this boy in a friend way. His name's Ethan and he likes action movies and I like action movies, but I don't always go on about them. He talks about some movies and I know for a fact that he hasn't seen them because when anyone asks him questions he never knows the answers, but he always *pretends* he's seen them. And he smells of cheese-and-onion crisps. I like cheese-and-onion crisps, but I don't want to always be smelling them."

"But apart from that, Jiu-Jitsu is good?"

"Brazilian Jiu-Jitsu."

"Sorry. Brazilian Jiu-Jitsu is good?"

"It's good. Although I don't like it when my arms are trapped and I can't move."

Valkyrie winced. "Yeah. I'm the same."

"Can you do the splits?"

"I can, actually," said Valkyrie, quite used to these whiplash topic changes by now, "but not in these jeans. Can you?"

Alice dropped into the box splits and shrugged up at her. "Yeah."

"That's pretty cool."

"Thanks," Alice said, springing back to her feet and doing a little dance.

"You're a bundle of energy, aren't you?" Valkyrie asked, unable to stop another laugh.

"I have my moments," said Alice. "Did you hear what Dad did yesterday? Oh, God, it was so embarrassing. Wait till he tells you. Dad!"

Alice charged back into the house and Valkyrie followed. They found their parents in the kitchen, arguing.

"If you don't want to go to golf," Melissa said, "don't go."

"But I have to," Desmond whined.

"You're a grown man. You don't have to do anything you don't want to do when it comes to a hobby you don't even like."

"But all my friends are doing it."

"If all your friends jumped off a cliff, would you do it, too?"

"I don't know," Desmond said, sitting heavily in a chair by the table. "If it looked cool, then probably."

"Dad," said Alice, "tell Stephanie about what you did."

"Not this again," he moaned.

Valkyrie grinned. "What did you do, Dad?"

He rolled his eyes. "We were sitting here yesterday morning, and we were talking about all the sorcerers and Cleavers who stand outside all day long, keeping watch, protecting us, and I thought that they might like a cup of tea. So I ran the idea past your mother, who told me no, don't do anything nice for them."

"I didn't say that," Melissa interrupted. "I just said that Stephanie had made it clear that we shouldn't acknowledge them – that it would be too dangerous and also it would risk exposing them to the neighbours."

"Anyway," Desmond continued, "your mum went upstairs to have a shower, and I was left in the kitchen, with the kettle, and mugs, and a tray, so I thought that I'd just break the rules, just this one time. So I made five or six mugs of tea, got some chocolate-chip cookies, put them all on the tray, and walked out to the front gate."

Melissa struggled to stop her smile from spreading. "Tell Steph what you said."

193

He sighed. "I said, 'I know I'm not supposed to do this, but I thought you might want a break.'"

"And who did you say this to?"

"Well, no one," Desmond answered. "They were invisible, weren't they? They had that invisible cloaking ball thing, hiding them from view."

"I was out of the shower by this stage," Melissa said, "and watching from the upstairs window as my adorable husband has a full-blown conversation with the gatepost, even though you'd specifically told us that none of our security detail would be stationed anywhere near the gate. I watched as the man I fell in love with spoke to thin air and held out his tray full of mugs to no one at all."

"Oh, Dad," said Valkyrie. "When did you realise there was no one there?"

"When no one took the tea."

"And how long did that take?"

"A few minutes."

"And, when no one answered immediately, did you not think you might have got this wrong?"

"I just thought they were really professional. Like those sentries with the fluffy hats outside Buckingham Palace, the ones who can't react to tourists."

"Oh, Dad," she said again, and then her phone buzzed. "OK, I gotta go. Father, please try not to embarrass yourself while I'm away."

"Absolutely no guarantees," Desmond warned.

She gave him a hug, then pulled on her jacket and grabbed her helmet.

"I wish you wouldn't ride that motorbike everywhere," Melissa said as Valkyrie kissed her cheek. "It's really dangerous."

"Mum, it's fine. It's actually a lot safer than you'd think."

Alice gave her a big hug. "Maybe one day I can ride on the back?"

"Not a chance," said Valkyrie, kissing the top of her head. "It's way too dangerous."

Sunday-morning traffic was light, and she made it to Ironpoint Gaol a half-hour ahead of Skulduggery. She parked the bike and leaned against it.

Jagett was here already, standing in the sun, ignoring her. She thought about calling over to him, but decided against it.

The Phantom pulled up, and Skulduggery got out. An SUV followed behind, and Ragner clambered awkwardly out.

"How are you feeling about this?" Valkyrie asked Skulduggery as he came over.

"The level of sarcasm I could wield at this point would be considered a deadly weapon," he told her, "so instead I shall answer with understated sincerity: I'm not feeling the best about this."

Finally out of the car, Ragner joined them. "Greetings, Valkyrie," he said, a worried smile on his face.

"Hey there," she said. "How's Eraddin?"

"Very good," Ragner said. "He has much relief that the death threats were not a personal slight on his character. I am not so pleased with how things have turned out, but I have gladness in my heart that my friend is safe."

"I take it you and your brother don't get along?"

"We do not." They watched Jagett, standing just out of earshot. "When we were five years old, he challenged me to a duel in the Arena of Blood. My father waived the usual rules and allowed it to proceed. Jagett failed to kill me that day; our father has never let him forget it, and my brother has never forgiven me for not dying. My family, Valkyrie, it is complicated."

The doors to the gaol opened and the warden led a squad of Cleavers out. They carried a black coffin between them, made of some metal Valkyrie didn't recognise. Large circles of sigils were carved into it, and criss-crossing the whole thing were black chains, similarly inscribed.

They set the coffin on to a horizontal metal lattice that had been set up earlier, and Jagett came over to watch as keys went into locks and sigils were deactivated and countered, glowed brightly and then faded. Chains slithered off.

The warden turned to them. "Are you sure about this, Arbiters?"

"Just open it," growled Jagett.

Skulduggery nodded.

The Warden shook his head, then gave the order, and the Cleavers pulled the coffin open.

Quietus was bigger than his son. Tall and broad. Immense, was the word that popped into Valkyrie's head. Massive chest, massive arms, legs that seemed impossibly thick. He had long hair, black and grey, like Jagett, and a beard and a wide face. He should have been sleeping – the coffin was designed to sedate its occupant into unconsciousness – but he was watching them the whole time.

"Quietus of Gaunt," Skulduggery said, "you are to be transferred from our planet to your own, where you will live out the rest of your days in this coffin. This is the reward you will receive in exchange for one piece of information that you will furnish to us. Do you accept these terms?"

Quietus looked at him like he was contemplating whether or not to respond. Finally, he spoke in a voice that rumbled. "Where is my son?"

Jagett went down on one knee, his head bowed. "I'm here, Father, ready to do you—"

"Where," said Quietus, "is my other son?"

Ragner hesitated, then stepped into his father's view.

A grim smile rose to Quietus's mouth. "The traitor," he said. "The betrayer."

"They need the dimensional frequency of the Void World," Ragner said.

"And for this, I get to languish in my prison at home instead of languishing in my prison here? What difference should it make to me?"

"This universe is ending, Father," said Jagett. "We must leave."

Quietus sniffed the air. "Yes. The air is heavy with imminent destruction. Skeleton – you think the solution to your problem lies on the Void World? Then if I am your only hope, I would demand more from you. I would demand my freedom."

"Demand away," said Skulduggery. "You've heard the terms of the only deal you're going to get."

"Then I have nothing to say to you."

Jagett got to his feet. "Father, you cannot stay here." Quietus looked at him and Jagett wilted. "I mean to say... our universe needs your strength. It needs your leadership. Transferring you back to Gaunt is surely one step closer to—"

"Only I possess the information you need to save your entire universe, skeleton. If you can do without me, you may put me back where you found me."

Skulduggery watched him. "Warden," he said at last, "can I have a moment of privacy with the prisoner?"

"He's all yours, Detective," the Warden said, and the Cleavers followed him back to the gaol.

Skulduggery motioned for Valkyrie to stay where she was, and he walked up to Quietus and held his hands out. The air around them rippled, preventing their words from escaping.

"What is he doing?" Jagett asked.

"I have no idea," said Valkyrie.

When they were done, Skulduggery dropped his hands and turned to them. "We've reached an agreement," he said. "We'll take custody of Abrogate Raze and return Quietus to the Dire Dimension. Before he goes through, Quietus will tell us where to find the Void World."

Quietus's face betrayed no emotion, but Valkyrie could sense how pleased he was.

"What did you say to him?" she asked.

Skulduggery tilted his head at her. "We negotiated."

She didn't press it. Didn't ask what Skulduggery had promised him to get him to change his mind. Priorities, she reminded herself. Solve the immediate problems, then worry about the new ones.

Ragner and Jagett arranged a dozen small metal triangles on the ground in a circle. Once they were in place, the triangles started to vibrate. The space between them shimmered and a ribbon of energy, deep blue like the sea, flowed to each one, connecting them and expanding to fill the circle. Simultaneously, another circle appeared beside it.

The brothers wheeled the lattice into the space between the metal triangles, then stepped away.

"Skeleton," Quietus said, "come here and I will tell you how to get to the Void World."

Skulduggery hesitated, then walked into the circle. He leaned close and Quietus spoke to him, and Skulduggery nodded. He moved back and closed the coffin lid, sealing it, then stepped out of the circle.

When he was clear, the triangles lifted off the ground, swallowing the coffin. At the same time, the other circle also lifted, revealing an identical coffin, still wrapped in chains. Ragner and Jagett carried this coffin to the lattice, resting it upon the struts. No one made a move to open it.

"Did you get what we need?" Valkyrie asked Skulduggery. When he didn't answer, she said, "Skulduggery?"

He looked away from the coffin, and tilted his head at her. "Yes," he said. "Yes."

"Are you OK?"

"Not especially."

He went quiet again, so Valkyrie looked over at Jagett.

"You have twenty-four hours to leave this world," she told him. "You're here illegally, but Supreme Mage Creed will allow you a one-day grace period. After that, we will hunt you down and turn you over to the Gaunt authorities."

Jagett smiled. "You fret for no reason. I will be walking upon my home soil before nightfall. Today is a good day for the future of the Dire Dimension."

"I foresee very little will change," Ragner said. "Our father may have been returned home, but he is still imprisoned, and he will remain so."

"Until someone lets him out, my brother. Rest assured, our father will rule Gaunt once again and this will not be good news for some of us."

Jagett pressed a sigil on his belt and he vanished.

"Huh," said Valkyrie. "Can we get one of those?"

"It is not that impressive," Ragner said dismissively. "What is really awesome, however, is a fully electric Sports Utility Vehicle with heated steering wheel to keep your hands warm. A mode of transport that is both cosy and impressive."

"I think I'd rather have a belt teleporter."

Ragner shook his head sadly, and looked at Skulduggery. "I am hoping all this was not a mistake that will cost lives."

Skulduggery didn't say anything as Ragner got in his SUV and drove off.

Valkyrie looked at the new coffin, then at Skulduggery. "That's your dad, then?"

"That is he."

"You gonna open it, say hi?"

"No."

She nodded. A moment passed. "I can't imagine what you must be feeling. Like, the rage alone must be tearing you apart. The hatred. If it were me, I don't think I'd be able to handle it. I think I'd be screaming and kicking the coffin and setting it on fire or something. You must be going through a hell of a lot right now."

"I am," said Skulduggery. "Thankfully, I have you to keep my mind off it."

"Ah," said Valkyrie. "Sorry. So what're you going to do with him?"

"We'll secrete him away where no one will ever find him."

"We as in you and me?"

Skulduggery shook his head. "We as in me and my siblings."

She realised he was looking up and she followed his gaze as six figures drifted out of the clouds and began to descend.

37

They flew just like Skulduggery tended to – standing upright, as if they'd just stepped out of a restaurant and were waiting for the car to be brought round.

"The one in the middle is Carver Gallant," Skulduggery said, referring to the handsome but serious man with the blond hair and the nice suit. To his right was a dark-haired woman in jeans and a long coat, and beside her a petite blonde who looked no older than Valkyrie herself.

"Then you've got Confelicity Divine and Apricity Delight. You already know Uther, of course." Uther Peccant, the old, grouchy teacher from Corrival Academy.

"That's your brother?" Valkyrie said. "I've met him, like, a hundred times. Why did you never mention it?"

"You've met him a maximum of four times," said Skulduggery, "and we've always had other things to talk about. The gent in the colourful waistcoat is Fransic Catawampus, and the one on the end is Bayard Muchly."

Fransic touched down beside the others and shook his head, like he'd been daydreaming about other things the whole time. Bayard was a stupidly gorgeous man who looked immediately bored.

"Valkyrie," Carver said, shaking her hand, "it's very good to meet you."

"You can all fly," Valkyrie said, which wasn't the smartest thing in the world to say, but it was out now, so she figured it best to just go with it. "But you're not all Elementals."

"We are, actually," Confelicity said, "but we're other things as well."

"Being magically ambidextrous runs in the family," said Skulduggery. "Though I'm a little behind when it comes to mastering other techniques."

"On account of the effort it took to keep himself in one piece after he died," Apricity said, stepping up to wrap Valkyrie in a hug. "Hi there. I've read so much about you, it's like I'm meeting a celebrity."

"Uh, thank you."

"A celebrity that nobody likes and people still blame for the unthinking murder of thousands of people."

"That's me."

Apricity grinned. "I like you. We're going to be best friends."

"No, you're not," said Skulduggery. "After we do this, we're all going to go our separate ways, like we always do."

"We don't go our separate ways," Bayard said. "You go your separate way, and the rest of us hang out together."

Skulduggery tilted his head. "You do?"

"You know we do," said Confelicity. "I told you we do. I invited you to come along. You said you were busy."

"I am busy an awful lot. What do you do when you *hang out together*?"

"We each have our preoccupations. Some of us solve problems. Play chess."

"Try to track down our errant siblings," Fransic said, his voice quiet and his smile small.

"And how is that going?"

"Haven't found them yet."

"That's surprising."

"Is it?" Fransic asked. "They are frightfully intelligent people."

"So are you."

"No, we are terribly intelligent people. They are frightfully intelligent. It's a completely different kind of intelligence."

Skulduggery nodded. "Good point. Uther, you're glaring at me rather pointedly."

"That's how I always look at you," Peccant said.

"Hi," said Valkyrie. "Before, when we'd meet, I didn't know you were his brother. So... hi."

"Miss Cain," he said, and that seemed to be the end of it.

"Apologies for the change of topic," Bayard said, "but can we now discuss the fact that our beloved father is lying in a coffin before us when we all promised each other that he would never again return to this dimension?"

"Circumstances have changed," Skulduggery said.

"Circumstances tend to do that. It's why promises matter."

"They've changed in what way?" Carver asked.

"I assume you've been keeping up with current events?" Skulduggery asked.

"Naturally."

"The being known as Obsidian poses a direct threat to this universe. A means of containing and/or defeating him lies on the Void World. We needed to take Abrogate back in order to learn the location of the Void World. It was a simple exchange."

"He's the God of the Apocalypse."

"I am aware."

"He killed our mother," Bayard said.

"I'm aware of that, too."

"But you weren't there," said Apricity. "You weren't there to watch it happen. You don't have those memories."

"Accepting Abrogate's return was the only way we were going to learn the frequency of the Void World."

"You should have consulted us," said Carver.

"I did consult you."

"No, you alerted us, after you'd made your decision. You didn't consult us because you knew we'd object. You knew we'd have sought another way to gain that information. But you didn't want to wait."

"I couldn't afford to wait," Skulduggery said.

"And you wonder why we're angry with you?"

"Not at all," said Skulduggery. "I know exactly why you're angry with me. I always have."

Bayard scowled at Fransic. "Are you going to say anything?"

"I have said something," Fransic responded.

"Are you going to say anything else?"

Fransic sighed, and looked at Skulduggery. "Please understand that I was perfectly happy to keep relatively quiet."

Skulduggery gave a gentle nod. "Of course."

"You have a problem, Skulduggery," said Fransic. "You are a terrifyingly intelligent man, but you think you are smarter than all of us, that you alone can see all the angles. You think you know best."

Confelicity smiled apologetically at Valkyrie. "I'm sorry, but I think we need to talk to our brother alone. Family business. I hope you understand."

"Of course," Valkyrie said. "I've got to report back to Creed anyway. Skulduggery?"

Skulduggery took out his phone, tapped at the screen for a few seconds, then put the phone away. "The co-ordinates," he said.

Valkyrie's own phone buzzed in her pocket and she nodded to him, then nodded to the others. "Nice meeting you all."

In return, she got a range of smiles, nods and, from Peccant, indifference, and then she got on her bike and slipped on her helmet.

When she got back to Roarhaven, she hopped the kerb, slowly passed the bewildered guards, and parked at the door to the Dark Cathedral. As she took the elevator up, she transferred the co-ordinates from her phone to a piece of paper, because Creed was boringly old-school. He was in his office alone, still hunched over the Nexus Helmet, his thick fingers making surprisingly nimble adjustments to the headset.

"Got them," she said, tossing the paper on to the desk. He barely glanced at it before returning his attention to his work.

"This is good news," he said. "Good news, indeed. I'll have a Shunter open a portal and send a team of our best people and, finally, we'll have something to hold Obsidian."

"Yeah," Valkyrie said, and frowned. "Sorry, what's this about sending a team?"

"Our best team, of our best people."

"See, that's what I thought you meant. The thing is, Skulduggery and I, we pretty much do this sort of thing ourselves, you know? We don't, like, pass it off for someone else to handle."

"I completely understand," said Creed, putting aside his work and looking up at her, "but I'm afraid there is no other choice. I don't trust the skeleton, and you're too valuable to risk sending to another reality. What if you're trapped there? What will then happen to the Faceless Ones that are currently held inside you if you're unable to return? No, no, I'm afraid I must insist that you stay home."

Valkyrie watched him. "Yeah," she said, even slower than before. "It's just, that's not how we do things."

He sighed, and stood, and spoke to her like she was a child. "Valkyrie, we don't know how dangerous the Void World will be."

She stifled a sudden blast of anger. "It's the Void World. There's nothing there."

"We don't know that – but, even if it's true, we don't know what the environment will be like. What if there's no oxygen? No atmosphere? What if the ground is made of lava?"

"Then sending me and Skulduggery would be your smartest move. My suit supplies me with oxygen, and he doesn't need to breathe. Plus, we can both fly. Can your best people fly?"

"Two of them can, yes. I understand that you want to go and I understand that you're used to getting your own way. But you have a responsibility now. There is an untold number of Faceless Ones waiting to pass through you into this world. You are the Child and the Mother. Your place is here. You see that, don't you?"

"Damocles, I'm going to say this once: you ever talk to me again like you're talking to me right now, and I will break your jaw. You get me?"

"Have I done something to offend you?"

Her anger flared and lightning hit the walls, sparking off the chains, before she forced it down and smiled. "That was my only warning."

"I thought we were allies."

"And I respect you as such. But you either return the favour or I'll be doing this alone."

"I see," said Creed. "I have offended you, in whatever fashion, and I'm truly sorry. But it is my fervent opinion that you should not be part of the expedition to the Void World. It is simply too dangerous."

When Valkyrie left his office, her fists were clenched. A priest came up to say something with a smile on his face, but he backed off when he saw her expression. She called Skulduggery.

"Where are you?" she asked.

"Driving back. You sound annoyed."

"I am annoyed. Creed won't let us go to the Void World."

There was a moment of amused silence. "He won't let us?"

"He said he doesn't want me doing anything risky."

"Has he met you?"

"He's going to send a team instead."

"It's adorable that he thinks we'll do what he tells us."

Valkyrie grinned. "Finally – someone speaking sense."

"They're not going to shunt, are they?"

"No. His Shunters are afraid they'll just be shunting into, like, a world of instant death or something."

"So they're going to reprogramme one of the portal devices," Skulduggery said.

"Why do I bother calling to tell you things that you've already figured out yourself?"

"I sincerely don't know. They'll need time to adapt the device, so keep an eye on them and, when they move, we'll move."

"Sounds good to me."

"In the meantime, to take our respective minds off our respective troubles, I thought we might search Serpine's place of residence, to try to solve at least one of our little mysteries. Shall I meet you there?"

Another grin. "Oh, I rather think you shall."

38

The house was tidy. There were no ornaments and no pictures. The cupboard had one dinner plate, one side plate, one cup and one saucer. A knife, fork and spoon were all that rattled in the cutlery drawer. The fridge was empty save for milk and cheese. There was a tiny cactus on the windowsill.

"Wow," said Valkyrie, "it looks like a serial killer lives here."

"Are you surprised?" Skulduggery asked, leading the way up the stairs.

"Kinda, yeah. Serpine has more personality than... this."

They entered the bedroom. The bed was perfectly made. Among the clothes in the wardrobe was the grey suit. There was nothing else of note.

"So many clues," Valkyrie said, then raised her eyebrows at Skulduggery. "So, that was your family, huh?"

"Minus our three more murderous siblings who are still out there, plotting murderous plots, yes."

"They seem nice. Bayard is hot."

"So he tells me."

"Are they all as smart as you?"

"I don't know," Skulduggery said. "They'd need to try to kill me before I could make a reasonably accurate judgement on that issue."

"Is that likely to happen?"

"Any time soon? Probably not."

They went downstairs.

"It must have been nice when they came back," she said. "I mean, for all this time you've been alone, and then suddenly you have your brothers and sisters again."

"I wasn't alone," Skulduggery said. "I had you." He turned on the basement light and then led the way down, and Valkyrie watched him for a moment without moving. He turned on the steps and looked up. "Are you coming?"

She cleared her throat. "Yeah, cool," she said as gruffly as she could manage, and followed him.

On the shelf against one breeze-block wall there was a jar with a lump of flesh floating in a murky solution the colour of urine.

"Ah," said Valkyrie, poking at the glass to make the lump of flesh move. "He kept it."

"Your first attempt at a new hand?"

She nodded. "I needed a few goes before I got it right. It's relatively easy to regrow a limb for myself, but regrowing it for other people is actually sort of tricky. We had four failed attempts before I got it right."

"And after every failed attempt?" Skulduggery asked, peering into another jar on another shelf.

"We had to chop it off."

"So he's been complaining about me letting his hand get cut off once, and not complaining about you chopping his hand off four times?"

"I'm cuter than you. Also, I was doing it to help."

"There are three jars."

"Sorry?"

"Four failed attempts, four chopped-off hands... only three jars."

Valkyrie joined him, looking around. "Huh," she said.

The first attempt had resulted in the lump of flesh. The second was a hand that was all thumbs. The third had eight fingers and two thumbs.

"The last is missing," she said.

"What went wrong with that one?" Skulduggery asked, conducting a search of the rest of the basement. There wasn't much down there, though, so it didn't take too long.

"It kept growing," she said. "It wasn't ballooning out or anything, but the wrist kept growing longer. I knew I could do better, so I chopped it off, started again, and this time I got it right."

"And what did you do with the hand?"

Valkyrie shrugged. "We put it in the bag with the others and Serpine said he was going to burn them. Obviously, he didn't."

"How much did that fourth hand grow?"

"Like, four or five centimetres over a week, something like that. What are you thinking?"

He looked at her and didn't say anything.

Valkyrie laughed. "No. Come on. That's silly."

"Is it?"

"Yes," she said. "Skulduggery, the hand didn't grow itself a new Serpine, OK? I was helping Serpine grow the hand, not the other way round."

"And you're sure it couldn't have backfired in some way?"

"Like, am I absolutely, positively certain that it didn't backfire? No. Obviously not. This is magic we're talking about. There are unintended consequences to the simplest of things, and growing someone a new hand is not a simple thing. So, yes, it's possible, but it's just silly."

"When you eliminate the impossible, whatever remains, no matter how silly, must be the truth."

She folded her arms. "So you're saying that I accidentally grew a new Serpine, and he's the one who killed Scure."

"Yes."

Valkyrie thought about it. Thought about it some more.

"Dammit," she said. "I grew a new Serpine, didn't I?"

"I think so."

She turned and stormed up the stairs.

"Say hi from me," Skulduggery called after her.

She walked out of the front door and flew to the City Guard headquarters, where she demanded to be taken to Nefarian Serpine's cell.

He was dozing on his bunk when she walked in. He sat up, surprised. "Are you breaking me out?"

"I am not," Valkyrie said, standing with her arms folded as the door slammed shut behind her. "Why didn't you destroy the hands, Nefarian?"

He pursed his lips. "You've been in my basement."

"Yes, we have. Why didn't you destroy the hands like you said you would?"

"Honestly? They're good conversation pieces."

"I'm sorry?"

"People come in, they see the hands, they ask what's up with the hands, and the conversation starts. It's an icebreaker. From there, you move on to topics not involving hands."

"You think hands in jars make a good icebreaker?"

"Put it this way, Valkyrie: if you visited someone in their home for the first time, and you noticed that they had jars of hands on the shelves in their basement, wouldn't you want to know more?"

"Tell me something, Nefarian – how many people have you invited back to your house?"

He made a face, as if the entire notion repulsed him. "None. Why would I invite anyone back? No. Never."

"Then why would you need an icebreaker?"

He opened then closed his mouth.

"Where's the fourth hand?" she asked.

He looked away.

"Where's the fourth hand, Nefarian? What happened to it?"

"Nothing happened to it. Why would you even ask that? I didn't get round to buying a fourth jar, that's all."

"I'm going to ask you something, and I want you to think twice about lying to me. The fact is, depending on the answer, I might

211

want you to lie to me, but it's in your own best interests not to do that. Nefarian, as stupid and silly as this sounds, as ridiculous as it is, did the fourth hand go on to actually grow a new you?"

"Yes," Nefarian said quietly.

"Oh, dammit."

He stood. "Did you know that was going to happen? I didn't even think it'd be possible. I put it away, I put all the hands in the freezer, and, when I took it out again, it had grown an arm up to the elbow. I didn't know what to do, so I put it back. I left it for a week, and when I checked again it had a shoulder."

"Why didn't you destroy it?"

"Why would I destroy it? I was growing an extra body in my freezer. If ever I was injured, I had a spare. I think everyone should have one! It could very well be the way of the future!"

Valkyrie massaged her temples. "OK. OK then. I'm not going to even... Let's just move past that. Where is the body now?"

Nefarian hesitated. "A secure location."

"You're sure about that?"

"Of course."

"You haven't put it together yet? Nefarian, you've been arrested for a murder you claim not to have committed. The only explanation is that you were in two places at the same time. The only explanation for *that* is that your spare body is alive."

Nefarian looked at her. "No," he said.

"Yes."

"It can't be alive. There's no consciousness there."

"Maybe it's fooling you."

"It's an empty shell, Valkyrie."

"Tell me where it is, and I'll go look."

He shook his head. "You'll destroy it."

Her phone buzzed. Creed's team were preparing to open the portal to the Void World.

"Listen," Valkyrie said, putting the phone away, "I'm not going to destroy it. If it's like you say it is, if it's just a collection of spare

212

parts, if there's no sign of life whatsoever, then fine. I'll believe you. We'll leave it alone. But if I'm right, and it's alive, then it killed Robert Scure and it wants you to be executed for it. Don't you want us to find out if that's what's happening?"

Nefarian chewed his lip. "I *would* like to be released from jail."

"Then tell me where your second body is. I have to go and visit an alternate world right now, but the moment I'm back, I'll check it out."

"And you won't destroy it if you don't have to?"

"Nefarian, come on. Trust me."

39

Every morning and evening now, there was compulsory worship in the Corrival chapel, where a priest would come over from the Dark Cathedral and lead all the students, and most of the staff members, in prayer. Just about everyone, from what Omen could tell, resented every last thing about this painful half-hour – apart from the pupils and teachers who were already devout and, of course, the priest.

That day Omen just couldn't do it. He couldn't spend another minute on his knees, reciting the insane lyrics of some ode to a group of transdimensional super-fiends. So when he was faced with the chapel doors, the doors that all those other students were filing through, he turned and walked the other way, and felt pretty damn good about it.

It was the first time he'd felt good about anything in a while. Even the leather strap that he dug out of his pocket and placed over his bracelet filled him with anger. This was Crepuscular's trick, yet another instance of his cleverness, his sneakiness, his untrustworthiness.

Omen was an idiot, without a doubt – that had never been in question – but he hated the idea of anyone taking advantage of his idiocy. And for what? To prove some ridiculous point to Skulduggery Pleasant, to prove that Crepuscular Vies was a better sorcerer?

Omen had thought they were friends, but the truth was that he'd been little more than a prop to be used in Crepuscular's psychotic game.

He heard footsteps, remembered there was always a prefect on patrol in the hallways during prayer time, and quickly stepped to the corner. He peeked round, saw Filament Sclavi striding towards him.

"Hey!" Filament shouted. "Who is that? Show yourself at once!"

Obviously, Omen wasn't going to turn himself in and get sent down to the detention cells, which sounded bloody awful, but there wasn't a whole lot he could do about it apart from run and hide, and he wasn't about to do that. He wasn't a child. He was halfway down the corridor when he realised he was already running, and he thought to himself, *Oh, I* am *a child. That makes sense.*

He heard Filament's running footsteps and jumped, bringing the air in to boost him halfway to the next junction. He landed and staggered, almost fell, but got a hand to the corner and whipped round, somehow managing to keep upright.

"Stop!" Filament screeched from somewhere behind him.

Omen grinned, and ran on.

He got to the stairs and took them three at a time, his legs starting to burn when he reached the top. He risked a backward glance and caught a flash of Filament's furious expression. He'd never liked running when he was younger – his legs were too short, and then they were too ungainly – but he was starting to see the appeal as he led the pursuit up and down stairs and through wings. He thought he might be able to lose Filament by cutting through the corridor bisecting the faculty offices, but the prefect seemed to be gaining, and Omen's enthusiasm and enjoyment were deserting him along with his stamina.

A door opened ahead of him and Mr Peccant stepped out. Omen managed to stop right before he crashed into him. Peccant glared, then heard Filament running up and motioned Omen into his office.

Omen lunged in and hunkered down behind the door, struggling to get his breathing under control as he listened to Filament staggering to a stop.

"Sir!" Filament proclaimed.

"Yes?" Peccant responded.

"Sir, the student..."

"The student? The student what?"

"The student who... He ran into your..."

"For heaven's sake, boy, stop your panting and form full sentences!"

Omen listened to Filament suck in a deep, deep breath. "The boy in your office, sir," he said.

"What are you talking about?"

"The student. The one who ran in just now."

"The one who ran in," echoed Peccant.

"He's skipping prayers, sir. I need to..." Another deep breath. "Sorry, sir. I need to report him and bring him to detention."

"I see," said Peccant.

"Apologies for panting, sir."

"Your face is red.'

"Apologies for the red face, sir. I chased him from the chapel."

"Chased who from the chapel?"

"Whoever's in there, sir."

"What do you mean? There's no one in my office."

A baffled moment for poor old Filament. "Sir?"

"There's nobody in my office, Mr Sclavi. You're mistaken. Run along now, if you can."

"Sir, but I saw him. I saw him run in."

"You're wrong. I was standing here the whole time and I didn't see anyone. Better get back to prayers, Mr Sclavi."

"Sir—"

"Get back to prayers, I said!"

"Yes, sir."

There was a moment of silence, and then Filament's footsteps trudging away.

Peccant stepped into his office and closed the door, then tapped the doorframe. Omen recognised the sigil that sound-proofed the room.

"Thank you," he said as Peccant went to his desk and sat. Omen had been here once before, after falling from the library balcony. Peccant had saved him that day, had dragged him in here, to safety.

"Causing trouble again, are we?" Peccant asked, picking up his pen.

Omen shook his head. "I just didn't want to go to prayers."

Peccant grunted. "An inclination I can understand. I never was one for the worshipping of deities, especially the kind that stand outside your window for weeks on end."

"Filament will tell someone about this."

"I imagine he will. He has that look about him."

"I wouldn't want to get you into any trouble, sir."

"It's a bit late for that, Darkly. How's the search for that brother of yours coming along?"

"They haven't been able to find him," said Omen. "Not yet."

"The Network newscasters don't seem to hold out hope for his safe return," Peccant said, writing something in the margins of the paper he was correcting. "They seem to think this Obsidian persona has completely subsumed him."

"Yes, sir."

"But you don't think that?"

"No. Auger's still in there. I know he is."

Peccant nodded. "Good. Someone needs to have faith in the boy. It's what makes the world go round."

"Sir?"

"Faith, Darkly. Faith. If a person can't have faith in his brother, who can he have faith in?"

"No one, sir."

"What?" Peccant said, looking up. "What nonsense. If you can't have faith in your brother, have faith in your sister, or your

217

parents or cousins or friends or neighbours. Have faith in your fellow humans, Darkly. There's always someone to have faith in."

"Sorry, sir."

"As well you should be."

"Do you have brothers, sir?"

"I do. Four of them. Five sisters, too."

"That's a big family."

"Back when I was a child, everyone had big families."

"Did you have faith in them?"

Peccant observed him. "I did," he said. "In some of them, I still do."

Footsteps approached – what sounded like Filament's, and a pair of high heels.

Peccant sighed, and stood. "Back behind the door, Mr Darkly," he commanded, and Omen hurried over.

"Mr Peccant," came Duenna's voice as she knocked. "Mr Peccant, I would like a word."

"I have a choice few for you," Peccant muttered as he tapped the sigil and then opened the door, blocking Omen from sight.

"Mr Peccant," Duenna said, "this student has interrupted me at prayers with what I can only imagine to be a lie, or at the very least a mistake. Mr Sclavi, please repeat what you told me."

Filament's voice – hesitant to start. "I saw... like, I chased a student. He was missing prayers and I told him to stop and he ran and so I chased him, and he came in here."

"And you're absolutely positive he came in here?" Duenna asked. "There's no chance you may have been mistaken?"

"None, miss."

"But, when Mr Sclavi told you what had happened, Mr Peccant, you insisted that no such student had run in. Do you see my dilemma? Who am I to believe?"

"You're to believe your staff," said Peccant. "Kids are stupid. There have been studies that prove this. Sit in on any of my classes and I can confirm it beyond a shadow of a doubt."

218

"Uther – can I call you Uther? Uther, did a student run into your office?"

"No one ran into my office, Prunella. I don't allow running."

"My name is not Prunella."

"That's hardly my fault. Would you like to check? Would you like to conduct a search of my office to verify the veracity of my statement?"

"Oh, I think any student would have had ample time to scurry away by now, Mr Peccant."

"Then are we done here? I have marking to get back to."

"No, Mr Peccant," Duenna said, her voice growing harder, "we are not done. Prayers are mandatory for students and faculty, so why weren't you in the chapel?"

"If I'm to pray, I pray on my own time, and in my own way."

"I'm afraid that just won't do. That won't do at all. Prayers have not been worked into our timetables just to offer thanks and love to the Faceless Ones, but also to ensure that the worshipping is done in accordance with the rules. Staff are encouraged to pray on their own time, absolutely, but they are also expected to attend the scheduled sessions."

"Principal Duenna," said Peccant, "you may be perfectly happy to dance round what you're meaning to say, but I do have work to get back to – so please make your point and leave me to it."

"Mr Peccant... I am unused to being spoken to in such a manner."

"Then I'd get your hearing checked, because people have been saying things like that about you for the last seven years."

Omen tried to picture Duenna's face right at that moment, but nothing he could imagine seemed to do the trick.

"I will not stand for such insubordination," she said in a voice Omen could barely hear.

More footsteps now. Heavier. Two sets, marching in unison.

"And what the hell is this?" Peccant asked. "City Guard officers on school grounds? Why do we need police officers in school?"

"Security is paramount," Duenna responded. "Sedition can start from the most unlikely of places."

Peccant laughed. "You mean here? You think a school is an unlikely place for sedition to start? Dear God, you really don't know anything about students at all, do you? This is precisely where sedition should start. In the minds of the young and the curious. This is where thoughts of rebellion should spring from: the mind of the teenager, bolstered by great works of great art. It is in the classroom where freedom festers, under the stale floorboards of authoritarianism. You dare to think you can control them? You can't stop progress with ignorance. If you try to prevent a society's evolution by putting your foot down, the foot will be crushed by the turning of the wheel. Do you see that? Can you even comprehend the enormity of your growing irrelevance?"

"Officers," said Duenna, "please arrest Mr Peccant."

Omen listened to the clinking of a short chain and the heavy click of shackles closing.

"Oh, I do apologise," Duenna said. "Did I interrupt your little speech?"

"Some revolutions are televised," Peccant said. "Others don't have to be."

Omen listened to them take him away.

40

Creed's team were ready.

Because they couldn't be sure that opening a dimensional portal to the Void World wouldn't flood the immediate area with life-cancelling energies, they decided to open the portal in a warehouse in the middle of Dublin in the middle of the night. Which was nice of them.

Valkyrie and Skulduggery walked in and Creed's team turned to them.

"What are you doing here?" Pike said. "You can't be here. This is a restricted area. The Cleavers should have stopped you."

"The Cleavers aren't going to stop the Child and the Mother and her faithful sidekick," Valkyrie said with a big, cheery smile. "We're just here to wish you luck."

"To say *bon voyage*," Skulduggery added. "To tell you that our hopes and our dreams go with you. When you step through that portal, alongside all your weapons and equipment, you're taking the very future of this world in a little carry-on bag, the kind you'd take on an aeroplane, for example. It wouldn't take up too much room in the overhead compartment, but you want to know where it is at all times, so you tuck it under your seat. That's where we'll be. Tucked under your seat. With you in spirit. With you, beside you, but most of all beneath you. We are profoundly grateful that it's you guys who are going. When I asked Valkyrie who was on the team, who'd be the ones making the journey, I was worried."

"He was worried," said Valkyrie.

"I was. But, when she told me who was going, there is only one word to describe how I felt."

"Very relieved."

"Two words to describe how I felt, with one of them being an adverb, there to do nothing but modify the adjective, and the adjective... well, that's the important one, is it not?"

Valkyrie nodded. "Probably."

"You have to leave," said Pike.

"Absolutely," Skulduggery responded. "But first, if I may, I have prepared a short speech."

"We really don't have time to—"

"Adventure can be a cruel mistress," Skulduggery said, walking between the members of the team and patting some of them on the back. "She can be unkind and merciless and, at times, sadistic. She can whittle you down to the nub of who you are, of who you think you are, and who you imagine yourself to be. But adventure calls to you. You can hear her voice in the wind."

"In the wind," said Valkyrie.

"You can hear her voice in the roar of the sea."

"The roar," said Valkyrie.

"And in the low, tremulous murmur of the sun."

"Tremulous."

"Thank you," said Pike. "Now, if you'd both just leave the—"

"Adventure," Skulduggery said loudly, "is a nine-letter word, and each one of those letters is as important as the next. Adventure wouldn't be adventure without all nine, would it? With only eight, for example, it would be aventure, which isn't a word. It's almost a word, but not quite. Each letter stands for something important. A is for the astonishment you will most certainly feel while setting foot on the Void World. We don't know what's waiting for you. We don't know if there's anything *to* wait for you. We don't know much."

"We don't," said Valkyrie.

"D," Skulduggery said, "is for death. That's what you're risking. That's what you might have to face when stepping on to the Void World. It might be a nice death, soft and cosy and smelling of rose petals. It might be a squishy death, where your body is pulverised by something big and heavy."

"Like a foot," said Valkyrie.

"V is for Valkyrie because she'll be here, cheering you on. In fact, she has written a song she'd like to sing to you."

"No, I haven't."

"You have, and I think it's time you sang it. Don't be shy. We're all friends here. Even him." Skulduggery pointed to the guy beside Pike.

"If you don't leave the area immediately, we'll be forced to call the Cleavers and have them remove you," Pike said.

"Fine," Valkyrie said irritably.

"Thank you."

"I'll sing the song."

"What? No."

She cleared her throat and started nodding her head. The team stared at her. Ten seconds went by. Fifteen.

"This is the instrumental part," she explained.

"Right, that's it," said Pike. "I'm calling the Cleavers."

Skulduggery held a small, smooth stone, and he pressed the sigil carved into it and the pain disks that he'd attached to the backs of Pike and two others lit up. Those nasty little contraptions delivered an intense burst of debilitating agony as Valkyrie's hands crackled with lightning, hurling the remaining team members off their feet. Pike was the last one to collapse, and when all six were unconscious, Valkyrie picked up a small silver case, and joined Skulduggery at the portal device.

Her necronaut suit flowed over her clothes. She pulled up the hood, and set the mask over her face.

Skulduggery activated the device and the portal opened, a

doorway of riotous, colourful energy. He reached out his hand and Valkyrie grinned and took it, and they stepped in, breaking through the colour, and a vast pale blue sky opened up above them. Their feet kicked dust. The land was barren. In the distance, dark mountains kept low to the horizon.

This was not the first time Valkyrie had visited another dimension, but it was still pretty cool.

"How's the air?" she asked.

"Not breathable," Skulduggery replied, sounding far away. "Keep your mask on."

The emptiness of the world prodded at her mind. In the last few years, she had grown used to a background hum of activity that only she could sense, as the world she'd grown up in buzzed around her. But here there was no activity. There was no life. There was only nothingness, and the absence was sending gentle fingers of discomfort pressing into her temples, into the point right between her eyes.

They approached the only object in sight: a small, broken boulder – the Void meteorite. One side had been smashed open, exposing the jagged innards that glistened, here and there, with tiny dots of the purest black. Mevolent had done a pretty thorough job of excavating all the obsidian.

Valkyrie took three metal nails and a hammer from the silver case. "I hate to say it – after all the trouble we went to beating up Pike and the others – but they could probably have done this without us. I mean, it's right where Quietus said it'd be, you know?"

Skulduggery nodded. "We may have been unnecessarily harsh."

"Think they'll understand?"

"Probably not."

"I'd say they'd forgive me, though. I'm the Child and the Mother, after all. But you..."

"They will not be pleased with me."

She crouched, and hammered the nails into the boulder at regular intervals. Every time the hammer struck, she winced.

"Are you OK?" Skulduggery asked.

"Grand," she said. "Just a headache."

Once the nails were secure, Valkyrie pressed the sigil on the hammer. The nails pulsed once, and the boulder lifted off the ground.

"Will there be enough meteorite?" she asked.

"For a prison cell? No. But the stone could be laced into iron bars. It might be enough to hold him."

"Or shackles."

"Stone shackles," Skulduggery said. "The next big thing."

Pain darted behind Valkyrie's eyes and she scowled.

"Valkyrie?"

"Dammit," she muttered. She dropped the hammer and squeezed her eyes shut, trying to hold it back, but the vision burst out of her and her eyes snapped open, and images of things that weren't there played out around them.

They were in a concrete corridor, and China Sorrows was lying dead beside an empty life-force bomb. The first time Valkyrie had experienced this vision, China had been lying dead in a field of broken glass, blood everywhere. Now, there was no blood, there was no broken glass, and China was almost unrecognisable. Her life force had been drained, reducing her to a mere husk of empty skin and brittle bones.

"This is different," Skulduggery murmured.

The corridor went away and the Whistler stood in darkness ahead of them. Sometimes he whistled 'Blue Moon' – sometimes 'Dream a Little Dream of Me'. Today he was silent, and still.

Valkyrie tottered, and Skulduggery had to hold her up. "I'm OK," she said, stepping away, determined to stand on her own.

Things were definitely different. The first time, she'd seen the thousands of refugees from Dimension X trudging towards an uncertain future. She'd seen the misery etched on their faces – the same misery she'd seen in person, years later. They weren't in the vision any more. Neither was Cadaverous Gant, or Saracen Rue.

But Creed was, approaching an image of Skulduggery, his suit in smoking tatters as he tried to get to his feet.

"You actually think you're going to win?" Creed asked.

That scenario flew apart as the Plague Doctor jumped through a window and disappeared, and then Tanith materialised, her sword in her hand.

"It didn't have to be this way," she said.

Valkyrie watched herself – her future self – circle Tanith in the opposite direction.

The ground cracked and flew apart, dissipating Tanith, and honest-to-God monsters started crawling out of the Earth.

"This is still the vision, right?" Valkyrie asked.

"Still the vision," Skulduggery confirmed as they watched the monsters trample cars and snatch up the screaming people trying to flee. Around them, police sirens wailed and they heard President Flanery's voice crackling through a badly tuned radio station.

"On this day," Flanery intoned, "America declares war on the sorcerers."

Bright flashes made Valkyrie jerk back, explosions in the distance – impossibly huge explosions that filled the horizon with mushroom clouds. A sudden wind, impossibly strong, tore houses and lamp posts out of the ground and tossed cars and trucks, and the light came and the light burned it all and then there was Valkyrie herself, dropping to her knees. This is when she died, she knew. She'd seen it again and again – dying on her knees.

Obsidian stepped into view. Her future self looked up at him and laughed and said something and he waved his hand and it all went away.

"Huh," Valkyrie said softly, the headache receding. "So that's how it—"

But the vision wasn't over yet because now the image shifted, and Valkyrie was suddenly watching herself, right here on the Void World, watching the vision, watching as Skulduggery walked up behind her, slapped a pain disk on to her neck and pressed the sigil on the stone and the Valkyrie in the vision contorted in agony and fell.

Valkyrie whirled, the vision washing away. "You're going to attack me?"

Skulduggery laughed at the suggestion, but stopped when she noticed the pain disk in his hand. "Yes," he said, and flicked his wrist, but Valkyrie was already ducking out of the way. The disk sizzled as it passed her ear.

"Wow," she said, straightening.

"Damn," he said, taking off his hat and setting it on the ground.

Valkyrie's right foot slid behind her and she bent her knees slightly. "Don't try it," she said, her hands crackling.

"Well," he responded, "I kind of have to now."

"This won't end well for you."

"You forget – I taught you everything you know."

"That's amazingly incorrect."

He shrugged. "I taught you some of what you know."

"I'm not twelve any more. I can do things—"

He swiped at thin air and a gust of wind knocked her sideways and Skulduggery lunged. She brought her arms up to fend off the punch or the grab, but he kicked her instead, his foot slamming into her shin. She grabbed him to stay upright and he moved past her, twisting her arms. She countered and his elbow clunked into her mask and she bit the tip of her tongue. He had hold of her right wrist and bent it back towards her, but she sent a wave of energy straight to her fingertips and Skulduggery snapped away from her, stumbling backwards.

Valkyrie shook her arm out. "Like I was saying, I can do things I couldn't before. You're not going to win this."

"You're overconfident."

"And you're underestimating me."

"Not at all," said Skulduggery. "I just have faith."

She smiled. "You're hoping I won't hurt you."

"I've decided to believe that a part of you recognises the fact

227

that I'm only here to help and, when the time comes, I'm trusting you to hesitate."

"One of the things you did manage to teach me was never to hesitate."

"Seeing as how you were never the best student in the world, I'm trusting you to have skipped over that part of the lesson."

"And now you're insulting my—"

He threw fire. The flames exploded against her mask and Valkyrie stepped back, eyes shut on instinct, immediately realising her mistake but then, of course, it was too late. Skulduggery's shoulder hit her midsection and his arms wrapped around her legs, scooping her feet from under her. She hit the ground and he was on top, but immediately turning her, slipping an arm around her throat from behind. He had his hooks in, his feet twisted round her thighs. She went to flood her body with magic, but he dug the knuckles of his free hand into the side of her neck and the flash of pain cancelled out her thoughts. The strangle came on. The mask gave her some protection, but not enough. She tried flooding her body with magic again but, again, he dug his knuckles into that nerve cluster.

Valkyrie tapped the skull medallion on her belt and her necronaut suit flowed away from her. She gasped, her eyes bulging, and Skulduggery released his hold in an instant and called her name as he crouched over her. She tapped the medallion and the suit came back and she blasted him and he went flying backwards. She pulled down the mask as she rolled to her hands and knees, sucking in air and blinking away tears.

"Nicely done," Skulduggery muttered.

"Thank you," Valkyrie responded.

They both got up and moved closer, till they were standing just outside striking distance.

"So what's the plan?" she asked. "You take the meteorite back to the resistance?"

"This isn't about the meteorite. This is about you."

"Oh," she said. "You take me back to the resistance. I get it. OK. To do what? Convince me to switch sides? Convince me to act against my children?"

"To help you, Valkyrie."

"You have been helping me. Fighting by my side these last few weeks, like you're supposed to – that's how you help me. I don't need the other kind of help. I suppose the rest of the resistance are waiting for us on the other side of that portal, are they?"

"All we want—" Skulduggery began, but Valkyrie jumped and spun and slammed her foot into his chest. She landed, channelling her magic into her muscles, and kicked low and then high, just like she'd trained, just like the drills she'd run with Coda Quell, catching Skulduggery by surprise. She blasted him with crackling energy and he tumbled into the dust. She ran after him. He snapped out his hand, but Valkyrie vaulted over the rippling air, landed with one foot on his shoulder, driving him to the ground. She flipped backwards, avoiding his grasp.

He got up slowly, warily, brushing the dust from his suit. "All that Cleaver training's paid off."

Valkyrie shrugged. "It's always good to have a few surprises ready."

"I couldn't agree more," he said, and held up the smooth stone with the sigil carved into it.

Valkyrie cursed, slapped her pockets, swept her hands over her shoulders, searching for the pain disk that wasn't there because of course it wasn't, and she looked up and Skulduggery leaped into her, his knee crunching into her chest.

She staggered and now Skulduggery slapped the pain disk on to the left side of her face and charged, the hammer flying into his hand as he took her through the portal. They landed in the warehouse, tripping over the unconscious forms of Creed's team, and Valkyrie seized up, muscles knotted, teeth grinding together, as pain hit every synapse in her brain. The world went white, and then she was lying on the floor, and Skulduggery was handcuffing her hands behind her back. When they locked, her power went away and her suit flowed back into the amulet.

"Are you OK?" he asked, lifting her to her feet. "Valkyrie? Are you OK?"

She mumbled something as the door opened and China Sorrows and Tanith Low walked in.

"We've got to move," said Tanith.

"Hello, my dear," China said softly, taking Valkyrie's chin in her hand. "There's no need to panic, if panicking was on the horizon. We're your friends and we only want to help you."

Valkyrie shook her head. "What are you doing? What's happening?"

"Send the signal," Skulduggery said. "Get Fletcher in here."

China tapped her wrist and a small sigil rose to the surface of her skin and glowed briefly, before fading away.

They waited.

Skulduggery tilted his head. "Something's wrong."

Tanith took out her phone and made a call. She frowned. "He's not answering."

"He's been compromised," said Skulduggery, taking his gun from its holster as he moved to the door. "We're going to have to fight our way out."

"Fight who?" China asked. "There's nobody there."

"There will be. Take Valkyrie, and this." He passed her the hammer. "The meteorite will follow wherever that hammer goes."

China gripped Valkyrie's arm.

"Walk away," Valkyrie said. "All of you."

"Not without you, dear," said China.

The door burst open and City Guards ran in.

While Skulduggery and Tanith fought them off, Valkyrie twisted her arm free and slammed her forehead into China's nose. Cartilage broke and blood sprayed and Valkyrie stomped on the inside of her ankle and China shrieked and went down, clutching her leg. Valkyrie jumped, her knees to her chest, swinging her wrists beneath her. She landed, hands now in front, and dug a handcuff key from her pocket. She freed herself, got her suit back on, and retrieved the hammer.

China grabbed her wrist. "You're not yourself," she said, perfect teeth bloodstained and gritted against the pain.

Valkyrie pulled away and stood. She blasted a hole in the ceiling and Skulduggery stopped beating up the City Guards long enough to look round. Energy crackling, she flew up, out through the hole she'd made, the Void meteorite following along behind.

41

The burn on Frightening's shoulder got infected, and for a few days Tyler's mom wanted to take him to hospital and Tyler's dad argued against it, and they got mad at each other while Frightening lay in bed with a fever, too weak to do much more than sleep. When the fever broke, and he realised how much time had passed, Frightening insisted on leaving. Tyler's parents objected until he finally convinced them that his being there might put everyone in danger. They got really quiet after that, and didn't argue with him any more.

Tyler's dad went to borrow a car from Tyler's uncle that Frightening could drive to Houston. It wasn't much of a car, his dad said, but it wouldn't break down and it wouldn't draw the attention of any traffic cops, and Frightening accepted the offer with thanks. While he waited for Tyler's dad to get back, he sat in the kitchen with Tyler and Mila and told them about South Africa. Mila said she'd always wanted to visit, but Tyler reckoned she was just sweet on Frightening so she'd say pretty much anything to impress him, even though she had a boyfriend that she swore she loved.

They heard a car pull up outside and they all thought it was Tyler's dad, but when Tyler's mom answered the door she had a wariness in her voice that made them all go quiet.

"How can I help you?" she asked.

"Afternoon, ma'am," said a lady. "My name's Agent Frost, and this here is Agent Dale. We're from the FBI and we're looking for a man you may have encountered lately. This man. Have you seen him?"

There was a pause as Tyler's mom examined whatever they were showing her.

"No," she said, "sorry. I don't know him."

"He's a very dangerous individual, ma'am."

"Then I hope you find him."

"Mrs Clonston, isn't it?" asked the man, this Agent Dale. "Mrs Clonston, is your husband home, or maybe we could speak to your kids? We've been asked to conduct a thorough search."

"My husband isn't here right now, but he'll be back soon."

"It's very important that we find this individual before he hurts anybody else."

Frightening looked at Tyler and Mila, put his finger to his lips, and slipped out of the kitchen.

"I get that," said Tyler's mom, "but I don't know where he is."

"He killed two Federal agents last week," said Frost. "Close by here, actually. You know the Madison farm? That's just up the road, isn't it? That's where he killed them."

"I haven't heard anything about it on the news."

"We're trying not to start a panic."

"Maybe if you started a panic, you'd find someone who's seen him. If you'll excuse me, I have to get back."

A creak of a door hinge, suddenly stopped.

"Mrs Clonston," said Agent Dale, "would it be possible to search the premises?"

"No," Tyler's mom said. "It definitely would not."

"You're not hiding something, are you?"

"Get off my property." Movement. "What are you doing? You can't come in here. You can't come in—"

His mom gave a cry and Tyler and Mila burst out of the kitchen, ran to the front door as Frightening emerged from the living room, colliding with Agent Dale and slamming him into the wall. Agent Frost had fire in her hand, but Frightening batted her arm to one side and the fire went out, and he grabbed her and threw her over his hip.

Dale punched him, punched him again, kicked him in the chest and Frightening caught him with those eye-blasts as he lunged, and Dale was thrown back, hit the wall and collapsed.

Frost scrambled up, whipping a gun from her jacket and Frightening turned, but it was like he couldn't see her, and he grabbed at nothing. Tyler's mom tackled Agent Frost from behind, wrapping her up in a bear hug, pinning her arms by her sides. Frost cursed and kicked and Tyler's mom grunted, but didn't let go. She was a nurse, and she was used to people struggling.

The air rippled and Tyler's mom hurtled off her feet and Tyler sprang to catch her. The impact took them both to the ground and Mila was there, grabbing their arms, dragging them up.

Frightening had regained his sight, and he glared at Agent Frost and she glared back. The gun was on the floor between them.

"We're not here to hurt anyone," Frost said. Moving slowly, she took a pair of old-fashioned handcuffs from her pocket. "Just put these on and come quietly. No one else has to die."

Frightening didn't answer, and Frost tossed him the handcuffs and immediately dived for the gun and Frightening's eye-blasts struck her just as she grabbed it. She flopped like she was boneless, the gun spiralling out of her hand, and she lay there, unmoving. Frightening backed away, hands out in front to ward off any further attack.

"Are they down?" he asked. "Tyler, are they both down?"

"Yes," Tyler croaked.

Frightening nodded. "Nobody move, if you please. It takes a moment for my eyes to start working again."

Tyler's mom put her arms in front of Tyler and his sister and moved them back as Tyler's dad stepped into the house, Frost's gun in his hand and pointed straight at Frightening.

"Who the hell are you?"

42

Valkyrie sat in Creed's chair, her feet up on the massive desk. "You knew that we were planning to beat up your little team and go to the Void World ourselves."

Creed closed the door behind him. "I knew you would be unhappy with an order that told you otherwise."

"So you set us up," she said. "Tell me I can't do something, forcing me to do it against your wishes, and pave the way for Skulduggery to seize his chance to whisk me away. You knew we were going to try something, and you knew *he* was going to try something."

"I suspected," said Creed. "But I didn't force you to act, Valkyrie. You were the only one to make that decision."

"But you expected it."

"I was reasonably sure it would happen, yes."

She put her feet down and leaned forward. "I don't like being used as bait, Damocles. Next time you think up a trap in which I'm the lure, I'd appreciate it if you tell me ahead of time."

"And I would appreciate it if you followed my instructions," said Creed. "But I have accepted that that's never going to happen."

"God, you're annoying," she said, standing. "And not in an attractive way. Not in an annoying-but-undeniably-sexy kind of way. You're just annoying. You make me want to fry you where you stand."

"If that is your wish, I know I can't stop you."

She glared at him. "So annoying."

"It was, sadly, necessary. Now you know what I already knew: that Skulduggery Pleasant cannot be trusted, and he's not your friend."

"Of course he's my friend."

"He betrayed you."

"He was trying to help me."

"He betrayed the Faceless Ones."

"He could only have betrayed the Faceless Ones if he'd ever pretended to follow them – which he never did. He made it quite clear that he was staying by my side because of me and me alone. He thought I needed help."

"But now you can see that he's the enemy, yes?"

Valkyrie sighed. "Technically, yes."

"And he needs to be put down, along with the rest of the resistance."

"If we have to do it, then sure. But if there's a chance to save them, to let them see the light, we'll take that opportunity."

"You have far too much faith in those people."

Valkyrie shrugged. "If it's a crime to have faith in your friends, throw me in jail, but don't really because I'll kill you."

There was a knock on the door and Cerise, the High Sanctuary Administrator, stepped in.

"Apologies for interrupting you, Supreme Mage," she said in her usual calm manner, "but an urgent matter has been brought to my attention that I felt I needed to communicate to you as soon as possible."

Creed frowned at her. "If it's urgent, Administrator, why have you wasted time coming here in person when a phone call would suffice?"

"My apologies again, sir," Cerise said. "You are, of course, entirely correct."

"What is it? What is the urgent matter?"

"It's the Cleavers, Supreme Mage. They're gone."

Creed didn't respond, so Cerise kept talking.

"Those coming to the end of their shift left as scheduled, but their replacements failed to turn up. We can't find any Cleavers anywhere. Not here, not at any of the Sanctuaries around the world."

"And when were you told about this?"

"Just a few moments ago, Supreme Mage."

"And you walked over here, did you?"

"I walked quickly, sir."

"You wasted time, Administrator."

"I apologise."

"One might think you have deliberately wasted time."

"Heavens."

"Leave," growled Creed, and Cerise bowed and quietly left the room.

Valkyrie raised an eyebrow. "Did you see that coming? You didn't, did you?"

"Try not to sound so pleased," Creed replied. "This affects you just as much as anyone else."

"Not really, though. The Cleavers walk away, the City Guard steps in to fill the gap here, Sanctuary agents fill the gap around the world, and everyone is stretched so thin that the system breaks down. Chaos and anarchy take over. All your little plans crumble to dust. And me? I'm still the Child and the Mother. So I'll leave the panicking to you, if it's all the same, and I'll just continue on my way."

She strolled to the door, but stopped and turned slowly. "Oh, Damocles? With all the Cleavers leaving their posts and everything, does that mean the prisons are unguarded?"

Creed's eyes widened.

Valkyrie shrugged. "Interesting." Then she left.

43

Coldheart Prison was a place of sounds.

There were the sounds from the convicts that drifted from the tiers of cells embedded in the rock walls – the idle chatter, the bored laughter, the occasional shout and curse and threat – but those could be found in any prison or gaol around the world. What separated Coldheart from the rest was the hum of magic that flowed through the pipes and cables – the power that kept the island floating through the clouds – and the call of the wind as it sneaked in through cracks and crevices, and up from the vast chasm at the prison's base.

Walking the corridors – some simple tunnels cut out of rock, some pristine hallways – Temper was reminded of his journey in the *USS Nautilus* in August 1942. He'd never liked the idea of submarines: the thought of being trapped in a tube under the ocean made his heart constrict. But the sounds it made – hauntingly strange, like nothing else he'd ever experienced – had stayed with him. Coldheart was like that, in a way – hauntingly strange, unique to itself, and also utterly terrifying if he thought about it too long.

"Here we go," Skulduggery said behind him. "Look miserable."

The warden, a man named Ritanical, rushed over to meet them, flanked by two gruff-looking sorcerers. He glanced at the handcuffs around Temper's wrists and then switched his attention to Skulduggery.

"Detective Pleasant!" he said. "The Cleavers! They're gone!"

"Gone?" said Skulduggery.

"They vanished! The Teleporter, too!"

"You have a Teleporter?"

"It's in the new regulations – we need to have a Teleporter on duty at all times in case of emergency."

"But isn't this an emergency?"

"Yes!"

"So where's your Teleporter?"

"We don't have one!"

"Isn't that against regulations?"

"That's what I'm trying to tell you!"

Skulduggery chuckled. "Well, I won't tell if you won't, Warden. I'm just here to deliver a prisoner."

"Detective Pleasant, you're an Arbiter. Surely you can use your influence to call for reinforcements? This is, as I said, an emergency. All I have are a dozen sorcerers to maintain order in a facility that needs a hundred and twenty Cleavers, minimum!"

"A hundred and twenty?"

"Minimum!"

"And you have twelve?"

"Yes!"

"Warden, it sounds to me like you have a staff shortage."

"Yes," Ritanical said, "I do!"

"How long has Coldheart been back in service? Two weeks, isn't it? That's not very long at all."

"What are we going to do?"

"I'm no expert on prisons," said Skulduggery, "but if I were you, if I were warden of this entire facility, if the responsibility fell on my shoulders and my shoulders alone... I don't know. I'd probably panic."

"But... but I'm already panicking!"

"Then why do you need reinforcements? You're doing great on your own!"

"I don't understand why you're not seeing the severity of the situation! Our Cleavers are gone! Our Teleporter is missing!"

"He's not missing."

"I assure you he is!"

"No. I know exactly where he is."

The warden frowned. "Wait, how did you even get on to the island?" His phone beeped and he looked at it, his frown deepening. "It says here that Skulduggery Pleasant is wanted for crimes against Roarhaven."

"Can I have a look?" Skulduggery asked, taking the phone from him. "Oh, so it does. There's something else here, too. The sparrow, it says. The sparrow flies south for winter."

The handcuffs dropped from Temper's wrists and he grabbed one of the sorcerers while Skulduggery snapped his hands at the air and the warden flew backwards. The sorcerer tried to pull away, but Temper cracked his elbow into the guy's jaw and he crumpled. He left Skulduggery to deal with the last guy and raised his hand to the security camera. Hansel shot out, smashed through the camera lens, and then retracted into Temper's palm.

Skulduggery laid the second sorcerer on the ground and they walked on, side by side. They got to the chasm where the wind howled up from beneath, and Temper operated the console. A cell of metal and glass rose from the depths of the chasm and turned slowly in mid-air, and the skeleton in the orange jumpsuit nodded to them.

"Hello, Skulduggery," said Cadaver Cain.

"Hello, me," said Skulduggery.

44

The jumpsuit hung off Cadaver like a sheet on a clothes horse. The skeleton's skull was fractured, held together by metal staples. He looked at Skulduggery and Skulduggery looked back at him and neither of them said anything for a while.

"I don't get what's going on," Temper muttered.

"He wants to say that I must know what he's going to say," said Cadaver, "but he doesn't want to be the first to speak."

"And he wants me to say that so he can tell me that he doesn't know what I'm going to say, because all the futures he's already seen have been rendered moot by the arrival of Obsidian," Skulduggery responded. "Can you even do it any more? Look into the future?"

"I don't know," Cadaver replied. "You cut off my link to the Viddu De, and my magic has been bound since you arrested me, so I have no way of knowing if it will still operate. I suppose you'll just have to let me out of this cell and we'll see."

"Amazingly, I don't see that happening."

"You'll have to let me out eventually if you want to know what the future holds."

"Or I'll just muddle through on my own."

Cadaver tilted his head. Skulduggery tilted his. Neither of them said anything for a while.

Temper sighed. "Now what are you doing?"

"Running through the possible conversations," said Skulduggery.

"In your heads? Each of you are running through the possible conversations in your heads?"

"When we reach the conclusion of one, we go back and start again," said Cadaver.

"But you don't know what the other person is thinking."

"Of course we do," said Skulduggery. "We're using logic and anticipating the other's counter-argument."

"Right," Temper said slowly. "So who's winning?"

"I am," said Cadaver.

"He is," said Skulduggery. A moment passed. "Now we're even."

They were quiet again.

"Impressive," said Cadaver.

"I thought so," said Skulduggery.

"Stop," Temper said. "For God's sake, stop. Do either of you have any idea how annoying it is to stand here and know you're the dumbest person in the room?"

"No," Skulduggery and Cadaver said at the same time.

"You can't just look at each other and imagine the argument, all right? You just can't. It's not how we do things. Cadaver, you want us to let you out. Skulduggery, you don't want to let him out. Start the argument there."

Skulduggery shook his head. "We're already beyond that."

"We've agreed that I have to be released," said Cadaver. "Now we're discussing what comes next."

"Then what does come next?" Temper asked. "How can we trust you?"

"That all depends," said Skulduggery, "on the information we have that he doesn't. He's already noticed that the Cleavers are missing, and has surmised they've left their posts in response to drastic steps taken by Damocles Creed."

"And Creed would only have taken drastic steps once he was close to achieving his goal," Cadaver said. "That, plus the fact

242

that it's just the two of you here, means that Valkyrie has, indeed, become the Child of the Faceless Ones."

"Her judgement is compromised," Skulduggery told him. "There are thousands of Faceless Ones already here."

"Undetectable?"

"To mortals."

"And Obsidian?"

"He's killing their worshippers," said Temper. "Small-scale stuff – like he hasn't seriously started yet."

"But he's noticed Valkyrie," Skulduggery said. "He'll be going after her. She's in danger."

"And you think that fact will ensure that I do, in fact, help you."

"Yes."

"Then I have three conditions."

"Yes to the first two, no to the third."

"The third is non-negotiable."

"The third will not happen, as you well know, and you don't care because you just put it in there to make sure you get the first two."

Cadaver tapped his fingers against his chin. It made a pleasing hollow sound. "Very well," he said. "We have a deal."

"I have no idea what's going on," Temper said as Skulduggery pressed and swiped the buttons on the console. The front wall of the cell faded away.

"I'm going to need a great big gun," said Cadaver, floating over the chasm towards them. "And a change of clothes."

45

It was all over the school: Skulduggery Pleasant was a bad guy. He'd been designated an enemy of Roarhaven and a member of the resistance. Omen did his very best not to care. He wasn't nearly as successful as he'd liked to have been.

Morning assembly was a more subdued affair than normal. People were getting ground down by the relentless persecution, by the overwhelming feeling of helplessness that had started to seep into every part of their daily lives. Smiles were seldom seen.

"It has come to our attention," Duenna said from the stage, "that some students have been abusing the trust we have placed in them. Certain individuals, and they know who they are, insist on confronting members of the faculty with baseless accusations and pointless arguments. This is very disappointing. How do you expect to be treated like adults if you continue to behave like children?"

She shook her head. "You have left me with little choice, I'm afraid. From now until further notice, all use of magic by students – with the exception of prefects – is curtailed as punishment."

She took the controller from her pocket and tapped it three times. Across the hall, bracelets glowed briefly with binding sigils, and Omen's magic faded to a dull, almost imperceptible ebb.

The hall was quiet but for the rustling of sleeves being pulled back. Omen waited for someone to complain, waited for the shout to go out. But no one, apparently, wanted to be the next student hauled away to the detention cells. There was nobody left willing to make a stand.

Omen sighed, took a deep breath, and shouted, "You can't do this!"

"You can't take our magic!" someone else shouted, and then everyone was shouting, roaring at the stage. The teachers standing behind Duenna didn't say a word, but they glared daggers at the principal's back. Prefects strode up and down the lines, ordering students to be quiet, and Filament came for Omen.

"I knew it'd be you eventually," he said, snarling out a grin as he grabbed Omen's arm and led him to the door.

Omen didn't resist. He just kept his eyes on Duenna, noting the look on her face, the confusion over why no one was obeying her.

She couldn't understand why the students weren't simply doing what they were told. She couldn't fathom why the teachers weren't supporting her. She was too limited a person, possessed too limited an intellect, to comprehend these things.

For the first time, Omen looked at Principal Duenna and saw not authority but weakness. And he smiled.

46

The headache that pierced China's brain had nothing to do with the broken nose that Valkyrie had inflicted upon her the previous day. The nose, like the broken ankle, had been mended without problem once China had got to a healer. No – the headache, so severe that she had to stop walking for a moment with one hand reaching out to the wall to steady herself, was a mere aftershock of the psychic attack that had put her in a coma ten months earlier. A gift that kept on giving from her beloved daughter.

The headache faded and China took a deep breath, righted herself, and walked through the door ahead.

"China," Cadaver said, turning to her, "it is so good to see you."

He was dressed in a black shirt and trousers and a long black coat. China found it interesting that he seemed to have chosen a new uniform, as much to define himself as to separate him from Skulduggery. What did the new outfit declare but *look how different I am, look how casual and carefree I have become, now that I've thrown off the shackles of useless nobility*. There was always the possibility, of course, that Cadaver was using these clothes to make people think exactly that, and lead them to assume they had started to figure him out, so China didn't put too much stock in this immediate analysis.

"I have some understanding of the languages of magic," he said, gesturing to the sigils he'd carved on the walls, "but it's nothing compared to your vast wealth of knowledge. With this room, I'm trying —"

"I can see what you're trying to do," said China.

He tilted his head at her. "Do you think it will work?"

"Perhaps."

"I could certainly use your guidance."

Her fingertips glowing, China moved to the nearest wall. She took a moment to examine what Cadaver had already carved there, and got to work. Her nails cleaved through the plaster and brick like she was swirling her hand through soft ice cream.

"It's good to see you," Cadaver said as he worked on the opposite wall.

She carved, and didn't answer.

"When I'm from, you're not quite... yourself."

She slowed her movements, pressing her nail in deeper, then rotating it slightly, sweeping upwards, and then continued on. These letters demanded perfection in their execution.

"I haven't been able to visit you in years," Cadaver continued. "In the future, as you can imagine, they like to keep me away from my old friends."

"Is that what we are?" she asked. "Old friends? I've often wondered."

"That's one aspect of what we are," he replied. "There are others. You're not going to ask about your future self, are you?"

"I don't see the point. That future will no longer happen, so that version of me will no longer exist."

"You're not curious about who you could have become?"

"I'm curious about a great many things, Mr Cain, but not about that. I'm curious about the fact that you've agreed to help our cause when, according to you, there is no future. I'm curious as to what you hope to achieve. I'm curious why you wanted me here, when we both know you're perfectly capable of finishing this room by yourself."

When he spoke, the sound of his voice had shifted, and she

knew he had turned and was looking at her. She worked on. "Would you believe I just wanted to talk to you, after all this time?"

"I'm sure that's one of the things you wanted, yes," she said.

"I'm helping you, despite the apparent futility of our actions, because there is always a chance that we might subvert our fate. We've done it before."

"And do you believe we can do it again?"

He hesitated. "I don't know."

"A rare admission of fallibility."

"I'm not used to not knowing. The Viddu De allowed me to see every possible path to the future – but they appear to have cut off their link with me. I am feeling quite adrift."

"So all you have to rely on is your faith in the people around you," said China, turning.

"Yes. Isn't it horrible?"

"Quite."

"If this works, you understand what people will say about us, don't you?"

China nodded. "They'll call us optimists."

"A dreadful accusation."

"Simply horrid."

"And demonstrative of a severe misunderstanding of what pessimism actually is."

"To a detective," China said, "I imagine it's everything."

"To any reasonable intellect, it is."

She turned again, and went back to work. "You ask me if I'm curious," she said, "but you're the oddity here, Mr Cain. The future in which you exist has been undone. You are, literally, from nowhere. The fact that you're even here to partake in this conversation is undoubtedly a testament to some esoteric law of quantum physics. I wonder, if you were to – somehow – survive here for the next seventy-two years, and catch up to the point in the timeline when you travelled back, would you cease to exist in that same instant?"

"I do hope I'm around to find out."

China glanced over her shoulder at him. "Isn't that fascinating? It's enough to make one fight to avert the imminent end of everything, just to see what would happen next."

"I'm glad I can be a source of inspiration for you, China," Cadaver said, and resumed his work on that side of the room.

"I take my inspiration wherever I can find it," she responded, pausing for a moment to calculate the perfect arc of a letter that no one had written for over 2,000 years. She achieved it without flourish, but with a pleasing sense of personal satisfaction. "Where have you been taking *your* inspiration from? These gods of yours?"

"The Viddu De."

"Dead gods from a dead universe. They sound delightful."

"They have their moments."

"And they taught you to see all possibilities at once, I believe? That must have been nice. Useful, too, I'd imagine. Now it's no longer a mystery as to why Lord Vile was never defeated on the battlefield."

The tone in Cadaver's voice was one of amusement. "Vile, my dear China, was arrogance personified, as you well know. He quickly grew bored of winning with ease and refused to use the gifts the Viddu De had bestowed – as much to tempt the fates as to seek new challenges." Something new crept into his voice. "Vile didn't see the things that were to come. He didn't see the effect they would have on him."

"You speak of Lord Vile as if he were a different person."

"He both was and wasn't."

"You are, were, and apparently always will be, a complicated person, Cadaver Cain."

"I'm not the only one, China Sorrows."

When they were done, Cadaver left, escorted by Temper Fray and Dexter Vex, and Skulduggery entered, carrying a Soul Catcher. China pointed to a circle on the floor.

"We will be safe in there," she said. "At no time can we step outside the circle. To do so would be to leave ourselves open to possession. If this individual is as powerful as you seem to think, we can take no chances."

Skulduggery looked around. "Are you sure this will work?"

"Not entirely," she admitted. "But it stands a better chance than wishing."

They stepped into the circle. Skulduggery held the Soul Catcher in one hand, and with his other he traced a sigil into the globe.

A bolt of energy sped from the Soul Catcher, arcing out in different directions like comets, rebounding off the walls and ceiling and floor. They all met in the middle and the comets became butterflies of light, swirling round each other, tighter and tighter, until they collided and gradually formed an image. A shape. A person.

"This is new," said the shape, in Malice's voice.

"I expect you to be on your best behaviour," Skulduggery responded. "Otherwise the room gets deactivated and your Soul Catcher is returned to its cell."

"Is that Skulduggery or Cadaver?" Malice asked. "I can't see properly. I can make out a hat, though. Skulduggery?"

"It's me. Cadaver's in the other room."

"He's walking around free?" Malice asked, "I wouldn't trust him, if I were you. He's sneaky."

"I'm aware. As I was saying, if you misbehave in any way, this conversation is over."

"Who is that with you? Is that Valkyrie?"

"I'm afraid not," said China.

"China Sorrows," said Malice, enjoying the name. "Oh, China, how delightful. We have such fun in the future, we really do. I get to know you so well."

"So I was told," China said. "You kill me, apparently."

Malice laughed. "But not before I have utterly, utterly broken you. I thought, and I don't mean to be rude, but I thought you'd be harder to break. It didn't take long, though, and it didn't take much. The key was to remove your ability to read. Once you'd lost that, it was as if you'd lost your passion. I think you only continued to live out of sheer habit."

"You may indeed have broken my future self, my dear girl," China said, "but you haven't broken me. Please don't waste your time with lazy intimidation. It doesn't become you."

Malice laughed, her form solidifying a little more. "I like you. You're feisty."

"Be careful," Skulduggery said. "You're very close to misbehaving."

"My apologies, Skulduggery. But can I ask a question, in all seriousness? What happened? Why am I like this? Creed was supposed to find a way to send me back to my own time."

"Your own time doesn't exist any more," said Skulduggery.

The shape didn't respond for a moment. "What happened to Valkyrie?" she said at last. "Where is she? Why isn't she here?"

"Valkyrie is with Creed. She's taken your place as the Child of the Faceless Ones."

"Is she OK?"

"If you're asking if she's a winged harpy, no, she's not. She didn't fight it this time. She embraced it. Physically, she's unchanged."

"And the Faceless Ones?" said Malice. "I'm trying to expand my consciousness beyond these walls, but I can't quite manage it."

"The Faceless Ones are here," said China. "Some of them, at any rate. Intangible right now, but they won't stay like that forever."

Malice's shape settled enough to make out her features. "I'm happy for her. I'm happy she's still her. I feel sorry for my younger self, of course. She's going to miss out on so much. An indescribable amount. That's sad. But someone has to be the Child of the Faceless Ones and if it's not going to be me, then I'm glad it's my sister."

"How very magnanimous of you," Skulduggery responded. "So we're going to need your help in fixing her."

"Fixing?"

"Healing. Returning her to normal."

Malice laughed. "There is no normal, Skulduggery. Not any more. This is who she is. It's who she's going to stay."

"I won't accept that."

"It's not up to you."

"Everything is up to me," Skulduggery said.

"You came back from the dead because you willed it, and now you think you can do literally anything you set your mind to, is that it?"

"I see no reason to start doubting myself now."

She laughed again. "You are delightful."

"But I'll need your help."

"And why would I help you? Valkyrie is the most powerful person on the face of the Earth and she's going to change everything."

"And then?" Skulduggery asked.

"And then what? She lives happily ever after."

"No," he responded. "You don't believe that. Remember who we're talking about here. Valkyrie Cain might be beaten, but she will never be defeated. She's going to find her way back from this. Even if I do nothing, the old Valkyrie will return. At some stage – it might be next week, it might be next century – your sister will reassert herself and she will hate what she's done as the Child of the Faceless Ones. You know she will."

Malice watched him.

"I'm asking you to save her from that torture. She's blamed herself and hated herself enough. We can't let it happen again. We can't let her hurt anyone. We can't add to her burden. She's going to come back and when she does she will have needed us to do everything we could to bring her home. Tell me, Malice, am I wrong about any of that?"

"Probably not."

"So the question is," said China, "what are you going to do?

252

Are you going to contribute to the suffering she'll go through later, or will you help us bring her back before she does something she can't undo?"

"This is ridiculous," said Malice. "You can't just argue your way out of what's happening. You can't just convince me to work against the Faceless Ones. These are my *children*."

"No," Skulduggery said. "Not in this timeline. Not any more. You're in quite a unique position, Malice. You've been cut off from the events that made you. You can reinvent who you are. You can prioritise the people you love and fight for them."

"I love the Faceless Ones."

"More than you love Valkyrie? More than you love your parents?"

"My parents are dead."

"Those parents – the ones you lost – are never going to exist any more. The parents that do exist are alive right now, and if you don't fight to save Valkyrie, and if she doesn't fight to save the world, those parents will die."

"You don't know that," Malice said.

"They'll either die or live in abject terror for the rest of their lives. And what'll happen to the younger version of you? Valkyrie became the Child of the Faceless Ones to ensure that her sister has something approaching a normal, happy life. I'm not going to let that moment of bravery, that sacrifice, be in vain. Are you?"

Malice didn't answer for a moment. "So what do you need me to do?" she asked.

47

Omen sat in his detention cell. There was no clock, and his watch and phone had been taken from him, so he had no way of knowing how long he'd been here or how long he had left to go. He was hungry, though, and thirsty, and he needed to pee.

Then the door opened and the prefect, Grey, nodded to him. "Detention's over," he said, walking away.

Omen followed him out, and stopped. Grey stood next to Never and Axelia. Behind them were Kase and Mahala and a dozen other students.

"This is the only area where the bracelets don't record what we say," Grey told him. "If we want to talk, this is the place to do it."

"Talk about what?" Omen asked, though he already knew.

"This can't go on," said Axelia. "We can't just stand by and let Duenna get away with what she's doing. Creed's oppressing the city, Duenna's oppressing the school... we have to do something. Things aren't going to get better on their own."

"OK," said Omen.

"We're hostages," said Never. "No one wants to say it, but that's what we are. Duenna isn't letting anyone leave. Parents aren't allowed to visit. We're being held here to make sure that mages around the world do what Creed tells them. The resistance don't have a chance if we stay as hostages – so we need to break free."

"And you're the person to lead us," said Kase.

"Ooooh," said Omen, "I don't think that's the best idea."

"We voted," Never said. "We decided. You're in charge."

"In charge of what, exactly?"

"This. Us. Everyone here and, to be honest, most of the students in Fourth, Fifth and Sixth Years. We're not involving anyone in Third Year and below because they're absolutely tiny and so adorable, even the weirdly tall ones."

"I see," said Omen. "And what am I supposed to be leading you into?"

"That's up to you," said Mahala. "Kase and Never and I, we're used to Auger knowing exactly what to do, even when he was making it up as he went along. That's what you're going to have to do now."

"OK, wait – so we're all agreed that we have to do something, and we're all agreed that we will do something, but I have to decide what that something is?"

"Exactly," said someone down the back.

Omen thought about it, and shrugged. "We won't be able to do anything without our magic, so the first thing we do is get rid of these bracelets. We'll need to steal Duenna's remote control without her knowing."

"Ah," said Never, "a heist. Subterfuge, planning, trickery, distractions. Loving it already."

"Or," said Axelia, "we hit her with a chair."

Never frowned. "Not exactly subtle."

"Does it have to be? Duenna's working with Creed, so she's a bad guy. When this is over, one way or the other, are any of us prepared to have her as our principal? No. So why even attempt anything subtle? We should just hit her with a chair and get it over with."

"That's certainly one way of doing it," said Omen.

Never looked at him. "You want to be sneaky."

"I do."

255

"You want to steal the remote and figure out how it works."

Omen smiled at his friend. "I want to clone it."

"Oh," said Axelia. "And then return it without her even realising it was gone?"

"I know we'd all rather just get it and press it and all the bracelets come off, but that won't really do anyone a whole lot of good if they can just make us put the bracelets back on. We have to time it right. It'll mean we'll all have to keep going around without magic and I don't like that part, I really don't. But we've got to be smart here. If you're being tortured and you realise the chain is loose but the door is locked, there's no point in leaping off the torture table. You've got to endure the torture until the door is open and you can run out."

Axelia made a face. "I'd rather not be tortured at all."

Never made another face. "When did torture come into it?"

"I have a question," Kase said. "Do any of us know how to figure out how the remote works?"

"Crepuscular said all the information we'd need is in our magic-science textbooks," Omen said. "We just have to go looking for it."

"Who's Crepuscular?" asked October Klein.

"Wears a bow tie," said Never. "Has adventures with Omen. Cool guy."

"Not so cool any more," Omen said.

"I stand corrected. We hate him." Never frowned. "Wait — have you still been having adventures? Have you been leaving the school?"

"Oh, yes. Sorry. I've been able to hide my bracelet's signal, so I've been sneaking out for the last few weeks."

"And you didn't tell me?" said Never. "Your best friend? I am shocked, appalled, horrified and aghast."

"The good news is I'll be able to hide your bracelets' signals, too. At least, I hope I will. The entire plan depends on it, actually, because we'll need everyone here working together to figure out how to clone the remote. That means spending an entire night in the Science Block, using school equipment, and we can't let anyone suspect what we're up to."

"Of all the people in all the world," said Never, amazed, "who would have thought it'd be Omen bloody Darkly who found a use for our education?"

48

The teacher sat with her wrists shackled to the top of the heavy table. She'd been there for close to an hour, in that little room, and she was nervous, and her mouth must have been very dry. There was a cup of water beside her, but the chain on the shackles was too short for her to be able to drink from it. That little touch had been added to all City Guard interviews at Hoc's command. He was quite proud of it.

He smoothed down his uniform and entered the room suddenly, making Militsa Gnosis jerk in her seat.

He didn't say anything as he took his own seat opposite her. He put the file he was holding on the table, moved it slightly, and finally regarded her.

"Thank you for coming in," he said.

There were at least a dozen responses to that line that he always seemed to get in return. The most popular was, "I didn't have much of a choice," but that was usually uttered by angry, defiant people. Gnosis looked neither angry nor defiant. She just looked scared.

"Protocol would dictate that I identify myself and inform you of the precise reasons why you're here," Hoc continued, "as well as lay out the rights you currently possess, but I think we can safely bypass all of those formalities, don't you?"

Militsa hesitated. "Why?" she asked.

"Why what?"

"Why are you bypassing them?"

"Because you're here on matters relating to the criminal activities of the so-called resistance. As such, the normal rules do not apply. Under the Extraordinary Measures Act, we are able to hold you, without charge, indefinitely."

Hoc hadn't thought it was possible for Miss Gnosis to grow any paler.

"I don't have anything to do with the resistance," she said.

"Would you be at all surprised to learn that every single member of the resistance that we have caught and interrogated has said something resembling those exact words? Probably not. Miss Gnosis, you are a Necromancer, yes?"

She nodded.

"Not many Necromancers out in the world these days. Ever since the Passage debacle, your kind have been laying low – no doubt hoping the rest of us would forget how they tried to kill, what was it, three billion? Four billion people?"

"Only a few Necromancers knew that's what the Passage entailed," Gnosis said. "The rest of us were lied to. We had no idea—"

Hoc held up a hand to silence her. "The Necromancers aren't on trial here, Miss Gnosis. I'm just trying to get an idea of who you are. I prefer this, the personal approach, where I look you in the eye and judge you for myself. When we're done here, the Sensitives will come in and extract every last strand of truth from your mind, but their methods can sometimes have unintended consequences. Psychological damage and whatnot. This portion of our investigation is every bit as important as the later, more unpleasant portions – so please, do try to enjoy yourself."

"Could I... Could I have some water?"

Hoc smiled. "There's water in that cup. Would you describe yourself as socially liberal, Miss Gnosis?"

"I suppose."

"A yes or no answer would be appreciated."

"Then yes."

"Would you describe yourself as being, perhaps, anti-establishment?"

"I work at a school."

"A yes or no answer, if you please."

"No," said Gnosis. "I work at a school. I can't be anti-establishment if I work in the establishment."

"Can't you? You've never heard of dismantling something from the inside?"

"I'm not dismantling anything."

"Are you a worshipper, Miss Gnosis? A devout follower of the Faceless Ones?"

She adjusted her posture slightly. "Of course."

"Is that easy? As a Necromancer, you have your own system of esoteric beliefs, do you not?"

"I did, yes. But after the Passage I found myself doubting the Necromancy way. When the Faceless Ones returned, I realised I'd been wrong my whole life, and I gladly accepted them into my heart."

She said that far too fast, like a line in a play recited by an untalented actor.

"I see," said Hoc. "That is good news. I'm sure it was quite a shock, though, for your girlfriend at the time to turn out to be the Child of the Faceless Ones."

"It was," Gnosis replied.

Hoc opened the file. "According to my notes, your relationship with Valkyrie Cain ended soon after."

"That's right."

"Might I enquire as to why?"

"I'm... I'm afraid that's personal."

"And I'm afraid I'll have to insist."

Gnosis nodded, and took a moment. "I was overwhelmed."

"In what way?"

"Valkyrie had gone from being my girlfriend to being the emissary of the Faceless Ones overnight. I couldn't... I wasn't strong enough to deal with that."

"That's very honest of you. Do you think of yourself as a good person?"

"I try to be."

"Again, a yes or no answer would be preferred."

"Yes."

Hoc nodded. "And yet, six months ago, you killed a man."

She stiffened.

"An assassin, according to my notes. A Ripper named Coda Quell."

"It was self-defence."

"It's quite a feat to kill an ex-Cleaver."

"I didn't mean to do it."

"Quite a feat again to kill an ex-Cleaver by accident."

"He attacked me, I defended myself. I didn't want to hurt him, but I was scared."

"And I'm sure the power boost didn't help."

"Yes," she said quickly. "Yes, that's right."

"And here's where we get into trickier territory," said Hoc. "We all knew about the boost that sorcerers were going to get to their power on *Féile na Draíochta*. It's a well-known phenomenon, and the whole reason we have a Festival of Magic in the first place. The plain fact of the matter, Miss Gnosis, is that you should have been prepared to compensate for the fact that your Necromancy powers would be stronger for that twenty-four-hour period."

"I panicked. I didn't have time to—"

"And, unfortunately, that raises further questions. You, yourself, know full well the work that has gone into widening the Source rifts. Isn't that one of your areas of expertise? In order for the Faceless Ones to physically manifest in our reality, we have to flood this universe with magic. Every sorcerer in the world will soon be almost twice as strong as they were six months ago. But can you be trusted with this level of power? You've already killed one person. How many more victims will you claim?"

"None," said Gnosis, panic flaring behind her eyes. "I'm not a killer."

"But you are."

"That was self-defence!"

"Miss Gnosis, I'm going to have to ask you to calm down."

"I am calm! I'm not going to kill anyone! I didn't want to hurt Coda Quell, but he came to kill *me*! He wanted Valkyrie for himself and he thought I was his only obstacle and all I did was defend myself!"

"You're being unruly, Miss Gnosis."

"This is ridiculous! I'm not a member of the resistance and I never have been! I'm a teacher! I don't want to hurt anyone, I just want to teach, and do research, and live a normal life! I'm not a bloody terrorist and I'm not a bloody murderer!"

The door burst off its hinges and hit the opposite wall, barely missing Hoc, who launched himself out of his chair and sprawled across the desk as Valkyrie Cain barged into the room. Hoc clambered down on the other side and backed away as Cain strode up to him, put a hand round his throat and picked him up off his feet, her eyes blazing with terrifying white energy.

"You," she said, and when she spoke he could see the energy crackling down deep in her mouth.

Hoc tried to answer, but his words were being squeezed back. He tried peeling her fingers away, but they were made of steel. Three of his officers came running in, two with their guns drawn, one with a sword in his hand, but when they saw Cain they faltered, and came no further.

Cain tightened her grip and Hoc felt his larynx about to rupture.

"Valkyrie," said Gnosis, the chain not letting her stand. "Valkyrie, let him go."

Cain ignored her, her eyes narrowing, her snarl growing.

"Valkyrie!"

She squeezed tighter, and then dropped him, and Hoc slumped to the floor, gasping. The energy faded from Cain's eyes, and she pointed behind her, at the desk. "Release her."

One of the officers hurried forward and in moments Gnosis was on her feet and rubbing her wrists.

Cain turned to her. "Militsa—"

"Don't talk to me," said Gnosis, and walked out.

The officers averted their eyes. The last of Hoc's blood froze in his veins.

Cain looked back at him, and slowly hunkered. She put a hand on his shoulder. "It is taking," she said softly, "every last ounce of self-control that I have not to kill you for this. Why you thought this was acceptable, I do not know. How you thought you could get away with this, I have no idea. Why you thought I wouldn't hurt you is beyond me."

Hoc's mouth was so incredibly dry. "I... I would have been remiss in my duty not to explore the possibility that she was involved in some way with the resistance."

Cain nodded, and squeezed, and Hoc screamed. She straightened as he fell back, clutching his shoulder and screaming some more, and walked out.

49

Valkyrie knocked on the door. Militsa opened it, her eyes hardening when she saw who it was.

"Hey," she said.

"I just wanted to check that you got home OK," Valkyrie said. "Wanted to see if you were all right? Are you all right?"

"I'm good, yeah."

Valkyrie nodded. "That was... You've got to understand, I didn't know he was questioning you. When I found out, I went straight there."

"I believe you."

"He shouldn't have done it. I mean, how stupid is he? What did he think I was gonna do when I found out? Did he think I wouldn't mind?"

Militsa shrugged. "The advantages of having an ex-girlfriend people are scared of."

That stung, the way she said *ex*. "Why did they even pick you up in the first place?"

"You wouldn't understand," Militsa said, walking into the house.

"Give me a chance," said Valkyrie, hurrying in after her. "Is it a Faceless Ones thing? Did you not attend a prayer service or something? Because I don't mind that. I don't go to them myself. I don't think anyone should who doesn't want to."

"It wasn't a Faceless Ones thing."

"Then was it a resistance thing?"

They got to the kitchen. "Never mind."

"So it was," said Valkyrie. "You said something about the resistance, something that might indicate that you possibly support what they're doing in some way, and you were arrested, right?"

"Basically."

"I told Creed, he can't have the City Guard arresting people who disagree with him. When it's all done, everyone will be able to feel the love that the Faceless Ones are offering and no one will even want to resist any more. He just has to give it time."

"All I said was that the members of the resistance are good people."

"But you said it in front of a City Guard officer?"

"Shouted it, actually. Right in his face."

Valkyrie laughed. "Well, you must have known they'd arrest you."

Militsa started walking towards her office. "I did, aye."

"Then why did you do it?" Valkyrie said, following.

"Because I knew you'd storm in to save me."

Valkyrie hesitated. "You... wanted me to come save you?"

"I did."

"That's why you got yourself arrested?"

Militsa shrugged as she entered the office.

"So why did you want me to save you?" Valkyrie said, walking in after her. "So we could talk? So we could talk like we're talking right now?"

"That's exactly it," Militsa said, but her voice was sad, and Valkyrie frowned.

The office was dark, the lights off, but even in the gloom Valkyrie could tell that the desk and the bookcases and the clutter were all gone, and then Militsa bolted out of the room and the door slammed shut as sigils lit up around Valkyrie and an energy ricocheted off the walls like a thousand bullets of light, leaving criss-crossing trails that she could practically taste. She sensed a purpose within that energy – a focus, a consciousness, and she knew who it was before all those little bullets came together and coalesced into a figure, tall and strong and smiling.

"Hello, Malice," she said.

"Hello, sis. I hope you don't take it personally, Militsa leading you into a trap and everything. Desperate times and desperate measures. But you're looking well. Being the Child of the Faceless Ones must agree with you."

"I can definitely see why you liked it so much. Do you miss it?"

"I do. It fulfilled me."

"Me too."

"But now it's gone," Malice said. "And it never actually happened. And you've taken my place."

Valkyrie smiled. "And doing it better."

"Is that what you think?"

"I don't know if you've been able to look outside, but the Faceless Ones are standing on every horizon. When I visited the future, I didn't see a single one."

"Because they had a universe to conquer."

"Is that where they were?" Valkyrie asked. "Travelling the cosmos? Conquering alien worlds?"

"You'll find out, sister. They get bored after a few years of standing around."

"Maybe in your future. In mine, they'll do what I tell them."

Malice laughed. "Is that right? You'll be the one issuing orders, then? You'll be the one telling a race of gods, fourteen billion years old, what to do? Oh, I hope I'm around to see that."

"I doubt you will be."

"And what are you going to tell them to do? Keep standing on horizons? Look scary?"

"Pretty much. I'm going to tell them to take care of the Earth while I'm away."

"And where will you be?"

266

"Travelling the cosmos," said Valkyrie. "Conquering alien worlds."

Malice folded her arms. "That's their job. That's what they're meant to do."

"Not any more," Valkyrie said. "I'll take one or two with me as backup, in case I need them, but I'll be doing all the work. I'm a bit of a control freak, as it turns out. I don't trust anyone else to do the job properly – not even my own children."

"They're not your children," said Malice. "*You're* the Child, remember?"

"I'm the Child and the Mother," Valkyrie told her. "Did people not call you that? No? Oh, dear. Maybe it's a title Creed came up with, just for me. I suppose I have an advantage over you, though. When you were the Child of the Faceless Ones, you *were* a child. And then it took another few years until you could face the Child of the Ancients and move to the next level. Until you could grow up, basically. But me? I'm a grown woman, with years of experience handling untold amounts of power. I don't have to face the Child of the Ancients. I don't have to prove myself. I was born for this, Malice. Every trauma I've been through, every moment of torture, has been preparing me for the role I took from you."

The energy that formed Malice's figure crackled with hostility. "And that's who you're going to be, is it? Valkyrie Cain: Conqueror of Worlds? Terror of the Cosmos? You think you have the power to do that?"

"No," said Valkyrie. "I'm not Darquesse any more. I'm not a god. But I do respond well to a challenge."

"You'll die out there."

"Probably. It sounds fun, though, doesn't it?"

A reluctant smile twitched at the corner of Malice's mouth. "I suppose."

"So what's the plan here?" Valkyrie asked. "Are you supposed to tug at my heartstrings? To snap me out of it?"

"Of course not," Malice said with another laugh. "That wouldn't have a chance of working. Skulduggery has it in his head that it's only a matter of time before the real Valkyrie reasserts herself. What he doesn't understand, what none of them understand, is that that Valkyrie isn't coming back. There's nothing to snap you out of. You aren't possessed or brainwashed. You've just been... added to."

"Have you told them that?"

"Dude, I tried."

"Then why are we here?"

Malice sighed. "Listen, I should be happy that the Faceless Ones have returned. I shouldn't really care that it wasn't me who brought them back. I should be consoled by the fact that they're here at all, right?"

"Right."

"Only I'm not. Valkyrie, I'm resentful. I'm bitter. I can't stand that the Child of the Faceless Ones is someone else. I can't stand that you, my own sister, whom I love, whom I lost decades ago and have only just found again, has robbed me of this impossible privilege. I'm sorry if that makes me petty, or mean-spirited, or somehow small, but that's the truth. That's my truth. Do you understand?"

"So why are we here, Malice?"

"Basically? If I can't be the Child of the Faceless Ones, then nobody can."

Malice became streaks of light that sliced into Valkyrie's chest and took her off her feet. She hit the ground and writhed, hands at her head, screaming as Malice tore through her system.

50

Temper opened the door and Skulduggery and Cadaver rushed in. Cadaver pulled Valkyrie's hands behind her back and Skulduggery shackled her wrists, but still she screamed and squirmed on the floor.

"Malice!" Skulduggery called. "Leave her! Malice!"

Valkyrie continued to thrash, smacking her head against the floor.

China stalked in and slapped her hand against the far wall. Streams of dancing light left Valkyrie's body and formed a figure in the middle of the room. When the figure solidified, Valkyrie finally slumped, and didn't move.

"I told you to leave her," Skulduggery said, straightening up.

"My apologies," said Malice. "It was hard to hear in there, what with all the screaming. She's fine, though, and I did my part, so now you honour your side of the deal by letting me go."

"There is no 'our side of the deal'," Skulduggery said.

"Then why did I help?"

"You didn't," Cadaver said. "You did what you did out of bitterness and resentment, remember?"

"I'll have you know that what you heard was part of a private conversation and should not be used against me."

Cadaver took the Soul Catcher from his coat. "Back you go."

"I can help more if I stay out here," Malice said quickly. "Being stuck in that thing is... well, it's boring. And it's weird. And it does

269

things to your thoughts. It's not nice, and after what I've done to further the cause of freedom and justice and other noble ideas, I think I should be allowed to roam free. I'm energy, for God's sake. What harm can I do?"

"A lot," said China.

Malice glared at her. "You know, I preferred you with scars."

"Back in the Soul Catcher," Cadaver said.

"I have more to offer."

"Back."

"I've got insight. Literally, I was inside Valkyrie and I saw all kinds of stuff in there. Stuff that not even she knows about. Useful stuff."

Skulduggery tilted his head. "Such as?"

Malice tilted her own head. "First, I want guarantees."

"You're bluffing."

"How dare you!"

"If you have something useful to tell us, tell us now. We'll decide how useful it is, and figure out what to do with you then."

She thought about it, then shook her head. "No. I've changed my mind. I'm not going to tell you."

"OK."

"Aren't you going to argue?"

"No," Skulduggery said, and Cadaver tapped the sigil carved into the Soul Catcher and Malice howled as she was sucked into it.

There was a moment of quiet.

"I believed her," Temper said. The others looked at him and he shrugged. "I did. She sounded like she'd seen something important, then decided not to tell us."

"I believed her, too," said Militsa, from the doorway.

"The question, then," said China, "apart from what it is she saw, is why did she decide not to share it."

"Leverage," Skulduggery said, using the air to lift Valkyrie off the floor.

"Or she's protecting the Faceless Ones," said Cadaver.

Skulduggery nodded. "If she saw something, a way to hurt them that Valkyrie doesn't consciously know, we'll need that information."

"She won't tell us," said Cadaver. "She saw an opportunity to gain her freedom, then thought better of it. We can't waste time on that now. We're deep in enemy territory and we need to get Valkyrie out of here before we're discovered. We can't afford to let things go horribly, hilariously wrong right now. There'll be plenty of time for that later."

51

Frightening Jones was tied up in the basement and Tyler's dad wasn't letting anyone down there to see him.

The handcuffs that the fake FBI agents had with them, the ones inscribed with all those weird symbols, seemed to stop Frightening from using his magic to escape, but, even if he managed it, he'd still have to deal with a locked basement door and Tyler's dad, who was now camped outside that door with a handgun in his lap.

He was not taking the magic thing well. Tyler's mom wasn't, either, but at least she was handling it better than her husband.

Mila spent most of her time making Tyler repeat what he'd seen that night at the Madison farm, like hearing the same story over and over again would let magic suddenly make sense.

"Sorcerers," she said, keeping her voice down. They were in her room and she was cross-legged on her bed and Tyler was sitting on the floor. "There are sorcerers. Good and evil sorcerers."

"He didn't say *evil*," Tyler corrected. "He just said *bad*." Tyler wasn't altogether sure why that mattered, but it just felt like it did.

"Bad sorcerers," Mila breathed. "That is messed up."

"Yeah."

"And Dad won't even let us talk to him. I mean, this would change the world, do you realise that? If this got out, it would change everything."

Tyler did realise that, but he pretended he didn't because Mila looked like she was thinking things through.

"What does that mean for religion?" she asked. "If there's magic in the world, if it's actually real, does that mean there's a greater chance that there is some sort of God out there somewhere, or a lesser chance? And, if people find out, will they start worshipping these sorcerers? You know what people are like. Religions and cults start at the drop of a hat. Will we all start worshipping Frightening Jones?"

She wondered at that, and shrugged. "I mean, that wouldn't be altogether bad. What? He just seems like a nice guy. Why do you have that stupid look on your face? God, grow up, Ty, would you?"

"Sorry."

"And what about politics?" Mila continued. "There'd be a new bad guy, wouldn't there? So all the old enemies and rivals that exist now, would they reach out to each other to face a new threat? This could lead to world peace."

"I don't think they would," Tyler said. "I think they'd shrink back instead of reaching out. It'd probably make things worse."

"Maybe." Mila was quiet for a bit. "You know... if we could get into the basement, we could record what Frightening says, maybe put it online. We could show people what's really going on. I mean, we could actually change the world, Tyler."

"We can't."

She made a face. "Why not?"

"Because of the bodies." The bodies of the fake FBI agents were wrapped up and stored in the freezer shed while Tyler's parents decided on the wisest course of action.

"Ah, yeah," said Mila. "That's, like, hiding evidence or something, isn't it? It's definitely disturbing a crime scene."

He nodded. "The crime scene was definitely disturbed."

Mila sagged back. "So we can't change the world and become super-famous and get endorsement deals all because our folks moved some corpses into a shed. Typical."

"Typical."

"I swear, though – if anyone else announces the discovery of sorcerers while we have a real-live one chained up in our basement, I will sue our parents for, like, severe loss of potential earnings."

"That's a good idea."

She flopped back on to her bed. "I'm full of them."

52

Duenna and Vice-Principal Noble walked towards the chapel, exchanging a few words as they went, but mostly staying silent. Funny how none of the teachers would walk with them. When they got to the doors, they gave the City Guard their phones – and Duenna also handed him the remote, which he placed immediately in a bag that he folded and placed in a tray on his desk.

Omen followed Duenna in, keeping an eye on the cop as he passed. Now that the woman in charge was gone, the guard went back to slouching, his gut once again smoothing out the creases on his uniform. He didn't even look at the students as they filed in – he just stared into empty space, bored out of his mind.

In the chapel, Omen found a spot to kneel between Never and Axelia, and, when the priest started to drone, they began to whisper.

"Anyone know what the cop's name is?" Omen asked.

"Limerence," said Axelia. "He's not the brightest. When Duenna asked for an officer to be stationed here, I don't think they sent the cream of that particular crop."

Never shuffled a little closer. "That's good, right? If he's thick, he'll be easier to steal the remote from, won't he?"

"Maybe," said Omen. "But stupid people aren't curious people, and curious people are the easiest to distract."

Never raised an eyebrow. "So his stupidity might, in fact, be a strength? Curse my innate intelligence."

"We could always just hit him with a chair," said Axelia.

Omen frowned at her. "What is it with you and chairs?"

She shrugged. "I imagine they're good for hitting people with. I don't know – I just always wanted to hit someone with furniture."

"You're a strange girl, Axelia."

"Every girl is a strange girl, Omen. You just have to get to know us."

53

Temper stood beside Skulduggery and they watched Valkyrie wake. The room they were in was small, the only light streaming through the two-way mirror set into the wall.

Valkyrie examined her surroundings, then looked at the mirror, smiling. "You can't keep me in here forever," she said. "Sooner or later, one of you will feel sorry for me, or I'll fool you into believing that the old me has come back, and then I'll escape and get back to doing what I was doing and nothing will have changed. So why bother? Just save everyone the hassle and accept defeat."

The door opened and China walked in. "Do you really think any kind of defeat will be accepted with Skulduggery involved?"

Valkyrie sighed. "I know it's a long shot, but I have to try. There's literally nothing you can do to stop me. Even if you get every Sensitive you know to try to push me down, to subdue one part of me in favour of another, I'm too strong. The real me will resurface eventually."

China sat in the chair opposite her. "This is the real you, is it?"

"In all my glory."

"Skulduggery doesn't think that's true."

"I know what Skulduggery thinks. Malice told me. He thinks he can convince the old me to reassert herself by appealing to, what, my sense of decency? My love for my family and friends? My love for Militsa? I can still love all those people, I can still be a decent person, and also be the Child of the Faceless Ones. They're not mutually exclusive."

"I'm sure they're not, dear. But that's not what Skulduggery thinks."

"That's what Malice told me he thinks."

"Do you really expect Skulduggery Pleasant to explain his plan to Malice? She was an integral part of it, we needed her to distract you, but there was no chance that we would ever actually trust her with the truth. There was no telling how she would have reacted. She's a Child of the Faceless Ones, too, after all, albeit once removed."

"So what is it?" Valkyrie asked. "What's the plan?"

China sat forward, her elbows resting on her knees, her finger-tips pressed together. "We have a working theory," she said. "We don't think you've changed – in many respects, you're still the Valkyrie Cain we all know and love. We just think you're being influenced."

"By the Faceless Ones."

"By your psychic connection to them, yes."

"I'm not psychically connected to them now," said Valkyrie. "The moment you bound my magic, the connection was lost."

China shook her head. "It's been muted," she said, "not lost. We think, in order to break their hold over you, that link needs to be severed."

"And how do you plan on doing the severing?"

"That's my job."

Valkyrie nodded. "You're going to tattoo some sigils on to me. You really think that'll work? The Faceless Ones are quite loud."

"Then there will need to be a great many sigils. We're going to be here for a while, Valkyrie. You may suffer some discomfort. I do apologise for that."

"It won't make a difference. Say you shut their voices out of my head, say you're actually capable of doing that – so what? I've already been changed, China. It's too late. Can't you see that?

Don't you understand? I'll still be the Child and the Mother of the Faceless Ones even if I can't hear them."

"True," China said, "but that's a problem we'll deal with once we have the old Valkyrie back in control."

"There is no old Valkyrie," Valkyrie said, losing her patience. "I am the old Valkyrie. I'm the new Valkyrie. I'm the only Valkyrie left."

"Well," said China, smiling, "I certainly hope that's not true." She stood up. "Let's get to work, shall we?"

"We should leave them to it," Skulduggery said.

Temper nodded. He'd had no great desire to watch China carving tattoos into Valkyrie anyway. "Is everything in place?"

"The building has been scrubbed, but keep an eye out for anything we've missed," Skulduggery said. "Evacuation is in an hour."

"I won't be late," Temper said.

He passed rooms of maps and files and notes, all carefully arranged to look as authentic as possible. The real files were already off-site, safe in boxes stacked in a corner of their next temporary base. This whole resistance thing was one long pursuit, slowed down enough so that it was both unbelievably dull and terrifyingly tense.

Temper stopped, a frown on his face. Light danced beneath the closed door of a room that should have been abandoned. He drew his gun and crossed over to it, moving quietly. He listened at the door, then pushed it open.

Cadaver Cain lay on the floor next to the Soul Catcher containing Malice. His clothes still had a shape to them – they still looked like they were worn by a normal, flesh-and-blood person – but his skeleton itself was flat on the floor. The Soul Catcher pulsed with crackling light, and then some of that energy flowed from the Soul Catcher into the skeleton, and the bones clicked and realigned and Cadaver sat up suddenly, tilting his head at the gun levelled at him.

"What the hell were you doing?" Temper asked.

The air rippling around him, Cadaver floated to his feet. "Investigating," he said. "Malice had information we needed. I decided to get it."

"You run this past Skulduggery? China? Anyone in charge?"

"That must have slipped my mind. You can put the gun away."

"I don't think I will. It looks like you've forgotten the terms of your parole. You do nothing – nothing – without express permission from one of us first."

"You mean to say that you still don't trust me?"

"I mean to say."

"Then you won't be interested in what I learned, I presume?"

"Why don't you tell me, and I'll decide?"

Cadaver adjusted his sleeves, pulling them down ever so slightly. "A short while before the Activation Wave was triggered, Valkyrie and Skulduggery broke into the Dark Cathedral with the Sceptre of the Ancients, planning to use it to destroy the Eye of Rhast and derail Creed's plans."

"They told me," said Temper. "She tried to use it and the damn thing exploded."

Cadaver nodded. "The black crystal that powered the Sceptre, the katahedral, shattered."

"So?"

"When it shattered, it released all of that katahedral energy."

"So?"

"Energy like that, Temper, doesn't just evaporate. It has to go somewhere. Be stored somewhere."

"And where'd it go?"

"Into Valkyrie."

Temper frowned. "But that would have killed her. Anything that black lightning touches, it turns to dust. Even gods."

"Everything, it seems, apart from Valkyrie Cain."

"How's that possible?"

"My theory is that the energy chose a vessel that had already demonstrated its ability to contain and wield massive amounts of power."

"So she absorbs it without being damaged by it," Temper said, lowering the gun. "And it's still there?"

"That's what Malice detected when she was poking around. Valkyrie probably isn't even aware of this energy inside her, but it's there, and I think it can be called upon."

"She'd be able to wield it? To use the black lightning without it killing her?"

"If it hasn't killed her yet, I doubt it will do so now."

"Wait a second," said Temper. "Are you actually saying that Valkyrie might be able to kill the Faceless Ones?"

Cadaver tilted his head happily. "Isn't magic wonderful?"

54

The straps and chains and ropes held Valkyrie down while China's fingertips moved over her skin, her touch hot but not painful – not exactly. China linked the new sigils with some of the ones she'd already tattooed on to Valkyrie's upper arm. The swirls and swoops and dashes, the points, the curves, the edges and corners, they were all of the deepest black. Her hands and arms, her shoulders, running down her chest, her back, swirling across her belly, down her legs, around her feet and up the other side. Her neck, too, and her face, and across her eyelids and over her ears.

One day became two and China took breaks often, and every time she left the room, pale and exhausted, Valkyrie shouted at her and cursed her and begged her to stop. Every tattoo dulled her connection to her children. She couldn't hear their thoughts, not with her magic bound, but the channel between them was open, like a radio searching for a signal. The quiet hiss of static was reassuring, a balm, a promise that they were still out there, that she'd see them again, hear them again, feel them again. But the sigils were taking her away from them, bit by bit and piece by piece. It was quieter now, in her head, and lonelier, and there were thoughts surfacing that she didn't want surfacing, and everything was going wrong.

When China came back into the room for the final time, Valkyrie explained to her why she should stop. She used logic and reason and remained calm. She promised China everything she had ever wanted, promised to deliver to her the biggest collection of magical artefacts ever assembled in one place.

China ignored her, and got back to work.

Valkyrie's promises turned to threats. The threats turned to screams. The screams turned to sobs. The sobs turned to begging.

China didn't stop. China just worked.

55

They'd found him. The City Guard had been after him for days, ever since he'd escaped from their dirty, smelly dungeon. It was inevitable, really. Sebastian was just surprised that it had taken him so long to screw up.

He tried to step back into the shadows, hoping his clothes would hide him, but the City Guard officers frowned and came into the alley, and he knew he wasn't going to get out of this without a fight.

"Hello," he said, stepping out in front of them.

They stopped. Stared.

"You're under arrest," the first cop said, like he couldn't believe he was saying those words.

"Yeah," said Sebastian, somewhat miserably.

"Come quietly."

"No," said Sebastian, even more miserably.

The first cop went for his gun and Sebastian flung his hat into his face and followed that with a punch that sent the cop stumbling. His partner backed off, fumbling at his holster, and Sebastian lunged, jabbed his fingers into the guy's throat. The gun clattered to the ground and Sebastian hammered his fist into the hinge of his jaw.

Sebastian turned and the first cop fired point-blank into his chest and it hurt like hell, but the bullet didn't go through. They grappled, and Sebastian put him on the ground and hit him until he was unconscious.

He made sure both guards were out of it, rubbing the soreness out of his chest as he did so. He retrieved their guns, dismantled them and let the pieces fall, then put his hat back on.

"Unnecessary," said a voice behind him and Sebastian spun. Nuncle stood there, eating a stick of celery. "Should have just walked by them, boy. That's what I would've done. Saves on all the hitting, you know?"

"How did you get out?" Sebastian asked, frowning.

"Out of where? I've been to many places, so you're going to have to be a tad more specific."

"The dungeon," said Sebastian. "How did you get out of the dungeon?"

"I followed you, didn't I?"

Sebastian shook his head. "You would have been caught. I was almost caught, and you were well behind me."

"Aye, I was. But I have a knack for blending into the background, so I do. I passed right by them."

Sebastian checked around him, making sure no one was sneaking up, then glared. "You want to know what I think? I think you're working for the City Guard. Commander Hoc. Damocles Creed. I think you were sent in to spy on us, and you told them what we were planning, and now you're here to lead them to me."

"Oh, right," said Nuncle. "So I'm a spy now, am I?"

"I think so."

"That's exciting. I've never been a spy before. I hope I enjoy it."

"If you're not a spy, then how did you find me?"

"I never lost you, boy. I was behind you the whole time, more or less."

"No," said Sebastian. "You weren't."

"I could teach you, if you want. Old Nuncle makes a grand teacher, so he does."

"Look, just what do you want? Why are you here?"

Nuncle smiled. "Why are any of us here? That's a question for the ages, is it not? Why are we here? What is our purpose?"

"I know what my purpose is."

"You think you do."

"Hey, look, you're free to hang around here and ramble on, but I'm leaving before more cops come to arrest me."

Nuncle nodded and smiled, and Sebastian made his way to the rooftops – where Nuncle was waiting for him.

Sebastian stared. "How did you do that?"

"I just want to talk to you, lad."

"Are you a Teleporter?"

"I'm just an old man looking for a conversation."

Sebastian sat on the low wall running along the edge of the rooftop. He was tired of running and hiding. The truth was he was tired of not having anyone to talk to, either.

Nuncle sat before him, cross-legged. "The universe is waking up."

Sebastian raised an eyebrow behind his mask. "Was it sleeping?"

"Oh, aye. Oh, it was. It's been sleeping since it was created. But now it's waking. You and me, we're part of that. We're part of its brain."

"You're obviously the crazy part."

Nuncle laughed.

"I'm sorry," said Sebastian, "do you actually believe the universe is waking up, or is it just something you say so people will think you're interesting? The universe isn't alive."

"Course it is, boy. It's alive, it's waking, and it's becoming aware."

"The universe is not a person."

"But it is sentient like a person."

"It's cosmic dust and rocks and suns and gases and a whole lot of empty space. That's all."

"That's depressing, that is. Is that really how you view existence?

Tell me this and tell me no more – are you sentient? You are, aren't you? You're aware of yourself – you're aware of your own existence. Right? You think, therefore you are. So you are sentient... But is your foot sentient?"

"What?"

"Or your hand?" said Nuncle. "Or your ribcage? Or are you sentient because your body contains a sentient mind? Yes? So, for the universe to be sentient, all it needs is for something within it to possess this quality. And that is what we are. We are the sentient mind of the universe, and because we are so young as a species, the universe is still in the process of waking up."

Sebastian blinked at him. "Uh-huh. And what happens when it's fully awake?"

Nuncle smiled. "Then we expand. Our thoughts begin. Our synapses fire. We look around and we understand. A being of Darquesse's power – she knows this. She is this."

"Darquesse isn't a universe."

"Not yet."

"You're being confusing just to confuse me."

"I'm sorry, lad. Sometimes that happens. I've lived a long time, see?"

"How long?"

Nuncle shrugged. "How long have you got?"

56

While Valkyrie screamed and threatened and cursed and begged, a part of her didn't mind so much what was happening. She was the Child and the Mother, absolutely, and that wasn't anything she could change right now, but she'd never been a big fan of the Faceless Ones. She'd fought against them, in fact. Hell, she'd even killed a couple.

And she knew that all this love she felt for them had been imposed on her. It had taken almost a week for it to seep through after she'd absorbed the Activation Wave. The first morning she woke up, she was fine. Nothing had changed. The second morning, pretty much the same. The third morning, she was feeling a little odd, like a new side to an old argument had opened up in her consciousness. From there, it snowballed, and she found herself taking their side in discussions with others. Militsa found that very upsetting and they broke up. Skulduggery found it upsetting, but he figured the best thing to do was stay by her side so he could at least try to steer her in the right direction.

It was a nice thought, but ultimately fruitless. He'd have been better off doing what Militsa had done.

Valkyrie missed Militsa. She missed a lot of things about her old life. She missed her friendship with Skulduggery, and she missed her family, and her dog.

So China worked away and Valkyrie raged, but at the same

time she smiled in a secret place, and willed China to work faster. With every hour that passed and every new sigil tattooed, she felt a little bit more like herself.

But then it all went wrong.

Through tear-streaked eyes, she watched the door burst open. She watched sorcerers come pouring through, and China turning, raising her hands. There was a flash of purple and China hit the wall and there were people all around Valkyrie now, and Damocles Creed himself strode into the room and knelt by her and touched her face like she was his long-lost daughter.

"You're safe," he said to her softly. "You're safe now."

She cried.

57

Prayers.

Omen watched as Officer Limerence held out the bag and Duenna dropped her phone and the remote into it without even looking at him. He closed the bag, folded it, and put into the tray on his desk.

The moment Duenna disappeared into the chapel, Axelia emerged from round the corner, sipping a coffee. She didn't even glance at Limerence as she walked towards the chapel doors. Omen feared that the cop wasn't going to notice her, but at the last moment he snapped out of his daydream to hold up a hand.

"Oi," he said. "No food or drinks during prayers." Axelia looked around for somewhere to put it and Limerence gave a loud sigh. "Give it here."

"Oh, thank you," Axelia said, and tripped as she stepped over to him, hurling the coffee into his chest.

Limerence howled. While Axelia apologised profusely and threw a fresh handkerchief at him, a group of passing Sixth Years formed a wall, shielding the desk from the eyes of any teachers as Omen crept up from behind. He snatched the bag from the tray, replaced the remote with the fake they'd made in the school workshop – just an empty chunk of plastic – and put it back. Then he scrambled away, the remote in his pocket, and the wall of Sixth Years drifted casually apart. Omen joined them as they filed into the chapel, Axelia coming up behind him.

"Wow," she whispered. "Your plan worked."

"You sound surprised."

"Aren't you?"

"Yes," he admitted. "I'm bloody astonished."

58

Watching China being interrogated by the Sensitives was not a pleasant experience. She sat in a room not unlike the one they had been in in that cold resistance headquarters, with her wrists chained to the table, her black hair plastered to her face with sweat. The Sensitives were sweating, too. China's defences were formidable.

The door behind Valkyrie opened and Creed walked in, joining her at the window.

"She'll break," he said. "Everyone breaks."

"You might need a few new Sensitives to do it, though," said Valkyrie. "Looks like she's wearing out these two."

"Possible." A moment passed. "And how are you feeling?"

She looked at him. "You're worried."

"Not at all."

"You're worried China managed to block my link to the Faceless Ones. You're worried that your only line of communication has been cut."

"A reasonable concern."

"You can relax," Valkyrie said, tapping her arm. Sigils appeared, rising briefly to the surface of her skin before fading away again. "Even if it would have worked, China didn't have time to finish. Besides, your little project seems to be coming along nicely. Pretty soon you won't even need me – you'll be communicating with the Faceless Ones yourself."

"The Nexus Helmet is intended to be an emergency backup, in case anything does happen to you. I pray that we will never need it."

They watched as one of the Sensitives broke away from the silent interrogation, blood running from his nose.

Creed pressed a button on the wall. "Get those idiots out of there and send in people who can do their damn job."

"Yes, sir," came the nervous voice on the other end. A moment later, the heavy door opened and the two Sensitives left, allowing China a moment to sag in her chair.

"I want to talk to her," Valkyrie said.

Creed hesitated. "Do you think that's wise?"

"No interruptions," Valkyrie said, walking out.

She stepped into the interrogation room and closed the door behind her. China looked even more tired up close.

"You had me in a room just like this," Valkyrie said. "It even had a two-way mirror. Did that make you feel secure, knowing you were surrounded by the resistance?"

"How many did they catch in the raid?" China asked.

Valkyrie could have lied, could have picked a number to see if the expression on China's face changed. But she decided to tell the truth. "None," she said. "They must have seen what was coming and teleported out. We managed to grab a few documents, though, so our people are going through those as we speak." She sat. "How are you feeling?"

"I have a migraine."

"Having those Sensitives bashing against your mind like that can't be much fun. You could make it easy on yourself, you know. You could let me in. I'm not as good as they are, but I'd be a hell of a lot gentler."

"I'm sure you would, dear."

"Is that a no?"

"Sadly, it is."

"China, this is inevitable. They will break into your mind. No

293

matter how long it takes, they'll do it. The more you fight it, the more damage they'll do. You have a beautiful mind. Please stop resisting."

A slight smile curled one corner of China's lips. "You still manage to care, even after I spent all that time carving those sigils into you?"

"You're my friend," said Valkyrie. "You were doing what you thought was right. You think I'm under the Faceless Ones' control, so of course you're going to try to free me. How could I be mad at you for that?"

"You *are* under the Faceless Ones' control."

"I wish I could make you understand how wrong you are, but there's no way for me to do that, is there? I just have to hope that you'll eventually come round."

"Hoping isn't very practical. We could have hoped that you'd snap out of this delusion and reject the Faceless Ones, but where would that have got us? Instead, we decided to act."

"And look at the results."

"Is it ideal?" China asked. "No – but what is these days?"

"China, your idea didn't work. You covered me in sigils to set me free and nothing's happened. I'm still connected to the Faceless Ones, I'm still the Child and the Mother. I still hear them in my head and they hear me. This is a bond that can't be broken."

"That's because I didn't finish."

"China, what are you even doing? You're making excuses now?"

"Excuses are for the weak, you know that. In order for the sigils to break you free, I needed to connect you to a conduit of power I simply didn't have access to. Now I do."

"What kind of conduit?"

"This place. This entire building is a conduit for power. You know this already."

Valkyrie smiled. "So you needed to be here in the High Sanctuary in order to complete what you were doing?"

"Indeed I did."

"Well, we're here. Now what? You're going to break free from those shackles and overpower me?"

"Something like that," said China. She turned her head, and her tone changed. "Lock down this room."

"What? Who are you—"

A sheen spread across the door and Valkyrie's thoughts expanded until they were too large to fit in her head, and it was all she could do to watch as the shackles snapped free from China's wrists.

"I made specific alterations to certain parts of this building," China said, standing and moving round the desk. "In the unlikely event that I was ever deposed as Supreme Mage, I needed a system in place to ensure that I'd be treated fairly. Voice-activated security measures are but one of my modifications."

Valkyrie tried to move, but couldn't. She tried to speak and could only mumble.

"No one can hear you," said China. "No one can see what's happening, either. That glass has been treated. They now see only what they expect to see – you and me talking." China hunkered down in front of Valkyrie, the tips of her fingers glowing. "Which gives us plenty of time to complete our work."

59

While the rest of the school slept, Omen and eighteen others sneaked out of their dorm rooms and met in the Science Block. Tapping the remote and holding it up to show them, he resisted the urge to touch any of the sigils that started to glow along its surface.

"You know what we have to do. We have all the books we reckon we'll need, but we're going to be relying on everyone who's been paying attention in class for the past few years. That's not me."

"We know," someone said.

"We have the next eight hours to figure out how to clone this remote. No matter what, it's being switched back in the morning. If Duenna notices what we're trying to do, she'll just start all over again and we won't have a chance. But we should be fine. We can absolutely do this."

"So long as we figure out how to actually do what we need to do," said Never.

"Yes," said Omen happily.

The door opened and Gerontius stuck his head in. "We might have a problem."

Filament Sclavi and three of his fellow prefects stalked the corridors like dim-witted cats hunting for a gang of clever and noble mice who only wanted to do the right thing and help other mice.

Omen watched them peer round a corner, and then creep off in the direction of the Arts Block.

"They're looking for us," Never whispered. "They must know something's up."

"That's the problem with involving other people," Axelia said softly. "The more they're talking about something, the higher the chances of being overheard."

"They'll find us eventually."

Omen nodded. "We'll have to grab them."

"And do what?" Never asked. "Tie them up? Gag them for the next few weeks? I mean, I'm all for stuffing them into a cupboard somewhere, but teachers might notice."

"Then what do we do?"

"We lead them away."

"For the next eight hours?"

Everyone went quiet.

Never's eyes narrowed. "Hold on. They know something's going on, but they don't know what. So we'll just get up to mischief, get ourselves caught, and they'll march us down to detention, thinking they've foiled whatever we've dreamed up."

"A trip to raid the kitchen," Axelia suggested. "We've done it before. Everyone knows it happens. We'd be breaking the rules, but wouldn't get in too much trouble."

"I like it," said Omen. "Also, I'm a little hungry, so..."

"Oh, no," Never said. "You're not getting caught."

"God, no," said Axelia.

"What? Why not?"

"Because you're the leader."

"Yeah, but I'm not very good at it."

Axelia slapped him lightly on the shoulder. "Shut it, please. We need you free to improvise if anything goes wrong. Plus, if all of us are taken to detention, we can't continue with the plan, can we? Never and I will get ourselves caught."

"Or just Axelia," said Never.

She scowled.

"Or both of us," Never said glumly.

Axelia hissed and pulled them away from the corner as Filament and his buddies reappeared. Omen turned to hurry away, but his footsteps squeaked on the floor. He looked at his friends with wide eyes, and Never and Axelia immediately linked arms and strode round the corner like they had no idea who was approaching from the other side.

"Ah, poo," Omen heard Never say.

He flattened himself to the wall, listening to Filament giving two of the prefects the order to escort the naughty students down to the detention cells. Multiple footsteps squeaked away on the floor, but Omen didn't move. He kept his eyes on the corner, just waiting to be discovered.

"Should we wake Duenna?" he heard the remaining prefect ask.

Filament sounded scornful. "Wake her up for this? Two students out of bed? This isn't worth it. It's barely worth us waking up for."

"Then why do you have that look on your face?"

"Because Never and Axelia Lukt only get into trouble with Omen Darkly, and we haven't caught Omen Darkly, have we?"

"You want to go looking for him?"

"Oh, we could. We could definitely waste our time doing that. Or I could just check his dorm room. What do you think? Might that be easier? To check if he's asleep in bed or out here, breaking curfew? Might that be a better idea?"

"You're really sarcastic."

"If you stop saying stupid things, I'll stop being sarcastic about the things you say. Now don't say anything at all, if you please. I need to focus."

Filament was in Omen's Teleportation module, and in the last week he'd finally managed to teleport without assistance – something Omen, and many students, to be fair, still couldn't manage. But it had taken him a while to focus in the way he'd needed to, so Omen still had time.

Not much time, but time.

So Omen took off his trainers and socks, backed away from the corner, and turned and ran.

He sprinted for the stairs, risked breaking both his ankles as he hurtled downwards. He cut across the Combat Arts Block and took more stairs down, grabbing the banister at the bottom and whirling round it to sprint off towards the dorms.

Bare feet slapping the floor, he burst through the swing doors and ran on, rounding the next few corners by ricocheting off the outer walls. He got to his corridor. The door to his dorm room was still closed. He got halfway there and Filament teleported into the space ahead of him and Omen put on the brakes, but instead of whirling and catching him, Filament lunged for the bin and puked into it.

Omen crept past him, the faint sounds of his footsteps totally obscured by the violent upchucking into the trash receptacle. He made it into the room, whipped off his T-shirt and his jeans and pulled on his dressing gown, messed up his hair a little more than usual, and poked his head back out of the door.

Filament spat a few times, then straightened up and wiped his mouth. He turned and jumped when he saw Omen looking at him.

"You feeling all right?" Omen whispered, squinting at him.

Filament blinked. Then pointed at the bin. "I vomited. I'm not used to teleporting."

"I heard. What are you doing up? It's, like, the middle of the night. Do you usually walk around, fully dressed, in the middle of the night?"

Attempting to claw back some of his authority, Filament glared. "You don't get to ask a prefect what they're—"

Omen put his finger to his lips. "Voice down, man. Gerontius and Morven are still asleep."

Filament's glare intensified. "Where are Never and Axelia?"

"Sorry?"

"Where do you think they are right now?"

"Is this a trick question?"

"Answer me or I'll put you in detention!"

"Keep your voice down, Filament. I'm assuming Never and Axelia are fast asleep in their own beds, which is where I should be right now. In my bed, I mean. Not theirs. That'd be weird."

Filament folded his arms. "And you've been here all night, have you? Then why are you all sweaty?"

"That's a very personal question."

"You're breathing hard."

"I sometimes dream I'm a dog and so I kick out in my sleep a lot."

"Do you have any witnesses to back up your claim that you've been here all night?"

"I suppose Gerontius and Morven are my witnesses," said Omen, "although they're asleep, too." He indicated Filament's chin. "You've got a bit of vomit on your... never mind."

Filament wiped his sleeve across his chin.

"I'm going back to bed," said Omen. "You have a nice night, OK?"

Before Filament could formulate a response, Omen closed the door.

60

It was working. It was actually working.

The communication channel she'd had, that quiet static that let her know she was still connected to her children – it cut off all at once and she could have cheered, but instead she wailed, could have danced, but instead she struggled against the bonds that held her. That was a moment, a moment of victory. It was nice.

Gradually, she took control of her body, and she stopped struggling. Taking control of her mind took a little longer, but, like a conquering army sweeping over enemy territory, she planted her flag in every battleground until it was all her once again. The old Valkyrie. The real Valkyrie.

"Is that you?" China asked. Her voice croaked with exhaustion.

Valkyrie looked down at herself, looked at all the glowing tattoos on her skin. She smiled weakly. "It's me."

"You're sure?"

"Pretty much."

"I'm going to have to trust you on that one," China said, and helped her stand.

Valkyrie's stomach rumbled and she needed to pee. Hobbling slightly, she turned to the two-way mirror. Practically every part of her body was covered in sigils.

"These are all to keep the Faceless Ones out of my head?" she asked.

"Among other things," said China.

Valkyrie turned, looking over her shoulder at the rest of the tattoos. "Pretty cool," she said, and tapped the smallest sigil on her arm, allowing her fingertip to follow its curve. Like a light being dimmed, the tattoos faded to invisibility.

"So what are your current feelings towards the Faceless Ones?" China asked, watching her carefully.

Valkyrie took a moment before answering. "They're still my children," she said. "I don't have that blind devotion to them any more, but I still love them. It's weird. On the one hand, I want to protect them from anyone who wants to hurt them, and on the other I want to destroy them, because if I don't, they'll kill billions of people. So... I'm conflicted, you know? But I'm also aware that there's only one outcome here. They have to be destroyed. There's no argument to be made for anything else. These are the Faceless Ones we're talking about."

"You're probably the only person in the history of the world, with the exception of Malice, who knows what they're truly like," China said. "Beyond the monstrous exteriors, beyond the death and destruction, and beyond anything that's ever been written about them. You know more about the Faceless Ones, you have a deeper understanding of their race, than Damocles Creed or Mevolent or any scholar could ever even conceive of."

Valkyrie nodded. "Without getting too American about it, they're a bunch of jerks."

China laughed.

"I'm serious," Valkyrie said, too exhausted to join in. "That's exactly what they are. The Faceless Ones are nasty. They're my children, absolutely, but they're sadistic and petty and mean-spirited, and they're only happy when they're spreading fear. All those people who worship them? The Faceless Ones drink in that energy, they take it, absorb it, and they despise them for it. They actually despise their own worshippers. They think they're pathetic."

"And you've got no qualms about helping us destroy them?"

Valkyrie sighed. "I don't want to do it, but I have to, and I'm not going to hesitate. They're bullies, right? They're bigger and stronger and they're demanding that the mortal world hand over its lunch money. I don't care who you are, whether you're the bully's best friend or their mother – it's clear who the bad guys are. See a bully, smack a bully: that's always been my philosophy."

"Words to live by."

Valkyrie finished dressing. "So what's the plan? How are we getting out of here?"

"We're not," said China. "You have an opportunity to retrieve the Void meteorite – we're going to need it to subdue Obsidian. So you get some sleep, then carry on like you've been doing, and, when the moment comes, you strike, take the meteorite and escape."

"I'm not sure that's going to work. Creed's Nexus Helmet will be finished tomorrow. If it works like they think it will, he'll be able to communicate with the Faceless Ones."

"And they'll tell him what you're up to," finished China. "Yes, I see the problem. It's not ideal, certainly, but our options are limited. In which case, you'll have to forget about sleep and try to find the meteorite before Creed has his first conversation with them."

"And what about you?"

"Creed has to be confident that everything is going according to plan, so I'm afraid you'll have to put my shackles back on."

"The moment I have the meteorite, I'm breaking you out of here. I swear."

"Oh, Valkyrie," said China, "I'm depending on it."

61

Temper ordered a non-alcoholic beer and took it to the table in the back. It was a weeknight and the bar was quiet and playing country music, and the Packers were losing to the Rams on the TV above the bar, but no one was paying them much attention. A couple of minutes later, Dexter walked in with his boyfriend, a large man called Rasmus whom Temper had only met a few weeks earlier. Rasmus went to get them some drinks and Dexter came straight over.

"You're limping," Temper said.

"Got shot," said Dexter.

"Bad?"

"Had worse."

"This before or after you had the conversation with Alaric Sake?"

"During," Dexter said. "He'd been expecting us. Seems Creed has put the word out: the resistance are making house calls on Sanctuary officials, so carry a gun and make sure it's loaded. Didn't make much difference. I took it off him and sat him down and told him who'd been making his life miserable. By the time I was leaving, he was thanking me, and told me not to worry about the carpet I'd been bleeding on."

"How nice of him."

A bunch of good ol' boys came in, laughing and talking loudly, and Rasmus passed them on his way to the table. He put the drinks down – non-alcoholic beers all round – and nodded as he took his seat. "Temper," he said.

"Rasmus."

"He tell you he got shot?"

"He did."

"It's getting too dangerous to send people out alone."

"Hopefully, we won't have to send anyone out any more," said Temper. "We've been planting the seeds of doubt and discontent for the last few weeks and now we're seeing the results. The German Sanctuary's collapsed – did you hear that? Once the mages discovered how compromised their Council of Elders was, they walked out."

Dexter raised an eyebrow. "And have they all joined the resistance?"

"Not yet," Temper admitted, "but we need to give them a little time before we approach them. Still, it's a result. It's a win."

"Yes, it is," said Rasmus, and raised his glass. "Here's to winning."

They clinked. Temper liked Rasmus. Dexter had a habit of going through boyfriends and girlfriends without much thought or consideration, especially after Saracen's death, so it was nice to see him find someone he could slow down with. Rasmus was big and burly and as calm as a still lake. He was good for Dexter. Temper hoped it would last.

"Any word on Valkyrie and China?" Dexter asked.

Temper shook his head. "And we have no way of finding out. If everything's gone well, Valkyrie is already back on our side."

"And if our bad luck continues to hold?"

Temper grimaced, and didn't answer.

Three men and two women came in, all looking like they'd had a hard day at the office and just wanted to unwind. The men had their ties loosened and the women took off their jackets as they settled into the booth on the opposite side of the bar. The shoes they all wore were good shoes – expensive – but the suits were cheap enough to not stand out, yet brand-new. One of the men, the tallest one, hadn't even ironed the folds out of his shirt yet. They glanced at the bar staff and they glanced at the good ol' boys, but they didn't glance over at Temper's table. Their eyes didn't even flicker that way.

"What an odd bunch of unconvincing mortals," said Dexter, taking a sip of his drink.

"Oh, damn," Rasmus muttered. He was a big guy, but he wasn't a fighter.

Dexter smiled at him like he'd made a joke. "We're going to do our best to get out of here without any trouble, but I don't like our chances. The moment this goes sideways, get to the car and drive."

"I'm not leaving you."

"I appreciate that, but Temper and I will stand a better chance if it's just the two of us."

Rasmus hesitated, then nodded.

"Well," said Temper, "I'm gonna see what I can do about splitting up their happy little group." He got up, walked towards the restrooms, glancing at the game on the TV as he did so. Three of the men in the bad suits wandered over to block his way.

"I know you?" said the tall guy.

Temper smiled back, all friendly-like. "Don't think so."

"You sure I haven't seen you around?"

"I'm not from here."

"Where you from?" asked the tall guy's friend, the one with the expensive haircut. "You sound New York. You sound Brooklyn. You from Brooklyn?"

"You ask an awful lot of questions, fellas. I'm not gonna lie to you, I feel a little under the microscope here. I feel like you're intimidating me."

"There a problem here, buddy?" said one of the good ol' boys, speaking directly to the tall one.

"Nothing to concern you."

"That fella there, he was just enjoying a drink with his friends, wasn't bothering nobody, and then you and your lot walk in and the whole temperature of the place plunges. Now, seeing as how this is our regular watering hole, as it were, I feel obliged to inform you that you ain't welcome here."

The tall one smirked. "Is that so?"

"That is so, as a matter of fact."

The tall one nodded, and snapped his hand at the air and the good ol' boy hurtled back.

It all went to hell after that.

The sorcerers attacked and Rasmus tried helping, but it was Temper and Dexter doing the work, defending the astonished mortals even as they were defending themselves. Hansel and Gretel shot out of Temper's palms, burrowing into shoulders, snatching guns from hands, latching on to throats, giving him the time he needed to get in close.

Then a blast of energy hit him, sent him reeling, and one of the sorcerers grabbed him, wrapped her arm round his throat, had his right arm twisted behind his back. She pulled him about the place, not giving him the chance to get his feet beneath him.

Dexter went down and one of them, the tallest of them, had picked up the gun, and he pointed it right into Dexter's face and there was nothing Temper could do. They were outnumbered and they were going to die here, the resistance would fail and Creed would win, and Temper roared and all of his rage came shooting out through his chest in a stream of light and darkness and there was a scream and the tall guy went down.

The Gist lashed out, catching another sorcerer in the chest, sending him spinning across the room even as it flew to the corner and twisted, turned, came flowing back, mouth opening impossibly wide and all those teeth flashing. With its claws, it lifted another sorcerer off the floor and flung her behind the bar.

The woman holding Temper let him go, tried running, but

307

the Gist got her before she'd got more than five steps. Temper dropped to his knees, the sounds growing dull. There were more screams and gunshots and above it all was the terrible tortured sound of the Gist itself, shrieks that were becoming laughter. Temper tried to breathe but couldn't. Tried to regain control but couldn't. He tried to remember one good thing about his life but failed. There was a woman, a woman with short dark hair, an assassin. He couldn't remember her name.

The Gist was too strong. The Gist took everything good about him and swallowed it. Temper tried to resist, tried to fight, tried to hold on, but there was nothing he could do, nothing he could grip, and Temper tried to shout out in fear and desperation and loss, but even that shout was taken from him as he flowed into the Gist and the Gist was all there was.

The bar grew silent. The football still played on the TV. The Packers were still losing.

"Temper?"

Dexter got to his feet.

"Yes," said Temper, but his voice sounded weird.

"You OK?"

Temper turned to him and watched Dexter's expression change.

"I'm fine," said Temper, and smiled with all his teeth.

62

The plan worked perfectly.

Omen was exhausted, but that didn't affect the plan one little bit. After he'd beaten Filament back to his dorm room, he'd snuck out again, rejoining the others in the Science Block as they worked to clone the remote control. Eyes bleary and thoughts clouded with brain fog, they finished it with a few minutes to spare. It wasn't pretty – it was a clunky little contraption with basic sigils carved into it, about the size of a phone – but they were all sure it'd work. Pretty sure anyway. Relatively sure.

But it was all they had, so they clung quite happily to the possibility as they sneaked back to their dorm rooms just in time to emerge for morning prayers.

Omen kept the cloned control in his pocket. He wasn't going to risk anyone stumbling across it – it was far too important to take a chance like that. In his other pocket, he had the actual remote, the original. Granted, he didn't have Never or Axelia – they were both still in detention, and probably would be for most of the day – but he had everyone else in place to switch it with the fake remote. The fact that he was exhausted and that everyone helping him was exhausted had no impact on the plan whatsoever.

Just like the previous evening, he watched Duenna drop the remote – the *fake* remote – into the bag that Limerence was holding out. He watched Limerence put the bag in the tray on his desk. He watched Kase stumble into Mahala and Mahala stumble against the table, and when Limerence got up to tell them off, Omen sneaked up unseen, whipped the fake remote out of the bag and stuffed it into his pocket, then dropped the real remote into the bag in its place.

The plan worked perfectly. It was at that point that everything else went wrong.

Limerence happened to glance back, must have seen Omen out of the corner of his eye, and whipped round. Omen froze, the bag containing the remote still in his hand, hovering over the tray.

There was a moment when Limerence's expression didn't change, and Omen wondered if he might still be able to get away with this. But then Limerence frowned.

"Hey," he said. Then he roared, "Hey!"

It was over. Omen knew, in that instant, that it was over. Being caught like this, with Duenna's remote in his hand, would mean more than detention. It would mean more than expulsion. It would mean arrest. It would mean questioning. It would mean sitting in a cell, unable to help, unable to do anything, unable to fight for Auger. He couldn't do that. He couldn't allow that.

Omen threw the remote into Limerence's face and he bolted.

The air closed round him for a moment as the cop attempted to stop him, but Omen's friends blundered between them, cutting off Limerence's hold, and Omen ran on. By the time he got to the stairs, an alarm was ringing out through the whole school. The doors started to slam shut.

Omen lunged through the front door before it sealed, stumbled down the steps and out into the street. He wrapped the leather strap around his wrist, took off his blazer and tie as he walked quickly away, stuffing them into the first bin he came to. A City Guard patrol car passed, braking sharply outside the school gates. Omen kept walking.

He made it to the gym on Ascendance Street, a gym he'd never actually trained in, but where he was a fully paid-up member, and went straight to his locker. He got changed into jeans and a T-shirt and transferred his phone, wallet and the cloned remote into the jacket that he pulled on. He grabbed his go-bag – Crepuscular had taught him to always have a go-bag for emergencies – and put on a baseball cap with a sigil stitched into it that would disrupt any security cameras he happened to walk by.

He left the gym and joined the flow of pedestrian traffic until he could hop on a tram. He had hoped to take it right up to Shudder's Gate, then grab a lift out of Roarhaven entirely – but the exit was blocked by the sudden arrival of extra City Guard officers. Omen put his head down and the tram passed, looping round to take him back into the heart of the city.

He ate at a café, then spent the day walking through various bookshops, examining each shelf, trying to look like he wasn't wasting time while he waited for something to occur to him. Having a go-bag was all well and good, he realised, but he also needed a plan for what to do once he'd grabbed it.

He popped into another café to use the toilet. When he was done, he looked at himself in the mirror. He looked like a scared little boy. He realised his phone was in his hand, realised he was waiting for permission to call Crepuscular and plead for help. Permission from whom, he didn't know. He scowled at his reflection as he put his phone away. He slung his bag over his shoulder and left the toilets, and walked straight into a City Guard officer.

The cop would probably have passed him right by were it not for the fact that Omen jerked back and then froze.

The man frowned at him. "You OK?"

"Yes," said Omen. "Thank you."

The frown deepened. "What's your name?"

"My name?"

"There's a Corrival student everyone's looking for," the cop said. "Is that you?"

"I'm not a student," said Omen, attempting a laugh. "I mean,

I was a student, but that was last year, so I'm not a student any more. I'm nineteen years old. Thank you. How old are you?"

"What's your name?"

Omen's mind went blank.

"Did you hear me? What's your name?"

"Derp," said Omen.

"Derp?"

"Filament Derp, yes."

"What kind of name is Derp?"

"It's French."

"It doesn't sound French."

"Do you speak French?" Omen asked him.

"A little."

"Do you, though?"

"Not really."

"Then Derp is French for *irony*."

"Huh," said the cop. "I didn't know that."

"Not many people do. Apart from, like, seventy million French people."

"Where are you headed now?"

"I'm on my way home."

"Where do you live?"

"That way," Omen said, pointing.

"I suppose you'd better get back, then," said the cop, "assuming you are who you say you are. There's no reason why you wouldn't be, is there?"

"None that I can think of."

The cop nodded, smiled, and then lunged, grabbing fistfuls of Omen's jacket and slamming him back against the wall. "*Petit imbécile!*" he roared. "*Pensais-tu que je ne connaîtrais pas ma propre langue?*"

"Please," Omen gasped. "I can't understand a word you're saying!"

"I'm French, you buffoon!"

"You can't be," Omen gurgled. "You didn't know what Derp means."

The cop went to shout even louder and Omen struck him under the chin with the heel of his palm, swept his legs, then crunched his face into the ground.

"I'm really sorry," he said, and ran out of the café.

There was another cop sitting in a patrol car outside and his eyes widened when he saw Omen's face, and Omen turned left and just sprinted, didn't know where he was going or who was even after him any more, he just knew that he had to run.

It had started to rain by the time he couldn't run any more, and, when he'd staggered to a gasping, panting stop, he realised he was outside Doctor Synecdoche's medical clinic. Sirens cut through the night, getting closer, and Omen went to knock just as the door opened and he was dragged inside.

63

The shield had gone up, a dome of energy that covered Roarhaven. Instead of making the people beneath it feel safer, however, it seemed to have had the opposite effect. Everyone was jumpier today. Suspicious.

Certainly the High Sanctuary personnel that Valkyrie managed to speak to were suspicious of her motives whenever she raised the subject of the Void meteorite. It would have been downright insulting if she wasn't actually planning on betraying them all. Besides, Valkyrie was far too tired to be insulted, and she didn't have the time for it, either. Her only hope, as she joined Creed in his office, was that the Nexus Helmet just wouldn't work. If she could have that stroke of good fortune, then maybe, maybe, she could get some sleep and search for the meteorite while able to form coherent thoughts.

Two of the High Sanctuary's top scientists fitted the helmet carefully on to Creed's head. With its many towers and spires, it as much resembled the Dark Cathedral as its more obvious counterpart – the helmet Mevolent wore into battle. The scientists adjusted the tightness and checked the lenses, ran all kinds of tests while Valkyrie leaned against the wall, struggling to stay awake. Once they were finished, they backed away like they were retreating from an unstable explosive. The whole time, Creed kept looking out of his office window at the Faceless One standing over Dublin.

"This is a momentous day," said the priest, Eliezer. "A day that will live forever in legend and myth, when the mind of an exceptional sorcerer reaches towards the divine, and makes contact with the Faceless Ones for the first time."

Valkyrie yawned. "I'm literally standing right here."

The priest blinked at her. "Sorry?"

"I've already made contact with them."

"Oh," said Eliezer, blushing. "Yes. I meant... I only meant that the mind of an exceptional, uh—"

"Male sorcerer?" Valkyrie prompted. "Is that what you meant?"

"No! No, not at all!"

"Then...?"

"I just meant that today is a great day because... because..."

"Because a dude is about to do what a girl did ages ago?"

Eliezer swallowed. "Yes."

"Silence, please," said Creed.

Eliezer bowed. "A thousand apologies."

Valkyrie raised an eyebrow. "Get on with it."

Creed did an impressive job of ignoring her. "I am ready," he said.

The scientists looked nervous, like they knew that if this went wrong they'd probably be killed in some horribly petty way. They nodded to each other, and activated the helmet.

Valkyrie felt the rush of sensations, of words and feelings too alien to be fully comprehended by a flesh-and-blood brain flow through the helmet and Creed stood up out of the chair, his legs rigid, his hands curled, the tendons in his neck so taut she looked away in case they snapped. The Faceless Ones probed Creed's mind and did it not delicately. They barged around in there, flinging his thoughts to the rocks, stomping through memories like they were puddles, uprooting the trees that formed the forest that was his personality.

Valkyrie felt all this and it gave her a headache. To Creed, it was agony.

She tapped the amulet on her hip and her necronaut suit flowed over her clothes. Just in case.

The stomping subsided, and some Faceless Ones withdrew from Creed's mind and some remained, and she felt their curiosity, and their puzzlement, and Creed's head turned and he looked at Valkyrie, his eyes narrowing behind his helmet. She could almost pinpoint the moment Creed and the Faceless Ones figured out she was no longer under their influence.

Dammit.

White lightning burst from her torso and the people around her went flying and she hurried to Creed, taking the handcuffs from her pocket.

But Creed knew what she was about to do, or the Faceless Ones did, or maybe there wasn't a whole lot of difference between them at this point, and something new rushed in through the helmet. Not feelings, this time, not sensations, not even thoughts.

But power.

It hit Creed and he jerked back and the shockwave knocked Valkyrie off her feet. She went rolling over the priest's unconscious form and got up again to see Creed shivering violently.

He took a deep breath and straightened, and looked at her.

Valkyrie caught him with a lightning blast that smacked him against the wall and dropped him to his knees. She ran to him, twisted his right arm, went to attach the handcuff, but he tore his hand away, grabbed her as he stood, lifted her into the air and slammed her to the floor. Her suit absorbed much of the impact and she lit him up when he reached for her. He staggered, growling in pain. She stood.

He looked at her, glared at her through the eyeholes of the mask, and she glimpsed the magic behind that glare right before it hit her. It tore the floor away and burst the wall outwards. The necronaut suit protected her body, but Creed's power shredded her face as she flew backwards. She tumbled with masonry and choked on blood and clouds of dust and she fell, with the rain, from the Dark Cathedral.

She couldn't see, and didn't know which way was up and which was down, and didn't even try to fly. Instead, she pulled her magic in and reinforced her body's integrity and she fell all the way to the street below and collided with the ground and the ground cracked.

Valkyrie lay there, bones broken, organs failing, listening to the cries of alarm and running feet and the sound the rain made. She watched, through tear-filled eyes, the people around her – some coming to help, some running the other way. She couldn't blame them.

Creed landed close by. She tried to rise but couldn't.

"They see you now, Valkyrie Cain," said Creed. His voice sounded weird in the helmet. "The Child and the Mother and the Traitor. You are the proof they never needed that humankind is beneath their consideration. The faithful will be rewarded. The blasphemers shall be punished. Your world changes now, in this moment."

Something shifted, like the temperature turning sideways, and Valkyrie's eyes flickered over to Khrthauk as it shimmered, and all its ridges and tentacles and mass and mandibles slowly developed shadows as the light from the sun hit this being and couldn't pass through any more. It had become solid. It was visible – not only to sorcerers but now to everyone. To the whole world.

She looked back at Creed as his boot came in and he kicked the consciousness out of her.

64

Around the world, the Faceless Ones announced their presence.

Impossibly massive monsters became visible, became tangible. They stood on the horizon, bigger than mountains – but it wasn't just horizons on which they stood. They crushed cities underfoot and blocked out the sun. Passenger planes crashed into their flanks unnoticed, and fighter jets sent their missiles to explode against limbs, tentacles, twisted torsos and claws. Not a thing made them flinch, for mountains do not flinch.

And then the smaller monsters came up out of the Earth.

The Shalgoth broke through the roads and the pavements and the streets, bursting water pipes, snapping cables, cutting power. They swiped at cars and trampled pedestrians. They grabbed those who tried to run with their claws or pincers or tentacles. Those they flung away screamed and the screams merged with the alarms and the sirens.

Some climbed up through the floors of office buildings, crashed through homes and schools and hospitals.

The Shalgoth emerged first in Dublin. A few minutes later in Melbourne. Then Philadelphia, Moscow and Berlin. Next came Liverpool and Cape Town and Cairo. City after city. No country was spared.

The police responded first and the monsters didn't notice their bullets. The militaries of the world struck next. Some of the monsters, the ones without armoured hides, howled in pain and outrage and lashed out in devastating fury.

As this footage filled the airwaves, as panicked reports of death and destruction scrolled ever faster across the screens of terrified mortals huddled together, there were new reports of people doing astonishing things, of throwing fireballs, of shooting energy from their hands and eyes. Of flying.

The Faceless Ones had announced their presence and immediately unleashed the Shalgoth upon the world, and the sorcerers rose up to fight them.

65

The front door splintered under the blast of energy and the sorcerers walked into the Edgley home like they were masters of the world. Three of them, one City Guard and two murderous thugs, upturning furniture as they passed through the house. They called out for Valkyrie's parents, for her little sister, enjoying every moment of their new-found freedom to hurt mortals in public. They were loving this. All the nasty little daydreams they'd been storing away were now rushing out into the universe, manifesting in reality.

Tanith had another dose of reality waiting for them.

She dropped from the ceiling. They whirled, but her sword sang, and in moments they were dead.

"You can come down," she called, sheathing the sword beneath her coat. "Go straight out the door, though. Don't look over here."

Desmond came down the stairs with Alice at his side, his hand clamped over the back of her head, making sure her face was buried in his shirt. Melissa came after them, carrying their bags. Neither even glanced at the bodies.

A minivan pulled up outside, splashing through puddles on with the wet road, as Tanith caught up with them. The door slid open. Beryl, Fergus, Carol and Crystal were already seated, and of them only Crystal looked calm. Valkyrie's parents turned to Tanith.

"We're not going anywhere until you give us a straight answer," Desmond said. "Where's Steph? Is she OK?"

"She's fine," Tanith lied, looking up the road for enemy reinforcements. "She's busy. She sent us to get you to safety."

"She said you're the enemy," Melissa said.

"If you didn't trust me, you wouldn't have let me into your house," said Tanith.

Desmond grabbed Alice's jacket off the rack, one-handed. "Where's our security detail?"

"The Cleavers have joined us, and the sorcerers who were here have been called back to Roarhaven. Please, we don't have time for this. Everything will be explained when you get to where you're going."

"And where is that?"

"I don't know," Tanith said. "It's safer if I don't know. You're Valkyrie's only weakness, and if they get to you, they'll get to her. I can't know where you're going because if they catch me, they'd find you."

"We should go," called Fergus from the minivan.

Desmond ignored him. "We're not her weakness," he said, anger in his voice. "We're her strength. Tanith, you tell us what's going on right now, or we're not going anywhere. Those monsters, the ones on the news – they're real?"

"Yes."

"And Stephanie's on their side, or she's on our side?"

A hesitation. "She was on their side," Tanith said, figuring that honesty would be the fastest way out of this. "She was converted, but she's better now. I think she's on our side again."

Melissa frowned. "You think?"

"I haven't seen her in a while."

"Is she OK?"

"I don't know."

"I want Stephanie," Alice said, and started crying.

Desmond patted her back. "It's going to be OK, sweetheart. Stephanie's the strongest one there is. She's the hero."

Tanith nodded. "She is the hero, but if they catch you, that's the end of her. You get me? You have to go. You'll be taken somewhere safe and remote and you'll have a team guarding you. Get in the van and leave. Now."

Melissa pointed at her. "You keep my daughter safe."

"I will."

They got in the minivan.

66

It was first period when the phones started going off.

"Hey, now," said Mr Martinez, "you know the deal with this stuff. Phones off in class."

Tyler looked around as everyone started getting calls and texts and Mr Martinez stopped complaining, and took out his own phone. Tyler's cell buzzed. It was a message from his mom.

GET HOME NOW

Students were running in the hall. Some of them were crying. Panic spread through the air and Tyler opened a social-media app and tapped on a video.

Helicopter footage of what remained of Houston filled the screen. The city burned around a monster that looked like a jackal turned inside out. It swiped at buildings with its massive claws and the buildings toppled into the fire. The monster's head was lost in clouds of smoke.

Tyler grabbed his bag and joined the stream of kids flowing out the front door. He found Mila and they ran home. The door to the basement was open.

Tyler was first to the stairs, beating Mila by a mere moment. They got to the bottom and Tyler's dad was standing in front of

Frightening with the gun pointed at his head, and Frightening was on his feet with his hands up.

"You tell me!" Tyler's dad shouted. "You tell me what the hell is going on or I swear I will pull this goddamn trigger!"

"Dad!" Mila cried. "What are you doing?"

"Get upstairs, kids!"

"Dad, no!"

"The monsters!" he said. "You think they don't have anything to do with these sorcerers? That what you think? They brought them here! They probably unleashed them!"

Tyler stood between his dad and Frightening. "Dad, Frightening's a good guy. He's trying to help. He saved me, remember?"

Tyler's dad pushed Tyler to one side. "Tyler, go upstairs! Both of you, go to your rooms!"

"Dad, no!"

"Cooper!" their mom shouted.

"Mom!" Mila yelled. "Down here!"

Their mom came running down. "Cooper, what the hell are you doing?"

"He knows something!" Tyler's dad said, waving the gun in Frightening's face. "He knows what's going on!"

"So why are you pointing a gun at him? Put that thing down!"

"The monsters are killing people!"

"Yes!" the mom roared. "I know! And everyone's scared and none of us know what to do! You know who else is scared, Cooper Clonston? Your mother! She's sitting at home right now and you know that she's watching cable news and it is blowing her little mind! She's alone and she's scared and she's waiting for her son to come fetch her and bring her back to his house where she can stay with family until the world figures itself out! Isn't that so, Cooper?"

Tyler's dad stared at her. Then he said, "Yeah," and he stopped pointing the gun at their captive.

67

It was three weeks after the Faceless Ones had appeared to mortals, and thousands – tens of thousands – of Shalgoth had crawled out of the ground to begin their attacks. Omen still watched the mortal news channels with a cold, sick feeling in his gut.

He watched shaky camera footage of people running from the Shalgoth, cars being hurled into buildings, power lines being ripped down, and fires raging across cities on which Faceless Ones stood. Journalists, reporting from war zones that had popped up on their own front doors, showed video of sorcerers using magic in broad daylight, in full view of the world's media, all the old rules forgotten in a last, desperate attempt to save as many lives as possible.

He became aware of a presence in the room and looked round. Doctor Synecdoche – Reverie, as she insisted he call her – stood in the doorway, her face drawn and pale, her eyes fixed on the screen. Omen muted the TV and the clinic fell into silence. The only sound was the rain against the window.

He knew that look on her face by now. "You have news," he said.

Reverie came in, sat in her armchair by the fireplace. It was late and she looked tired. "It's Valkyrie," she said.

"She's been spotted?"

"She's been arrested."

"But she's the Child and the Mother," said Omen. "She's one of them."

"My last client of the day – she just left – said her wife was passing the Dark Cathedral a few weeks ago, the day the world went crazy. She said she saw Valkyrie on the road outside. Actually *on* the road, lying on it. Someone in a mask or a helmet was kicking her – from the muscles, it might have been Creed himself, but she said it was hard to tell. Cathedral security came running out and they shackled her, and the City Guard closed off the road and activated cloaking spheres and everyone was told to move along or be arrested."

"And you're only hearing about it now?"

"Everyone's too afraid to talk. They don't know who's listening."

"But... wait. If they arrested her, that means she's their enemy, right? So is she on our side? Is Valkyrie a good guy again?"

"It... it looks like it. But they've had her for weeks, Omen. *Weeks.* For all we know, she's dead."

"No." Omen couldn't help it: a spark of hope flickered inside him. "If she was dead, Creed would have announced it. She's alive, and they have her, so she'll escape. She'll escape or Skulduggery or the resistance will free her."

"I hope you're right, Omen, I really do." Reverie looked miserable. "But everything's different now. No matter what happens, we can't go back to the way things were."

"Skulduggery will find a way, Doctor. Valkyrie will find a way. I know them."

"I'm afraid there's only so much that even Skulduggery Pleasant and Valkyrie Cain can achieve." She took a deep breath. "But I think we should refocus on getting you out of Roarhaven. The City Guard have tolerated me because my clinic provides care for people who don't want to be seen by High Sanctuary doctors, but I'm too closely linked to members of the resistance."

"You think they'll come to arrest you?"

"It's always been just a matter of time and, given the speed with which events are unfolding, I don't have much of that left. I'm expecting—"

Reverie's eyes flickered away from him and she frowned. Omen followed her gaze, and snatched up the remote to unmute the TV.

"—away from school," his mother was saying.

His father stood by her side, wearing the gravest and most serious of his expressions. They were making this statement from the steps of the High Sanctuary.

"Ever since he lost his brother, Omen's behaviour has been erratic and deeply out of character. He is not a troublemaker, he is not a rabble-rouser, he is not a rebel. He is an ordinary little boy who is scared and easily influenced."

Caddock nodded. "The Darkly family stands with Supreme Mage Creed, with the Church of the Faceless, and with the High Sanctuary. We have no tolerance for this ridiculous, murderous resistance, who are doing far more harm to the fabric of our society than they realise."

He put an arm round Emmeline's shoulders. "We lost Auger when, through circumstances beyond his control, he became Obsidian. We will mourn him. We will remember him. We will honour him."

"But Omen has chosen to abandon us," said Emmeline. "He has betrayed the family legacy. He has stained forever the family name." She bravely steadied her quivering bottom lip. "From this day on, Omen Darkly is no son of mine."

Reverie crossed over to Omen, took the remote from his hand and clicked off the TV. He kept staring at the screen.

"Omen..."

"They've disowned me?"

"Omen, they're under a lot of pressure."

"Everyone's under a lot of pressure. Everyone's scared and worried and panicking. But they... they've disowned me?" He laughed. He actually laughed.

There was a knock on the door.

They looked at each other. The doctor's apartment was on

the top floor of her clinic, and to get up there would require bypassing the security measures on street level.

"Get to the spare room," she said.

Omen hurried through the apartment to the room with the spare bed and the secret escape hatch. He closed the door, but not all the way, and looked around for a weapon. The leather strap on his wrist successfully hid his bracelet's signal, but did nothing to stop it from nullifying his magic. He picked up a lamp and wrapped the cord round its base.

The doctor opened the apartment door. He heard her talking. Heard someone responding. No shouting. No cries. Then he heard footsteps leading back to the living room.

"A nice place you've got here." A man's voice. American. Omen recognised it, but couldn't place it.

"Thank you," said Reverie. "Could I ask what this is about, please?"

"Of course, of course," said the man, with a smile in his voice. "You're entitled to know what brings someone like me to your door, after all. Do you know who I am?"

"You're Silas Nadir," said Reverie. "The serial killer."

"Former serial killer," Nadir said. "I've been adjusted. Up here. Three Sensitives went into my head and sorted me right out. I'm better now."

"I'm not altogether sure that something like that is possible," said Reverie.

"It is," Nadir responded, and his voice moved. He was walking round the living room, probably examining the books in the book-case, picking up the framed photographs, and generally intruding into Reverie's home. "And, now that I'm a productive member of society, I have dedicated my life to helping people find the true way, into the light of the Faceless Ones."

Reverie paused. "That's an interesting prosthetic."

"Do you like it?" Nadir asked. "When my hand was cut off, I was... upset. I was overcome with feelings of anger. I felt the need to punish everyone in order to gain some sense of vengeance. But it's when they were attaching the prosthetic that they sent the Sensitives into my brain. They figured since we're fixing one part of him, why not fix it all?"

"It works well, does it?"

"My brain or my hand?" Nadir said, and chuckled. "Both work great, thank you. My thoughts are nice and clean and, as of today, my new appendage has yet to spill innocent blood."

"And why are you here, Mr Nadir?"

"Ah! To the point, Doctor! I like that! A student called Omen Darkly – I believe you know him – has run away from Corrival Academy and I am one of many who have been asked to find him. His parents are very worried about him. The world has changed – it's a lot more dangerous than it used to be."

"And you care, do you?"

A laugh. "There was a time when I wouldn't have given a damn about the well-being of a silly teenager, but I've changed, along with the world. Now all lives are precious to me – especially the life of one so young. My childhood was not a happy time for me – in many ways, it made me the person I became – so, if there is anything I can do to help this missing student, I am willing to do it."

"And why did Omen run away?" Reverie asked.

"Now, Doctor, whoever said I was looking for Omen Darkly?" asked Nadir, a note of triumph in his voice.

There was a short silence. "You did," said Reverie.

"I did?"

"At the start, yes."

Omen could just picture Nadir shrugging. "Oh. Well, who knows why he ran away? Kids are stupid. I used to run away all the time."

"And do you think he came here?"

"Do I think who came here?"

"Omen Darkly."

That note of triumph again. "Whoever said I was looking for Omen Darkly?"

"Mr Nadir, are you feeling OK?"

There was another pause. Nadir cleared his throat. "Yes. I'm fine. Thank you. I'm checking here because the boy knows you, and might come to you if he's in danger."

"Why would he be in danger?"

"I didn't say he was in danger."

"You said he might come here if—"

"I know what I said," Nadir snapped, and Omen tensed. A moment passed. "I'm sorry. That was rude."

"Mr Nadir, you've gone quite pale."

"Just a headache."

"I don't know where Omen is, Mr Nadir. I haven't seen him."

"I get headaches."

"If you give me the name of your doctor, I can call to—"

"What do doctors know?" Nadir snarled. "They don't know what the hell they're talking about. They tried to get me to stay in that little room for more observation. Look at me. Do I look like I need more observation? I'm of no use to anyone talking about how I'm feeling or what I'm thinking. I should be out here, helping people by knocking on doors. Where is he, Doctor?"

"I don't know."

At the sound of a stumble, Omen left the room and took five long, quiet steps towards the living-room doorway.

"I know he's here," said Nadir. "You think I'm stupid, Doc? You think I came up here without knowing what I know? What kind of serial killer do you think I was? A goddamn amateur? I stalked. I planned. I took my damn time. Omen Darkly's been missing for weeks and most of the people sent to look for him think he made it out of Roarhaven, but I know better. I've been talking to people. All kinds of people. I spoke to your neighbours. I spoke to your clients. Some of them really didn't want to tell me, but I made them."

"What did you do to them, Mr Nadir?"

"I asked them some questions," Nadir said, his voice tight. "Asked if they'd seen anything. Heard anything. Suspected anything."

"Mr Nadir, you're hurting me."

"I'm gonna do more than hurt you. Where are you hiding him?"

"I'm not hiding anyone."

"You think I won't kill you, Doc? You think I won't—"

There was the sound of someone being hit and Nadir grunted and there was a scramble and Reverie cried out and Omen ran in. Nadir had Reverie on her knees, his left hand yanking her hair, his right arm raised. Instead of a right hand, he had what looked like a large spider made of black metal sprouting from his wrist, and all of those thin arms thrashed at the air.

Nadir turned, saw him, and Omen threw the lamp and it cracked open on Nadir's face. Reverie scrambled up, Omen grabbed her and they left the apartment, running down the stairs. The door ahead was open and they plunged into the night.

"Get to the resistance," Omen said.

She held on to his arm. "You're coming with me."

He freed himself. "I'll be fine. Run!"

He took off, and Reverie hesitated, then forced herself to run the other way. A moment later, Silas Nadir burst out, saw Omen, and sprinted after him.

Nearly slipping on the wet road, Omen risked a glance behind him, saw that he was actually increasing his lead. He allowed the possibility that he might be outperforming someone physically to bolster his stamina, and tried to lose the maniac behind him down a maze of alleys that led to Oldtown.

It was going pretty well until three gunshots went off like explosions and Omen came to a staggering stop, his hands up as he turned, wincing, expecting to catch a bullet in the chest. But Nadir just trained the gun on Omen as he staggered after him, then leaned against the wall, sucking in lungfuls of air. His face was flushed and sweating. Omen could have run on forever.

Nadir tried to say something, then changed his mind and focused on his breathing. He hunkered down, leaning back against the wall, the gun wavering slightly in his left hand.

Omen waited.

"If you hadn't..." Nadir began, before a sudden intake of breath derailed the conversation. He shook his head. Breathed in. Breathed out.

Then a big man stepped into the light, and for a moment Omen thought it might be someone from the resistance come to rescue him, but his hopes were dashed against the rocks of reality, then stomped on by the oversized feet of the murderer-for-hire, Tancred Bold.

"Found him," Tancred called.

"You didn't... find him," Nadir gasped. "I... found him. I caught him. Go away."

"Hush, little murderer," said Tancred.

Reznor Rake sauntered through the rain. "Omen Darkly," he said, smiling as though greeting an old friend, "the world throws us back together, eh? It's fate, is what it is."

"I'm the one who found him," Nadir said, getting his breathing under control.

"You're the one who found him first," Reznor corrected. "But we've been following you, and now we're the ones who found him second. But so what? We're all on the same side, am I right? We're all working for Creed."

"I guess," said Nadir.

"Actually, no," Reznor said. "We're not on the same side at all. See, we have a history with Omen. He lost us money and he lost us work. Our reputation was severely damaged by this kid."

"Damocles Creed wants him brought in for interrogation."

"Creed can have him when we're done with him."

Nadir squared up to Reznor, showed him his spider hand. "You really want to tangle with me, Rake?"

"Oh," said Reznor, "probably not. But he will."

Tancred punched Nadir so hard, when he hit the ground his feet started twitching. Reznor and Tancred approached Omen.

"Don't look so worried," said Reznor. "We're not going to hurt you if you don't do anything that makes us hurt you."

"If you're not going to turn me over to the City Guard, then what do you want with me?" Omen asked.

"It's like we said to the serial killer – you damaged our reputation. Until recently, we were a safe pair of hands. Hire us to do a job, we did the job. Hire us to kill someone, that person got killed. Hire us to steal something, that something got stolen. Hire us to do both? Both got done. But then you took the Obsidian Blade from us, and we failed to deliver on a contract, and our reputation hasn't recovered. We were beaten by a bunch of, and I don't mean this in a negative way, a bunch of stupid schoolkids. You see how that would affect our standing in the killing-and-stealing business?"

"I can see it."

"So we've been looking for ways to regain that lost ground. This is nothing personal, by the way. You beat us fair and square. Or rather you beat *Tancred* fair and square, and that guy in the Cleaver outfit beat *me* fair and square."

"I was outnumbered," Tancred grumbled.

"So we've been looking around," Reznor continued, "searching for some way back to the top of the heap, and it turns out that all we had to do was wait a while until our old friend Omen Darkly got himself mixed up with this resistance we hear so much about on the Network. Now we're thinking, if we get Omen, and we place Omen in a precarious situation where his very life is on the line, his brave friends in the plucky resistance ought to come running to his rescue. Am I right?"

"You want to use me as bait?" Omen asked.

"That's about the long and short of it, yeah."

"It won't work. I'm not actually a part of all that."

"See, I don't think that really matters. What matters is that

Skulduggery Pleasant and his friends know you, and like you, and are willing to risk it all to come to your rescue if you get a message to them."

"And why would I do that?"

"Because we'll cut bits off you if you don't," said Tancred.

"Hey, now, come on, you don't have to threaten the kid," Reznor said. "We're not going to cut bits off you, don't worry."

Omen glared. "I won't lead them into a trap."

Reznor frowned at him. "You realise we're going to cut bits off you, right?"

"I'm not bait. I won't do it."

"We'll make you," Tancred growled.

"Then fine, I'll do it."

"Really?"

"Sure," said Omen. "But I'll slip a code into the message so that they know it's a trap."

Tancred leaned in. "You'd better not."

"You won't know either way," said Omen.

Tancred glanced at Reznor. "Damn," he said.

"I have a counter-proposal," said Omen.

Reznor laughed. "Oh, this'll be good."

"I won't help you regain your old reputation," Omen said, "but I will help you make a new one – a stronger one. Creed's got China Sorrows in a jail cell, and Valkyrie Cain, too. He'll expect the resistance to try to save them. He won't expect you two to free them before that happens."

Now Tancred laughed. "You want us to rescue China Sorrows and Valkyrie Cain?"

"Yes."

"You want us to act against Damocles Creed? To act against all these Faceless Ones standing around and the monsters that're popping up all over the world?"

"Yes."

"Why should we?" Reznor asked, his expression thoughtful.

"Because we're going to win," said Omen. "Skulduggery Pleasant and Valkyrie Cain and everyone in the resistance, they're going to win. Creed is going to lose. The monsters are going to be beaten and the Faceless Ones are going to be exiled. They've run away before and they'll run away again. They've proven that. Everyone who's working alongside Creed will have everything taken away from them. Right now, yeah, it's safe to be on Creed's side – but that's going to change, and when it does it'll be too late to switch. You'll be hunted. You'll be captured or killed."

"And what if you're wrong, and the resistance fails and Creed wins?"

Omen shrugged. "Then I'll probably be dead, so I won't much care."

Reznor chewed his bottom lip, then pointed at Omen. "You stay right there."

They stepped away to confer and Omen waited. Silas Nadir's feet had stopped twitching and he lay on the ground, safely unconscious. It had stopped raining.

Reznor and Tancred came back.

"We've talked it over," said Reznor. "What you're proposing is a huge gamble. A massive, ridiculous gamble. It all comes down to who we think will win. And who can possibly know that? Talk to a dozen different Sensitives, ask them to tell the future, and they'll come back with a dozen different visions."

"It *is* a tricky situation."

"Add in the minor detail that your entire argument stems from the fact that you'd say anything to get out of this situation – so you and your suggestion, by the very situation you're in, are already compromised."

"This is very true."

"But that doesn't change the fact that – even though you might well have been making it all up as you went along – you make a very good point."

"A very good one."

"So we've decided to work with you," said Reznor, "and rescue Valkyrie Cain and China Sorrows. But first some ground rules. You do what we say, when we say it. You don't try to run away, or turn us in, or act to harm us or inconvenience us at any stage."

Omen nodded. "If I can help it."

"At all."

Omen nodded again. "At all, if I can help it."

"I swear to God, kid, there's something about you that I just want to punch, you know?" Reznor sighed. "Come on. Let's get you out of here."

68

This was it. This was the speech he'd be remembered for. These next few minutes would be his legacy.

"We're live in five," said the guy with the headset, "four, three," then he held up two fingers, then one and then pointed, and the red light on the top of the camera came on.

"My fellow Americans," said Flanery, "my fellows humans, I speak to you today on a matter of grave importance. This is a day that will go down in history as the most important day in human existence. A day when we, humanity, stand up against the terrors that threaten us, and begin to fight back.

"We have seen, in the last few weeks, devastation on an unprecedented, unimaginable scale around the world. We have witnessed the emergence of previously unknown animals of astonishing size and the chaos and destruction they are leaving in their wake. While they stand there, motives unknown, we have seen other animals attack and kill people in our cities and towns, on our farms and ranches, in our trailer parks and apartment complexes... Nowhere is safe from what many people are calling *monsters.*"

Flanery paused for dramatic effect. He'd gone off-script slightly there, but he thought it added a common touch that the speech was otherwise lacking. His team had advised him not to use the word *monster* – they said it would cause panic in the populace – and he'd agreed, but right now, with all the lights and the camera and the fact that the world was watching, he'd realised that he'd look stupid if he didn't call them what they were. He'd also been advised not to use the phrase "nowhere is safe", but he figured the only way that people were going to be reassured is if they were first fully aware of the dangers that were facing them.

"I have mobilised the full might of the American military to battle these monsters, and we have already seen incredible victories across our wonderful strong nation."

Another slight deviation from the script that wasn't strictly true, but his advisors had told him that a victory was possible and probably even inevitable, so he doubted he'd ever have to walk back those words.

"We have also seen a secondary threat emerge," he continued, really getting into the sombre mood now, really selling it with the grim jutting of his jaw. "Men and women, demonstrating abilities one could only call magic, have been shown in footage broadcast on social media and news networks, appearing to battle these monsters. It seems that whatever war they are fighting has spilled out of the shadows, and the casualties are people like you and me. These wizards and witches are the enemy. They may look like us, but they are not us. If you see one, call the police immediately. Do not engage, and do not try to be a hero. Barricade yourself in your home and don't come out until they have left the area."

Flanery shook his head as if he was thinking of all the lives senselessly lost. Then he looked up.

"A select few members of my administration first learned of the existence of so-called magic late last year. We kept it from you, the American people, so as not to cause widespread panic – and alert our enemies to the fact that we knew of their intentions. We wanted to better understand the situation before we told you. This is not something I was pleased with, but being president means making the tough decisions."

He put some steel behind his eyes. "So let me assure you that we are not defenceless. Some months ago, I personally instructed our very best scientists and doctors to infuse this magic into the fighting men and women of our military. I saw this coming and I prepared, and so our soldiers have been given amazing powers – superpowers – to protect American lives, American land and American interests."

If this speech had been delivered in a stadium, the people would have gone crazy at that last line. They would have screamed and cheered so loud they'd have gone hoarse. It was a damn wasted opportunity to be saying these words in the stillness of the Oval Office. Flanery made a mental note to fire someone over that decision.

"But what use is all this if and when our allies fall?" he asked. "What use is it to be the most powerful country in the world if the rest of the world is on fire? So I have decided that I will lead not only the fight-back here in America, but also in every other country that needs our help. In the coming weeks, we will make available our top-secret system of providing superpowers to the soldiers of each country who asks for our assistance."

Those who could pay, anyway.

"Tomorrow these super-soldiers will be deployed on American soil, and the world can watch as we turn the tide, as we use the wizards' own magic against them and against these abominations. Our brave heroes will combine magic with the most advanced weaponry and tactics this world has ever seen. On this day, America declares war on the sorcerers – and we will emerge victorious."

He smiled with appropriate grimness. "God bless you, and God bless the United States of America."

69

Tyler's grams was taking an afternoon nap and his mom was working a double shift and his dad sat forward, rubbing his hands together like he did whenever the fights were on and he wanted one particular guy to beat another particular guy.

"Here it is," he said. "This is gonna be good. You kids watching?"

"Yeah, Dad," said Mila.

School was closed and the internet was spotty at best thanks to all the downed lines, so cable news was their only window to the outside world. Their dad wouldn't even let them leave the house unsupervised any more.

He pointed at the screen as the soldiers advanced down the street. "There they are. Those are our boys. You see 'em?"

"Our boys and girls," Mila corrected, too worn out to get annoyed.

Tyler's dad nodded quickly. "Those are our boys and girls, absolutely, sweetheart. Absolutely. They're just like us – normal, like us – but super-charged full of that magic. Frightening Jones and all those others, they think they're better than us? Stronger than us? Uh-uh. Not with these fellas. Not with these fellas and ladies – sorry, sweetheart."

One of the smaller monsters, the kind that was bigger than an SUV but smaller than a semi-truck, was caught out alone. The chyron that flowed from the bright red LIVE banner on the bottom of the screen identified the city as Los Angeles.

Tyler couldn't help it: he sat forward, just like his dad. This was the first real test of Flanery's super-magical-warrior soldiers, and it was being broadcast live across the world. This was a big deal, and possibly signalled a turning point in the war.

The soldiers kept advancing, accompanied now by the thunder of their automatic weapons. The bullets annoyed the monster. It roared its displeasure. Then the soldiers let their guns swing back on their straps. Their hands lit up.

"Here we go," Tyler's dad said, grinning like a kid at Christmas. "Good old American muscle!"

The monster lumbered towards them. One of the soldiers lost his focus and his hands stopped glowing. Another one just stood there, hands up and teeth gritted, like he'd forgotten how to make the energy leave his body. The rest of the soldiers actually managed to release their streams of energy.

They hit the monster and were ignored, and the monster reared back and its belly convulsed. When it dropped back down, it vomited a thick flaming liquid that struck a police van on the far side of the street and scorched through it. Then it turned its head, and the liquid seared through the soldiers.

"I'm... sorry," said the news anchor, her face pale, "we seem to have lost the signal. We'll... We're trying to re-establish... We'll be back after this commercial break. Don't go away."

Tyler's dad sagged back in his chair.

70

Tanith slowed to a stop, put her foot on the street and frowned at the building ahead. An ice-cream parlour, painted a pleasing yellow. On a nice day, in a world without monsters killing everyone, it might have been a lovely place to stop by. But today it was too still, for some reason. It just sat there, this building, like it was waiting for something.

There was movement inside, movement behind the windows, and then the whole front of the building burst towards her and a Shalgoth came stumbling out. This was a big one, two storeys high and bloated. Tanith twisted the throttle and the back wheel spun and she turned the bike and shot forward, the monster right behind and snapping at her with its great lobster claws.

The bike screamed down the street and she shot across the intersection and the Shalgoth came barrelling after her, throwing parked cars out of its way, snapping lamp posts, roaring at her the whole time. She veered left and it was a mistake, but she had to keep going, and she slalomed between wreckage and rubble.

The sounds of destruction behind her stopped and instantly she turned the bike, barely avoiding the Shalgoth as it landed. She juddered down some steps and was off again, the monster launching itself into the narrow space between the buildings above. It scuttled overhead, tearing chunks out of the masonry on either side. Tanith lowered herself in her seat, the wind ripping at her hair as broken bricks hit the ground all around her. One of them struck the front wheel and the bike wobbled and Tanith sprang off. She curled up and tumbled through the air. The bike skidded along the street on its side, leaving a trail of sparks, and she landed with one foot on its front cowl and the other on the exhaust, surfing it to slow her momentum and then springing off again when the Shalgoth tried to drop on her.

She sprinted round the corner, almost froze when confronted with the squad of soldiers waiting there.

She ducked and they opened fire and the Shalgoth bellowed its anger. Keeping low, Tanith scrambled forward, and one of the soldiers grabbed her and pulled her behind them.

"Cease firing!" yelled the officer in charge, and in the sudden silence the Shalgoth roared, its skin coated with pinpricks of blood. "OK, squad," the officer said, "conventional weapons are once again proving ineffectual. I guess it's magic hour."

He took a bag from his pocket and, one by one, the soldiers pulled out a little square of paper inscribed with a sigil. At the officer's nod, they each popped the Splashes into their mouths, and these exhausted, drawn, shaken men and women suddenly straightened, their shoulders squaring and their smiles spreading. Energy started to crackle from their hands.

"Let 'em have it," the officer said, and the soldiers strode forward, blasting the Shalgoth with energy streams. The monster recoiled with every hit, roaring now in actual pain.

"Expose that belly for me!" the officer shouted, pulling a rocket launcher from the back of the truck. The others laughed, some whooped, and one of them took out his phone to record this for posterity.

Tanith watched the Shalgoth rear back. "Hold on," she said.

"Naw," said the officer, aiming. "You just stay right there and bear witness. Clear!"

He pulled the trigger and the rocket flew and hit the Shalgoth square in the belly in an explosion of fire and flesh and pink liquid. The soldiers cheered and the Shalgoth toppled, its guts slipping out of its ruined torso.

Tanith frowned. No, not guts.

A dozen creatures came slithering from that mess, finding their clawed feet and sprinting forward. The soldiers panicked, loss their ability to focus their ill-gotten magic, and scrambled for their weapons – but the creatures were on them before a shot was fired, tearing through them.

Tanith ran.

She leaped over a car and the smaller Shalgoths leaped after her, every bit as agile. She flipped over a pile of rubble, her sword skewering the creature that tried to snatch at her. She jumped from a ruined wall to a neighbouring building, and ran straight up the side of it. The creatures scrambled in pursuit, their claws slicing through brick.

She got to the roof, but they were gaining.

A window smashed above her and Skulduggery came tumbling through, tangled up with one of the creatures. He twisted at the last moment, crunching the monster's head off the rooftop, and then rolling to his feet.

"Rejoice," he said, "you're saved."

Tanith ducked a claw and slashed back in return. The creatures had them surrounded. "Yeah," she said. "I certainly feel saved."

A fireball came from nowhere, exploded across the back of one of the creatures, and Cadaver Cain landed beside them.

"*Now* you're saved," he said.

Skulduggery muttered something and the creatures dived at them.

71

"I'm not going to hurt you," said Temper, and meant it. He didn't want to hurt Kierre. He loved Kierre. He remembered loving Kierre. He remembered what that felt like.

Or he thought he did. He frowned. Did he remember it, or did he merely remember remembering it?

Kierre walked in and the heavy door shut behind her and locked. Temper tried to smile in a non-threatening manner.

"I don't know what to do," Kierre said.

She was sad. Temper could tell she was sad because of the way her mouth didn't smile. The corners turned downwards. Temper turned the corners of his own mouth downwards, too, in order to demonstrate that he was also having sad feelings.

"They're saying we should kill you," said Kierre.

"Who is saying this?" Temper asked.

"Everyone."

"Why? Why do they want to kill me? I'm their friend."

"You were their friend," Kierre said.

"I'm still me."

"You're not you, Temper."

"Kierre, look at me. Of course I am. I'm Temper Fray."

"You're Temper Fray's Gist. You overpowered the real Temper. He's gone now, he's been gone for almost a month, and you're all that's left."

She was right.

"You're wrong," said Temper. "It didn't take over. I fought back. I won."

"Have you looked in a mirror lately?" she asked.

He smiled. "They won't let me have a mirror. They won't let me have sharp things."

"Before they put you in here, they let you see yourself, didn't they?"

Yes, they did.

"No, they didn't," he said.

"You're lying, Temper. I saw the footage."

He laughed, caught out. "Yes. They let me see myself. I don't get what the big deal is. I'm still handsome, right?"

"You're very handsome, Temper."

"I've still got a killer smile, don't I?"

Kierre took a pause. "Are you being funny?" she asked.

He smiled, running his tongue over his sharp teeth. Yeah, his teeth had grown. So had his fingernails. His fingers, too. His hands, his limbs, his torso. He'd been a tall man, but now he was taller. He'd been a strong man, but now he was stronger. A fast man, a smart man, a powerful man, and now he was faster and smarter and oh, the power that flowed through his veins made every bit of him tingle. All he wanted was to bound across to this woman he loved and kill her. He loved her so much he wanted to eat her up.

"Do you think they should kill me?" he asked her.

"I don't know," Kierre answered. "You're too dangerous to let loose. It would be kinder to kill you than keep you locked in a cage for the rest of your life."

"I'm not dangerous."

"You're every bad thought Temper ever had. You're every cruel instinct. You're every murderous impulse. You're a killer. You're a thing. You're not the Temper I knew. Not any more."

He watched her. "Let me out of these shackles."

"I loved you."

"Let me out."

"Goodbye, Temper."

He flung himself at her and the chains snapped taut, his claws almost at scratching distance from her face, and Kierre just stood there, unflinching.

"If you love me," he growled, "you'd let me kill you."

She left him in the room, alone.

72

Beneath the High Sanctuary were the holding cells. Valkyrie had stayed there once or twice, and knew them quite well. But beneath the holding cells there was a dungeon. Until she'd been chained up there, on her knees, she'd had no idea they even existed. As far as dungeons went, however, she'd been imprisoned in worse.

Her clothes were filthy, and stank. The necronaut amulet was still on her belt, but the suit had retreated from the magic-binding sigils glowing on the shackles that had rubbed her wrists raw and bloody.

Creed came to visit, still wearing the Nexus Helmet. She wondered if he ever took it off these days. She wondered if he showered with it on. Slept with it on. He probably did. He probably ruined a perfectly good night's sleep by keeping that ridiculous contraption on his stupid head.

Valkyrie would have killed for a good night's sleep. She would have killed to be able to stand up straight, for that matter.

"The Faceless Ones love you," he said.

She grunted.

"They love you and you betrayed them."

She wondered what kind of mood she was in today. Sometimes she was cocky. Other times she was angry. Recently, she'd just been frustrated and annoyed and miserable. Each time he entered the dungeon and said those words – "The Faceless Ones love you" –

Valkyrie discovered what kind of mood she was in for the day. Her life was nothing if not one endless stream of delightful surprises.

"Now, come on," she said, "that's not fair." Ah, today was a cocky day, it seemed. "I only loved the Faceless Ones because they'd messed with my head. If anyone should be mad here, if anyone should be doing the torturing, it's me."

"You are the Child and the Mother of the Faceless Ones."

"And, as their mum, I'm telling you to let me go."

"You have their brethren inside you."

"It sounds weird when you say it like that."

"I have many knives," said Creed. "I could cut them out of you."

"You tried that," Valkyrie said. The scars on her body were not even healed, and she smiled and showed missing teeth. "You had your healers repair me from my fall just so you could break me apart again."

Creed nodded. "And I know you're not afraid of disfigurement. I know you can repair yourself far better than our healers ever could, given the opportunity. I know you can regrow limbs if you ever get a chance to use magic again. You rightly see physical pain as transitory. I know that torture can only have a limited effect on you."

She nodded. "I accept your surrender."

"There will be no more torture. You will not be physically harmed again. I will instead focus on that which cannot be repaired – the world outside these walls and the people in it. They can't be replaced as you would replace a finger, or an eye, or a limb. I am aware that hope sustains you – hope for yourself and for your loved ones. The hope that this unpleasantness will pass and things will return to normal.

"But, of course, I am in the process of removing normal as an option. The role of your Sanctuaries has always been to keep magic from the mortal population of this planet, yet since you've been here, they have been given proof beyond all doubt that magic exists and the universe is a much more terrifying place than they could ever have imagined."

There was a screen on the wall behind him that lit up with news reports showing the Faceless Ones looming over the skyline and the streets crawling with Shalgoth.

"Release the rest of the Faceless Ones," said Creed.

When he'd first shown her these news reports, she'd wanted to believe the footage was doctored, that it was special effects, that it wasn't real. But she knew the truth. Magic had been shown to the world in the most awful way possible.

"There is no hope," said Creed. "You can't return to normal after this. But, if you release the Faceless Ones that are currently inside you, our Dark Gods will call off the Shalgoth. Mortal lives will be spared." The screen went dark. "If you don't, they will let the Shalgoth continue destroying your cities and killing your people."

"No," said Valkyrie. "If I release them, it's over. The mortals those monsters are killing, they'll die anyway, and more of them. All of them."

"Not all," said Creed.

"No," she said. "Just the ones your gods don't want to immediately eat."

Creed came closer. "The people you're trying to protect are dying. You're failing them."

"I'll fail them more if I do what you want."

"But you will do what we want. Your capitulation is inevitable. You're helping nobody, Valkyrie. Your resistance means nothing. There's no hope for you. You've been here for over three weeks. No one has come to save you. Roarhaven is impenetrable. There is no escape, or rescue, or triumph. The world has changed. The world you knew is over."

She shook her head. "Not yet. We can do something. We can still do something."

"You can't."

"Yes, we can. You don't know us. You think you know us, but you don't. There is a way to save the world, there is a way to fix this, and we will find it."

Creed shook his head. "You're in the most secure building on the face of the Earth. Skulduggery Pleasant and your allies are busy fighting and dying against the Shalgoth. If there is a way to save the world, you won't be part of finding it."

"There's always a way."

"Not for you."

She cracked a smile. "So long as I'm here, I'm alive. And, so long as I'm alive, I have a chance."

Creed looked at her. "Yes. You do." He sounded sad. "Very well."

She frowned after him as he walked to the door. "Very well what?"

The door opened and he turned to her. "So long as you're here, you have a chance. So long as you're alive, you have a chance. We cannot allow that to continue."

"You're not going to kill me. I still have your gods' little brothers and sisters inside me."

"And we will be unable to save all of them. Such is the sacrifice you're forcing us to make."

She lost any semblance of the smile.

"Those sigils that China Sorrows carved into your flesh prevent the Faceless Ones from sharing your mind like they're currently sharing mine," said Creed. "To remove the sigils, we'll have to remove the flesh."

Valkyrie went cold.

"Once they're sharing your mind, you will release as many of their brethren as you are able to before you die," he said, and left.

73

This one was bipedal, over twice Tanith's height, narrow-hipped and wide-shouldered. Boils covered its pink skin, and its head was squat, its eyes small, its arms so long its clawed fingers dragged on the ground when it walked.

"I'm going to call him Spot," said Cadaver.

"You called the last one Spot," Skulduggery said.

"But he didn't last long, so the name never got the chance to stick. This one's bigger. He looks like he'll have more of a chance to establish himself."

"Will you stop naming the monsters?" Tanith asked, peeking out at it from behind the rubble.

Cadaver tilted his head at her. "Why? Does it make it harder to kill them if they have a name?"

"No," she said. "It's just stupid."

Cadaver made a scoffing sound. "If we didn't do things just because they were stupid, we'd never do half the interesting things that we do."

"He has a point," said Skulduggery.

"You two are meant to have genius-level intellects," Tanith responded. "Isn't it an insult to your own intelligence to willingly do stupid things?"

"No," they both said.

The Shalgoth stalked the area outside a corner store in which cowered at least a dozen terrified mortals. It knew they were close, but it hadn't seen them. Not yet.

"We have to lead it away," Tanith said. "Cadaver, it's your pet, so that will be your job. Once it's clear, Skulduggery and I will evacuate the mortals."

"Why can't I evacuate the mortals?" Cadaver asked.

"Because you have neither a façade nor a trustworthy head," said Skulduggery. "The mortals would panic."

Cadaver sounded offended. "There is nothing wrong with my head."

"Its shape is strange and off-putting."

"Then we'll swap and you can lead Spot away."

"We are not swapping heads," Skulduggery responded.

The discussion was, thankfully, derailed by machine-gun fire, as a half-dozen soldiers advanced on the Shalgoth from a side street. Backing them up were another five soldiers firing tightly controlled energy streams that kept the monster off balance.

"Ah," said Cadaver, "some competent mortals. A rare sight, indeed."

Two more soldiers ran through, leaping at the Shalgoth, tearing at it with superhuman strength. The monster squealed and flailed, trying in vain to dislodge its attackers who now had knives in their hands. They hacked through its flesh. One of the soldiers slipped, grabbed on to the monster's leg, and skewered its knee. It stumbled and fell and the other soldiers crowded round, blasting the thing to bits.

Once it was dead, they cheered, slapped each other on the back. One of the gun-wielding soldiers slapped an energy-throwing soldier too hard, and a scuffle broke out, and before Tanith could figure out what was happening they were screaming and shooting at each other and within moments they were all lying dead.

Tanith stared. Skulduggery looked away. Cadaver laughed.

74

Valkyrie woke to see China on her knees on the opposite side of the room. The chains that held her glowed with the same sigils as the ones holding Valkyrie. "You're still alive."

China managed a weak smile. "As are you."

"They torture you?"

"Naturally."

"Did you tell them everything?"

"Naturally."

"Think it helped them in any way?"

China shook her head. "We planned on my capture. Everything I knew was already out of date when I was caught. I have to admit, Valkyrie, that I am most upset that you're not free. I don't suppose you managed to steal the Void meteorite before you were apprehended?"

"I didn't. We should have just run."

"Ah, you live and learn. I suppose I should have known it was going to go wrong. This was one of Skulduggery's plans, after all."

"You know the problem with Skulduggery's plans?" Valkyrie asked.

"They rarely work?"

"Apart from that. I've noticed that his plans are really just starting points, you know? They're designed to get us into a situation, and they do that well, but then it all falls apart. The reason, I think, is that he's always so super-confident that he can improvise his way out of it when things go wrong."

"Yes," said China. "Yes, that's him exactly."

"And that's fine for Skulduggery. It all seems to work out for Skulduggery. But for the rest of us?"

"The rest of us find ourselves in chains, in a dungeon, about to be tortured." China paused. "Granted, that also happens to Skulduggery a lot."

"Yeah," Valkyrie admitted. "OK, maybe he's just not very good at plans."

"I'm inclined to agree with you. I see you've lost a finger."

"I have, yes." Valkyrie wriggled the remaining fingers of her left hand. "But that's OK. I wasn't using it. They've been focusing lately on mental torture, you know? Sometimes, in fact, I feel that mental torture is almost worse than physical torture. But then I experience physical torture and I go, nope, physical torture is way worse."

China nodded. "It hurts more."

"It does, right? Hey, I just want to say thanks for this. You got yourself captured and you've been in chains for weeks and you did it all to help me. I really appreciate it."

China smiled. "I knew there was something special about you the first time we met, that day in my library. You kept your faith in me, Valkyrie, throughout it all, no matter what I did or what I'd done. You forgave me. You made Skulduggery forgive me. I am where I am now because of you: on my knees, in chains, in a dungeon."

"You're welcome."

"It makes you wonder, though, why we've been put in the same room."

"I'm guessing Creed wants to torture you in front of me," said Valkyrie.

"That's what I was thinking, but I was hoping you'd be too polite to say that part aloud."

"Ah, sorry. There I go again, blundering my way past social niceties. For years, you tried to teach me how to be a lady, but I never listened."

An arched eyebrow. "Being a lady isn't about politeness or manners or decorum, my dear – it's about approaching life with dignity and strength. You're the very definition of a lady."

"Ah, well." Valkyrie grinned. "*Enchantée.*"

"That's really not how you use that word."

"Oh. Sorry. Hey, now that I have you here, do you know anything about the Hosts?"

China smiled. "I should have known you'd be on that particular case."

"Wait, what? You're investigating them, too?"

"I've heard rumours about their recent activities, yes, and then Solace appeared in a dreadful attempt to distract me from continuing my enquiries. I am curious, however, as to how they appeared on the radar of Valkyrie Cain."

"It's a long story."

"I don't think either of us are going anywhere soon, dear."

"Good point. Do you remember Crepuscular Vies?"

China nodded. "What about him?"

"Until recently, he's been getting into what we used to call *adventures* with Omen Darkly. You know, helping people around the world, stopping bad guys, that kind of thing."

"So he's been manipulating Martin Flanery, he's probably the one who killed Abyssinia, *and* he's been helping people around the world? I confess, I'm confused. Is he or is he not an enemy?"

"It gets even more complicated than that. See, we actually met him, about a month ago. He used to be Fregoli Cleft."

China raised an eyebrow. "I could have sworn he was dead."

"Not dead, just captured. Tortured."

"There's a lot of that going around."

"Crepuscular blames Skulduggery for not saving him, for believing he had died, and for not coming to rescue him. He claims he's over it, that he is in no way bitter or resentful, and he's been partnering with Omen to prove that they're a better team than Skulduggery and me."

"Well, I don't know about you, Valkyrie, but that certainly sounds like someone with no unresolved psychological issues to me. And yet what has this got to do with the Hosts?"

"Crepuscular has twenty brothers and sisters," Valkyrie said, "who were involved, at some point, with that particular secret society. We're trying to find out if any of this is as sinister as we suspect. Skulduggery wasn't even sure if they really existed."

China smiled again. "That's just because he cannot fathom the existence of a secret society who would not want to have him as a member. He conveniently forgets that people like this prefer to stay anonymous – and he's anything but anonymous."

"So they're real? They actually exist?"

"They actually do."

"How do you know?"

"They invited me to join them. I said no, of course. I had little interest in joining yet another secret society. I was a founding member of two already and honorary chairperson of a third – where did they expect me to find the time?"

"Who are they?"

"They all work in various Sanctuaries around the world, safe-guarding the mortals from magical threats. They were, and are, what would be considered, to use the parlance of the day, 'good guys'. At the same time, they aren't naive enough to view the mortals as entirely placid creatures – they know they have the potential to hunt us down and destroy us. So this group, the Hosts, came up with the Doomsday Protocol."

"This last-resort weapon I've been hearing about," said Valkyrie.

"Actually, it was more like a last-resort set of instructions than an actual weapon. Combine that with a small number of dedi-cated mages – twenty of them, to be precise – and they could apparently take down the mortal power structures within hours, if not minutes. The world would be thrown into chaos, this is true, but then the Sanctuaries would be forced to take over and restore order. It's not what any of them want – but it is a better outcome than every single sorcerer being burned at the stake."

"These dedicated mages," Valkyrie said, "what do you know about them?"

"The Twenty are assassins, warriors and butchers, bred to obey."

"OK, so if Crepuscular's brothers and sisters are the same twenty warriors who are going to be sent out to destabilise the world in case of an overwhelming mortal threat, and it seems like they are, then what would count as an overwhelming mortal threat?"

"I'm sure I don't know," said China. "Perhaps a situation where magic has been revealed to the world, and a president has unleashed an army of mortal super-soldiers as he declares war on all 'wizards'? Maybe that would qualify?"

"President Flanery did that?"

"Commander Hoc showed me the press conference before he dragged me in here."

Valkyrie chewed her lip. "So Crepuscular went to all this trouble to start a war that would force the Hosts to activate the Twenty, which would then put the Sanctuaries in charge of the world? It's a whole lot of work for something that any sorcerer could kick-start quite easily, isn't it?"

China thought about it. "Then it's not about the end result," she said. "It's about something in the lead-up to the end result."

"Maybe it's not about what the Twenty will actually do – maybe it's just getting them into a position where they're able to do it. If they were active right now, if they were among us, waiting for the signal to act, Crepuscular wouldn't need them to be unleashed, would he? But if they're hidden away, if they're somehow trapped or isolated, he'd need a global emergency to free them."

"And that's his ultimate goal? To free his siblings?"

"If my family was trapped somewhere, I'd do whatever it took to rescue them. Wouldn't you?"

"Let's not dwell on what I would do, Valkyrie. If that is the case, if he's done all this to ensure that his siblings are unleashed, as you put it, the fact that they would then go on to overthrow mortal civilisation might be a sacrifice he'd feel is worth it."

"We need to explain to the Hosts what's happening," Valkyrie said. "Once they know how everyone is being manipulated, they won't unleash the Twenty, right?"

"It isn't their decision," said China. "The Doomsday Protocol is triggered by world events. Once certain things happen in the mortal world, it will begin, and no one will be able to prevent it."

"Then we stop the Twenty. We get one of the Hosts to tell us where the Twenty are being kept, and we stop them."

"Every Host is being watched by the High Sanctuary, making it extremely difficult to get to them undetected."

Valkyrie frowned. "How did Creed know to start spying on them?"

China smiled. "I'm the one who issued the surveillance order. I like to know what people in power are thinking."

"Is there a way you can get a message to any of them without Creed knowing about it?"

"I've done it before," said China, "I daresay I can do it again. Of course, for this to happen, we would both need to be free."

"Oh, I wouldn't worry about that," Valkyrie said, smiling. "I have a feeling that's going to be taken care of any... moment... now." They both looked at the door. When it didn't burst open, Valkyrie sighed. "I don't know why that never works."

"It is a mystery, my dear."

75

They found a woman, a sorcerer, with a bullet in her leg at a looted pharmacy.

"We were trying to help," she told them through gritted teeth as Skulduggery did what he could for her injury. "There was a busload of mortals with Shalgoth closing in and we gave them time to get out of there. There were six of us. Then these soldiers turned up, more of Flanery's super-soldiers, and they opened fire. Two of us... They got two of us. Shot them dead. I got away, but there are three more they took prisoner."

"Where are they keeping them?" Tanith asked.

"The mall, down that way. But I don't know if they're still alive. Have you seen – ow!"

"Sorry," Skulduggery said.

"It's OK." The woman shook her head. "Have you seen what they're doing to us? To mages? They're executing us. Either a firing squad or a hanging."

"I've seen," said Tanith.

"And that's just the soldiers. Have you seen what the mortals are doing? They're burning mages at the stake. Can you believe that? Can you actually believe what they're doing to other human beings? Goddamn savages."

"We'll get your friends back," Skulduggery told her. "If at all possible, if they're still alive, we'll get them back."

Tears ran down the woman's face, but Tanith doubted she even knew she was crying. "It's not going to be easy. These super-soldiers... the things that are giving them their power—"

"Splashes."

"—the Splashes, yeah, they're making them unstable. And I don't just mean physically. Yeah, they're jittery and they don't know how to control their magic and I've seen more than a few of them actually combust, but it's making them unstable mentally, too. I've followed the press conferences and I've heard Flanery's speeches. I know they're supposed to be the best of the best – super-powered Navy SEALs, totally in control – but they're a pack of roided-up lunatics boiling with aggression. They're killing each other as much as they're killing the Shalgoth."

"We've seen that, too," Cadaver said.

The woman looked between Skulduggery and Cadaver. "What's the deal here anyway? I thought there was only one of you."

"There is," said Skulduggery. "He's from the future."

"Hello," said Cadaver.

"Cool," the woman said.

They left her there and travelled to the mall, entering through an open skylight. Crouching among the rafters, they looked down at the food court, where the soldiers had cleared a space. The three sorcerers sat on the ground, their hands shackled behind their backs. There were nine soldiers – five of them were eating and chatting and the other four sizzling with power and spending their time glaring at the sorcerers like they wanted to tear them apart.

"I have a plan," Cadaver said quietly.

"Your plans are terrible," said Skulduggery. "We'll do my plan."

Cadaver shook his head. "Your plans never work. They appear deceptively simple, but they rely on your opponents reacting with logic and good sense, which they're never capable of."

"I much prefer a plan that overestimates the intelligence of my enemies than a plan that underestimates the intelligence of my friends."

361

"I'm not underestimating anyone."

"Your plan won't work," Skulduggery insisted.

"And your plan is doomed to failure."

"Stop, the both of you," said Tanith. "Why don't you tell me what your plans actually are, and then we'll vote on the best one?"

"Excellent idea," said Skulduggery. "Cadaver creates a distraction, leading some of the soldiers towards the east entrance. The soldiers that remain will suspect that an attack is coming and we're not going to disappoint. I'll draw their fire towards the west, allowing Tanith to drop down behind them and free the prisoners. Tanith and the prisoners will then attack the soldiers from behind. When they're down, Cadaver will lead the first team back towards us, but on the lower level. We'll have the high ground, we'll demand their surrender, and if they refuse, we'll overwhelm them."

"That won't work," Cadaver said.

"If executed correctly, I guarantee it will be successful."

"If everything goes perfectly, yes – but this is the real world, and not everything goes perfectly."

"Then why don't you tell us your plan?" Tanith asked.

"Fine," Cadaver said. "I lead the more volatile soldiers along the promenade to our left – they're eager for a fight, and won't be able to resist a fire-throwing skeleton. The other – some would say inferior – fire-throwing skeleton attacks the remaining soldiers from the other side, distracting them long enough for Tanith to manoeuvre into position and free the captives. Once this group of soldiers is dealt with, I lead the volatile soldiers back towards here, where we attack them in a pincer movement."

Tanith frowned. "That's the same plan."

"No, it isn't," said Cadaver.

"It's not the same plan at all," said Skulduggery.

"It's the same plan," she said, glaring. "It's the exact same – I don't believe you two."

"On a superficial level," said Cadaver, "I admit that there are similarities."

"But similarities are inevitable when faced with this enemy in these surroundings," Skulduggery said. "Some overlap is to be expected. But the plans aren't the same."

"Fine," Tanith said. "Then how about this? Skulduggery, you do your plan."

He nodded. "Superb choice."

"This is a mistake," Cadaver warned.

"Oh, don't worry," said Tanith, "because, while Skulduggery is carrying out his plan, you'll be doing yours."

Cadaver tilted his head. "Combining the plans? That's a risky endeavour."

"Not when they're both the same."

"We'll try it your way," Skulduggery said. "But I don't like our chances."

They combined the plans. It worked.

76

Reznor Rake and Tancred Bold strode through the High Sanctuary and Omen hurried along between them. He had expected them to put him in handcuffs in an effort to portray him as a prisoner they were taking in for questioning, but they'd laughed at the idea, and Tancred had said, "Nobody cares about you, kid."

Turns out they were right.

The City Guard didn't even glance at Omen as he passed, and the few sorcerers he saw were too busy glaring at the City Guard to notice him. There was a tension in the building, an electricity that crackled between those in uniform and those not. It wouldn't take much, in Omen's opinion, to set them at each other.

"What if it doesn't work out?" Tancred asked as they took the elevator down. "What if the resistance don't beat Creed?"

"They will," said Omen. "They've got Valkyrie back on their side."

"Valkyrie Cain is formidable, don't get me wrong," said Tancred, "but the Faceless Ones are already here. Those monster things—"

"Shalgoth," said Reznor.

"—are already killing people. The world has already been changed. We're betting everything on Creed being defeated, but now I'm wondering – what if it doesn't happen?"

There weren't even any guards when the elevator doors opened.

Passing locked cells on either side, they headed for the dungeon entrance.

"It's a risk," said Reznor. "But when have we ever played it safe, eh? We rescue China Sorrows and Valkyrie Cain, we get them out of this place, and we'll have it made. Yeah, we might have to lend a hand in the fight against Creed, but so long as we're paid well, so long as the rewards are what I expect them to be, this'll all be worth it."

"I hope you're right," Tancred grumbled.

"Of course I'm right. When am I ever wrong?"

Reznor led the way down into the dungeon, where Valkyrie and China were sharing a cell.

"Omen?" Valkyrie said, clearly astonished to see him.

Omen went up to the bars. "Are you better?" he asked. "Are you back to being normal?"

She blinked at him. She was cut and bruised and missing teeth and a finger, but she seemed remarkably upbeat. "Yeah," she said. "Yes. I... are you rescuing us?"

"Only if you're against Creed and the Faceless Ones."

"I totally am," she said, smiling. "You came to rescue us. That's so cool."

Reznor cleared his throat.

"Oh," Omen said quickly, "this is Reznor Rake and Tancred Bold. They're here to rescue you, too. They, um, they need to be paid, though."

"I'm sure suitable payment can be arranged," said China, "so long as you get us out of here."

"Working on it," said Reznor, and he and Tancred went searching for the keys.

"What's it like out there?" Valkyrie asked.

Omen glanced between Valkyrie and China. "It's pretty bad," he said. "The monsters, the Shalgoth, they're everywhere. It's on all the news channels – the mortal news and the Network. The Americans and the Russians and the Chinese, they've started dropping bombs on their own cities. Not nuclear bombs, not yet, but huge, huge bombs. They say eleven million people have died so far, they think, and thirty-six million are missing."

"What are the Sanctuaries doing?" Valkyrie asked.

"Some of them are fighting back. Most, the ones that the Supreme Mage controls, aren't doing anything."

"Not officially," Reznor said, coming back with a set of keys in his hand, "but some of the Sanctuary mages are disobeying orders – they're out there fighting the Shalgoth, trying to help the mortals."

"Stupid bloody mortals," Tancred grumbled. "Their soldiers are shooting at mages. They think everyone with magic is part of the attack. We should leave 'em to the monsters, see how they like it."

Reznor got the door open and hurried over, trying to fit each of the smaller keys into the shackles. When he found the right one, he freed Valkyrie first and she gasped as magic flooded her system.

"Give me a moment," she murmured, her eyes closing. "There are a dozen doctors in this building and I have to find the best one to... There we go."

Her flesh rippled and the cuts healed and the bruises disappeared and her finger regrew on her left hand.

"Whoa," said Tancred.

Valkyrie got up, came over and hugged Omen while Reznor freed China. Omen didn't know what to do, so he hugged her back.

"Thank you," she said softly. "And I'm sorry for losing my way."

"You're grand," he said, shrugging as he hugged.

She gave him a squeeze, and stepped back. Even her teeth had regrown. "I'm sorry for how we treated you – me and Skulduggery. I'm sorry we didn't treat you as an equal."

He blinked at her. "Don't worry about it. I mean, like, I'm not an equal, so obviously—"

"Of course you're an equal," she said. "You might not be as powerful or as experienced as we are, but I wasn't as powerful or as experienced as Skulduggery when I was starting out. That doesn't mean you're any less valuable."

He blushed. "At least you weren't using me to make a point."

"At least there's that. Any word from Crepuscular lately?"

"Not since LA."

"Good. That's a complicated situation he's got going on. It's probably best to stay away."

Omen nodded, and China joined them.

"Shall we leave?" she asked.

Valkyrie went first, hurrying up the stairs to the cells. "Reznor and Tancred – I don't believe I've heard of you. Good guys or bad?"

"Hovering round the middle," said Reznor, "with some occasional dalliances with proper villainy."

Valkyrie glanced back. "But so long as you're paid, you'll fight for us? Fair enough. I've known a few people like that. Word of warning, though – you betray us, I've got some very nasty friends."

Reznor was about to reply, but he was interrupted by someone knocking.

"Excuse me?" came a voice from one of the cells. "Is that Valkyrie? Valkyrie Cain?"

Valkyrie paused, then opened the slot in the door next to her. A face peered out, all green eyes and great hair. It took Omen a moment to recognise Nefarian Serpine from his pictures.

"I thought it was you," Serpine said, looking pleased. "What a stroke of luck this is. Seeing as how you're escaping, I was wondering if you wouldn't mind taking me with you. Creed seems determined to execute me, but won't tell me when. He has a lot going on, you know? My execution's already been pushed back twice, and I've reached the point where I've just given up. So maybe let me out of here and we'll all run off together, what do you say?"

"Sure," Valkyrie said, "I'll let you out. You do one thing for me first, though."

"Anything."

"Tell me how you were in two places at once."

Serpine sighed. "Are you still talking about that? It wasn't me, Valkyrie. Whoever you spoke to, whoever killed Scure, wasn't me."

"I don't believe that."

"Then do you believe me when I say that I don't know? Because I don't."

"I'm sorry," China said to Valkyrie, "but do we really have time for this? The thing about being in enemy territory is that it's always best to leave it at the earliest opportunity."

"I agree with China," said Serpine, "and may I say how wonderful it is to see you again, Miss Sorrows? Valkyrie, you seem absolutely certain it was me you were talking to and I sincerely don't know how that could be, but ordinarily I wouldn't doubt you in the slightest. So now yes, I, too, am stuck with a conundrum: I know I didn't kill Robert Scure, but I believe you when you tell me I did. It's as much of a mystery to me as it is to you, so if you let me out of here and we do, in fact, escape, I will help you in whatever capacity you require in order to solve this riddle."

"Promise?"

"On my honour. If that isn't sufficient, on your honour."

"Fine," she grumbled, and opened the door.

He stepped out of the cell, smiling as his magic returned. "Look at us – what a merry band of malcontents we are. Shall we press on?"

"After you," Valkyrie said.

Serpine bowed graciously and led the way to the door. It opened and a City Guard ambled through, his eyes widening when he saw them. He fumbled for his gun, but Serpine grabbed his wrist, twisted, wrenched the weapon free and cracked the butt against the cop's temple. The City Guard crumpled, and Serpine turned to them. "Do you have an escape route planned, or are you hoping that we can all just walk out of here?"

Valkyrie looked to Omen, who looked to Reznor, who glowered.

"I just thought we'd fight our way out," he said. "I didn't expect things to go so smoothly. I thought there'd be alarms going off and people shooting at us."

"Not an unreasonable expectation, in fairness," Valkyrie said, shrugging. "So, Nefarian, the answer is no, we do not have an escape route planned."

"There aren't many guards," Omen said, "so sneaking out mightn't be that difficult."

"We'll sneak as far as we can, and then fight if we have to," said Valkyrie. "Once the alarm sounds, everyone get out however they can, OK? Omen, you stay with me."

Omen nodded. "Thank you."

They carried on, and it went fine until they got to the foyer, at which point there were City Guard officers running in and people were shooting and everyone was shouting. Serpine went one way and Reznor and Tancred another, and Valkyrie grabbed China and Omen and suddenly they were flying, and Omen clung on and squeezed his eyes shut as they burst into the open air and flew, crackling, over the city wall.

Her ability to steer hampered by her passengers, Valkyrie landed – a little roughly – a few minutes later, and used Omen's phone to call Fletcher.

"What do we do now?" Omen asked. "I mean, like, what do you think Creed's going to do now that you've escaped? Is he going to be angry?"

"You're worried that he'll take his anger out on innocent people," said Valkyrie. "Maybe your schoolfriends?"

"Would he?"

Valkyrie glanced at China, and China shrugged and said, "He may very well do exactly that."

"OK," Valkyrie said. "OK, that's a reasonable assumption, that someone will have to suffer for what we've just done. So we give him something else to focus on. We don't allow him time to take his anger out on anyone."

"What are you thinking?" China asked. "A resistance attack? Something grander?"

"Something much grander," said Valkyrie, and she looked towards the Faceless One standing over Dublin. "I reckon it's time to start killing monsters."

77

When this was all over, when Sebastian could finally take off his ridiculous costume and go back to normal life – if, indeed, there was anything resembling a normal life to go back to – he wondered what the world would look like, and if there would be this many lunatics roaming its streets.

The Obsidian worshippers, the Nulls, were growing in number, with more disaffected citizens joining their ranks every day, but he still didn't know what it was they actually believed in. *The end is coming*, that was one of their chants. *The end is nigh*. They prowled Roarhaven like bad-tempered alleycats, dishevelled and flighty and quick to anger, and the other citizens of Roarhaven, those who might be charitably labelled 'normal', had started to avoid them wherever possible.

"Unfortunate people," Nuncle decided, watching them from the rooftops.

"Unfortunate?" Sebastian said. "They're going around beating up strangers and scaring everyone."

"Because they're lost," said Nuncle. "Because they're sad and scared. They're so sad and so lost and so scared that they think they want the world to end and for it all to be over. They have an overabundance of pain and sorrow and they don't know what to do with it except share it with whomever they meet."

"I've got a word for people like that and it isn't *unfortunate*."

"I'm sure you do," Nuncle said, smiling. "But everyone is carrying around a little bag of pain, Sebastian, and that pain informs everything they do. I wish things could have been different for them, but life by its nature is pain."

"Well, that's depressing."

"Is it?" said Nuncle, frowning. "Why?"

"Because if the nature of life is pain, then the point of life is pain."

"Oh, no, my boy, I don't agree with that at all. The fact of the matter is that there is no point *at all* to life."

"Well," Sebastian muttered, "that's much better."

"People place too much emphasis on the *point* of things," said Nuncle. "As if that matters. As if it makes a difference. There is no point to life. There is no grand goal you must achieve in order to judge whether the life you've lived is worthy or worthless, is a success or a failure. Life is life. It's there. It's lived. It passes. People navigate their way through to the best of their ability, carrying their little bags of pain around with them, seeking out happiness where they can, comfort where they find it, and contentment if at all possible. That's all there is to it."

"Sounds simple."

"There is, indeed, beauty in simplicity."

"So those Nulls down there are missing the point by thinking there is a point, where they really should be accepting the fact that nothing means anything so why get depressed about it?"

"You're quite right when you say that nothing means anything, but their depression is added to their bag of pain. It might be helpful to think of this bag as more of a burden, held on the shoulders, threatening to overbalance you. You might want to walk in a straight line through your life, but your burdens make you stumble one way or another, and when you look back, as you die, you discover that the journey you've taken has been anything but straight."

"Hold on," Sebastian said, frowning, "are we talking philosophy?"

"Perish the very thought, my boy," Nuncle responded, horrified. "We are merely discussing the fundamental nature of existence."

"Oh, OK."

"I would never try to trick you like that."

"That's good to know."

Nuncle suddenly turned, inhaling deeply. "Do you smell that?"

The air filters in Sebastian's suit were excellent, but even so it took him a while to detect the faint aroma on the breeze.

"Food," Nuncle said, drawing the word out. "Food, glorious food. Are you hungry, Sebastian?"

"I'm never hungry," Sebastian said, trying to keep the misery out of his voice. He dearly missed experiencing taste. Sometimes, at night, he lay awake, imagining the first morsel to pass through his mouth once he could take this mask off.

"I like food," Nuncle announced. "It becomes quite addictive after a while, doesn't it? Do you mind if I pop down to get some?"

Sebastian blinked. "Sure," he said. "I'll stay right here."

Nuncle grinned. "Be back in a moment!"

And then he was gone, scampering towards the stairs, and Sebastian turned and immediately ran for the edge of the roof. He knew this part of the city well, and knew which gaps were jumpable and which were not. He jumped, landing on the adjacent building and jogging onwards.

He liked Nuncle, he did, even if he didn't remotely understand the man. The conversations they had, while rambling, always felt like Sebastian was preparing for a test he'd never take. Plus, he had no idea where Nuncle had come from or if he could even be trusted. The fact of the matter was that Sebastian was better off alone – especially for what was to come next.

He'd been focused lately on evading capture by the City Guards and avoiding run-ins with the Nulls, but too much time had passed. He had to rescue Darquesse, and he had to do it now.

Despite the things she'd done, despite the atrocities she'd committed as her old self, he couldn't allow her mistreatment to continue. The thought of her being hurt – being tortured – by Commander Hoc and his pack of thugs boiled his insides. He wasn't her father, he knew that, he was well aware of that, just as he was well aware that, in general, she needed him about as much as she needed anyone – which was not at all. But he'd raised her. He'd held her as a baby, he'd rocked her to sleep, he'd watched over her and worried about her and had been delighted – initially – with every stage of her rapid development. The moment she said her first word to the moment they were having full-blown conversations may have passed in hours rather than years, and her first step to her first flight may have been a matter of minutes, but he was there for it all.

More than that, he realised now, he wouldn't have missed it for anything. She had given him joy. When he'd put on this suit and undertaken this mission, he expected hardship and loneliness and sacrifice, but he hadn't expected pure, undiluted happiness. He hadn't expected love.

He wasn't her father because she didn't have a father, but he was the closest thing she had to one, and, despite how bizarre it all was, she was his daughter and he loved her.

And he was going to save her, no matter what.

78

When the universe began, there were monsters already here.

They watched the universe being born, these monsters, these First Gods, who were called many things but, as the countless eons passed, they became known as Those Who Slumber, Whose Names We Dare Not Speak Lest They Rouse to Waking. They watched whole races of other gods, of lesser gods, being born. Out of these races, after all this time, only the Faceless Ones were still potent, and out of the Faceless Ones, the one whose name was Khrthauk was a legend, even among its own kind.

Valkyrie knew this legend. She knew what Khrthauk had done, knew how savage and ruthless and cunning it had been when it came to slaughtering the other gods. She knew how merciless it had been when the Ancients had risen up, how furious it had been when the Faceless Ones had been forced to retreat to another reality.

Khrthauk had been one of the first Faceless Ones to come back. It stood over Dublin amid ruined and trampled buildings, over the obliterated corpses of the city's dead, and Valkyrie knew it felt nothing but pleasure at all that pain.

She flew closer and Khrthauk turned slightly, and she felt its attention shift as it acknowledged her presence. She sensed its hesitation, and confusion, and also the bond between them, and for a moment it was overwhelming, the love she felt for this thing.

It was hers, it was of her, and in that moment she wished it no harm, and knew she would protect it from anyone and anything that tried to hurt it, that tried to destroy it.

But she fought against that moment, and pushed aside those feelings, and once she was past them they faded until they were nothing but a niggling part of her.

"Hello, my love," she said.

Khrthauk made a sound, a roar and a whine and a moan, that, were it directed at Valkyrie, would surely have burst her eardrums.

"I can't allow you to live," she called, using words it did not understand. "I just can't. You had your chance, you and the others. You ruled the universe. You were worshipped here. But you don't belong on this world any more, and this universe is better off without you."

She drifted closer, and put a hand on its hide. It was rough, and sticky, and surprisingly warm.

"I'm sorry," she whispered.

She called forth the katahedral energy inside her and it passed from her hand into Khrthauk. The creature recoiled, its flesh rippling, and Valkyrie flew backwards to avoid its thrashing, both hands straight in front of her, black lightning leaping from her fingertips. It poured out of her and she screamed as the Faceless One screamed and the patch of hide she'd just been touching turned to dust and the dust spread over its massive body and then it came apart, crumbling like an old statue, collapsing into a mountain of its own remains.

Valkyrie kept flying backwards, staying out of the dust cloud, tears streaming down her face.

"I'm sorry," she said again.

Then she frowned, and turned, looking into the distance. On the horizon, there was a flash.

Eyes widening, she launched herself upwards, the wind ripping at her hair, and a beam of energy, as wide as an ocean liner, screamed by beneath her. She abruptly changed course, speeding for the ground before the Faceless One gathered itself for another attack, and hid herself behind the curvature of the Earth.

"It's war now, baby," she whispered to the world.

79

Four Sensitives crowded into Valkyrie's mind to make sure there were no Faceless Ones lurking there, maybe tucked behind some childhood memories or squeezed between her doubts and fears. When she was cleared for duty, Dexter gave her a quick tour of the resistance headquarters while they waited for Skulduggery to get teleported back from monster duty. It was a lonely old building, thirty miles outside Chicago, and most of the lights didn't work. Not the most impressive of facilities.

"We're stretched pretty thin," Dexter said.

Valkyrie was sitting in the small kitchenette as he made her a coffee. He looked tired. He had cuts on his face and his hand was bandaged.

"All of our resources are being put into protecting people from the Shalgoth – we haven't been able to move against Creed in any way lately. But now that you're back..." He glanced over. "Is it true? You killed a Faceless One?"

She nodded, letting tendrils of black energy dance between her fingertips. "Looks like I'm a walking Sceptre of the Ancients," she said, "for as long as I can evade their attacks anyway."

"And now that they know you're coming?" he asked. "Now that you're a confirmed threat?"

"They're going to catch me," Valkyrie said. "Today, tomorrow, next week – sometime soon, I'm going to be a second too slow."

"Yeah. And that's true of us all." Dexter put the coffee in front of her, and sat.

"We haven't really spoken in a while," Valkyrie said. "I don't just mean when I was stuck in a dungeon. We haven't really spoken since we got back from Dimension X. You doing OK?"

"You mean without Saracen?" said Dexter. "I've lost friends before. You adjust to the loss, you make room for the gap in your life, and you move on. You have to."

"I really liked him."

Dexter smiled. "Everyone liked Saracen. Not as much as Saracen liked Saracen, but pretty close."

Kierre of the Unveiled walked in, stopping when she saw who Dexter was talking to. "Valkyrie. I was not aware you had returned."

"Just arrived," Valkyrie said. "I heard about Temper. How is he?"

"He lost control of his Gist," she said. "We have him secured in the basement."

Valkyrie frowned. "Can he be helped? Healed?"

"They say nobody comes back from something like that."

Valkyrie didn't know what to do, didn't know how to react, so she went over and took Kierre's hands. "I'm so sorry," she said.

Kierre looked at her, hesitated and blinked. "Thank you." She stepped away. "Dexter, we have been called to provide reinforcements for Tanith Low and Cadaver Cain."

Valkyrie frowned. "Wait – Cadaver's in the field?"

Dexter stood. "Like I said, we're stretched thin. Take care of yourself, kid."

He left, and she went back to drinking her coffee until Skulduggery appeared in the doorway, and she knocked over her chair as she sprinted into his arms.

She cried and he patted her head as he hugged her, and she muttered into his shirt.

"Pardon?" he said. "I didn't quite catch that."

Valkyrie detached herself just enough to speak. "I'm sorry," she said. "I'm so sorry."

"Whatever for?"

"For working with the Faceless Ones."

"Oh," he said. "That."

"Thank you for sticking by me."

"You were merely overwhelmed by a maternal instinct to protect your evil children. I was a parent, too, once – there's no need to explain yourself."

She wiped her eyes. "It's not really the same, though, is it? You were an actual parent to a flesh-and-blood child, but I was just a conduit to a race of evil gods."

"I suppose you're right. It isn't the same. You don't know what it's like to be a parent to a flesh-and-blood child, and I don't know what it's like for a race of evil gods to be born through me as they pass from one reality to another. I don't know what it's like to be filled with all that history and memory and sensation. They're two different experiences – but I'm certainly not qualified to decide which is more valid." His head tilted. "It can't have been easy, to destroy the one over Dublin."

Valkyrie nodded. Gave a brittle smile. Waited. "Well?" she said.

"Well what?"

"Aren't you going to apologise for not breaking me out of the dungeon?"

"Not at all," Skulduggery said. "Roarhaven had its shields up. I could no more get into the city than a moth could get inside a bulb. Besides, I have unwavering faith in you. I knew you'd get out eventually, and, in the end, did my gamble not pay off?"

"Omen had to come and rescue me."

"See? My faith in you was rewarded."

"But I didn't break myself out."

"No, but you were there to be broken out, weren't you? You can't break someone out of a dungeon without there first being someone in the dungeon to break out, now can you?"

"I... what?"

"The fact is you're welcome, Valkyrie. Now, moving on – we've had reports of the other Faceless Ones moving. Slowly, and ponderously, but definitely moving. Almost as if they're looking for someone."

Valkyrie sagged. "It won't take them long to find me. I reckon I'll need to keep moving myself, every few hours, or they'll be able to pinpoint my position. I'm probably endangering everyone just by being here right now. Do we have a plan?"

Skulduggery nodded. "The plan is for you to stay alive."

"Excellent. I love this plan. How do we do that?"

"I have no idea."

"The plan started off great, then went seriously downhill, I hope you don't mind me saying."

"OK," he said, "before this slips into doom and gloom, we've got to remember that things *are* looking up. Thanks to me, you are now free."

"Once again, you didn't do anything."

"You are also our weapon. You can destroy them. This is something we didn't have earlier, and now we do. That's to be celebrated. Yes, the Faceless Ones, the Shalgoth, Creed and his followers are all hunting for you as we speak, but we can use this to our advantage. If everyone is looking to kill *you*, nobody is looking to kill the rest of us."

"Silver linings," said Valkyrie without enthusiasm.

"The approach we take is simple," Skulduggery continued. "The resistance spreads out. We keep an eye on the Faceless Ones. Whenever one strays too far from the others, whenever one becomes isolated, Fletcher will teleport you to that location, you'll take out the Faceless One, and you'll teleport away again. One by one, we can cut down their numbers."

"That sounds good," said Valkyrie. "Provided I can sneak up on every one I go after, there's even a chance I won't be horribly killed before I get close."

"But that still leaves us with a problem," said Skulduggery. "What do we do about the Faceless Ones still inside you?"

"I destroy them," Valkyrie said. "Burn them out of me."

He hesitated. "And are you sure you'll be able to do that? I'm well aware what the Faceless Ones mean to you."

"It's them or us, Skulduggery. I have no difficulty in deciding who's more important."

"And what of your stance on killing?"

Valkyrie's gut twisted. "They're gods. They've lived long enough and they've brought pain to enough worlds in enough realities. They had their chance to be a force for good, they had their chance to be kind, and all they care about is power. They don't deserve life."

"What do you need us to do?"

"Nothing," said Valkyrie. "I just need a few hours alone, somewhere quiet and out of the way. When I do this, I'm going to be lit up like a Christmas tree for a short time. The Faceless Ones are going to come for me."

Skulduggery put his hand on her shoulder. "When?"

She took a breath and let it out. "Find me somewhere isolated, and let's get it over with."

80

Tyler and his dad went along to the town meeting in the hall where they usually held raffles and fundraisers, and the mayor stood up at the podium. Standing behind him was a nervous young woman Tyler had never seen before.

"Thanks, everyone, for coming along tonight," the mayor said. "Now, we've all seen the news and we've read the papers and I know we're all scared and anxious and wondering what's next and what's gonna happen and what we're gonna do about it. Well, I can tell you that the Federal Government is promising aid to any state that requests it, though they've encouraged the governor to sort it out with the resources already available. With that in mind, we have a representative from FEMA here to talk us through our options. Doctor?"

The nervous woman got to her feet and approached the microphone. "Thank you, uh, Mr Mayor, but I'm not a doctor and I'm not a FEMA employee. My name's Maria and I'm, that is, I've worked with them in the past but, really, I'm attached to an adjunct facility that, um, well, to be honest, I specialise in cataloguing different types of soil, but occasionally I'm brought in to advise on—"

"We get it," said Mr Lemire, standing. "You're a big-shot scientific expert. We don't need your credentials, lady – we just need to know what FEMA's gonna do."

"I'm sorry, I think there's been a mistake."

"There ain't no mistake, Doctor. FEMA's the Federal Emergency Mandate Association, is it not?"

"Again, I'm not a doctor, and it's the Federal Emergency Management Agency, actually."

"It don't matter what the letters stand for! What matters is what it means! What matters is what it does! So what are you gonna do about this emergency?"

"Just to point out again, sir, I am not actually a FEMA official."

"You're the closest thing we got to it, ain't ya?"

"Well, I – I guess so."

"Then what are their secret plans?"

"Secret plans?"

"Their top-secret plans! We all know they got scenarios in place and once the scenario stops being a scenario and starts being a thing that's happening, they have a plan to deal with it!"

"Well, I mean, sure, they have plans to deal with earthquakes and hurricanes and chemical spills and... Sir, they don't have any plans to deal with monsters the size of mountains and monsters that come up out of the ground."

"Just tell me this, lady – who we gotta blame?"

"I'm sorry?"

"Who sent them? Because we all know somebody sent them!"

There were a few grunts of agreement.

"So what're we talking about here?" Lemire continued. "The Russians? The Chinese? It's the Australians, ain't it?"

"Why would it be the Australians?"

"Somebody sent the monsters!"

"Now, come on," said the mayor, stepping forward to speak into the microphone. "She's probably not allowed to tell us on account of it being top-secret and all."

The mayor stepped back and Maria resumed her position, frowning. "No, actually, that's not why I can't answer that. Sir, ladies and gentlemen, I don't know who sent the monsters, or if anyone sent them at all. Take a look at the news – the monsters are everywhere. They're in Russia and they're in China and, yes, they're even in Australia. Why would an enemy country send monsters to destroy cities in America and also use them to destroy their own cities?"

The crowd went silent for a moment, then Lemire sneered. "Plausible deniability."

Tyler looked at his dad and his dad sighed. "These idiots don't know anything," he whispered. "Let's go."

81

Emmeline and Caddock Darkly stood before the Supreme Mage's desk like errant schoolchildren. Commander Hoc stood behind the desk for once, at Supreme Mage Creed's broad, muscular shoulder, and it was all he could do to stop himself from grinning.

"Your son is a terrorist," the Supreme Mage said, his voice somehow sounding even more powerful coming from behind the Nexus Helmet.

"That's a lie," Emmeline said sharply. She immediately bowed her head. "Apologies, Supreme Mage. I just meant that Omen is a good boy. He's always been a good boy."

"I saw you reading your statement from the steps of the High Sanctuary. Those were not the words of parents who believe their son is a good boy."

"With respect, Supreme Mage, we agreed with your office that it was important to come out and denounce his actions."

"Yet you waited almost a month to do so."

"The fact is that Omen may have fallen in with some people who've associated with the resistance, but I promise you he has nothing to do with them."

"Principal Duenna seems to think that he has direct involvement."

"She's wrong."

"In fact, Principal Duenna suspects your son of working with the resistance in order to undermine her position at the school."

"Why would the resistance give a damn about Corrival Academy?"

"That's where they seek to recruit the next generation of terrorists," the Supreme Mage said.

Caddock attempted a scornful laugh. "Supreme Mage, forgive me, but all of this sounds highly dubious. I know Duenna – I've known her for a long time – and she is nothing if not prone to bouts of self-indulgent paranoia. It doesn't surprise me in the least to learn that she believes there's a conspiracy to oust her from her position, but it does surprise me to learn that she's blaming it all on Omen."

"And yet," said the Supreme Mage, "Omen absconded from the Academy after attempting to steal Duenna's property. Is this not so, Commander Hoc?"

Hoc gave a sharp nod. "It is, Supreme Mage. The device in question is a remote control of sorts, used to maintain order among the student body. It was only thanks to the training and quick reflexes of Officer Limerence that the boy's attempt at thievery was foiled."

"There you go," the Supreme Mage said. "Can you explain your son's actions?"

"We cannot," Caddock admitted, "but I'm sure there will be a simple explanation whenever we actually find Omen to ask him."

"Duenna sending out search parties was an outrageously reckless decision," Emmeline said. "Omen is a sensitive boy and this would have terrified him. It probably sent him running into the arms of these resistance people – at least *they* weren't dispatching killers to hunt him down."

"Silas Nadir has been thoroughly rehabilitated," said the Supreme Mage.

"There's an old saying in my family, Damocles: once a serial killer, always a serial killer. Omen is not a threat to Duenna, or to the school, or to Roarhaven. We understand that you have a lot going on, but we are here to ask you to let our son come home."

"Four days ago, you announced to us all that he was no longer your son."

Emmeline faltered for a moment. "Because you ordered us to."

"I ordered no such thing."

"Your office did. Your representatives told us they could guarantee leniency if we thoroughly denounced and disowned him."

"My representatives misspoke."

The Darklys stared at the Supreme Mage in horror.

"What can we do?" Emmeline asked quietly.

The Supreme Mage watched them. "Reparations will have to be made."

There was the slightest of hesitations. "Of course," Emmeline said.

"You have, I believe, amassed a considerable fortune due to Auger being the Chosen One."

"We have," said Caddock.

"But now Auger has become Obsidian, and is a direct threat to not only our way of life, but also the Faceless Ones themselves. By rights, I should be punishing your family, not granting it favours."

"What do you want, Supreme Mage?"

"Three-quarters of everything you own to be transferred to the Church of the Faceless."

Hoc watched the Darklys pale. Caddock looked like he needed to sit down, but Emmeline stayed impressively tall.

"And, if we do this, you will allow Omen to return? He will face no criminal proceedings?"

"I will consider the matter settled."

"And what about Auger?" Caddock said, his voice little more than a croak. "If it's possible to return him to normal, if we manage that, can we expect similar leniency?"

"If the impossible happens and Auger returns and we are guaranteed that Obsidian will never trouble us again... then

388

perhaps we can discuss it. For a further three-quarters of your remaining assets."

If there was any blood remaining in Caddock's face, it deserted him at that point. "Very well."

The Supreme Mage waved a hand. "My office will be in touch," he said.

The Darklys, unused to being dismissed in such a way, hesitated for a long, awkward moment before walking out. It was glorious.

"Commander, report," said the Supreme Mage.

Hoc marched round to the front of the desk, and stood to attention. "Supreme Mage, we are ready to reduce Darquesse to energy and trap her in the Cage."

"And?"

Hoc's proud smile faltered. "And... and I wondered if you would like to witness such a momentous occasion."

"Momentous?" the Supreme Mage echoed, and Hoc knew he had chosen the wrong word. "My mind is filled with the thoughts of the Faceless Ones. Every moment that passes, I am witness to ideas and emotions and sensations that no human language could ever even hope to convey. What you are doing down in those squalid cells is nothing compared to what I get to glimpse through my connection to our gods."

"Of course, Supreme Mage. It was a ridiculous notion to even—"

"Your apologies mean less than you do, Commander. When you have done what I have instructed you to do, report back to me and I will give you your next assignment."

"Yes, sir," said Hoc. "Thank you, sir."

The Supreme Mage shifted his attention to a file on his desk, dismissing Hoc even more cruelly than he had the Darklys, and Hoc spun on his heel and marched out. He punched the elevator button. When the doors opened, he stepped in, his face impassive, and waited until the doors closed before sagging.

"Stupid!" he cried, bashing his fists against his head. "Stupid,

stupid! He doesn't care! He's talking to the Faceless Ones! He doesn't care about stupid, dumb things when he's communing with the gods!"

The elevator slowed to a stop and the doors opened and one of the priests tried to get in.

"Use the stairs!" Hoc screamed, and the priest jerked back and the doors closed and Hoc jabbed the button and sulked all the way down.

He composed himself, put a snarl on his face, and strode out of the elevator and out of the Dark Cathedral. He walked across the Circle Zone, flanked by City Guard officers, all the way to the High Sanctuary. There he left his escort behind and went into the deepest, darkest parts of that building, where the old Sanctuary squatted.

He burst through the doors and one of the scientists, a woman named Adroit, turned to him, her smile dimming when she realised he was alone. "Commander, is the Supreme Mage not—?"

Hoc glared. "Why would the Supreme Mage give a damn what we're doing down here, you imbecile? He's communing with gods. You think he cares about what you're up to? Just get on with it before I arrest you for wasting my time."

"Of course," Adroit said, ashen-faced, and led the way past the other two scientists, through to the chamber within.

Darquesse was on her knees in the Black Room, her arms twisted and locked out behind her, held in place with metal bars and shackles carved with binding sigils. Her hair was damp with sweat, and it clung to her face.

Hoc hunkered down before her. "I had a speech written," he said quietly. "It took me a week to write it and refine it. It needed to be perfect. But now it doesn't matter. You don't matter. No one cares what happens to you. You're no longer relevant." He stood, and nodded. "Throw the switch," he said.

Nothing happened.

"Doctor Adroit," he snarled, turning, "throw the—"

390

Adroit was on the floor, unconscious.

Hoc went for his gun and a fist came out of nowhere and punched him right on the nose.

Hoc squealed, hands at his face, his eyes filling with tears of pain as he went staggering back. He tripped and fell, and crawled to the wall. He pressed his back to it, tried pulling his gun, but it was gone. In all the mayhem, someone had stolen it. They'd stolen his sword, too. He was unarmed. Unarmed and unprotected.

A man appeared out of thin air, a man in a black outfit and black hat and a weird black mask. The Plague Doctor. In his hand, he held a cloaking sphere.

He put the sphere in his coat pocket and knelt by Darquesse. "You're OK," he said softly. "I'm going to get you out of here. You're going to be OK." He stood and pulled at the shackles, trying to figure out how to open them.

Hoc's gun had been tossed to the other side of the room, but his sword was right there. Pushing the pain of his probably broken nose to one side, Hoc scrambled to his feet and snatched up the weapon.

He swung and the Plague Doctor raised an arm and the blade should have sliced through, but instead it just thudded against the armoured material. Hoc tried moving back, giving himself room for another thrust, but the Plague Doctor did some sneaky martial-arts move and the sword flew from his grip and Hoc sank to his knees, his arm twisted, his blood-drenched face contorted.

"How do I release her?" the Plague Doctor asked.

"I'll never tell you!"

"You're going to tell me because we both know you're not a tough guy. How do I release her?"

"Burn in hell!"

The Plague Doctor twisted Hoc's arm more.

"The button on the wall!" Hoc screeched. "The blue one! Please let me go!"

The Plague Doctor shoved him away and Hoc curled up on the floor, clutching his sore arm. A moment later, the shackles securing Darquesse clicked open, the sigils fading.

It was as if he could see her flooding with strength. Her legs straightened, her shoulders squared, her head lifted. Her skin drank in the sweat and her hair rippled and was suddenly clean and healthy and it shone. She looked down at Hoc.

"Please," he gasped. "Please don't kill me."

She looked away, like she was barely aware of his existence, and took the Plague Doctor's hand and they disappeared. The door to the chamber opened and the other two scientists stepped in, eyes wide in alarm.

"Help me!" Hoc screeched. "I've been attacked!"

82

The multitudes of Faceless Ones flitting within Valkyrie's soul, like moths, waiting for their turn to pass into the world and take their place towering over the lands and cities and mountains – they knew something was wrong.

Now, instead of moths, they were angry flies buzzing against an unturned glass. She trapped them where they were and reached into herself, searching for that energy she had already used against Khrthauk.

When she found it, she studied it, examined it, watched it as it lay dormant. She stirred it a little, noted how it reacted, felt how the power was different from her own and yet still obeyed the same fundamental principles. Magic was magic, no matter the discipline.

She breathed deep and opened her eyes and called it forth and her body tingled. The fine hairs on the back of her neck stood up. Thin strands of black energy crackled between her fingertips. Fully aware of the devastation that this energy could cause – it scared her as much as it thrilled her – she kept it going, built it up. It didn't fry her. It didn't turn her to dust. She curled her hand and it became a ball that coalesced in her palm. To release it would be to destroy the room around her and so she drank it back in, reabsorbing it into her system.

Then she closed her eyes and directed this energy inwards.

It churned towards her soul, churned and built, and the Faceless Ones still inside her knew what was coming and they were panicking, trying to get out. They screamed at her, screamed in a fury she had never felt before. They were gods and they knew what she was going to do and they were powerless to stop her.

The black energy burst through her soul and obliterated every last one of them, and when it withdrew, and was safe, Valkyrie collapsed, suddenly crying, roaring with grief. She wanted to curl up, wanted to spend the rest of her life crying, but an awareness buzzed in the back of her mind and it forced her to get up, forced her to stagger to the door of this tiny cottage, out here in the middle of nowhere, and she looked west and saw the Faceless One called Rhgonnaleth moving its slow legs, turning, lumbering across the horizon towards her.

From the folds in its chest, there came a light and Valkyrie flew and the blast of energy that erupted from it missed her but only barely, throwing her sideways. She tumbled through the air, too exhausted to right herself, and a part of her welcomed the turmoil because just for these few seconds she didn't have to struggle.

She hit the ground, the necronaut suit protecting her, and she went rolling, finally coming to a stop on her back. She was too tired to run. Too tired to move.

Rhgonnaleth took a step, its great foot crunching through buildings and trees a few kilometres from where she lay. It looked down at her and she felt its hatred and anger boiling within an alien mind as it prepared to end her life.

Her campaign of destruction against the Faceless Ones hadn't lasted as long as she'd hoped. A small voice in the back of Valkyrie's mind noted how she'd been wrong – she hadn't been fated to die on her knees. She was going to die on her back, looking up at a god. She managed to raise a hand to it, and extended a finger.

Then Obsidian drifted into view, gazing up at the Faceless One, and Valkyrie felt Rhgonnaleth's attention flicker to the newcomer and it examined him, gauged his power, calculated the threat he posed. There was a moment of panic, but Obsidian was already waving his hand, and he wiped Rhgonnaleth from existence.

83

The news showed all these people leaving the cities. When the motorways got jammed, they left their cars and got out and walked. Thousands of people, tens of thousands, hundreds of thousands, maybe, some of them hauling suitcases, some lugging cat carriers, bags slung over their shoulders, holding scared little kids by the hand, leading dogs on leashes. Some of them, some of the people, carried nothing – they weren't even dressed for a hike – but they were part of the stream of all races and colours.

Tyler had seen refugees on TV before and that's what it looked like to him, except instead of a bunch of exhausted-looking people trying to get over the border into America, now it was a bunch of exhausted-looking people trying to get anywhere that didn't have a monster standing over it.

The news footage switched to three women and two men hanging from lamp posts by their necks. They each had a piece of paper taped to their chests. They all said WITCH. Tyler's mom turned the TV off, shaking her head.

"Where'll they go?" Mila asked. "The people?"

"The government will find them somewhere safe," said Tyler's mom, eager to get her mind off the hangings. "They might have to sleep in tents for a few nights, or maybe in school halls or something, but the government will take care of it."

"Goddamn government's responsible for it, more'n likely," Tyler's dad muttered.

"Cooper, hush," said his wife.

"You can't tell me this ain't part of their plan," Tyler's dad said, waving at the TV. "You can't tell me they didn't want this to happen. This is what they do, Cynthia! This is how they control us!"

"What nonsense. How is this controlling anyone?"

"It's carving up the population. It's dividing us. It's separating us from our neighbours. I'm not saying they started it, I'm not saying this is all the idea of the Federal Government, but I swear to you, they are complicit. Whoever's building those monsters, those wizards with the magical powers got in, probably years ago, and they've been working behind the scenes ever since to corrupt our country and weaken its people. You don't believe me? Look at what's been happening in the world even before the monsters arrived. This used to be a strong country – a proud country."

"Don't you try to tell me what kind of country this was," Tyler's mom said, in the voice she used when she was trying to keep her temper in front of the kids. "Don't you act like you know more and you've seen more and you understand more than the rest of us. Don't you act like you're the only one seeing things clearly. I see everything you do, but I don't see it through the same eyes, praise God."

"You're ignoring the truth."

"I'm facing the truth. I'm accepting the truth and not wasting my time trying to find things behind it."

"They're calling them sorcerers," Mila said, and her parents looked at her like they'd just remembered they had kids. "The wizards. I think they're called sorcerers."

"It doesn't matter what they're called," their dad said. "It's what they *do*. It's the *damage* they cause."

"But some of them might be on our side, Dad. I saw a video of one of them flying up near one of the big monsters, the ones over the cities? And he made it disappear. I mean, doesn't that sound like they're—"

"It's an act!" Tyler's dad said. "You gotta stop believing everything you see on your social media, Mila! You gotta start asking questions! You've all gotta start asking questions!"

Tyler and his sister looked at each other. Their dad was getting worse.

84

Valkyrie woke in a small bed in the resistance headquarters. Daylight streamed in through the blinds. She sat up.

"How are you feeling?" Skulduggery asked, walking in.

"Better," she said. "Much better. How long was I asleep?"

"Fourteen hours. Do you know what's going on out there?"

There was a bottle of water beside the bed. She took a long drink. "I can feel it. It's weird: my psychic connection to the Faceless Ones has been broken, but... but it hasn't really been broken, you know? It's like there's an extra strand of something that we don't have a name for yet."

"So you know what Obsidian is doing."

"Erasing them from reality," Valkyrie said. "Wiping them away. I feel every one of them when they go. They're not... It's not like they're dying. They just, I don't know... cease. They no longer exist."

"Do they know what's happening?"

"Oh, yes. Oh, they're all well aware, but at the same time they can't quite bring themselves to believe it. They've been alive for too long, you know? Yes, they've been beaten before, and they had to retreat from the Ancients, but they viewed that as a temporary inconvenience. They don't know how to process this."

"Are they scared?"

"Very scared. They're panicking."

"This must be hard for you."

"It's weird for me. I could have taken down a few more, but they'd have killed me eventually, so I'm glad that Obsidian is doing what he's doing. That boy is saving the world right now. But yeah, there's a part of me that's sad. It's a quiet part, though." She frowned. "Do you think we might actually get a happy ending out of this?"

"Do not jinx it," Skulduggery said. "China told me what you were discussing while you were waiting to be tortured."

"About Crepuscular orchestrating all this to free his family? You think it makes sense?"

"As much as anything. It's definitely a feasible conclusion. China's setting up a meeting with one of the Hosts – Grantham Arrant. If your theory is right, he'll be the one to confirm it."

"All right then," Valkyrie said, slowly getting out of bed. "I love it when we have a plan. Even though they tend to go horribly wrong."

"Before we go any further," said Skulduggery, "are you up for one more assignment?"

"I've literally just stood up."

"You don't have to go anywhere and you don't have to fight anyone, I promise. Are you strong enough?"

Valkyrie sighed. "Yeah. What have you got in store for me?"

He held up a hand for her to stay put, and walked out of the room. A moment later, Alice charged in.

"Stephanie!" she shouted, colliding with Valkyrie at such speed Valkyrie staggered a little, then put everything she had into the hug.

"Hey there," she said softly. "Hey."

Her parents entered the room, came forward at only a slightly reduced speed than their youngest, and for a moment there was hugging and nothing more.

"They told us what's been going on," Melissa said. "Are you sure you're OK?"

"I'm good," Valkyrie responded, blinking back tears.

Desmond broke off the hug to look at her. "Skulduggery explained it to us. He told us you loved the Faceless Ones like they were your children. Even though they're evil gods?"

Valkyrie shrugged sadly. "You'd still love us even if we did something bad, right? That's what it was like."

"So they were your family," Melissa said softly.

Valkyrie nodded.

"And you loved them like they were your family?"

"I suppose."

"My poor little girl," Melissa said, hugging her again. "I'm so sorry."

The unconditional love radiating from her mother, from her father and her sister, seeped through Valkyrie's defences and suddenly she was crying again, and that only made them hug her tighter.

"We'll be your family again," said Alice.

"Oh, sweetie," said Valkyrie, "you never stopped."

"And Militsa, too?"

Valkyrie hesitated. "I don't... I don't know about that one."

Alice looked towards the door and Valkyrie turned, saw Militsa standing there. Her parents took Alice and they all stepped back, giving Valkyrie space.

"Before you say anything," Valkyrie said, "there's something I need to tell you. I totally understand if I've ruined things between us. I know that you get what happened, I know that you get that my connection to the Faceless Ones was influencing me and everything I did and said, so I know that, intellectually, you know that none of it was technically my fault.

"But even though I know this, too, I don't think that changes anything. I still did the things I did and said the things I said – and I let this new love for these murderous abominations alter me. I don't blame you for breaking up with me. I would have broken up with me. Hell, if the situation had been reversed, I would have broken up with you.

"So we might never get back together. And that's awful, and it breaks my heart to even say it out loud, but I understand. Some things you can't scrub from your memory. Some things happen and they colour the way you think about a person for good, no matter what they might do in the future. There are actions or words that will taint a person forever. But before that happens, if it's going to happen, I need you to know that I love you, Militsa Gnosis. I love you with my whole heart. You're strong and you're smart and you're funny and you're decent. You're so incredibly decent. I love being with you, I love being around you, I love the person I become because of you. If we have to stay broken up and I have to go on with my life without you in it, then I'll accept it right here and now, I won't argue. I won't try to change your mind. I just need you to know what you mean to me."

"Uh-huh," said Militsa. "Is it my turn to talk?"

"Talk, nod, scowl, whatever, yes, go ahead."

"Thank you," Militsa said, and pulled Valkyrie into a kiss.

There was the sound of skittering paws, and Xena charged into the room and jumped, catching Valkyrie off balance. She tumbled to the ground and the dog bounded all over her, burrowing her head between Valkyrie's arms as she tried covering up, making her howl with laughter.

"Slobbery!" she gasped. "So slobbery!"

Valkyrie's family joined Militsa and they watched Xena's relentless attack.

"Go get her, girl," Militsa said.

85

Another Faceless One slouched towards Roarhaven from across the sea, no doubt churning tidal waves with every step. From where they stood on the roof of the library, neither Sebastian nor Darquesse could spot those waves – they could only see the monstrosity of a moving mountain coming closer.

"They're panicking," said Darquesse. "They'd forgotten what it was like to be scared, but they're scared now."

They watched Obsidian carve his way across the sky above their heads, towards the Faceless One.

"He is magnificent," Darquesse said.

Sebastian looked at her. "Can you stop him?"

"Maybe. I don't know. He operates differently from anyone else I've ever encountered. He is nothingness. I don't know if my power would work on nothingness. I could try. I could go after him right now and try to stop him."

"No. Not now. Not yet."

She smiled. "You want me to be ready. You want the moment to be right. You want everything to be in place, to be exact, to be precise."

"Yes."

"Are you sure that's all you want?"

"You're here to save the world. That's all I care about."

"In that case, I have more work to do. My plans were derailed." She smiled. "Until you came to save me."

"I couldn't leave you there. I had to at least try."

"Thank you for trying, Sebastian."

"You're welcome, Darquesse."

She smiled again, and flew away.

Sebastian turned and watched the Faceless One vanish: another god wiped from reality.

86

American cereal was delicious.

Omen had a third bowl of what would have been considered already a pretty high-sugar breakfast cereal in Ireland and the UK – but here in America was covered, in addition to its existing sweetness, in a sugary glaze that made every mouthful a wonderful delight. He ate alone in the small kitchen, people passing the doorway as he munched, too busy to even glance in. Valkyrie passed, talking with Tanith. They didn't notice him. He could have happily had this cereal for every meal of the day, with another sneaky few bowls just before bed.

He wondered, idly, if he was focusing too much on his breakfast as a way of distracting himself from worrying about his friends or his brother or the state of the world. He shrugged, and kept crunching those delicious berries that had tumbled with the flakes from the box.

Reznor Rake walked in, turned a chair and sat into it the wrong way round, like they did in the movies. He rested his elbows on the chair back and looked straight at Omen.

Omen couldn't eat if someone was looking at him, so he reluctantly pushed his bowl to one side.

"They're not going to pay us," Reznor said, like he expected Omen to do something about it.

"Oh," said Omen.

"You told us that rescuing China Sorrows and Valkyrie Cain would establish a brand-new reputation with the resistance that we could then build on."

"That's right."

"You said nothing about doing any of this for free."

"I didn't really think about that part."

"Me and Tancred, we get paid for the effort we put into stuff. That's our whole, entire way of operating."

"Have you spoken to anyone about this?"

"We went to speak to China Sorrows, who you'd imagine would be ever-so-goddamn grateful to us for getting her out of there before her execution."

"And what did she say?"

"She's not here. She's off having private meetings with various people around the world, apparently. The point is, you'd have thought she'd have made the time to talk to us."

"Everyone's really busy, though. Did you manage to speak to anyone else?"

"We took our concerns to Tanith Low, but she said she's not the leader here."

"Who is?"

"She said there isn't one. Said the resistance is more of a collective of like-minded individuals. She said there isn't a kitty. You know what a kitty is, kid?"

"It's a—"

"It's a fund of money for communal use, made up of contributions from a group of people."

"I knew that."

Reznor leaned closer. "Tancred and I are used to getting paid."

"I'm sure there'll be some reward when all this is over."

Reznor blinked. "Some reward?"

"And the new reputation you're building, I'm sure that'll come in handy later."

"Later?"

"You just have to give this a chance," said Omen.

Reznor jabbed a finger at him. "I want you to fix this."

"Me? How?"

"Use your influence."

"I have no influence."

"You're Omen Darkly – of course you have influence."

"I really don't, though."

"Kid, are you telling me that Tancred and I left a secure gig with Creed and his Faceless Ones buddies, where we were getting paid exactly what we were asking, to come here, to work with the resistance, who don't have any kind of discretionary fund or petty-cash system in place to pay well-meaning freelancers such as ourselves?"

"I'm... I think so."

Reznor stood. "This is bull."

"You did the right thing, though."

"This is such bull," Reznor said, and walked out.

Omen finished his bowl of cereal and took it to the sink to wash. He packed away everything and wondered what he was going to do for the rest of the day. He turned to go, and jumped back.

Obsidian stood by the door, observing him.

"Auger," Omen said, his heart thudding in his chest, "do you know me? Do you recognise me?"

Obsidian didn't answer. Didn't move.

"If you're going to wipe me away, just do it now. Get it over with. If you don't do it now, right now, then I'll know you're not going to do it. I'll know you recognise me and you remember me and you remember who you are. You're Auger Darkly. You were, I mean. That was your name, but you were going to change it. You were going to leave it behind. When you told me that, I didn't understand, but I..."

He faltered, then continued. "But I understand now. It's our parents, isn't it? The way they raised you – raised us – as if Auger Darkly was a brand, like the only thing that mattered was maintaining the influence that they only got because of you. I understand it now. They don't care about us. You were right. You were going to abandon the name and start over, and I'm going to do the same. I'm going to find a new name, a name I can be proud of, and I'm going to have a life and an identity of my own. I'm going to be right there with you, dude."

"Omen," said Obsidian, his voice distorted.

Omen's eyes were suddenly wet with tears. "Yes. Yeah, it's me. Auger, I've missed you. I thought you were gone. I thought I'd never see you again."

"Auger is dead," said Obsidian.

Omen went quiet.

"He loved you." Every word sounded painful, like it was being dragged through stone. "He loved being your brother. He was proud to be your brother."

"I need him to come back."

"There is no coming back," said Obsidian.

"Then who are you? If you're not Auger, who are you?"

"I am the nothing."

"You can't be nothing. You're talking to me. The person who's talking has a mind. You have a mind. So whose mind is it, if it isn't Auger's?"

"I am the nothing."

"You're my brother."

"Your brother is dead. I have his fading memories."

"What happens when they're gone?"

"Then all trace of Auger Darkly is gone, and there is only nothing."

"He won't let that happen. He'll fight. I know he will. He's always fought and he's not going to stop."

"His fight is over."

"But you won't be needed. When you get rid of all the Faceless Ones, you won't be needed any more. You can go away and let Auger come back."

"The Faceless Ones are one."

"OK."

"The Faceless Ones are one."

"Sure, the Faceless Ones are one. But, when they're gone, you can leave Auger alone, right?"

"There is no Auger."

"There has to be something. What's going to happen when the Faceless Ones are gone?"

"The Faceless Ones are one."

"What'll happen? What will you do next?"

"I am nothing. I am the end of everything."

Omen frowned. "What does that mean?"

Obsidian didn't answer, and Omen went cold.

"You're not going to stop," he said. "Once the Faceless Ones have been wiped away, you're going to start on the rest of us, aren't you?"

"The Faceless Ones are one."

"What are you going to do? Are you going to wipe us away? Humanity? The whole world?"

"I am the end of everything."

He meant it. The end of absolutely everything. The end of the universe.

"If you do that," said Omen, "you'll kill me. Auger will kill me."

"Death is not nothing. You will be nothing."

"I'll be dead."

"You will be nothing."

"Stop saying that!"

"He loved you."

"Auger! Auger, I know you can hear me! Please!"

"He loved you," said Obsidian. "And he wished he could have had more time with you."

He opened a tear in the space beside him and stepped into it. Omen rushed forward, but the rift healed and Obsidian was gone.

87

Valkyrie frowned. "The end of everything?"

Omen nodded. "That's what he said."

"And you're sure you didn't misunderstand him?" Skulduggery asked. "You're sure he meant that when he's wiped away the Faceless Ones, he'll be coming for the rest of us?"

"He'll be coming for the rest of everything."

"That is concerning."

The room was quiet. Tanith stood with Gracious and Donegan and Dexter and they all looked very grave indeed. Kierre stood alone, near the back of the room.

"At least we have a little time," said Valkyrie. "Obsidian will have to work his way through the thousands of Faceless Ones and they might be able to put up some kind of fight, which would delay him even further. That gives us an opportunity to come up with a way to stop him."

"Now all we have to do is think of one," said Tanith.

"The Faceless Ones are one," Skulduggery murmured. "He repeated that?"

"Four or five times," said Omen.

"Interesting."

"Is it?" Valkyrie asked.

"Isn't it?" Skulduggery countered. "It's curious. It's an odd phrase to utter once, let alone four or five times. I've known plenty of people who speak in riddles – usually sorcerers who hold themselves in too high regard – and it's always profoundly annoying. But the rest of what Obsidian was saying – he didn't speak in riddles, did he?"

"No," said Omen. "I mean, some of it wasn't exactly clear, but I understood what he meant."

Skulduggery nodded. "To be expected. Obsidian's mind has been drastically altered – to reduce his thinking down to the clumsiness of language must have taken some effort. I'm actually impressed that he managed to say anything at all to you."

"It was Auger," said Omen. "I know it was. He made the effort because of Auger."

"I agree. Despite what Obsidian said, there must have still been something of Auger left inside him. Which brings us back to the phrase 'the Faceless Ones are one'. Valkyrie, what do you think it means?"

She blinked. "Um... I dunno."

"Care to hazard a guess?"

"I haven't a clue. Who knows what someone like Obsidian means when he says something weird? He's operating on a different level."

"But you're the Child and the Mother," said Skulduggery. "You've had the Faceless Ones in your head. You've been in theirs. What do you think he meant?"

"I seriously don't—"

"Valkyrie!" Skulduggery shouted. "Give me an answer and don't think about it! *Don't think!* Don't wonder! Don't look so surprised! Just give me the first answer that pops into that ridiculous brain of yours!"

"My brain is not ridiculous!" Valkyrie shouted back.

Skulduggery kept shouting. "What did Obsidian mean when he said the Faceless Ones are one?"

"Just that the Faceless Ones *are* one!" she roared. "They're one! They're linked!" She stopped shouting as she went on, her voice gradually returning to normal. "They're different and they each think different thoughts, but there's a part of them that thinks the same thoughts, like a song playing in the background."

Skulduggery watched her in the sudden silence. "I see," he said.

She frowned. "Is that what he meant?"

"Perhaps."

"This link," said Dexter, "is it always there?"

"Always."

"Can you hear it?"

Valkyrie shook her head. "Not any more. I reckon I'm still receiving it, or at least I'm capable of receiving it, but I'm just not tuned into it right now."

"Why would Obsidian want me to know this?" Omen asked.

"I don't think he did," said Skulduggery. "I think Auger did. I think he managed – somehow – to get a message to you, through Obsidian's words."

"And that's the message? The Faceless Ones are linked? Why would he want me to know that?"

Skulduggery tapped his chin. "The link," he said. "The link. The chain. The rope. If there's a rope connecting all the Faceless Ones left in the universe..."

"Yes?"

"If there's a rope tied to everyone standing on a bridge and the person in front falls, what happens to the others?"

"They fall after him?"

"That's exactly what they do."

Valkyrie frowned. "If Obsidian... if he's worked out..."

Omen was getting annoyed. "What are you talking about? Please, just one of you tell me."

"Obsidian could have found a way to use the link," said Dexter. "What if he doesn't have to hunt down each individual Faceless One in order to wipe them from existence? What if he's worked out how to wipe away one, and then all of the others are wiped at the same time, because of the link that connects them?"

Omen hesitated. "He could do that? That could be done?"

"Maybe," said Skulduggery. "He could get rid of them all in an instant."

"And then he'd be moving on to the rest of us," Omen said. "But if he *can* do it, why hasn't he yet?"

"It might take preparation," Valkyrie said. "It's like when I have to do anything psychic – I need to stop everything else and focus on this new thing."

"So it could happen at any moment?"

They didn't answer.

"What are the Faceless Ones doing right now?" Skulduggery asked. "Who has the latest information?"

"I do," said Nefarian, walking in.

Valkyrie raised an eyebrow. "You made it to the resistance."

"You sound surprised."

"They let you in without killing you."

"You sound astonished."

"Serpine accompanied China back to us after you released him from his cell," Skulduggery said, "and we reasoned that we need all the help we can get. If that means using him as a human shield at the first opportunity, that's how far we're prepared to go."

This drew a thin smile from Nefarian. "Who would have thought, after all this time, that the two of us would be fighting side by side? It makes me miss the days when we were trying to kill each other."

"We've fought side by side before."

Nefarian waved a hand. "Everyone knows it doesn't count if it's in another dimension."

Skulduggery looked at him, head tilted, and Valkyrie felt the space between the two old enemies start to turn sharp.

"The report," she said. "What are the Faceless Ones doing?"

"They're not doing anything," said Nefarian. "They were moving. After you burned the other Faceless Ones out of your soul, Valkyrie, they all turned in this direction, started leaving the

413

cities behind. But then Obsidian showed up and wiped a few of them away and now they're just standing there. All around the world, they're just standing there."

"They know," said Valkyrie. "They know Obsidian's worked out a way to destroy them in one go."

"And they're scared stiff?" Tanith said. "Is that what's happening?"

"Maybe this is like an ostrich," said Omen. "You know the way they bury their heads in the ground when there's danger nearby?"

"Ostriches don't actually do that," said Donegan.

"They don't?"

"How are they expected to breathe with their heads in the ground?"

"I didn't say they were smart," Omen muttered.

"I don't think that's happening here," said Valkyrie. "I don't mean the ostrich thing – and I didn't know they don't do that, either, Omen, so don't feel bad – but the scared-stiff thing. They're not frozen out of fear – they're doing something. I can feel them working." She went to the window, looked out at the Faceless One in the distance. "Their energies are all over the place. I think they're changing."

Skulduggery tilted his head. "Changing how?"

"I'm not sure. I think they're altering themselves. Behind their fear and anger and confusion, there's a... hope. It's desperate, and reluctant, but it's definitely hope. They don't want to change, but they realise that they have to. If they don't, Obsidian will finish them."

"Are we worried about this?" Omen asked. "If they're changing, it might be into something worse – if that's possible."

"Maybe," Skulduggery said.

"We know how to fight the Faceless Ones," said Dexter, "and we know that Valkyrie can destroy them, but we have no way knowing if her power will be effective against Obsidian. If the Faceless Ones are devising a way to defend themselves against him, we should observe."

"We'll need to track Obsidian," Tanith said. "Donegan, you said you have a friend who can access Chinese surveillance satellites?"

"I said I might."

Skulduggery nodded. "Finding and watching Obsidian is our top priority. We'd better get on with it."

Nods all round, and the room began to empty.

"Serpine," Skulduggery said, "a moment?"

Nefarian waited, eyebrow arched, until it was just the three of them. Skulduggery walked up to him, flexing the fingers of his right hand before curling them into a fist. It looked like he was going to punch Nefarian. It looked very much like he was going to punch Nefarian.

Skulduggery punched Nefarian and Valkyrie wondered why the hell this surprised her.

Nefarian dropped to his knees and Valkyrie darted forward.

"What are you doing?" she said as Skulduggery shackled Nefarian's hands behind his back.

Despite the blood leaking from his lip, Nefarian chuckled and Skulduggery stepped away.

"It's Serpine," Skulduggery said, taking his gun out.

"I know," Valkyrie said. "I know it's Serpine. Why the hell did you hit him?"

Skulduggery shook his head. "This is *our* Serpine. The Serpine from this dimension. The one I killed fourteen years ago."

88

Valkyrie blinked. "I'm sorry, what?"

"Before you go shooting anyone," said Serpine, "the other Nefarian is in here with me – the one you like."

"I don't like either of you," said Skulduggery.

"I wasn't talking to you," Serpine responded, and looked at Valkyrie. "You can't let him kill me. You have to stop him."

"He's not going to kill you," Valkyrie said, frowning. "Skulduggery, tell him."

"I'm going to kill you," said Skulduggery.

"No, he is not. Skulduggery, put the gun down."

"He murdered my family. He murdered your uncle."

Valkyrie raised her hands slowly. "Hey. Hey, look at me. Do not shoot him, all right? Don't do it. I'm not understanding any of this, so would you please tell me what the hell is going on?"

"I don't know what's going on. I don't know how it happened. All I know is that the consciousness of the Serpine I killed is cohabiting that body."

Valkyrie reached out, fingers closing round the gun barrel. Skulduggery resisted for a moment, then allowed her to take the weapon away from him. She flicked on the safety and slid the gun into the waistband of her jeans. "You don't know how it happened," she said, "so work it out."

"It doesn't matter how it happened."

"It matters to me. Skulduggery, please. Stay calm, and figure it out."

Serpine laughed. "I'd forgotten how much fun this was. The decades following the end of the war, after the Truce, when I was on my best behaviour, were without a doubt the most boring of my life. But what made them bearable – what made them enjoyable – was knowing that Skulduggery Pleasant was out there, and he knew where I was, and he knew I was free, and he couldn't do a single thing about it. I can't begin to tell you how many nights I went to sleep with a smile on my face because of that."

Valkyrie waved her hand to get Skulduggery's attention, and then she pointed at her own eyes. She focused on the empty sockets of his skull, on the shadows that moved within, and she watched him suppress his anger, watched his body relax, watched that familiar cool return.

Skulduggery adjusted his cuffs. "I killed you," he said to Serpine, his voice smooth. "Fourteen years ago, I used the Sceptre, and the katahedral crystal exploded. When it exploded, the black lightning turned you to dust. That, by the way, was a wonderful moment. For centuries, people had been warning me of the damage vengeance would do to me. Before you embark on a journey of revenge, they said, dig two graves. They thought they were quoting Confucius – they weren't – but the wisdom of the words remained valid. Revenge is a self-destructive endeavour. Of course, so are unresolved issues of loss, grief and rage.

"In the moment, I was helped along by the fact that you were killing Valkyrie at the time, so not only was I doling out justice for my wife and child, I was also saving an innocent life. I had my revenge, and I felt fantastic."

"What a heart-warming story," Valkyrie muttered.

"But here you are," Skulduggery continued. "Sharing this body with the Serpine from the Leibniz Universe. How can that be?"

Serpine's smile grew wider. "I'll never—"

"Hush," said Skulduggery, slapping him over the head, "I'm still talking. Valkyrie, what do we know of the katahedral crystals?"

"They're also called hirranian crystals. Um, let's see... The Faceless Ones used them – well, they definitely used the one in the Sceptre – to kill each other in their wars. They acted as alarm systems: whenever someone who wasn't a Faceless One got near, the crystals would sing. They absorb the souls of the people they destroy, transforming them into energy, so the more people a crystal kills, the more powerful it becomes – and it's already started out powerful enough to kill a god."

"But, when I used the Sceptre, the crystal exploded."

Valkyrie frowned. "So it... it destroyed his body, dragged his soul out, but then... there was nowhere for the soul to go."

Skulduggery held out his hand and she gave him back his gun. He held it by his side. "So it stuck around. It stayed in the Sanctuary. It wasn't strong enough to make a nuisance of itself, which probably helped it evade the attention of all those Sensitives. A few years later, the Sanctuary was destroyed and we all moved to Roarhaven, but it stayed where it was."

"And they built a hotel around it," Valkyrie said. Her eyes widened. "I was there. I stopped by there, like, a month ago."

Skulduggery tilted his head. "Why?"

"I don't know. I wasn't planning on it. I was just riding through Dublin and I ended up outside the hotel. It was completely random."

"No, I don't think it was. Valkyrie, you're brimming with power."

"I *am* awesome."

"Some of that power is katahedral energy. You absorbed it when the new Sceptre blew up in your hand. Serpine's soul – what was left of it – must have been infused with a much more diluted strand of the same energy. It would have sensed you nearby. It could have drawn you in."

Valkyrie glared at Serpine, who winked at her. "And it hitched a lift. I brought it to Roarhaven. When I met with Nefarian – this

Serpine – the other Serpine's soul could have hopped into him."

"It must have seemed like fate was smiling on you," Skulduggery said to Serpine. "Not only was there a version of you from another universe whose mind you could jump into, but he had a spare body locked away, just waiting for you to make yourself at home. The opportunity, the timing... it was almost too perfect."

Skulduggery hunkered down in front of him. "But these wonderful, logic-shattering coincidences happen in threes, don't they? Fate smiled on you twice in rapid succession, so it's only fair that she add a twist, right? Before you could make one more move, Robert Scure walked in – one of the only Sensitives who could get past your psychic defences because he's the one who installed them, didn't he? That's the secret project you and he worked on, way back in the day. Did he sense something? Could he tell that there were two of you in there now? You couldn't run the risk of him saying anything – not with Valkyrie right there, not with her being so powerful. You wouldn't have stood a chance against her, not if she decided to take you in. So you shot her, killed Scure and ran."

"It took you long enough to work all that out," Serpine said with an exaggerated eyeroll. "I've been wanting to laugh in what passes for your face since I jumped into this body. How does it feel, Skulduggery, to know that your biggest triumph was nothing but yet another miserable failure?"

"It's not too bad, actually. It means I get to kill you again." He raised the gun.

"Oh, but you can't kill *me*," Serpine said. "There are two of us in here, after all – and one of us is on the verge of reforming. It's quite sickening, to be honest. I despise being this close to weakness. The sooner you get me to that second body, the happier I'll be."

"And what makes you think we're going to do that?"

"Because you have to. What, you're going to stop me from making use of a body that nobody else is using? You're going to stop the other Nefarian Serpine from regaining his independence?

He's still in here, you know. I may have subdued his consciousness with barely a struggle, he may be unaware of what's going on, but he's still here. You're going to trap him in with me forever? Really?"

"It's an option."

"No, it isn't. Because, when you let me inhabit a body of my very own, you'll have your enemy back. Admit it: you've been lost without me. We're a lot alike, you know. We need our enemies. I always needed you out there, Skulduggery. I needed a worthy opponent. And you? You needed me. You still do. You've allowed yourself to become dull. I can make you sharp again."

"Or I kill you here and now and save everyone the aggravation."

Valkyrie put her hand on Skulduggery's shoulder.

Serpine laughed. "See? She's made you weak. She's made you dull. I'm going to enjoy sharpening you up. It's going to be fun getting back to the good old days."

"You think we should let you go."

"I think you're going to, yes. You can't afford to lock me up – you know I'll only find a way to escape, and who knows what damage I might do on my way out? You're going to let me go because then I'll be able to hop out of this alternate version of myself, into my own body, and everything will be clean and clear and easy. You're the hero. I'm the villain. You get to track me down. Until one of us kills the other."

Skulduggery pondered the situation, then holstered the gun.

Serpine laughed as he got to his feet. "May I go now?"

"You'd better," said Skulduggery.

Smirking, Serpine strolled out of the room and Tanith barged into his shoulder as she hurried in.

"There's something happening," she said. "Obsidian's in New York, but the Faceless Ones there... something's happening. Val – you need to check it out."

Valkyrie's necronaut suit flowed over her clothes and she went to the window, opened it. "Don't kill Serpine while I'm gone," she told Skulduggery, and took off.

89

The building was alive with activity as the resistance tracked Valkyrie flying to New York. Omen found a room with no one in it, no one for him to get in the way of, and turned on the TV there. It was tuned to the Network, where they were reporting on a further crackdown on subversive activity within Corrival Academy. Duenna's smug face filled the screen and Omen immediately turned to a mortal news channel, but they didn't know what the hell was happening, so he turned it off and stood there and felt useless.

After a moment, he left the room and went down to the basement. Unlocked the door and stepped inside.

"There he is," said Temper, from the shadows.

Omen suddenly found that he had nothing to say.

Temper moved a little, into the light, and smiled. "Oh, come on, you can't be afraid of me, can you? We go back, you and I. We have history. You got me out of that cell in Coldheart, remember? You saved my life, kid."

"I remember," said Omen.

Temper held up his hands, showing the shackles. "And here we are again, huh? When will I learn, you know what I mean?" He chuckled. "There's a key around here somewhere, isn't there? Probably on the other side of that door. You would've seen it on your way in. Don't suppose you could go out there and get it for me, could you? I feel awful asking you this, Omen, I really do, but I'm going to need you to set me free again."

"I can't do that, Temper. You're not safe."

Temper let his hands fall. "Right," he said.

"Can I get you anything? Food or water or something?"

"I need the key, Omen. That's what I need."

"I'm sorry."

"You're sorry," Temper said, his voice softening as he took a step backwards. The shadows claimed his face. "So why'd you come down here? You came to check out the monster in the basement, that it? You wanted to see the claws? Wanted to see the fangs?"

"I wanted to see if you needed anything."

"The goddamn key, kid."

"They're looking for a cure," Omen said. "I heard them talking. As soon as all this is over and they have the resources, they're going to be searching for a way to reverse this."

"There is no reversing this. There's no curing this. It's not a disease or an injury. It's an evolution. You can't go back on an evolution, kid – that's not how it works."

"If it's impossible, then they'll do the impossible."

Temper watched him from the darkness, and laughed. Omen blushed, turned to go.

"Hold on," said Temper. "I'm sorry. I didn't mean to laugh. It's very nice of you to try and offer some hope at a time like this. But I'm happy the way I am. I don't need hope. I just need to be let out."

"I'm not releasing you."

"Then why are you here? Why'd you come down here? I mean, really?"

Omen hesitated.

"Oh," said Temper. "You want to talk. That's it, right? We've had some pretty good heart-to-hearts before this and now you're, what, feeling a little lost? A little out of your depth? So you came to see Temper Fray to get an honest opinion out of him. Hell, kid, I ain't going anywhere, so you may as well say what you gotta say, and then see if I can be of any assistance."

"I don't think you can help me."

"You got anyone else lined up as an understudy for me, though? Yeah, thought not. I'm here, you're here, so why don't we just try it and see where it takes us?"

Omen took a deep breath. "My parents disowned me," he said at last.

"So? You have terrible parents. You hate them."

"I don't hate them."

"It's OK to hate your parents if they're terrible parents."

"Maybe. Anyway, they disowned me and Auger... He came to see me, or Obsidian did, but I couldn't help him. I tried to help people at my school, but I couldn't do that, either, and then I came here because I wanted to help the resistance, but... Everyone upstairs, they all have their missions and their jobs and they know what they're supposed to do and they know what they can do, and then there's me, standing in the corner, waiting for someone to notice me while at the same time hoping no one does because I can't do anything."

"You can do plenty," Temper said. "You've been palling around with that Crepuscular guy, right? Getting into your own little adventures?"

Omen grunted. "That wasn't a partnership. Not really. Crepuscular had his own agenda and it had nothing to do with me."

"Everyone's got their own agenda," said Temper. "You have an agenda, don't you? You want to help people, you want to be useful, you want to matter. You got your priorities, same as anybody else."

"Right now, my priority is not to get in anybody's way."

"You know what you gotta do."

"I really don't."

"Yes, you do, you just gotta answer one simple question. Who can you help right now? If you can't help your brother, and you can't help the resistance, who else is there that needs you?"

"I don't—"

"Think about it, Omen," Temper said, coming forward once again. "Who else requires you to actually do something? What situation out there in the world can you affect?"

"I'm not sure that there's—"

"This isn't about being a hero, kid – this is about doing the right thing. This isn't even about succeeding – it's just about trying. Who needs someone to try? Who needs someone to care?"

"I suppose... my school," Omen said.

"Yes!"

"I have to get back there."

"You gotta help your friends!"

"I have to help my friends."

"Then what the hell are you waiting for?"

Omen smiled. "Thanks, Temper."

Temper lunged, his fangs snapping on the tip of Omen's nose and Omen jerked back, fell, and Temper screamed at him, chains rattling, spittle flying, and Omen scrambled up and got the hell out of there.

90

Valkyrie reached New York in time to watch Obsidian move towards the Faceless One called Lahsse, and Valkyrie watched its energies fluctuate. It burned with a fierceness that hurt her eyes and then its physical body bent inwards and folded in space, dissolving into an energy that compressed immediately. Lahsse was gone and in its place was a spark, a single spark, no bigger than the flame on a match head. Obsidian slowed his approach, gazing at this spark with curiosity.

More sparks flew in, dozens of them, burning their way into Valkyrie's eyeline. They joined with the first and it absorbed the essences of these other Faceless Ones, but didn't get any bigger. Then it flitted. It would have been too quick to keep track of, but Valkyrie was attuned to it now, and she traced its flight across the horizon. It absorbed more sparks and then it was gone.

She switched her attention back to Obsidian, who hung in mid-air, and wondered if he was processing what had just happened, the same as her, or if he was so different that she couldn't have recognised his thoughts even if she could see them.

The Faceless Ones had just reduced themselves to that single spark of energy. They had sacrificed their physical forms, sacrificed the power that had always been theirs, in order to escape eradication. There was no way back for them, Valkyrie knew. She had felt what they did as it was happening, and she had sensed their resignation. Their total and utter defeat.

After countless eons, after wars between gods and another war between gods and humanity, after a humiliating exile and a triumphant return, the Faceless Ones had surrendered. They were no longer a threat, no longer a consideration, and so Obsidian had let them go.

Because now he had other things to wipe away.

91

"Mr President, we have grave news. The big monsters, the creatures that were called Faceless Ones, do appear to have been vanquished, as we reported."

Flanery waited, looked round at everyone else crammed into the Oval Office, and frowned. "I can't see how you could call that grave news, though. Wouldn't that be good news? I'd call that good news. Jerry, wouldn't you call that good news?"

His Chief of Staff nodded quickly. "The best news, Mr President. Vanquished because of your quick thinking."

"That's right," said Flanery. "You think Paul Donovan could have done this? You think he'd be able to handle a monster invasion as well as I did? No chance. None. The guy's a loser."

"Sir, your quick thinking saved a lot of lives," General Sheckley said, "but that's not the grave news I mean."

"Ah!" said Flanery. "I knew it! Because that's good news. The big, huge monsters going away, that's good news. Not grave news."

"But the bad news, Mr President—"

Flanery bared his teeth and sucked in air. "What did I tell you? What did I tell all of you?"

The general, bizarrely, didn't look away in shame. "You asked us not to bring you bad news, sir."

"I told you. I told you not to bring me bad news."

"But this is important. Urgent. Vital, even."

Flanery sat back in his big chair. He'd had it brought in because it looked like a throne and it matched the big desk. The previous guy had had a small chair and it had made him look like a small man. Image was important, Flanery knew. Optics. It was all about optics these days.

The general continued talking as if Flanery had given him the nod to continue, and that just annoyed Flanery even more. "Our enhanced troops have been reporting heavy losses, sir."

"Our super-soldiers, you mean."

"Whatever you want to call them, Mr President, they're reporting heavy, devastating losses."

"Why? They have magic powers as well as the best guns."

"But they're going up against monsters and other people who have magic powers. Some of them have guns, too."

"But our guys are soldiers."

"Sir, as has been laid out in the reports we've sent over, the sorcerers we're fighting are hundreds of years old."

"Then they should be frail and weak."

"As detailed in our reports, sir, they are not frail and weak. They're hundreds of years old, their ageing has slowed, and they are fit and strong. They have fought in their own wars, and they have fought – alongside regular soldiers – in our wars. They are vastly more experienced – not only in wielding magic, but also in combat – than any of our fighting men and women could ever dream of being."

Flanery didn't like this guy. His voice was tight, like he was about to lose his temper, and nobody lost their temper with the President of the United States.

"The Faceless Ones are gone. Dead. Because of me. Because of my strategy. At this point, you should just be sending in our soldiers to clear up the mess they've left behind. What the hell is wrong with you? Can't you even do your job?"

"Sir, this conflict isn't even close to being over."

Now *that* Flanery laughed at. "Are you crazy? Are you not seeing what's going on? Turn on a TV, General! Everyone is hailing me as the greatest Commander in Chief who's ever lived!"

"This isn't about the goddamn news reports," Sheckley said, snapping out his words. "I am telling you the facts. I am telling you what is actually happening. I don't care what the news anchors say or what the journalist on the street is saying or what the opinion polls are saying – I am telling you what we actually know from actual intelligence our agencies have actually gathered."

The Oval Office fell silent. Sheckley's face was red and a vein pulsed in his gleaming forehead. Flanery felt his own face redden as rage spread upwards from his shoes. Nobody else in this meeting said a word. Nobody even dared look at anyone else.

"I defeated the Faceless Ones," Flanery growled.

"The Faceless Ones ran away!" Sheckley said loudly. "Nothing we did actually affected them in any way, shape or form! And as big as they were, and as much damage and death as they'd caused all around the world, they weren't doing anything! For the most part, they were just standing there!"

"You can't shout at me!"

"Yes, I damn well can!" Sheckley jumped to his feet. "The most immediate threat to the American public has been, and still is, those Shalgoth creatures! They're the ones actively seeking out and killing people! They're the ones we should have been focusing on – like we said! But, as usual, you didn't listen!"

"You can't talk to the president like this," snarled one of Flanery's aides.

"Shut up, you pipsqueak! You know what else you've done wrong, Mr President? You decided to go to war with the sorcerers! You decided to start fighting the people with the magic powers who, from the very first day, were trying to help us!"

"You're fired!" Flanery screeched, standing and almost knocking his chair over. "You're fired! You're fired! You're fired!"

"I will take my firing," Sheckley roared, "as a badge of honour, you incredibly stupid little man!"

The general stormed out of the Oval Office and Flanery screamed in unbridled fury. He picked up the phone and flung it to the far wall, but all those cables and wires meant that it snapped back, the receiver almost hitting him in the face. "Leave! Everybody leave!"

They all ran, all of them, scurrying out of the office like pathetic, snivelling mice. All except one man lounging on the couch with his legs crossed, a man Flanery hadn't even noticed was there.

Perfidious Withering waited until the door closed before speaking. "That was a very impressive display, Martin," he said in that plummy English accent.

"Get out."

The slightest raised eyebrow. "Oh, dear – somebody has lost his sense of humour, hasn't he?"

Flanery reached for the button that called in his Secret Service agents.

"Do you really want to do that, Martin?"

"I can get them to shoot you," Flanery responded, finger hovering. "They'd do it. And they're not ordinary agents, either. They've got magic. They're wizards now, just like you."

Perfidious smiled. "*Barba non facit philosophum.*"

Flanery recoiled. "What is that? Is that a spell? Did you just put a curse on me?"

"It's Latin, Martin. And by all means, press the button if you want a demonstration of the correct way to wield magic. I'm always good for a matinee performance."

Flanery hesitated, then sat with all the dignity he could muster. Which was an immense amount. "You're not welcome here."

"Before we get to that, I have a message to convey."

"Yeah? I've got a message to convey, too," said Flanery, and used his middle finger to scratch his nose.

Perfidious smirked. "How delightfully droll. Moving on, however, my employer is displeased with you, Martin. He has given you

430

ample opportunity to change your ways and come back in line and you have rebuffed every entreaty. This makes Crepuscular Vies very sad."

"I don't care what makes Crepuscular Vies sad," said Flanery, sneering.

"But you should. Mr Vies has guided you through some difficult times."

"I didn't need his help. I didn't need anyone's help."

"You needed an awful lot of help getting elected."

"You don't know what you're talking about."

"I'm talking about the Sensitive, the woman named Magenta Blithe. Do you remember her, Martin? The woman whose son Crepuscular arranged to be kidnapped? The woman who we forced to influence various senators and media personalities to support your nomination to the presidency?"

Flanery bristled. "I got where I am today because some of us are winners, and some of us are losers."

Perfidious stood. "And you, Mr President, are a loser."

Flanery went for the button and Perfidious flicked his hand and the desk slid halfway across the room.

"Circumstances have changed," Perfidious said, buffing his fingernails on the lapel of his blazer. "You're a part of that, absolutely. My employer has had to adapt and improvise around your blunderings – but adaptation and improvisation are what he excels at. His plans proceed regardless, and the end point is approaching. He has sent me here to say goodbye, Martin."

Flanery blinked. "He has?"

"You're free to do whatever you want. Continue giving those little magic Splashes to your troops. Ignore the damage it is doing to them, both mentally and physically. Mortal bodies are not meant to wield magic. I'm sure you'd know that by now if you ever bothered to read the medical reports your experts are sending."

Perfidious approached and Flanery stood up out of his chair and backed off.

"You're free to bask in unearned glory as misguided citizens chant your name. You're free to stand on an aircraft carrier and declare Mission Accomplished while the Shalgoth are massacring thousands in the streets of your fair nation every single day. You're even free to wage war against the very sorcerers who are trying to help you. My God, Martin – you're free to abuse your paltry reserves of power in whatever way you see fit."

"And... and you're going to let me?"

"Me?" said Perfidious. "This was never about me, old boy. I happen to like you enormously. You remind me of a painting of a great man that hangs in the National Gallery in London. Not the man, mind you. Just the painting. Large and brash and yet so very flimsy, set inside a gold-leaf frame. Surprisingly fragile for something so immense. No, this is about my employer, Mr Vies. This is a man who has acknowledged that you have confounded him at practically every turn. He thought he could control you. He admits now that he was wrong. He thought he could antici-pate you. Yet, at every opportunity to make the smart decision, you have veered most impressively away. You are uncontrollable, Martin, and entirely unpredictable."

"You're... you're not going to kill me?"

"Oh, dear me, no. I do not kill. That is a line I have not crossed in a very long time. Mr Vies sent me to act as liaison precisely because of this reticence. Between you and me – the friends that I feel we have become – some of Mr Vies' priorities have changed. I feel he has been influenced, in a positive direction, by his interactions with a good and noble young soul. To witness this transformation has been most heart-warming. And so he has sent me to deliver this final message, one of peace and goodwill, instead of coming here himself, and killing you. Mr President, it has been a singular experience interacting with you. Good luck in your future endeavours. You're on your own now. Be sure to make the most of it. *Valeas quam optime.*"

Perfidious Withering smiled, and left the Oval Office.

92

The Dark Cathedral was quiet apart from the sobbing.

Followers of the Faceless Ones, the guards and soldiers and priests, the priestesses in their robes and the worshippers clutching their copies of the Book of Tears sat on the ground or leaned against the walls and stared, just stared, at nothing, their eyes red-rimmed, their mouths agape. Their gods had abandoned them, had fled, and the faithful were lost. The City Guard, the officers who'd maintained the shield around the city's walls, had lost their focus. The shield had faltered. The shield had fallen.

Skulduggery and Valkyrie entered the Dark Cathedral and flew slowly upwards, witnessing sorrow on every level, and everyone was too distraught to even think about stopping them.

Damocles Creed sat in his uncomfortable chair. The Nexus Helmet was lying on its side on his desk. He no longer shared his thoughts with the Dark Gods because there were no Dark Gods, and he looked somehow smaller for it.

Creed watched them come in, took a moment to register who they were, and jumped to his feet.

"Guards!" he screamed. "Seize them!"

No guards came running in.

"Is this a bad time?" Skulduggery asked, enjoying the moment immensely.

"You heathens," Creed snarled. "You heathen scum." He fixed

his gaze on Valkyrie. "Betrayer. Blasphemer. May your eyes rot in their sockets and your tongue shrivel in your mouth."

"You're taking this better than I expected," she told him.

"This," he said, shaking his finger at her, "this is your doing."

Valkyrie perched on the edge of his desk. "What did I do? This was all Obsidian. He made your creepy tentacle-lords run away like little tentacle-babies."

"You murdered your own children!" Creed screeched.

"Let's leave the who-did-what-to-whom for another day," Skulduggery said. "Damocles, we have reason to believe that Obsidian will be coming here. We think he's going to want to finish off anyone who has the stain of the Faceless Ones on them."

"And that's you, big guy," Valkyrie said. "You and me."

"Let him come," Creed responded. "I will make him pay."

"We would love to see that," Skulduggery said, "but, before you die, we'd like to take the Void meteorite off your hands. It's not that we doubt your ability to make Obsidian pay – good on you, we like that enthusiasm – but we have no actual faith in your ability to do anything of the sort. So just in case you have that little old rock hidden away where only you can find it, we thought we'd pop by, pick it up, and leave you to your quick and amusing death."

Creed looked at them both and appeared, to Valkyrie at least, to be thinking it over. "Filth," he said at last, disproving Valkyrie's theory. "You're filth. You're degenerate, heathen filth. We had gods all around us. They had returned to us, even after everything we'd put them through. They had forgiven us, and returned, and they were about to usher in a paradise on Earth. But you couldn't abide that, could you? You couldn't abide happiness and unconditional love. You couldn't abide the very idea of living for something greater than you – living for the world. For the universe. For existence itself."

"Wow," said Valkyrie. "That sounds awesome. Pity that was only going to happen for a select few and everyone else was facing a lifetime of pain."

"The faithful shall be rewarded," Creed said. "That was the promise they made us."

The window disappeared and Obsidian drifted towards them.

"Dammit," Valkyrie muttered, letting the necronaut suit flow over her clothes.

"Creed, give us the meteorite," Skulduggery said. "It's our only chance to stop him. Creed!"

Before Obsidian's feet even touched the floor, Valkyrie let loose. White lightning flowed from her fingers. When that had no effect, she shook her hands, drew on another kind of energy, and blasted Obsidian in the chest with black lightning. He staggered slightly, but didn't fall, and didn't crumble to dust.

"Aw, hell," she muttered.

Skulduggery grabbed her, pulled her back towards the door, and they were about to run when Creed pulled a handgun from his desk. It was clunky, odd-looking, carved with sigils, and Creed pulled the trigger without ceremony and Obsidian jerked back, chips of black flying from his shoulder.

Valkyrie narrowed her eyes, examining the weird energy that twisted around the bullets in the gun. Meteorite-infused bullets. Creed had made a weapon out of it.

"Die," Creed whispered, and fired again and again, each shot sending Obsidian backwards, each cutting through his skin, cracking the surface and burrowing into what lay beneath.

Obsidian fell to his knees. Creed aimed at his head and pulled the trigger and the hammer clicked on an empty chamber. No more fancy bullets.

Creed dropped the gun, pulled a sword from a wall compartment. The handle was metal and the blade was jagged meteorite stone, and he took two long strides and prepared to swing for Obsidian's neck and Valkyrie raised her hand out of sheer instinct, white energy crackling, and Creed flinched, expecting the bolt that would send him spinning – but she hesitated. The sword in his hands was the world's only chance to end the threat of Obsidian.

Skulduggery reached out, lowered her hand, and she didn't object.

Creed's smile was entirely unpleasant – but, when he returned his attention to Obsidian, there was already a tear in space opening beside him and he was falling through. Creed cursed, slashing after him, cutting a swathe through his back, and then the tear closed up.

"Coward!" Creed screamed after him. "Come and face me! Come and die!" He turned, snarling. "You let him get away. I had him, I was going to end him, and you let him get away!"

Valkyrie glared, but didn't respond.

"We'll be taking that sword, if you don't mind," Skulduggery said.

Creed stepped back against the wall. The floor beneath him opened and he dropped into it and it resealed before Valkyrie even realised what had happened.

Skulduggery walked over. Stamped on the ground a little. "So old-fashioned," he murmured. "I love it."

He took Valkyrie's arm and led her to the window and they flew out. Someone was taking shots at them from street level, but they rose quickly into the clouds.

"Leaving aside the fact that we don't actually have it in our possession, there exists a weapon that can hurt, and probably destroy, Obsidian, and that's some sorely needed good news."

"I shouldn't have tried to stop him," Valkyrie said. Skulduggery adjusted the air around them so that he could hear her as they flew. "That was the moment, right there. Obsidian was taken by surprise. He was hurt. Even if we have the sword, how are we going to get close enough for it to do any good? If Creed had had any more of those bullets, he'd have used them. I messed up. Our one chance to stop him and I ruined it."

"Your instinct was to show mercy," Skulduggery said. "I really

436

don't think you should be apologising for trying to save the life of an enemy."

"I'm an idiot."

"Of course you are. You're a good guy." The clouds parted for them. "We're all idiots."

93

"Clear," Mendoza said softly, and his squad mates filed past him, their boots light on the ground, the flashlights from their weapons sweeping every wall, corner and doorway. Foster patted Mendoza's shoulder and Mendoza joined the procession, the stock of his gun reassuringly tight against his shoulder.

The building was dark, but showed signs of recent activity. The heating was on. Mendoza reached up as he passed underneath a light, pressed his fingertips to the bulb. Still slightly warm. They'd just missed the enemy.

The team moved further into the building, keeping watch for booby traps.

They reached the ground floor without encountering opposition, and declared the whole site clear. The lights were switched on and the forensics teams were called in to examine the computers and notepads and books that had been left behind. The National Guard set up perimeters outside. It looked like they were going to have to get through another night of not shooting anybody, when one of the technicians noticed a door that shouldn't have been there.

Mendoza and his team approached cautiously. Silently. The door wasn't in the building schematics. Whatever lay beyond was a recent addition.

The door was unlocked, and free of wires, alarms or explosives.

It opened to a set of stairs leading down into darkness. Mendoza went first.

The steps took them to a cold concrete floor – big, wide and empty. Across from them was another door. Making sure they weren't about to trigger any tripwires or step into any pentagrams, the team approached. There was a small, stubby key hanging on a nail beside the door. Mendoza nodded to Foster and Foster pushed open the door and they swarmed in, their flashlights cutting through the dark.

The room was empty except for a man sitting huddled against the far wall. His hands were shackled, attached to the wall by chains.

"Please don't hurt me," he sobbed, hiding his face from the glare of the lights.

"Identify yourself," Mendoza snapped.

"Please," said the man. He was African-American, and tall. "I own this building. Please, whatever you want, I can't help you. I don't know what's going on."

"What are you doing down here?"

"I don't know. Some people grabbed me. They said they'd be back and then they..." He wept. "They disappeared. They vanished, right in front of me! Please, they said they'd be back, please get me out! Are you police? Please get me out!"

"There's a key hanging from a nail," Mendoza said to Foster, nodding to the door. "Uncuff him."

Foster nodded, hurried away, was back a few seconds later. Mendoza swept his weapon round the room, expecting a dozen wizards to teleport in at any moment. They were experienced with Teleporters – they had one on their team – so he knew full well the danger they posed.

Foster undid the shackles, and suddenly stepped back.

"His hands," he said. "Jesus – his face."

The guy stood. He was a lot taller than he'd seemed. Mendoza turned his flashlight on him and he darted, opened up Foster's belly with one swipe of his right hand, and then something knocked the flashlight away and there was only screaming.

94

"What's wrong?" Cadaver asked as he plunged his fist through a monster's chest.

Tanith flipped over a slashing claw, twisting in mid-air to chop the claw from the wrist, and landed to take the head. "Nothing's wrong. Why would anything be wrong?"

The creatures swarmed them and they backed off down a narrow alley.

"You seem distracted," Cadaver said, almost shouting to be heard over the snarling.

"Well, I'm not." Tanith's sword slid into a creature's throat and she pulled it out again.

"OK," said Cadaver.

They fought in silence for another few seconds.

"Oberon told me he loves me," she said at last.

Cadaver clicked his fingers and filled the alleyway with flames, giving Tanith a chance to get her breath back. "I see," he said. "And did you respond in kind?"

"I told him I needed time to process it."

"If I could wince on his behalf, I would."

He cut off the fire and the remaining creatures clambered over their chargrilled brethren to get at them.

"I just haven't had a lot of luck when it comes to romance in the last few years," Tanith said, watching them advance. "Before

Celeste, there was Sanguine – kind of. Before him, there was..."

Cadaver pushed at the air and three creatures hit the wall so hard they died on impact. "Ghastly," he said.

"Yeah."

"One would have thought your complete failure to establish a romantic relationship with Ghastly Bespoke before he died would have prompted you to never make the same mistake again."

"It isn't the same thing." Tanith dodged a swipe and took a limb. "Oberon's great, don't get me wrong."

"But he's not Ghastly?"

"No, he's not."

"Ghastly Bespoke was a singular individual," Cadaver said. "If he'd been around after I lost Valkyrie, I doubt I'd have travelled the same path I seem to be on. So are you going to end this relationship with Oberon now, or wait a few weeks?"

"Who said anything about ending it?"

Cadaver didn't respond.

"Yeah," said Tanith, kicking a monster so hard its eyeball popped out. "I'm probably going to end it now."

95

The café was small and dingy and dark and it was packed full of Corrival Sixth Years, with a few Fifth and Fourth Years thrown in for good measure. When Omen entered, the chatter stopped and everyone looked at him. He hadn't seen them, hadn't even spoken to any of them, in a month. He had no idea how they'd—

"We saved you a seat," said Never, pushing a chair out. It squeaked on the floor.

Omen hesitated, then sat down. "I didn't expect to see quite so many of you."

"We tried to be subtle," said Kase, who was sitting beside Mahala, "but that didn't work out so great. I think we're all grabbing whatever chance we can to leave the school grounds."

"Is it really that bad?"

"Duenna's the worst," said Axelia. "The school's being run like a prison. They've even brought in the City Guard to make sure we're obeying the rules."

"Please tell us the resistance are planning something," Never said. "Please tell us they're coming to liberate us from our oppressors. I'm not even exaggerating, by the way."

Omen hesitated. "The resistance aren't coming."

The students groaned as one.

Omen held up his hands. "In their defence, they have a lot going on, and none of it's good. You've got to understand: as bad as things look, as depressing as the news reports are, it is so, so much worse out there. The Faceless Ones may be gone, but the Shalgoth are everywhere. Skulduggery and the others, they figure the safest place for everyone here is in school."

"That's because they don't know what it's like," said Never.

"So why are you back?" Axelia asked. "The City Guard are still looking to arrest you. If the resistance aren't coming to help us, why are you here?"

"Well," Omen said, blushing, "I thought seeing as how no one else is going to do anything, maybe I would."

Mahala frowned slightly. "You came back to help?"

"The world's going to hell," said Omen. "Everything's going wrong and the bad guys are in charge. So why not just fight back now, while we still can? If, you know, anyone's interested."

"Raise hands if interested," said Never, and everyone's hand went up.

96

The TV stayed off and nobody looked at their phones, and Valkyrie sat with her family and Militsa and filled her plate with food. They hadn't been able to agree on a Chinese meal or an Indian, so they ordered stuff from both and it arrived in the safehouse at the same time and now they mixed and matched, whatever they were in the mood for. Alice took most of the dumplings for herself. She loved those dumplings.

Skulduggery joined them halfway through, sat at the table with them, and for once Xena ignored him. She was focusing her attention on Valkyrie, and sat beside her, resting her chin on her thigh, gazing up lovingly.

"I feel like you two have business to discuss," said Melissa.

"It can wait," Valkyrie said, spearing a hunk of pork and popping it into her mouth. "I'm assuming it can wait anyway. Skulduggery, can it wait?"

"It can, indeed," he confirmed.

"I'd quite like to hear it, actually," said Desmond. "You told us some of what's been going on, but I'd love to be brought up to date. Or is it all top secret?"

"It's not top secret at all," Skulduggery said, "but I wouldn't want to worry anyone, or give them bad dreams."

Desmond shrugged. "I'll be OK."

"I'm pretty sure he was talking about Alice," said Melissa.

"I'll be OK, too," Alice said. "But now that everyone knows about magic, when we go home, can I tell my friends that Stephanie is a sorcerer and that she's saved the world?"

"Probably safest not to," Valkyrie said. "At least for the time being."

Alice put on a grumpy face, then ate another dumpling.

"All right then," Skulduggery said, shifting his attention to Valkyrie, "let's assess the situation. The Faceless Ones are gone."

"Not gone," she responded, sipping from her drink. "They're out there somewhere, a little spark flying about, but they're harmless."

"Are you sure they can't just reverse the process?" Melissa asked, a forkful of food hovering halfway to her mouth. "They turned themselves into a spark – can't they just turn themselves back?"

Militsa shook her head. "That's not how it works. They'd have used an awful lot of magic to reduce themselves down to this 'spark', as we're calling it. Now, by shifting their physical forms, by altering their entire species, they must have figured they'd be able to evade Obsidian for longer. On one level, this is quite an intelligent move. But they've sacrificed a huge amount of magic in doing so, and I doubt they'd have enough power to reverse the transformation. I agree with Valkyrie. I don't like the idea of them floating around free, but I don't think they pose a threat any more."

"The Shalgoth, unfortunately, do," Skulduggery said. "If anyone expected them to slink away after their masters abandoned them, I'm afraid they've been disappointed. That said, I feel we can leave this in the hands of the Sanctuaries."

"And what about Obsidian?" Desmond asked, munching.

"He's wounded," said Valkyrie. "Probably healing, if he's able. Creed has the only weapon that could be used against him."

"Obsidian is a major problem," Skulduggery said, nodding. "But, until he reappears, all we can do is wait."

Alice burped. "Pardon me," she said, and went back to eating.

445

Valkyrie dropped a sliver of chicken into Xena's mouth. "We still have the Serpine mystery to solve," she said. "We know why he killed Scure, but we have no idea how he managed to be in two places at once. It's not important, I get that, but he's not two people yet. He's still only one. So how was he able to do that?"

"Your life is so complicated," said Melissa.

"It just bugs me. I don't like mysteries that don't get solved."

"But the most immediate priority we have right at this moment," Skulduggery said, "is stopping Crepuscular Vies from activating the Twenty. The way things are going, he's going to push President Flanery into doing something incredibly reckless."

Desmond pointed at nobody in particular with his fork. "Flanery. Don't get me started on Martin Flanery."

Melissa patted his leg. "Nobody's asking you to, dear." She looked at Skulduggery. "When you say incredibly reckless, Skulduggery, what exactly do you mean? He wouldn't launch a nuclear weapon, would he?"

"Honestly? I'd say he's just waiting for a target big enough."

Everyone stopped eating. Apart from Alice.

"But we're going to stop it," Skulduggery said quickly, once he realised that he'd brought the mood down. "China has arranged a meeting with one of the Hosts, and once we're done here we're going to drive straight there. We talk to this gentleman, explain the situation, and work out a way to defuse the problem before anything is launched."

Valkyrie nodded, and tried to sound confident. "This is how we do it. We solve one problem after another until there are none left and everyone is safe."

"Then why are you wasting time eating a delicious Chinese/ Indian combination meal?" Desmond asked. "Shouldn't saving the world take precedence?"

She put down her fork. "Well, now that you've made me feel guilty about it..."

"Des," Melissa scolded. "Let her enjoy her dinner before sending her off to stop nuclear war."

"What does nuclear mean?" asked Alice as she chewed.

"It's a kind of power," Melissa told her. "Like electricity."

"So it'd be an electrical war?"

"The bombs would be worse."

"Much worse," said Desmond. "Millions dead. Millions more dying of radiation sickness. Nuclear winter, untold devastation, ecological disaster, economic ruin. The end times."

Alice shrugged. "Stephanie will stop it, though. Won't you, Stephanie?"

"Absolutely," Valkyrie said, standing up. "Skulduggery, let's get going. The world isn't going to save itself."

97

They drove into Dublin, avoiding the ruined streets, the parts of the city that the Faceless One had demolished, while the sky turned orange and red above them. It made Valkyrie strangely sad, seeing the sky so empty, not filled with ancient gods, their massive shadows falling across the land like storm clouds. She didn't comment on it and neither did Skulduggery, but then the silence became a comment and so she stirred herself to change the subject.

"Do you miss the Bentley?" she asked.

"I do," he said.

"The Phantom's nice."

"The Phantom is beautiful," he corrected. "The Phantom is, literally, one of a kind. But I've been through a lot with the Bentley."

"Remember when that guy charged into it? I had to jump into the canal to get away?"

"Ah, right back at the start of our adventures. Yes. I remember how he came apart in all that water."

"Magic is weird."

"It is, indeed."

"I wish we had the Bentley back."

"I don't think that's going to happen," he responded. "It's like our friend in the canal: if you meddle with the wrong kind of magic in the wrong kind of way, something bad is eventually going to happen. Things fall apart. The centre cannot hold."

"I've been thinking of those times a lot. The early years, you know? I look at Omen and Crepuscular – forgetting for a minute that Crepuscular seems to have been plotting against us for a while now – and I find myself disapproving of it all. Yet there I was, twelve years old, running around, almost getting killed every other week."

"It was a different time."

"Not really."

"But I was involved, and that makes all the difference."

She looked out of the window. "Would you change any of it? If you could?"

"That's not an easy question to answer. The law of cause and effect means that any slight alteration to the past would have a domino—"

"If none of that was a thing," she interrupted. "If you could go back right and, like, stop me from ever getting involved, knowing what lay ahead of me, would you do it?"

Skulduggery focused on the road ahead for a few seconds. "For my sake, I wouldn't change a thing," he said. "For your sake? I'd change everything."

The streets were quiet and dark and they found a parking spot easily. After a month of terror and monster attacks, most mortal businesses around the world were closed and shuttered – apart from supermarkets and restaurants. Most of these restaurants chose only to deliver, but a few of them – a very remote few – managed to stay open and welcome the bravest and most foolhardy diners in through their doors. When Valkyrie and Skulduggery got to their destination, the greeter welcomed them in with a worried look on her face.

"Did you see any?" she asked, checking behind them before she closed the door.

Valkyrie frowned. "Any what?"

"Monsters," said the greeter. "There was one spotted on Clanbrassil Street about an hour ago."

"There are no monsters here tonight," Skulduggery assured her, his façade smiling wide. "Just us regular people."

They joined China and an attractive man with grey hair and a very neat beard at a table at the back of the otherwise empty restaurant. Grantham Arrant stood as China sipped at a cup of tea, and shook their hands.

"Valkyrie, it's a pleasure to meet you," he said. "Skulduggery, I've come close to meeting you over the years, but I've always shied away."

"I suppose you don't get to be prominent yet mysterious by introducing yourself to a great many people," Skulduggery responded.

"Is that how China described me? I probably should be flattered." They sat. "What can I help you with? China said you had some questions about the Hosts."

Skulduggery tilted his head. "You don't mind answering them?"

Arrant smiled. "I don't mind you asking them. Whether I can, or will, provide answers is another matter entirely. What do you want to know?"

"We believe world events are being manipulated to trigger the Doomsday Protocol and activate the Twenty," said Valkyrie. "We want to get to them before this happens."

"If that's the way the world is headed, Valkyrie, you might not want to interfere."

"A man named Crepuscular Vies is pushing President Flanery to take a combative stance against the magical community," Skulduggery said. "This stance, the global situation we currently find ourselves in, is largely manufactured. Once we're able to get at the individual strands of it all, we'll be able to restore calm. We just don't want the Twenty to be activated when a peaceful resolution is possible."

Arrant frowned at them. "With all due respect, Skulduggery – I don't think this situation can be calmed. The Faceless Ones may be gone, but the Shalgoth are everywhere. Sorcerers are all over the mortal media. Mortals are terrified, and when they get terrified they get angry. They're hunting down people like us. They're executing them. They're holding public hangings and they're burning people at the stake in some countries. You're not going to be able to calm anything. The world is too far gone for that."

One of the waiters came over. "Can I take your orders?"

China smiled politely and Skulduggery shook his head and Valkyrie patted her tummy.

"I've already eaten, thanks," she said.

He frowned. "So... none of you are here for food?"

"No," said China, "but you may leave us to talk, if that makes you happy." The waiter giggled, and left them.

Valkyrie sat forward. "Do you know where the Twenty are?"

"I don't," said Arrant. "None of the Hosts do. Among the instructions they were given was an order to secrete themselves away for as long as it took while they waited to be activated. We hoped it would never happen, but..." He shrugged.

"What happens if they never *are* activated?" Valkyrie asked.

"After three hundred and thirty-three years, they will be released from their obligations, and another twenty will take their place."

Skulduggery pressed his fingertips together. "You seem confident of your ability to replace them."

"The Hosts are nothing if not persuasive," said Arrant.

Valkyrie frowned. "Something's not right."

"What do you mean?" China asked.

She kept her eyes on Arrant. "When you said that just now, about being persuasive, I got a feeling of... I don't know. Spite, maybe."

"From me?" said Arrant.

"Yes. And no. There's something else happening here. The longer I'm around you, the more uncomfortable I feel. You're not... You're not alone, are you?"

Arrant looked at her, and the expression of his face changed.

451

The smile changed. "Very good, Valkyrie. I didn't think you'd be able to detect me, but that's what I get for being overconfident. He warned me, yes he did. He warned me not to underestimate you."

China put down her cup. "Who are you?"

"A puppet," said Arrant, getting to his feet, "nothing more." He went to the next table and sat, and immediately his chin dropped to his chest and he fell asleep. But Valkyrie was already looking past him, to the old lady who walked slowly into the restaurant. She came to their table, and sat in Arrant's seat.

"Good evening, Solace," said China, like she wasn't surprised in the least to see her. "Would you like some tea?"

"Please," said Solace.

China poured her a cup, and Valkyrie looked at Skulduggery and he gave her the tiniest of shrugs.

Solace gently blew on her tea, and then sipped. "It's so nice to see you like this. In the quite radiant flesh. It makes a change from visiting you at night to inflict all that mental anguish."

"And you," said China. "To have you sitting across from me instead of standing at the foot of my bed, issuing threats – it makes me feel as though there is no bridge that cannot be crossed."

They smiled at each other.

"While I am thankful that we're using our words," Valkyrie said slowly, "this is probably a little too passive-aggressive to be actually useful. It really feels like you want to kill each other."

"If I wanted to merely kill her," said Solace, "she would be long dead by now."

China's left eyebrow flickered up when she glanced at Valkyrie. "I think I'm being thoroughly charming, considering the circumstances."

"Oh, you're just annoyed that I attacked you while you were delivering your speech in front of everyone in Roarhaven," said Solace.

"It did rather disrupt my plans, yes."

"It was one little coma. You can hardly blame me for the

damage it inflicted upon your aura of invincibility. If your subjects were so quick to doubt your competence, could they ever really have been called your subjects in the first place?"

"You tried to kill me, too," said Valkyrie. "Bit of an overreaction to me stealing your music box, but whatever."

"Oh, I wasn't mad at you for taking that box," said Solace. "It made me drowsy, up there in that tower. Befuddled. When it was gone, my thoughts cleared. It was a welcome change. I owe you my thanks, actually."

"Well, then – you're welcome."

"How long have you been controlling Grantham Arrant?" Skulduggery asked.

"Long enough."

"To what end? Do you want to see the Twenty activated?"

Solace smiled an old-woman smile. "What do you know of me?"

"You worked for Mevolent," said Valkyrie.

"Serafina," she corrected.

"Serafina," said Valkyrie. "You were one of her handmaidens. Caisson had gone after Skulduggery because he blamed him for the death of his mother. Caisson came out second best in that encounter, and you nursed him back to health. You fell in love, and the two of you ran away. You were gone for, like, a hundred and sixty years before Serafina found you and dragged you back. Caisson went after you and ended up killing Mevolent."

Solace nodded. "And then?"

"Serafina flew into a rage. She thought you'd killed Mevolent and she tracked you down."

"But?"

Valkyrie hesitated.

"But I told Serafina that it had been Caisson who had killed Mevolent," said China. "Serafina had him dragged away to be tortured for the next ninety years and I had Solace committed to Greymire Asylum."

"Where I languished," said Solace, "growing old and feeble

without my magic, until you arrived, Valkyrie, and stole my music box. You woke me up. Shortly afterwards, Caisson appeared at my window, like a fairytale prince. He was as handsome as ever, despite the scars, and he whisked me from my tower and I got to spend five whole days with him before he was murdered by Serafina's sister. I'll get to Kierre of the Unveiled in my own time, but you," she said, eyes on China, "are my primary target. You ruined my life first, after all."

"I must protest," said China. "Your life isn't ruined. It may still get better."

"Taking all this into account," Solace said, "could you answer me a question, Valkyrie? Why did China Sorrows, the beautiful, enigmatic ice queen famed for her ruthlessness, give up Caisson, her ward, instead of me? Whyever would she have done that? Would you like to know, Valkyrie? Would you, Skulduggery?"

"Solace is my daughter," China said, and took another sip of tea.

Solace laughed. "Oh, Mother, you never let me have any fun."

Valkyrie blinked, then looked at Skulduggery. His head was tilted at its surprised angle.

"It's jarring, I know," Solace continued. "She's barely aged since the day she had me – whereas I have not been as lucky. But do you know why she had me committed to Greymire? My mother loves me, in her way, but has never particularly liked me. I was always too clever for her – too obstinate. Would that be right?"

"It would indeed, dear," said China.

Solace nodded. "I was an unstable element in her precious, ordered little life. She couldn't bring herself to allow me to be killed, but she was evidently fine with locking me away in a tower while my husband was tortured for nine decades." She sat forward. "Growing up, nobody knew she was my mother, of course – she had far too many enemies – so she sent me off to work as Serafina's handmaiden and endure a life of crushing rigidity while she lived her own, far more glamorous, existence. I barely saw her as a child, as a young woman, and I didn't even know about Caisson until I found him, injured and alone."

"But none of this explains why you're involved here," Skulduggery said. "What's your connection to Crepuscular Vies?"

"I'm helping him," said Solace.

"You're helping him free his brothers and sisters. Why? How does that get you revenge on China?"

"Not everything is about revenge, and not everything is about my mother."

"Do you know what Crepuscular has done?" Skulduggery asked. "Do you know about Abyssinia, and Martin Flanery?"

"Oh, Skulduggery – if you have so many questions about Crepuscular, why don't you just ask him yourself?"

There was a shriek from the front of the restaurant and the greeter stumbled away from Crepuscular Vies, his checked – though undeniably stylish – suit failing to distract attention from his unique facial features.

He pulled a chair over and sat at their table. Nobody tried to kill anyone else. A promising start.

"Skulduggery," he said, "I like your tie. I'm more of a dicky-bow man myself, but I appreciate quality when I see it. Is it one of Ghastly's?"

"It is," said Skulduggery.

"I do miss Ghastly," Crepuscular said. "A thoroughly decent man, I always thought. I was sorry to hear of his demise – though it shocked me not in the least that Erskine Ravel was the one to kill him. I never trusted Ravel. He was always far too smooth for my liking."

"If only you had shared your keen insights with me back when they could have done some good."

"Before you left me for dead, you mean."

"Exactly."

"I understand that we're all on edge," Valkyrie said, "so I'm grateful for the restraint everyone is showing right now. But we do have some pieces of outstanding business to address. Crepuscular, we believe you've been manipulating Martin Flanery into declaring war on sorcerers, so that the Twenty – your brothers and sisters – will be activated. Would that be accurate?"

"It would," Crepuscular answered.

"And that is very understandable. I would do whatever it took to get my family released from whatever was binding them. I sympathise with your plight."

"Thank you, Valkyrie."

"What we're wondering is whether maybe there's another way to release them that wouldn't lead to the collapse of mortal civilisation. Do you think there might be?"

"If there were, I'd have found it."

"I see," said Valkyrie. "I see. So you view this course you're on as your only chance to free your siblings."

"I do."

"And Solace, without meaning to pry, I notice you haven't actually provided a reason why you're helping Crepuscular do this. You're angry at China, you're angry at Kierre, you're grieving the loss of Caisson – so how does the collapse of civilisation benefit you, or bring you any closer to your revenge?"

"Revenge is only a piece of what I'm after, dear girl. You see, I was robbed – robbed of time, robbed of my opportunity to taste the life that was denied me, first by losing Caisson, then by my mother committing me to Greymire. The person who sits before you in all of her elderly, wrinkled glory was a beautiful young woman once upon a time, with infinite potential. That potential has wasted away. Now I grasp at whatever is left."

"That's where I come in," Crepuscular said. "Have you figured it out yet? Why she's helping me? No? It's really not that difficult. Skulduggery, please tell me that you, at least, know what's going on."

"I do."

"I thought you might. Care to share?"

456

"Solace," Skulduggery said, "is your mother."

"Thank you!" Crepuscular responded. "Yes! Finally, someone is using their brain – or the ghost of their brain, whatever it is that's actually taking up space in your skull."

He fixed his eyes on China, and Valkyrie glanced at her and witnessed a rare phenomenon – a look of shock on that perfect face.

"Hi, Granny," said Crepuscular.

98

"Nope," said China.

99

Crepuscular laughed. "Do I make you feel old, Grandmother? I do so apologise."

China ignored him and looked at Solace. "You never told me."

"That I had children?" Solace responded. "Whyever would I? So you could ignore them like you ignored me? And, when you finally did remember they existed, would you lock them in a tower and take away their thoughts, too?"

"I would never have..." China faltered.

"You would never have what?" Solace pressed. "You would never have done what you did if you knew I had a family? I think that's a lie. If you were callous enough to even consider it in the first place, you're certainly callous enough to do it, no matter who gets hurt."

"It was a mistake," China said. "It was more than a mistake. It was wrong, and selfish, and cruel. It was evil. What I did to you was evil, and I am sorry."

"Does apologising make you feel better?"

"Nothing will make me feel better."

Solace smiled. "And why is that, Mother?"

"Because this isn't about me," said China. "It isn't about how I feel. I can't make up for what I did – not the act itself, nor the repercussions it set in motion. I'm not looking for forgiveness because I can't be forgiven."

"We agree on something," Solace said, her smile fading. "And what about what you did to Caisson?"

China shook her head. "I had no choice."

"You gave him to Serafina Dey to torture for ninety years."

"Better him than you."

"Wrong!" Solace roared, drawing anxious looks from the waiting staff. "Wrong! I would have taken his place gladly! I would have endured what he had to endure without hesitation if I thought it would have spared him a moment of pain! But you... you gave him to her. I cannot understand that. When I was born, you had me raised by others. My heritage, you told me, was a secret between us. Although I was brought up in the very castle you lived in, you treated me like a stranger whenever we met. You were consumed with worshipping the Faceless Ones, with worshipping Mevolent, with all your scheming and plotting – so consumed that you had no more love to spare for me.

"But Caisson... He wasn't even your son, but you still brought him up. As bad a mother to him as you were – and you were a bad mother to him – you still showed more love and devotion towards your ward than you ever did to me. And yet right when he needed that love the most, right when he needed that devotion, you betrayed him. You gave him to Serafina."

"To spare you."

"But why?"

"Because you are my daughter. Because blood is stronger than duty."

"Or because you saw an opportunity to rid yourself of both of us."

"No, I swear."

"You think your promise means anything to me?"

Crepuscular put his hands up in a calming gesture. "Mum, Granny, please stop the arguing. You've got your issues to work through, but you know what? Once we've all talked about it, once everything's out in the open, I truly do think that we'll be one big, happy family."

"I will not rest until she's dead," said Solace.

"There might be some bickering, sure, but what family doesn't bicker?" Crepuscular looked at Skulduggery and Valkyrie. "This is nice, isn't it? We might need some counselling sessions, but I feel like it's the start of a healthy dialogue."

"Are you done?" asked Valkyrie. "Is this little bit of theatre over with?"

Crepuscular raised an eyebrow. "My! Someone's in a mood! What's wrong, Valkyrie – are you jealous because, for once, not everything is about you?"

"That's exactly it," Valkyrie said, standing. Energy crackled around her fists, making some of the waiters gasp. "We're not going to let you unleash the Twenty."

"They're being held against their will," Crepuscular said, getting to his feet slowly.

"They chose this," Skulduggery said.

"They didn't know what they were choosing," said Solace. "The Hosts tricked them into service, just like they'd tricked me years before."

China frowned. "They tricked you?"

"Ah, yet another slice of information my mother isn't privy to," said Solace. "What a wonder that must be for you. The Hosts recruited me when I was a teenager. Mevolent had captured the good Mr Arrant. He languished in the dungeons for a few weeks before I was sent to deliver what meagre scraps the prisoners were being fed. We spoke. I helped him escape. From that moment on, I was a spy for the Hosts, passing on what little I knew of Serafina Dey's secrets.

"When I ran – when Caisson and I ran – the Hosts brought us both into the fold, and persuaded us to start a family – persuaded us to provide them with a new Twenty. Our children were trained to kill, to spy, to destroy... and to obey. Always to obey."

"This didn't really take with me," said Crepuscular. "I'm the middle child, you know? Number eleven. Slap bang in the middle of all this regimented living and rules and whatnot. I was the spare – wouldn't you say, Mum?"

"You were the unruly one," Solace said without humour.

"I caused some trouble," said Crepuscular, moving to stand behind his mother, hands on the back of her chair. "Started some arguments. Sowed some discord. But like I said – I was the spare. If they lost one kid during training, they'd always have me to take their spot. That was the plan anyway, but I hightailed it out of there the moment their backs were turned."

Valkyrie looked down at Solace. "So when Serafina took Caisson and you were committed to Greymire..."

"The Hosts told my children what to do," Solace said.

Crepuscular took her hand and helped her to her feet. China and Skulduggery also stood.

"They were ordered to seal themselves away and that's what they did. The Host took advantage of their conditioning. My children were never meant to be locked away like this."

"But surely the Hosts would be able to release them without you having to go to all this trouble with Flanery," Valkyrie responded.

Crepuscular shrugged. "Like I said, if it had been possible, I'd have done it. You think it's been fun, spending time with Martin Flanery? The man's a buffoon. But he is easily manipulated, and his hatred is very easy to stoke, so I figured out pretty early that all I had to do was turn up every now and then, prod him a little, and let him go spinning off by himself."

"Except now he's spun away from you," said Skulduggery.

Crepuscular grunted. "It's that Doctor Nye. It's a bad influence on him. But hey, he's about to do exactly what I need him to do, so what do I care?"

"How do we stop the Doomsday Protocol?"

"You can't," said Solace.

"You can't," said Crepuscular.

"I'm sure if we put our heads together, we can think of something," Skulduggery said, his hand moving towards his gun.

Crepuscular laughed. "We paid you this courtesy because we wanted everyone to understand why we are doing the things we're doing. It's no fun if you don't understand, do you see? If you think these are all random events occurring at random times, it saps the meaning from our intentions. You have to know. You need to know. We're going to make everything very clear, don't you worry. When the end comes, you'll know why you're the ones suffering the most."

Crepuscular teleported away, taking Solace with him. This drew more shrieks from the restaurant staff and a grunt from Valkyrie. She didn't know he was a Teleporter.

China shook her head. "If they request another meeting, please pass on my apologies, but I won't be able to make it." She picked up her handbag and prepared to leave.

"Hang on," said Valkyrie. "Shouldn't we talk about this? A lot has just happened."

"There's nothing to talk about," China said. "I had a child, my child had children, and now they want to kill me. That's the way of the world." She walked out.

When she was gone, the staff, huddled together, switched their attention back to Valkyrie and Skulduggery.

"That could have gone better," Valkyrie said.

"It could have gone remarkably worse."

"True, I suppose."

"But what they said about Flanery has got me thinking."

Valkyrie frowned. "That he's a buffoon? But we knew that. Literally everybody knows that."

"The other thing, about how easily he's manipulated. Abyssinia manipulated him and Crepuscular manipulated him... now I think it's time I manipulated him."

Valkyrie's eyes widened. "We're going to the White House?" Her hand went to her mouth. "I get to punch the president?"

"I go to the White House," Skulduggery said. "You stay here."

Valkyrie glared. "And why the hell would I do that?"

"I don't want to offend you," Skulduggery said, "but I'm scarier than you are."

"How dare you."

"To the untrained eye," he added quickly.

"I'm tall," she said, "and strong, plenty of people have told me how scary I am, and I shoot lightning from my hands."

"And I'm a walking skeleton."

"So why can't both of us go?"

"I need Flanery to focus on me. I need him to realise that the only person stopping me from killing him is me. I don't want him looking to you, the person with flesh and blood, for help. I need him to see me as his imminent and terrible demise. I need him to think that Death itself has come for him."

"But—"

"And I think you'll punch him too hard."

"But Skulduggery!"

"Valkyrie."

"But I wanna punch the president!"

"Next time."

"No," she whined as they walked for the door. "You always say that."

"Please don't sulk."

"Fine. Whatever. You go. I'll stay behind."

"I knew you'd understand."

"You suck."

"I know."

"Everything sucks."

"I know."

She left a huge tip by the cash register, smiled at the terrified waiters, and they left the restaurant.

"When you hit him," she said, "could you at least say, '*This one's for Valkyrie.*'"

"No."

"Could you be thinking it?"

"If I remember."

"And then say, '*Presidise this.*'"

"*Presidise* isn't a word."

"He won't know that."

"I'm not going to say it, Valkyrie."

She sighed. "Then what are you going to say?"

They reached the Phantom. "I'm not sure," he responded. "But, knowing me, it will probably be something eminently quotable."

100

The student protest was held at the main entrance to the school, out in the chill November air. Roarhaven citizens passed quickly by on the pavement just beyond the gates, keeping their eyes down, away from the signs and placards, in case one of the assembled City Guard officers caught them reading. Cars passed. No one honked in support.

That didn't deter the students. The protestors chanted and the younger students looked on and cheered and clapped. The cops, a dozen of them, watched, but didn't move to stop any of this from happening. Not yet.

The audience of younger students suddenly parted as the prefects came barging through, shoving the younger children out of their way. Filament brushed by Omen's shoulder, but didn't notice him, and Omen did his best to blend in better. Principal Duenna strode through the space created. Someone started whistling the Imperial March from Star Wars.

Duenna reached the protestors and the chanting died down. She took a few moments to read the signs and make note of the students who carried them. Then she said, "Detention to everyone still standing here after I count to ten. Away with you. Go on."

She flapped her hands like the pupils were nothing but pigeons she expected to fly off. The look of slight annoyance on her face became a narrow-eyed glare, but to Omen it was nothing more than a practised performance designed to make the protestors shrink back. When they neither flew off nor shrank back, her frown deepened.

"Go on," said Never, "start counting."

"All right," said Officer Limerence, glowering, "who said that? Which one of you said that?"

"I did," said Never.

"I did," said Axelia.

"I did," said Kase.

Then everyone, all of the students there, both in the protest and in the crowd watching, started chanting, "I did!" as loudly as they could and Limerence's jaw visibly clenched. Omen edged forward as the City Guards squared their shoulders and moved into position, forming a line between the protest and the gates.

"Disperse!" Limerence yelled. "Disperse immediately!"

The cops drew their batons and Duenna didn't make a move to stop them. Omen took a sports whistle from his pocket and blew it, and once the sharp note pierced the air the protesting students all dropped to one knee, their right arms held overhead.

The cops frowned, glancing at one another, then at Duenna, but she wasn't any more clued in than they were. Omen had been looking forward to this bit.

He took out the cloned remote and tapped the surface, and all around him bracelets clicked and opened and fell from wrists.

Omen blew the whistle again, and the first two rows of protesters pushed at the air and the space rippled and the City Guard officers hurtled backwards off their feet.

They hit the pavement outside the gates and sprawled, and Omen ran up to the sigil carved into the wall and traced his fingers back along its markings like he'd been shown, and the energy shield rose up, sealing Corrival Academy off from the rest of Roarhaven.

He didn't even see the protesters grab the prefects, didn't see the shackles snap on, but he made sure to hurry back through the crowd so that he could see the look on Duenna's face when she realised her authority had not only been questioned, it was now in tatters, and blowing in the wind.

101

After a busy morning of golf, Flanery returned to the White House where he told his assistant to hold all his calls. He had her close the door and he sat in the Oval Office alone and put on the TV that he'd had installed. He worked better when the TV was on, when he could see what people were saying about him.

CNN showed a poll where his approval rating was 83 per cent – an astonishing number by anyone's reckoning. The so-called experts tried to belittle that particular poll, tried to assign credit to the general feeling of terror gripping the country and the fact that the Faceless Ones had disappeared and everyone thought – 'without evidence' – that it was because of something the president had done. But they could belittle all they liked. Flanery was the greatest president who'd ever lived – and it was close to being official.

He was now seriously regretting having pushed to have the election postponed. If the people went out to vote right now, he'd win by a never-before-seen landslide.

"Martin."

Flanery looked up and cried out as a skeleton in a suit approached. He dived for the button on the desk, but the skeleton waved his hand and a gust of wind hit Flanery, sent him crashing into the wall beneath the window. Tangled in the curtains, he gaped up.

"Do you know who I am?" the skeleton asked, turning off the TV.
Flanery nodded.

"Who am I, Martin?"

"You're the... you're the skeleton. Skulduggery Pleasant. That's who you are. I know about you. They've told me about you. You don't scare me."

"Yes," said the skeleton. "You certainly don't look scared."

Flanery threw the curtain aside and clambered to his feet. He stuck out his chin. "You can't kill me," he said. "If you kill me, it'll be an international incident. There'll be consequences. I've left instructions with everyone on what to do. They'll drop bombs. You're Irish. I know that. We'll drop bombs on Ireland."

"No, you won't."

"You can't kill me. You're not allowed. You have rules. The Sanctuary won't let you kill me."

"You've declared war on us, Martin," the skeleton said. "The Sanctuaries are in disarray. Sorcerers are panicking. They're looking at their mortal friends and wondering if they'll have to hurt them. All because of you, Mr President."

"I'm just... I'm just protecting people like me."

"You've started a war you won't win."

"Oh, we'll win," said Flanery. "We've got magic *and* we've got the bomb. You think a few magic tricks will stop a nuclear explosion? You think it'll stop the radiation clouds? We'll blast you wizards into *nothing*."

The skeleton tilted his head. "You'll destroy half the world doing it."

Flanery sneered. "Then that's what I'll do. You think I won't do it? You think I'm afraid of what the people will say? They'll love me for it! Have you seen my numbers? They want a strong leader, they want a leader who does what he says he'll do, and if I say I'm going to drop a nuclear bomb on every Sanctuary around the world, that's what I'll goddamn do!"

"It never occurred to me that you'd be worried about what the voters would think," the skeleton said. "I thought you'd be more concerned about killing millions – billions – of innocent people."

"You see," said Flanery, shaking his head, "this is what everyone gets wrong. I'm the president. I'm the president of the United States of America. I'm the most powerful man on the planet. You know what I do, almost every day? I authorise drone strikes on enemy targets. I send people to kill terrorists. Once you've done that – and the first time I did, I have to be honest, it gave me a bit of a thrill – you realise that everyone's the same. Sending a drone to kill a terrorist is the same as sending a team to assassinate some tyrant or whatever, and that's the same as dropping a bomb on a bunch of people that I don't know and I don't care about in order to kill a few goddamn wizards and witches. It's all the same."

The skeleton didn't answer for a few seconds. "I came here to scare you into backing off."

"I'm not scared of you."

"No. But I'm scared of you." The skeleton took out a gun. "You're a psychopath, Martin. You're unfit for office, and you're too dangerous to let live."

Flanery couldn't take his eyes off the gun. "You're... you can't kill me."

"I'm afraid I have to."

"No," said Flanery, smiling. "You *can't* kill me."

Flanery thundered towards him. The skeleton fired and the bullet bounced off Flanery's chest and he tore the gun from the skeleton's hand and filled his fists with the skeleton's shirt and tie and jacket. He lifted him up and slammed him into the wall and then threw him – actually *hurled* him – into the opposite wall with enough force that he heard one of those bones crack.

Laughing, Flanery kicked his desk out of his way and charged over.

The skeleton thrust out his hand and the wind sent Flanery tumbling but, just like before, no pain came with it – not even

471

any exertion as he picked himself up. This was fantastic. This was amazing. Then, all of a sudden, the skeleton had flames in his hand and Flanery didn't know how to handle flames so he shrieked when they hit his arm and his jacket caught fire.

That was when the Secret Service guys burst in.

The skeleton turned and they shot him with the special gun, the one that fired that ink stuff that wrapped round the skeleton's midsection. A symbol started to glow and the skeleton cursed and some of the Secret Service guys attacked him and the rest of them came straight over, ripped Flanery's jacket off with the same magical strength that Flanery possessed, threw it on the ground and stomped on it until the flames were out. Then they turned, helped their buddies fight the skeleton.

They could have shot him, could have blasted him to dust, but Flanery had given them their instructions. They didn't need their guns anyway. Thanks to the Nye creature's little squares of magic, they were stronger and faster than the skeleton, though the skeleton seemed to be doing pretty well against them, all the same. There was no one Flanery could think of who knew more about fighting than Flanery himself – he'd never actually been in a proper fight, but all of his favourite movies were action movies, so he knew what the hell he was talking about.

The fight taking place in front of him, the one that was tipping over antique chairs and smashing expensive coffee tables, didn't have any of the cool kicks that Flanery liked, but it had plenty of elbow shots and fancy locks. Flanery didn't much like that kind of fighting – it was too complicated, and he couldn't really see who was winning. The Secret Service guys were getting thrown about – arms and wrists and jaws were being broken – but they didn't feel the pain and so kept going. Two of them grabbed the skeleton and the rest gathered round and pummelled him. It was one of the greatest things Flanery had ever seen and, because he'd been the one to start it, the victory was pretty much his.

When the skeleton hit the ground, Flanery barrelled forward

and kicked him, full force, in the head. He fell over doing it, but it was a great kick.

At Flanery's command, they picked him up off the ground, and congratulated him on doing an amazing job. Flanery didn't need their praise. This had been his first-ever fight and it was like he'd always known: he was a natural. If he hadn't been destined for great wealth and importance, he could have been a boxer, and probably a champion, too.

His assistant brought him a new jacket while he waited for the Teleporter to arrive. When he was properly dressed, Flanery peered closer at the skeleton, trying to work out how he moved. There were tiny, almost unnoticeable gaps between some of his bones, probably where cartilage and tendons and things would normally hold everything together. He was silent now, but it had been weird watching his jaw open and close when he'd talked before. He had no lips, no tongue, and nowhere for the sound to actually come from.

They teleported to Doctor Nye's laboratory and Flanery puked on to a Secret Service agent's shoes. When he was done, he wiped his mouth with a silk handkerchief and pointed at the skeleton.

"I think you should take him apart," he announced.

The two Nyes stopped talking to each other and paid attention to him, the way he liked it.

"I'm sorry?" said Doctor Nye.

Flanery pointed at the skeleton again to make sure everyone knew what he was talking about. "Take him apart. Like a car. See how he works, how he ticks. Maybe it's something we can use."

"We know how he ticks," said the doctor. "His essence contains his consciousness and holds his form – what some people call an aura."

"I know about auras," Flanery said, annoyed. "I know more than you'd think about auras. I want his examined."

"We would be happy to do so," said Professor Nye, the taller one. "In fact, I was about to suggest the same thing. We've studied souls before, but never one quite like this."

Flanery nodded. He really didn't care about whatever they were saying now. More stuff about souls. "Take his bones apart," he said.

"Of course," said Doctor Nye.

"I want to know how they work. How he stands up, and moves, and sits down. And I want to know how he talks."

Doctor Nye nodded. "We'll find out for you, Mr President."

102

The protective shield that covered Corrival Academy flashed a different colour every time somebody tried – and failed – to teleport in from outside. The City Guard attacked it from every angle, at every supposed weak spot. None of them got through. They must have known they didn't stand a chance – Corrival's shield was a miniature version of Roarhaven's – and they looked miserable as they were ordered to keep trying.

Omen watched them from the steps of the school. Every so often, a car would pass and honk in support of the students, and Omen would wave. It was a welcome development, and it annoyed the hell out of the cops.

Never and Militsa walked up and stood beside him.

"Victory," said Never.

"Victory," Omen agreed.

"Victory," Axelia confirmed.

Never sighed. "So now what do we do?"

"I have no idea," said Omen. "I mean, all of my focus was on unlocking the bloody bracelets and liberating the school and now that we've done that... I don't have a clue. How long will the food last?"

"We have enough for three more days," Axelia said. "If we all eat very, very little."

"A lot of parents are calling," said Never, "so we have a load of students being pressured to ask us to give up and drop the shield. Honestly, Omen, they hated wearing the bracelets and they hated how Duenna was treating everyone, but that just meant they were in a really strict school. Life was still normal, you know? They didn't have to think about what was going on in the world because they could just focus on classes."

"But now," Axelia said, "we've overthrown the school. We have the principal, a couple of City Guard officers and most of the teachers locked in the detention cells. We have prefects confined to their dorm rooms. We've posted guards and we're rationing food and we're surrounded by angry cops shouting threats at us. Everyone is really scared right now."

"Yeah," Omen said, watching the shield flash a different colour. "I really didn't expect to get into a siege-type situation. I didn't think this through at all, did I?"

Never shrugged. "You wanted to help, so you helped."

"I made things worse."

"You took a stand," said Axelia. "I know that it's landed us somewhere we didn't want to be, but a stand had to be taken. What, were we going to continue to allow ourselves to be treated like that?"

"Hell, no," said Never.

"Hell, no. It had to be done, so you did it. You came in, you organised, you freed us."

"I should have thought ahead."

Axelia shrugged. "Sometimes thinking ahead stops you from doing the right thing."

Never looked at her. "That's very wise."

"It definitely sounds wise."

A First Year ran up to them. "Um, sir? Mr Omen? Mr Darkly?"

"Omen's fine. You can call me Omen. What's up?"

"One of the prefects, sir. He got out of his dorm room. He hit someone and ran off when they were bringing him his lunch."

Omen's mood soured. "Which prefect?"

"Filament Sclavi, sir," the kid said, and saluted for some reason.

Omen turned to Axelia. "Double the guards at the detention cells and at every point where the shield can be deactivated. Make sure the guards are OK with hitting people, because they might have to." She nodded, and ran off, and he turned to Never. "We're going to have to search for him. Start teleporting – focus first on parts of the school that you know will be empty."

"Yes, boss," Never said, and vanished.

Omen winked at the First Year. "Nice job," he said, and the kid beamed with pride.

There was no way of telling where Filament would go – he just had too many options – but Omen hurried to the Combat Block, where he'd ordered the practice weapons locked away. Things were far too tense in the school to have a bunch of scared teenagers wandering around with access to tools of battle. Most of the practice weapons couldn't do lasting damage, but there were a few that the teaching staff used for demonstration purposes. No guns, thankfully, but plenty of edged weapons, and there was definitely one sharpened sword on the premises that he knew for sure was—

—he sagged—

—in Filament Sclavi's hands.

"What are you going to do with that, Filament?" he asked as Filament walked slowly towards him across the combat hall.

"What do you think?" Filament replied, giving the sword a flourish. "You're the leader in here. Everyone looks to you, the brother of the Chosen One, like you're some big hero. To take back the school, I have to take you out."

"By killing me?"

Filament shrugged like he couldn't care less, but panic danced in his eyes.

"You've never killed anyone before. Why would you want to start now? Have you thought about it? Thought about what it'd be like afterwards, I mean? I don't think I could handle it,

477

knowing I took somebody's life. I think it'd weigh on me. I think it'd suffocate me. But OK, let's say you kill me. Then what? You'll have to release Duenna, right? The cops we have down in detention, too? How many of our classmates do you think you'll have to kill to do all that?"

"I just have to kill you," Filament said. "Once the others see that I'm serious, they'll back off."

"Really? You think Never and Axelia will just back off after you kill me? You think Kase and Mahala will be scared of a sword? They've fought serial killers and monsters, Filament. Hell, most of the kids you'll be facing fought the King of the Darklands alongside Auger. You really think they'll be too scared to go up against you?"

Filament licked his lips. "It doesn't matter. I'll kill whoever I have to kill, starting with you."

"Why?"

"Because you're an enemy of the Faceless Ones."

"The Faceless Ones are gone, dude. They ran away."

"Then because you're an enemy of Damocles Creed."

"This isn't about Creed. He's not why I did this and you know it. It's about Duenna. This is a school. It's supposed to be about broadening your horizons and, like, finding out who you are and stuff."

"School is about learning to follow the rules," Filament said.

"Then school needs to change."

"You know, once upon a time, I thought we could be friends. That was stupid. I could never be friends with someone like you."

"Put the sword down, Filament."

"If you want it, come and get it."

"This is boring," said Jenan, stepping into the hall, and Omen felt his chances of getting out of there without violence dropping to zero. "If you're going to kill him, kill him. If you're going to stand there and threaten him, give the sword to someone who'll use it."

Filament frowned. "Like who? Like you?"

Jenan approached with a careless shrug. "I've done it before, and I've been looking for the chance to finish the job. Unless you've got your heart set on doing it?"

Filament had a moment of uncertainty, and then he lobbed the sword to Jenan. Omen pulled at the air to try to guide it into his own hand, but he wasn't very good at that. He wasn't very good at most things.

Jenan caught the weapon and gave it a flourish of his own, then set his gaze on Omen.

"This was inevitable."

Omen didn't have a reply, so Jenan continued. "The thing is, you were never supposed to be my adversary. My adversary, my arch-enemy, was meant to be someone else. Someone better. Someone like your brother."

"You wouldn't have stood a chance against Auger."

"I nearly killed him, though – remember that?"

"I remember."

"But it always came back to you," said Jenan, shaking his head. "It was always you standing there. It should have been somebody else. Anybody else. I deserved that. I deserved more than Omen Darkly."

"Sorry."

Jenan laughed. "You're always apologising. That's one of the things I hate about you. Always so meek. Scurrying around with your head down, trying to avoid people's eyes, trying to stay out of the limelight, trying to just get on with your day... I never apologise. Not really. My father taught me that. When I was a kid, he told me leaders don't say sorry. Even when – and this is where it gets funny – I genuinely regret something, I don't apologise for it."

"That is funny."

"I killed Isidora. Did you know that?"

Omen nodded.

"In Coldheart. We were standing over a... Anyway. Isidora was desperate to leave; she was really homesick and didn't want to be a part of Abyssinia's plan. She'd never wanted to join First Wave, I don't think, but she'd never been very good with peer pressure. So Abyssinia had to make an example of her, and she got me to do it.

"I was scared. I'd never killed anyone before. I'd thought about it – like, a lot – but it's very different when it's this vague thought in your head than when you've been told you need to execute someone. I didn't want to do it, actually. Right at the last moment, something clicked inside me and I realised – nope, I don't want to do this. I don't want to actually kill anyone, not for real. But then Abyssinia gave me a little nudge, a little psychic nudge, and I gave a little physical nudge and Isidora... I'll never forget her face. I'll never forget that look of, I don't know, horror, I suppose, as she fell."

"I'm really sorry that you had to do that, Jenan."

"There you go, apologising again," Jenan said, lip curling in annoyance. "Even for something that had nothing to do with you! You can't help it, can you?"

"I just wish you hadn't had to do that," said Omen. "It must have been horrible."

Jenan looked at him. "Yeah," he said quietly.

"Something like that, being used like you were, it'd send anyone spiralling."

"Is that what you think happened to me? That I was spiralling? No control over my actions?"

"You had control over them, but I think you were sent spiralling in a direction where every possible outcome was a bad one."

"Does that include attacking you and your brother?"

"It does."

"So it was both in my control, and out of my control?"

"Basically."

"You're pathetic. You're making excuses for other people's

480

behaviour. Why is that? So you can feel better about yourself? So you can go to sleep at night smug in the knowledge that you're a better person than I am?"

"This isn't about me, Jenan."

"Look," Filament said, "are you going to kill him or not?"

Jenan pointed the sword at him. "You shut the hell up."

Filament glared. "If you're not going to kill him, give me back the sword and I'll do it."

"Really?" Jenan said, laughing. "You'll kill him, will you? You'll go over there and stab him through the chest, will you? Sure! You go right ahead! Here!"

Jenan stalked over to him, pressed the sword into his hand and gave him a shove towards Omen. Immediately, Filament faltered.

"There," said Jenan. "It's not so easy, is it? It's very easy to say it and very easy to sound like you mean it, but not so easy to do it. What are you waiting for, Filament? Go on. Kill him."

Filament gripped the sword tightly and stared at Omen as if he was hoping that would be enough.

"You're like I was," said Jenan. "Big and strong and so, so tough. You're a leader, just like me. Just like my father. You know what leaders do, Filament? They make the hard choices. They do what weaker people can't. You need to kill Omen, so do it. Walk over there and kill him."

Filament didn't budge.

"What's stopping you? Are you worried that he'll beat you? He might. He's a lot tougher than he looks. But there are two of us, and I'll help you. I'll even hold him while you kill him. Would that make it easier for you?"

"Shut up," Filament said. "You're confusing me."

"That didn't take much, did it?" Jenan said, laughing again. "Maybe you're not like me. Maybe you're not a leader."

"I'm a loyal subject of Supreme Mage Creed," Filament said.

"Ah," said Jenan. "So you're not a leader. You're a follower."

Filament swung round, waving the sword in Jenan's face. "You're the follower! You killed Isidora Splendour because Abyssinia told you to!"

"That's right," said Jenan.

"You're not a leader at all!"

"No, I'm not. I'm a bully. The same as you. The difference between us is that I let myself get into a position where I killed someone. I didn't even hate her. I liked Isidora. She was my friend."

Filament sneered. "Omen isn't a friend of mine. He's an enemy of the Supreme Mage. He's an enemy of Roarhaven."

"Is he? Or is that what other people are calling him?"

Filament shook his head. "What are you saying? That I shouldn't kill him? You can't kill him so I shouldn't kill him, either?"

"I don't know what I'm saying, Filament. I came here to do it. I hate him. I hate him so much. He ruined my life." He sighed. "But he didn't, did he? He was just there. I ruined my life, all by myself."

"I should kill you both," Filament snarled.

Jenan spread his arms wide. "Then go ahead. Start with me."

Filament lowered the sword so that it was level with Jenan's stomach.

"Filament," Omen said softly.

"Shut up," Filament responded, tears running down his face.

"Don't do it."

"Shut up, I said."

Omen shut up. Jenan waited. Filament threw the sword to the other side of the hall. Jenan nodded, like he was almost sad that Filament hadn't gone through with it, and walked over to the door. He passed Omen without even looking at him.

103

The skeleton lay exposed and still, every individual bone held in place by a different-sized chained shackle.

"Is he still alive?" Flanery asked, peering closer. "Can he hear me?"

"He's alive," said Doctor Nye. "He hasn't said anything since we attached the chains, however. I'm trying to ascertain whether this is due to a sudden incapacity for speech or mere stubbornness."

Flanery reached out, then stopped. "Can I poke him?"

"By all means."

Flanery poked the skeleton's skull with his forefinger. "Not so talkative now, are you? Not so chatty. You came into my office thinking you could scare me. Thinking you could intimidate me. Me! The president of the United States! I built my empire from nothing! I fought and I struggled my whole life to get where I am today, and you thought that *you* could scare *me*?"

Flanery laughed. The skeleton didn't respond, and Flanery looked over at Nye. "Are you sure he's alive?"

"Quite sure," said the creature.

"Can you make him answer me?"

The other Nye, the taller one, the professor, ducked its head as it entered the room. "I have a theory about that, Mr President. I believe Detective Pleasant has shut down, sir. I've been reading up on our guest, and I've noticed an intriguing tendency to get himself tortured. Nefarian Serpine tortured him twice – the first time, right before killing him – and, more recently, the Faceless Ones themselves tortured him for close to a year. I believe that this somewhat unique history has resulted in a most unco-operative captive."

"Are we torturing him?" Flanery asked, really hoping the answer would be yes.

"Yes."

"Oh, good."

"But we are doing so as a mere side effect to our main objective," said Professor Nye.

"Which is to examine his soul," Doctor Nye said, irritated by the professor's interruption, "as per your instructions, Mr President."

Flanery nodded thoughtfully. "Yes, good. Yes. Is that what I instructed?"

"Yes, sir," both Nyes responded.

"Good, excellent. And what have you discovered?"

The Nyes smiled.

"You have arrived at a most significant juncture, Mr President," said Doctor Nye. "I am about to pluck Detective Pleasant's soul away from his physical form."

"*We* are about to," the professor corrected.

"Of course," the doctor said.

"OK then," said Flanery, "let's do it. Let's get it done. Is there a button to push? I think I should press the button. If it's important, I think I should do it."

"What a wonderful idea," said the professor.

"There, ah, there isn't one single button, sir," the doctor said.

"I wanted one," said the professor. "A big red button would be perfect, I thought."

Flanery nodded. "A red button. I was just going to say that. It should be a red button."

"I'm afraid we don't have a red button," said the doctor.

The professor clucked its tongue and shook its head, and the doctor looked even more annoyed.

"But I would be honoured if you would initiate the sequence, Mr President," the doctor said, indicating a series of switches.

Flanery walked over, examined the switches and nodded. "Excellent," he said. "This all seems to be in order. How many are there?"

"Sir?"

"Switches. How many switches?"

Doctor Nye glanced at the console. "Eighteen, sir."

"That's a good number of switches. OK, which ones will I press?"

Doctor Nye's long-fingered hand pointed to three switches. "These, Mr President, if you would."

Flanery nodded, sucked in his gut, and searched for words appropriate for such an occasion. "This is one small step for man," he said, and flicked the three switches.

Some lights came on, but nothing else happened.

"Thank you, sir," Doctor Nye gushed. "That was very well done."

"Did it work?"

"You have initiated the process, sir."

Flanery looked at the skeleton, and scowled. "He should be screaming."

"We have recordings of that, if you'd like to hear them," the professor said, coming forward. "Hours of it, actually. I was testing the capacity of his aura, steadily increasing the amount of pain he was experiencing. Astonishingly, I couldn't detect an upper limit."

Flanery frowned at him.

"I could have kept increasing the amount of pain and there would be no technical reason for me to stop."

Flanery's frown deepened.

"There was no limit to the pain he could suffer, sir."

"Oh," said Flanery. "Oh! So he kept screaming?"

"Yes, sir."

"And you have it on video?"

"Yes, sir. I can send it to your phone, if you'd like."

Flanery smiled. "I'd like that, yes."

104

China walked in on Valkyrie sitting cross-legged in the middle of the floor, her eyes closed and her breathing steady. A frown crinkled the space between her eyebrows.

Her eyes opened and she looked miserable. "Nothing. Less than nothing. I knew I'd never be able to find Skulduggery, and I've never met Flanery so any chance of zeroing in on his location was always a long shot, but I thought I'd at least be able to find Nye."

"Crengarrions are impervious to psychic probes," China said, helping Valkyrie to her feet. "It's just one of the reasons why nobody has ever trusted them."

"Any luck with your spies?"

China allowed herself a scowl. "No one has any idea where Nye's laboratory is."

"No one? At all? But you have an *army* of spies."

"I had," China corrected. "My time as Supreme Mage and my subsequent fall from grace have robbed my army of their great number. The few I have left are doing their best, but Nye has hidden itself well."

"So what do we do? How do we find Skulduggery?"

"To find a Skeleton Detective," a smooth, velvet voice said from behind them, "you need a Skeleton Detective."

Even as Valkyrie spun round, the delighted smile was fading from her face. Cadaver Cain stood in the doorway.

"May I?" he asked.

"Sure," said Valkyrie.

Cadaver walked in. "I don't ask for much," he told them, "just freedom. When all this is over, when the bad guys are defeated and Valkyrie Cain stands triumphant once again – instead of being locked back in my cell, as enjoyable as that was, I should like to remain free."

"You're too dangerous to remain free unsupervised," said China.

"You trust me enough to allow me to travel the world, killing Shalgoth."

"Desperate times."

"Hold on," said Valkyrie. "You can find out where Skulduggery's being kept?"

"I'll even help you free him. It's in my best interests to ensure his safety, after all. If Skulduggery dies, I stop existing."

"We know that's not true," Valkyrie said. "You're temporally shielded. If Skulduggery dies, you'll still be fine."

"In theory," Cadaver said. "I wouldn't be too keen to test that, however."

"Do you know where he is? Can you see the futures again?"

"Try as I might," Cadaver said, "I haven't yet managed to reconnect with the Viddu De, so that ability remains out of my reach. However, before our connection was severed, I saw where Crepuscular Vies had helped Doctor Nye set up his new lab. I have the exact address."

Valkyrie's hand lit up with crackling black energy. "Tell me where he is or I'll turn you to dust."

"No, you won't," Cadaver said. "Killing me will deprive you of your only way to get Skulduggery back – and, even if it didn't, we both know you wouldn't do it. You have killed, Valkyrie – but you're not a killer. Not yet anyway. I need your word that I will be allowed to go free once this is over. I demand freedom and amnesty."

"Skulduggery wouldn't approve," China said.

"But at least he'd be here," said Valkyrie. "Fine. You'll have your freedom and amnesty, but if you step out of line we're going to hunt you down. You have my word on all of that. Where is he?"

"Mexico," said Cadaver. "Shall we wait till morning, or...?"

"We're leaving now," Valkyrie said, walking out. "I'll get Fletcher."

When she was gone, Cadaver turned to China. "Might I make a suggestion?"

"No," China said, starting to walk away.

"I understand," Cadaver said, walking beside her. "You don't trust me and you are entirely right not to – but I trust you, and I trust your instincts, and I trust *in* your pragmatism."

China stopped. Sighed. Looked at him. "And what are you talking about now?"

"I was only going to suggest that now would be the perfect time to take Martin Flanery out of the equation," Cadaver said. "Once Skulduggery is back in the fold, his naturally occurring ruthless streak will surely be softened by Valkyrie's inherent good nature. This would be disastrous for any effort to take the necessary steps."

"You want to kill the American president."

"Yes."

"Then kill him. The world is in the middle of a great upheaval. What do I care about killing presidents at this stage?"

"That's good to know, China – it is – but by now Flanery is surrounded at all times by a platoon of his super-soldiers. A bomb would be needed, I think."

"So use a bomb."

"Doctor Nye has presumably installed security devices to protect Flanery from most kinds of attack."

"Cadaver, what do you want?"

His head tilted. "You have access to Abyssinia's remaining life-force bomb."

China watched him. "That's a high-yield weapon."

"Yes."

"Once it goes off, it will drain the life from every single living thing within a three-kilometre radius."

"I'm aware of its capabilities. If we use it right, we can get rid of Flanery and a good portion of his super-soldiers in the same instant."

China considered the implications of everything he'd just said. "There's nobody else on the planet who knows that the bomb is still in one piece," she said. "Do you understand how it's triggered?"

"I do."

"If we do this, it must remain secret."

"It will."

"And I feel duty-bound to add a rather annoying proviso: we must ensure that innocent casualties are kept to an absolute minimum."

"Absolutely."

China could feel a headache coming on. "I'll disable the shields around the bomb," she said. "You can set it off."

Cadaver bowed his acceptance of the terms of their deal, and she left. It wouldn't be the first time she'd conspired to kill an American president, after all.

105

Valkyrie had to wait almost an hour before Fletcher became available. When he appeared before her, his face was scratched, his hair was matted, and his clothes smelled of smoke.

"Sorry," he said. "Shalgoth infestation in Kaduna."

"Where is that? Africa?"

He nodded. "Nigeria. They do the best suya there. You ever have it? I'll take you some time, when there aren't monsters everywhere."

"Was it bad?"

He frowned. "It's great. Did I not say it was the best? It's delicious. They do it with these herbs—"

"I meant the infestation."

"Oh," Fletcher said. "Yeah. Pretty bad. Some people killed. We stopped it, though."

"You look exhausted."

He looked around for a seat, couldn't find one, and sat on the floor. "I'm a smidge tired, yes. How's my hair?"

"Disastrous."

"Bugger. So where am I taking you?"

"You'll be taking Cadaver and me to Mexico, as close to Guerrero as possible."

"I've been to Guerrero before, no problem. Why're you going with Cadaver Cain? Where's Skulduggery?"

491

"Not far from Guerrero, we think. He's been captured. He went to force Martin Flanery to back down and we haven't heard from him since. We think Flanery took him to Doctor Nye."

"Oh, hell. So this is a rescue mission? Count me in."

"No," Valkyrie said firmly. "You're too valuable to risk. All we need is for you to take us to Guerrero, and we'll handle it from there."

"Just you and this Cadaver guy? I don't trust him, Val."

"You've never met him."

"I've met Skulduggery."

"They're not the same person. Technically, they're the same person, but they're not the same person."

"How can you tell them apart? Does the future version have, like, an evil goatee or something?"

Valkyrie grinned. "No evil goatee. Though he's pretty distinctive."

As if he was waiting for his cue, Cadaver walked in, black coat swishing. Valkyrie pulled Fletcher to his feet.

"Fletcher Renn!" Cadaver said, like he was greeting his oldest friend. "In my time, you are quite rightly known as the greatest Teleporter who ever lived, do you realise that? It's thanks to you that the discipline began to thrive again. Some of your students went on to do amazing things, and it's all because of you. You have my every apology for all those times I was dismissive of you in the past. I was wrong, and I'm honoured for this chance to work beside you once again."

Fletcher stared at him through narrowed eyes, and then glanced at Valkyrie. "I really like him."

"Fletcher," she sighed.

"No, seriously, I prefer him to the other one."

"You humble me," said Cadaver.

"I love your coat."

Cadaver nodded. "It's very swishy."

"And those staples in your head are cool."

"I find they do lend me a certain ruggedness, yes."

"Can you two please shut up?" Valkyrie asked. "Fletcher, take us to Mexico, then come back here and get some sleep. You're no use to anyone if you collapse out there."

Cadaver put his hand on Fletcher's shoulder. "She's right, Fletch. You're our most important weapon against the Shalgoth. We can't afford to lose you."

"Will you be my dad?"

Valkyrie growled and stood on Fletcher's foot. "Teleport, dumbass."

Their surroundings changed in less time than it took to blink, and suddenly they were in the sun, standing beside a zebra enclosure.

"*Chilpancingo de los Bravo*," Fletcher announced. "Capital of Guerrero."

Valkyrie looked around. "We're in a zoo."

He nodded. "The *Zoológico Zoochilpan*. I once saw the saddest little monkey here, so I like to pop by occasionally and see how he's doing. Are you sure you don't want me to come with you?"

"We should be able to deal with what comes," Cadaver said, "but if we need backup, we'll call." He stuck his hand out, and they shook, and when Fletcher teleported away Cadaver tilted his head. "Why are you looking at me like that?"

"I see what you're doing," Valkyrie told him, and blasted into the air.

He followed, the air rippling around him. "What do you mean?"

"This charm offensive," she shouted against the wind. "You're trying to win people over to your side."

"My side is your side, surely," Cadaver responded.

"Your side is your own side, and you bloody know it."

He swerved north and she adjusted to match his trajectory.

"I'm trying to prove myself," he said.

"I've already promised you amnesty, so long as we actually rescue Skulduggery. You've got what you wanted."

"I will have my freedom and my amnesty, yes, but I have no

illusions about my status in this timeline. I am, quite literally, surplus to requirements. There's already one of me here – why does this world need another? The simple answer is that it doesn't – so I shall have to prove myself so valuable, so indispensable, that everyone – including Skulduggery – will have to wonder how they ever got along without me."

"Skulduggery does a pretty good job of that on his own."

"I agree. The world, as they say, might not be big enough for both of us. But I have to try."

Valkyrie didn't say anything to that, and they flew on, away from the cities and the towns, over green fields and woodland, into the mountains. They followed a road for a bit, making cars pull in sharply as they flew overhead, and Valkyrie got the feeling that Cadaver was searching for landmarks, or maybe trying to remember exactly where this laboratory was. Or maybe he was making all this up, and he had no idea where Doctor Nye was working, and was just waiting for his moment to attack her. But then he swooped lower and she followed, and they skimmed a rockface and found some steps cut into the stone.

They landed, and Cadaver led the way down to a steel door. He tapped the sigils carved into it, repeating a pattern three times and then reversing it, and the door clicked and swung open.

Inside, it was cool and dark. They reached the first corner. The place hummed with power and machines that beeped, but, so far, no actual people.

"At the risk of sounding like I'm trying to win you over to my side," Cadaver said as they walked, "it does feel good to work together again."

"Don't get used to it."

"Really? Let's not be so hasty. Maybe there will be a time when we'll partner up regularly – all three of us. We could be our own intrepid little gang of adventurers. Or, if Skulduggery is OK with the idea of sharing you, I could start out by having you on weekends..."

"Wow."

"It could work."

"I'm not a timeshare, Cadaver."

"Then maybe I should take on a partner of my own and we could team up in years to come. Perhaps Alice?"

Valkyrie pointed at him. "Don't even joke about that."

"She has magic – we all know that," he said. "She'll have to learn sooner or later."

"You won't be teaching her."

"Why not? I happen to think I'd be the perfect mentor. I've been through it once with you, so I can steer her away from all the mistakes we made."

"I don't know what I'm going to do about Alice, but I can guarantee that you will not be involved. I'm not putting my sister through anything like I went through. You don't do that to family. You don't do that to people you love."

Cadaver shrugged. "Very well."

They walked on.

A guard sat in a folding chair ahead, a gun on his hip and his eyes on his phone. Cadaver gestured and the guard flew off the chair, the air dragging him towards them. Valkyrie kicked him and he slumped over. They moved on.

"Can I ask you a question?" Cadaver asked.

"No," she said.

"Why have you never asked about my family?"

She frowned at him. "I've asked about them plenty of times. It's only in the last few days that I've got any kind of answer."

"Not my siblings," Cadaver said, "and not my parents – I mean my wife and child. As curious as you are, as obsessed as you get with uncovering certain details about certain things, why have you never asked about them?"

"I figured it was private," she said as they peered round the next corner. A technician in a lab coat passed from one doorway to another, reading the report in her hands. They waited till she was gone before continuing.

"You rarely care about privacy," Cadaver whispered.

"This is different."

"Would you like to know about them?"

"I already do. You've told me."

"I've given you snippets. Facts and names and dates and superficial things. What would you really like to know about them?"

She stopped, and looked at him. "What are you doing?"

"I'm being open. I'm sharing."

"If Skulduggery wanted me to ask those questions, he'd tell me. The only thing I want to hear from you is business."

Cadaver's head tilted. "Of course."

"Where exactly are we going?"

"I expect Skulduggery is being held in Nye's main lab, down this way. If I'm wrong, we get to explore this wonderful facility until we find him, but I'm me, so I'm probably not wrong."

A few more corners and they entered a large room stuffed with equipment. Skulduggery's skeleton lay shackled to one of the tables like the remains that had been excavated from a shallow grave.

Secured into a metal brace that hung from the ceiling was a glass cylinder the size of a thermos flask that writhed with energy. Valkyrie knew Skulduggery's aura instantly.

"They did it," Cadaver murmured as he and Valkyrie hurried over. "They pulled his soul from his body." He gazed at the skeleton. "Granted, this is weird, but I have to say I prefer him like this."

"Take the shackles off," said Valkyrie, trying to pull the cylinder from its mooring.

Cadaver passed his hand over a sigil on the table and all the shackles popped open with a metallic rattle. Valkyrie pulled the cylinder free and hurled it to the floor. It didn't break – it bounced. She blasted it with some white lightning, which only sent it skittering.

And Crepuscular Vies plucked it up.

Valkyrie tensed. "What are you doing here?"

"Helping," Crepuscular said. "This container is very tricky to open. It requires a magic touch, if you will."

Valkyrie raised her hand. "Give it back."

"But don't you want me to open it? I'm the only one who can. I told Doctor Nye to design it that way – as an insurance policy, you know?"

"Then open it."

He held the cylinder in his left hand, tapped it with the fingers of his right.

White energy crackled. "Open it, Crepuscular."

"I intend to," he responded. "That's why I came. It's all about timing, though. Skulduggery taught me that. Are you ready?"

"Nearly," said Cadaver, and Valkyrie turned to see Cadaver dumping Skulduggery's skeletal remains into a sack that he immediately tied off.

She lunged without thinking and he caught her with a punch to the stomach that doubled her over. Struggling to breathe, she fell to her knees.

Cadaver hunkered down beside her. "You were right not to trust me," he said. "I wish you absolutely no harm, but I'm afraid I can't have Skulduggery Pleasant running around while I'm active. He knows me too well. I don't like that. And don't for a moment think that he'd have been happy to have *me* running around, either. The moment the current situation was resolved, he would have hunted me down. This is purely self-preservation."

"Don't do this," she wheezed.

"I'm sorry. I have to. In a few years, maybe you'll see it from my side. Maybe you'll even forgive me. I hope you do. This world is infinitely more fun when you're by my side."

He straightened as Crepuscular joined him.

"I'm going to open this now," said Crepuscular, "freeing Skulduggery, just like I said I would. Only we're taking his skeleton with us. I don't know exactly how long he'll last without a physical form, but Cadaver reckons it won't be much more than three or four minutes before his consciousness starts to dissipate. If you have any last words to say to him, speak them now."

He placed the cylinder on the floor in front of her, then put his hand on Cadaver's shoulder and teleported them both out. The sigil on the cylinder pulsed and the glass cracked and then broke.

Valkyrie watched Skulduggery's essence swirling in the air before her. "Hold on," she said, forcing herself to her feet. "Just hold on. I'll find a Soul Catcher."

She started searching. The laboratory seemed to have every other glass container except what she needed.

Fine. She'd just need another kind of container. She ran out of the laboratory.

Three security guards – two men, one woman – passed in the corridor ahead of her. Valkyrie could have blasted them, but she needed one of them conscious so she charged. They heard her coming and turned and she caught the first one, the taller of the men, with a flying knee that launched him backwards. As she was landing, she hooked an arm round the throat of the woman, dragging her off balance, throwing her into her colleague as he went for his gun. She snapped a palm into his chin and kicked at the woman's leg but missed, and the woman lunged, headbutted her jaw, started shoving her away, giving her buddy the space he needed to draw his weapon.

Valkyrie jammed her thumb into the woman's eye and flipped her over her hip. She left her to her curses as she grabbed the male guard's wrist, not letting him raise the gun, and pushed him up against the wall. She slammed her elbow into his jaw and tore the gun from his hand and backed off, gun in a two-handed grip.

"Nobody move," she said.

The tall guard froze, halfway to his feet. The other guy held up his hands. His eyes were unfocused. He was ready to drop. The woman scowled, her hand on the gun in her holster.

"Slide them towards me," Valkyrie instructed.

Firearms skidded along the ground to her feet.

She was going to have to do this fast.

Slowing her breathing, focusing on the taller guard, she barged into his mind. He hissed, face screwing up, hands going to his head as he resisted. She switched her attention to the woman as she started forward and the woman cursed, dropped to one knee, trying to push Valkyrie out of her head.

Valkyrie retracted her thoughts immediately and sent them into the mind of the third guard, registering his surprise and his fear, and then his memories lay before her, but she didn't bother taking even a peek. She reversed out of there, clicked on the gun's safety before stuffing it into one of her deep pockets, and sent two handfuls of lightning into the tall guy and the woman. Then she grabbed the shorter guard, locking his arm painfully, and marched him to the laboratory.

Kicking open the door, she marched in, threw him down. "Your temporary home," she called out. "Skulduggery! Let's go! Move it!"

The guard got to his knees, started to say something and then he seized up, his face contorting. That lasted for a few seconds until he sagged, head dropping forward, chin on chest.

Valkyrie took a step towards him. "Skulduggery?"

The guard looked up. Opened his mouth. Closed it. Blinked. Raised his hands to his head and felt his face. "Oh, my," Skulduggery said in a voice that wasn't his own.

She hauled him to his feet and he wobbled, almost fell over.

"Oh, my," he said again.

"Bit of an emergency," she told him. "We have to move. Can you move?"

"This is extraordinarily disconcerting," he said, and then frowned. "Oh, I even sound strange. How odd. How very odd and, as I've previously mentioned, disconcerting."

She took out the gun, gave it to him. "Can you aim? Can you pull a trigger?"

He took the weapon, slid out the magazine to check the bullets, then slid it in again, racked the slide and flicked off the safety. "I can smell," he said.

"That's nice, dear," Valkyrie said, hurrying to the door.

Skulduggery followed on shaky, borrowed legs. "I'd forgotten what it's like to smell. Oh, I miss smelling things. The sea. The countryside. Fresh bread. Bread. I think I'm hungry. What does hunger feel like, again? Is it a pressure in your lower abdomen?"

"I think you need to pee," Valkyrie said.

"I need to pee," Skulduggery echoed. "Amazing."

An alarm went off.

Somebody shot at them and Skulduggery fired back and then they were running away from the shouts and the bullets. Valkyrie ran round a corner and Skulduggery followed, but careered straight into the wall and bounced off.

"Ow," he said, twirling. Valkyrie took hold of his arm and they raced on. "Pain in a flesh-and-blood body is different."

A guard burst out through a door ahead and Valkyrie jumped, kicked the door so that it smacked into the guard and he fell back and they kept running, leaving him sprawled on the ground behind them.

They turned another corner and Skulduggery hit it with his shoulder and almost went twirling again.

"Sorry," he said. "Finding it hard to co-ordinate."

A thick metal door closed before they could reach it and they turned left, bullets peppering the wall. Skulduggery returned fire and they sprinted onwards.

"I don't think I'm a very good shot any more," he said. "I'm not used to having eyes. It's harder to aim when you have eyes."

Valkyrie saw shadows on the wall of the bisecting corridor ahead and she shoved Skulduggery into a room and put her finger to her lips. He nodded. It was a storage room filled with boxes and crates. They crouched. Skulduggery's breathing was loud so she poked him with her elbow and mimed slowing down her breathing. He nodded and tried to follow her instruction, but did it weirdly, like someone pretending to breathe. She focused on the footsteps hurrying by the open door.

The alarm cut off. She could hear the shouting better now, heard the orders being issued. When the activity ceased in the corridor outside, she nodded and crept forward, and Skulduggery fell over.

Valkyrie spun, hurried back.

"Ohh," Skulduggery whispered.

"What's wrong? Are you hit? Did they shoot you?"

"My head feels light," he responded, his breathing picking up again.

She looked at him for a few seconds, then frowned. "You're hyperventilating," she said.

He looked up. "I am?"

"Yes."

"I see."

"Control your breathing."

"I thought I was. I'm sorry. I've quite forgotten how to do this."

"Stop talking. Lie there and relax."

"OK."

"But relax faster – we have to move." She pulled him up. "You good?"

"I'm super," he responded. "But I really do have to pee."

"Pee later. Escape now."

She led the way out, down the corridor, moving quickly but quietly. They barged through a door and two Doctor Nyes spun to look at them.

106

No, wait. Not two *Doctor* Nyes.

The one on the left, that was Doctor Nye, the creature that had cut Valkyrie open to carve a sigil into her heart, and never intended to let her leave. Its limbs weren't quite as long Professor Nye's, the creature from the Leibniz Universe who had tortured and double-crossed her. They stood side by side.

The doctor raised its long, bony finger, and pointed at Skulduggery. "It's you, isn't it? You've commandeered this mortal's body. How does it feel, after all this time as a skeleton? How does it feel to suddenly exist within a living shell? I imagine it would be quite a startling change. Is it? I would imagine it is. I would love to document your thoughts on this matter, and then maybe strap you to a table and record your reaction to the damage I inflict. Would you be open to this, purely for scientific purposes?"

"Not especially," Skulduggery told it.

The doctor waved aside his objection. "I was merely asking out of politeness. A push of the button beside me is all it will take to flood this room with a gas that will send you both to sleep before you can register its faint aroma – where you wake up after that is something neither of you have a choice in, I'm afraid."

Before Nye could reach for any such button, Valkyrie loosed a stream of lightning that would have struck it square in the chest were it not for the wall of energy that flashed up between them.

The doctor chuckled. "And you, Valkyrie, would you like me to tell you where you will be waking up?"

"Not interested," she said.

Skulduggery fired the gun, but the bullet sizzled against the same wall of energy. "Worth a try," he muttered.

"It's over," the doctor said. "For both of you. Cadaver Cain, as far as I am aware, is going to be keeping your skeleton locked away for use in an emergency, Detective, so you'll never be seeing it again. Tomorrow morning, I will separate your soul from that mortal's body. Crepuscular Vies, I understand, wishes for your soul to evaporate, and who am I to defy Crepuscular Vies' wishes? Once you're well and truly dead, I will examine the mortal to see if his soul has been affected in any way by sharing space with yours. He'll die, of course, but such is the price of science.

"But Valkyrie... you will get to live a lot longer. In fact, if I have my way, I'll keep you alive forever. You're such a unique specimen – a human with access to all sorts of magic we have yet to even categorise. Crepuscular is fascinating – his ability to wield a vast array of disciplines is beyond thrilling. But you, Valkyrie, you represent something we have never before seen. Because of everything that has happened to you, because of everything you've lost and gained, there is an argument to be made that you not only *wield* magic, but that you *are* magic. Isn't that magnificent?"

"That is very cool, yes."

Nye's wide mouth split into a smile. "You're being sarcastic because you have yet to fathom what this will mean for you."

"No," Valkyrie said, "I think I've got it figured. You came up with Splash. Then you came up with something that's a few steps beyond Splash – a way to take a sorcerer's magic and transfer it to mortals, if only for a short time. And now you look at me and you think – what would it be like to transfer *her* magic to other sorcerers? What would happen if I could transfer *her* magic to mortals? Would it be permanent? How would it affect their souls? That's what's going through your little head, isn't it?"

"It is," Nye admitted happily.

Valkyrie took the gun from Skulduggery's hand and pressed the muzzle into her temple. "And what happens to these plans of yours if I die right here and now, Doctor?"

Nye lost its smile. "You wouldn't."

"You're sure about that?"

"You're a fighter," said Nye. "Giving up isn't in your nature. You won't do it."

Skulduggery took the gun from her, but kept it pressing into her head. "She may not," he said, "but I would."

"This is ridiculous."

"We're getting out of here, Doctor, or Valkyrie dies."

"You won't kill her. I know you won't kill her. This is a bluff of outstanding stupidity." It reached for the button.

"Make one more move," Skulduggery said, "and I'll pull the trigger. Valkyrie's going to die on your table anyway – at least now her death will be quick."

Doctor Nye hesitated while, behind it, Professor Nye dislocated its jaw, opened its mouth impossibly wide, and chomped down on the back of Doctor Nye's head.

Doctor Nye squealed and struggled, but Professor Nye was bigger and stronger and held it in place.

Valkyrie stared. "What the hell?"

She became aware of a quiet slurping sound as Professor Nye started to swallow.

"Skulduggery," said Valkyrie, horrified, "what the hell?"

"Crengarrions can absorb memories from other Crengarrions by devouring their brainstem after death," Skulduggery told her as they watched. "It's their way of preserving traditions and it's supposed to be a great honour."

Professor Nye let Doctor Nye's body crumple to the floor, and it wiped its mouth as its jaw reset. "Apologies," it said. "I wish you hadn't had to see that, but I had little choice. I owe you – both of you – for things I have done in the past. This is my attempt to balance the scales. There is an emergency exit down the corridor to your right. It's at the very end and leads to a ladder that emerges at the uppermost peak of this mountain. If you hurry, you can get away without further interference."

"I don't get it," said Valkyrie.

Professor Nye looked at her. "You don't believe a creature such as I can regret their past actions? You don't think I, too, seek redemption?"

"Either that," Skulduggery said, "or by killing your alternate self you've just got rid of the only other being alive who knows the secret to transferring magic, thus ensuring that you are indispensable."

Nye shrugged. "I prefer my answer. You'd better run away now. Don't you have a world to save?"

107

There was a corner of the Corrival grounds where the protective shield fell just short of the wall. Hemmed in by the two walls, the spot was barely big enough for a person to stand in – but that's where Crepuscular Vies was standing as he waited for Omen to walk over.

"Thanks for coming," Crepuscular said. "I know that you could have ignored my message. I understand that you're mad at me."

"You don't understand anything," said Omen through the shield. "If you did, if you were even capable of coming close to understanding, then you wouldn't have used our friendship to score more points than Skulduggery Pleasant."

"So it's still a friendship?"

"No," said Omen. "Oh, no. No, it's no longer a friendship. You can get lost as far as I'm concerned."

Crepuscular took off his hat. "Can I explain myself, then? Would you do me that one favour? Surely you owe me that much?"

"I owe you?" Omen said. "For what, exactly?"

"Without wanting to hold this over you," Crepuscular said, "I have saved your life on multiple occasions."

"For all the wrong reasons."

"I helped you with Auger."

"To gain my trust."

"No," said Crepuscular quickly. "Well, not entirely. I also did it because I genuinely wanted to help."

"Why should I believe anything you say to me from now on? You know what I just realised? The people I can trust – that I can *actually* trust – are down to, like, three. I don't know which side Valkyrie and Skulduggery are on except, you know, their own, so I can't trust them. Auger's gone, apparently. That's what everyone keeps telling me. My brother's gone; he's not coming back; I've got to face reality. Hell, for all I know, those bullets Creed shot him with ended up killing him and he's lying dead somewhere and his body will never be found. And my parents. Ha! They're not even in consideration. I'm nothing to them and now they're nothing to me. I can count on Never, and I can count on Axelia, and maybe I can count on Miss Gnosis even though she's a teacher, and I thought I could count on you, but dear *Jesus*, I was so incredibly wrong on that one, wasn't I? It's embarrassing how wrong I was."

"Omen—"

"What, Crepuscular? What? How are you going to talk your way round this one? I'm very interested to know."

Crepuscular hesitated.

"I'm sorry," he said at last. "I'm sorry I misled you. Sorry I lied to you. I'm sorry I used you to prove myself superior to Skulduggery. You don't deserve that kind of treatment."

"And that whole proving yourself superior thing, in case I haven't spelled it out, is so bloody stupid."

Crepuscular nodded. "I know."

"That's easy to say."

"It's not, actually. It's very hard to say. I've put years into this, the idea that I can beat him by being better than him, by saving you where he couldn't save me. This has been my life, Omen. This has been the only thing that has driven me forward."

Omen looked at him. "That's sad and pathetic."

"I'm aware."

"And now you see sense, do you? Just like that?"

"Is that so hard to believe?"

"Kinda, yeah."

"I've seen sense because, for the first time, this narrative that's only existed in my head has met the real world, and it's hurt real people, and a real friend. So, yes, I now see sense. I see how stupid I've been, and I apologise."

"So, what? From now on, complete honesty, something like that?"

"Yes. I swear."

"OK," said Omen, "prove it. What else have you been up to?"

Crepuscular hesitated.

"Thought so," said Omen, about to turn away.

"We have Skulduggery Pleasant's skeleton."

Omen frowned. "His skeleton? What about the rest of him? His consciousness?"

"I don't know. We left that with Valkyrie. I don't know what happened there."

"Who's 'we'?"

"Cadaver Cain and me."

"You're... You've teamed up with the future version of the man you hate? To do what?"

"Take over. Creed has to be replaced. Roarhaven needs a new leader, even if it's only for a couple of days. Skulduggery would have interfered with that and so we removed him as an obstacle. I know how that sounds – it sounds like I'm the bad guy – but, if I have any hope of making it up to you, you deserve my complete honesty."

"And exactly how are you going to make anything up to me?"

"By seeing it through to the end."

Omen laughed. "Are you serious? After everything, you want us to be partners again? Why the hell would I agree to that?"

"Because of all the good we've done and all the good we can do. Omen, my motives may have been screwed up, but we saved lives. When everyone else was thinking big-picture stuff, end-of-the-world stuff, we kept helping the people who needed help right there and then – the people everyone else was ignoring."

"And that's what you want to keep doing, is it?"

"No. While we were saving lives, the people we trusted to save the world messed up. We can't let that continue."

"Whatever," Omen said, walking away. "Do whatever you want, but do it without me."

"I think we can save your brother."

Omen stopped, but didn't turn.

"I don't think he's too far gone," Crepuscular continued. "I think you can reach him. I think you're the only one who can. Auger's the Chosen One – if anyone can beat this Obsidian persona that's taken over, it's him."

Omen turned. "You'll help me find him? How, exactly?"

"That will take some work," said Crepuscular. "We'll need the High Sanctuary's full resources working on it – so Creed will have to be replaced."

"You're going to kill him?"

"No," Crepuscular said, "this isn't about killing anyone. We can remove him from office, throw him in a cell if we have to, and take over."

"We'll take over, will we? We'll take over the High Sanctuary? That's nuts. No one will listen to us. You think they'll obey your orders? No one even knows who we are!"

"No, but if they know Skulduggery Pleasant, then they'll know Cadaver Cain."

Omen frowned. "You want Cadaver Cain to run the High Sanctuary? To become the Supreme Mage?"

"It's the only way we'll be able to get Auger back."

"But that's not how anything works," Omen said. "The Supreme Mage has to be voted in, or appointed or something."

"Yes, they do," said Crepuscular. "Appointed by the Council of Advisors. Omen, recent events may have changed things up, taken some players off the board and put some new ones on, but I've always been good at improvising and adapting. I've been preparing for this for years. I need your help to see it over the finish line."

108

Marching through Nye's laboratory, Martin Flanery felt invincible.

It wasn't the Secret Service guys trailing after him, either, the ones brimming with magic. No, this feeling of invulnerability came from Flanery and Flanery alone. His muscles were popping. He could feel them. His hands were huge and mighty and capable of crushing steel. His legs were powerful – he could run fast and jump high and kick down a door. He could splinter bones beneath his feet.

He thought about how he'd beaten up the skeleton and he smiled a smile that threatened to rip his face apart but didn't. Couldn't. Nothing could rip his skin. No knife could cut him and no bullet could kill him. He was indestructible.

The smile dropped when he passed the table where the bones of Skulduggery Pleasant had been chained up, and where they weren't chained up any more. Nye was waiting for him, standing with its hands behind its back and its head bowed. Flanery wasn't afraid of it any more. How could he be afraid of something that he could snap like a toothpick?

"You failed me," he snarled.

The creature looked up. "I am here to work, Mr President. I do not co-ordinate this facility's security."

"You failed me!" Flanery roared, slamming his fist on to a table so hard the whole thing buckled.

"Of course, Mr President," said Nye. "I beg your forgiveness."

Flanery glared at him, hatred and revulsion broiling within him, on the very edge of leaping forward, grasping that scrawny neck and twisting it until it popped. Nye stood there, looking at him, like it was daring him to do just that.

"You think you're not replaceable?" Flanery said. "You think I'll go easy on you because you make the Splashes? There's another one of you, you idiot. What's stopping me from killing you right here and now and just putting the other guy in charge? It wouldn't even be murder. You're not even human. You're a creature. You're an animal. You're less than an animal. If I kill you, there'll be no monster-rights activists kicking up a fuss. No one will care!"

"You are right, of course," said Nye. "But I'm afraid I must correct you on one small point – there is only one of me. The being you knew as Doctor Nye met its demise when Valkyrie Cain and Skulduggery Pleasant escaped."

Flanery glowered. "They killed it?"

"Suffice it to say, it was killed. I'm sorry to tell you that I am the only Nye left. The good news, however, is that, while I already surpassed the doctor in every conceivable way, after feasting on its memories and experience, I am now twice the creature it ever was."

Before it had even finished speaking, the rage that had been burning in Flanery's chest flickered and faltered and went out, and took every bit of his strength with it. It was a horrible feeling, as if all his blood had been drained from him, and he sagged, almost stumbled into one of his Secret Service agents. Professor Nye watched him, a slight smile on its face.

"Are you feeling OK, Mr President?"

Flanery hated this part of it. "I'm fine," he mumbled, and stood up straighter. "I want another batch, though."

Those small, beady eyes narrowed. "You haven't used up the last batch already, have you? I warned you to pace yourself, to use them only when required."

"You don't warn me about anything, you got that? I'm the president, you ugly freak. You want my guys here to remind you of that?"

"No, sir, that will not be necessary. Another batch of the—?"

"The strength ones," said Flanery. "The ones to make me strong."

"Of course, Mr President. A new batch will be ready in just a few minutes. In the meantime, might I suggest a new Splash?"

"What kind?"

"A prototype, sir. I made two of them, just for you."

Flanery hesitated. "And what does it do?"

"I could explain, sir, but it would be far more effective if you were to just experience it. If you're too cautious, however..."

Cautious. Just another way of saying scared. "Give it to me."

Nye smiled. "Excellent."

It turned to a massive refrigerator, took out a metal box, made a big deal about opening it.

Flanery didn't like waiting. Waiting meant that somebody else had the power. He puffed out his chest. "I've been thinking," he said, "about the Splashes. Thinking of ways you could improve them." He spoke loudly, so that all the other scientists in the lab could hear him, and so that his Secret Service detail could appreciate how impressive he was.

"Yes, Mr President?"

"It came to me last night," Flanery continued, "I was thinking about them and I thought, you know what would make these better? Different flavours."

Nye hesitated. "Flavours, Mr President?"

Flanery nodded. "Right now, I don't even know what flavour they are. They taste of nothing. I put one in my mouth and I don't know what I'm supposed to be tasting."

"You're not supposed to be tasting anything, sir. They're flavourless."

"And that's your problem right there," Flanery said, snapping his fingers. "You need flavour. Everything needs flavour. Start off with something simple, like peppermint, or vanilla or chocolate, and then start introducing more advanced flavours like, I don't know, cookies and cream or raspberry ripple."

Nye looked at him. "I see."

Flanery knew that look, whether it was from a freak of nature like Nye or from one of his own generals, and he hated it. He felt himself starting to blush.

Holding the metal box in both hands, Nye held it towards him. Nestled in there were two squares of paper. Two Splashes.

Flanery picked up one of them, examined it. "How long will it take to work?"

"Immediately, Mr President."

"How long will it last?"

"Half an hour on the dot, sir. As always."

Flanery hesitated, but everyone was watching him, so he put it on his tongue and swallowed. He waited for something to happen, for that familiar strength to flood his system or the energy to start crackling, but there was none of that. There was no physical change at all, as far as he could tell.

For a moment, he wondered if Nye had miscalculated, or had perhaps simply failed, if perhaps its ambition had outstripped its ability, but such a thought did not last long. Professor Nye was far too intelligent, and far too cunning, to allow for the possibility of such an obvious failure. There were myriad ways in which that particular Splash could have been affecting him – it could have turned him into a Teleporter or a Shunter, or given him access to a thousand other disciplines. The possibilities, as he was starting to realise when it came to magic, were practically endless.

Flanery raised an eyebrow at the professor. "So what am I able to do now that I wasn't able to do a moment ago?"

Nye laughed softly. "I would like to answer that with a question, if I may?"

"By all means."

"One of the many projects that had stumped Doctor Nye when it was alive was its research into the Source of All Magic and how sorcerers, in turn, wield that energy. The doctor worked on the assumption that certain living creatures are more attuned to magic than others, but struggled to explain how they draw this magical energy from the Source portals. Would you have any idea how this is achieved, Mr President?"

"You're the expert, Professor. I know nothing about magic."

"But if you were to hazard a guess?"

Flanery sighed. "I don't know. I would imagine it has something to do with how receptive their cells are, since I expect the answer lies in the DNA strands, but I know next to nothing about..." He blinked. "Ah," he said, "you've made me smarter."

"Not only have I boosted your intelligence," said Nye, "but you will also find yourself drawing on the knowledge of everyone in your vicinity. In this case, the entire laboratory."

"I'm reading their minds? Wait – no. I'm absorbing facts, figures, theories – but I have no more insight into their private lives or inner workings than I did a few minutes ago. This is... this is fascinating."

"Yes," said Nye.

Flanery laughed. "This is incredible. My mind is... open."

"It is a wonderful way to be, is it not?"

"It is," said Flanery. "How many of those Splashes have you made?"

"Just two, Mr President – but I can make more."

Flanery considered it. "I don't want this mass-produced," he said. "I don't want this out in the world. We're not in the business of handing potential rivals an advantage, are we, Professor?"

"No, Mr President, we are not."

"We can supply our allies with all kinds of Splashes, give their soldiers all manner of physical advantages. Let them smash and destroy to their heart's content. Let bullets bounce off their chests. Let them hurl fire and throw energy. But we keep the Shunters and the Teleporters American, do you understand me? We keep the Sensitives American. As for the intelligence-booster... Well, I think I'll be the only one taking that."

"Of course, sir."

It was a surreal experience to be Martin Flanery in that moment, his weaknesses laid out before him. He had always thought of himself as the smartest man in the room, even in a room of certified geniuses. They just didn't have what he had, he'd told himself. They were bookworms, nerds, people who studied – cheated, basically – while he got by on his natural intelligence. He didn't need books. He didn't need learning. He was better than all of that.

But he could see now the emptiness of those ideas. He could see how they emanated from a place of worthlessness. His father had been a smart man – smart enough to build an empire through sheer grit and ruthlessness. His mother had been stern and unloving. Martin was raised to a life where money and power were all that mattered. Countless articles and exposés over the years had painted him as a man born into privilege, despising those who were less fortunate. He'd always accepted that portrait of himself, as reductive as it may have been, but he saw now that there were different kinds of privilege. Given the chance, would he have traded the privilege of wealth for the privilege of support? Of understanding? Of love?

"How are we with supply?" he asked, startled at the realisation that he could hold more than one thought in his head at the same time.

"Things are proceeding faster than anticipated," Nye answered. "I have refined the doctor's plans – streamlined them where necessary – and as a result our stocks are growing seven per cent faster than expected."

"I think it's safe to say that the right Nye survived," said Flanery.

"So kind of you, sir."

"Skulduggery Pleasant and Valkyrie Cain killed Doctor Nye

as they made their escape, you said? Or, actually, you didn't say that at all, did you?"

Nye bowed its head. "Doctor Nye's passing was tragic, Mr President, and we are all the poorer for it."

Flanery didn't respond to that. "Events certainly have conspired to make you quite invaluable, haven't they?"

"I suppose they have, sir."

"Although, now that I'm smarter than you, I'm sure I could figure out how to make those Splashes if I really had to."

"I'm sure you could, Mr President – if you were smarter than me."

Flanery looked at Nye and smiled, and Nye smiled back.

A machine chimed and a small door popped open, and Nye took out a metal box, the size and shape of a phone.

"To make you strong, sir," said Nye, passing it over.

Flanery pocketed the box while he examined the tables around him. He could spend the day down here, going through everything, taking it all apart and putting it back together better than before. Never in his life had he ever been interested in conducting research, in using an experiment to test a theory and progress a possibility, but today the opportunity was before him and it was almost impossible to resist.

An aide stepped in. "Mr President, sir, we have a situation developing in Seattle."

The world, it seemed, was full of situations, dragging him away from the things he most wanted. "The intelligence-booster," he said to Nye.

The professor plucked the second Splash from its box with a pair of long tweezers, and slipped it into a smaller box, no bigger than a stamp.

Flanery put it in his shirt pocket. "I want more of these."

"Yes, sir."

Nye bowed, the obsequious creature that it was, and Flanery led the way from the laboratory. Once they were out of range of the blockers, the Secret Service agent who'd taken the Teleporter Splash took a moment to picture their destination in his head. At his nod, his fellow agents linked up and Flanery joined them, and suddenly they were in the living room in the Executive Residence, each of them diving for their individually assigned puke buckets.

When Flanery had finished vomiting, another aide handed him a handkerchief to wipe his chin and three breath mints. Flanery chewed as he walked, eager to face this new challenge and figure out the best way to overcome it.

The Situation Room was alive with activity and his generals updated him on the various operations and Flanery hurried them along. They were used to talking slower, to explaining everything, to using simplified language – but today he was absorbing their words while reading the reports, both on screen and on paper, and everything and everyone was moving far too slow for his liking.

Shalgoth carnage in New York, Washington, Philadelphia and Dallas. Sorcerers battling monsters in Chicago, Seattle, Miami, Boston and Salt Lake City. A hundred other crisis points, and that was just in the continental United States. Around the world it was just as bad. Their allies needed help – they needed magic to give their soldiers a fighting chance.

This was all working out perfectly.

He ignored the shocked looks on his generals' faces when he started issuing orders. There was a moment of surprise, a moment of confusion, where they were realising that there was now a strategy at play, and then they snapped to it, got on the phones, started barking orders of their own. It was a beautiful thing, a magnificent thing, a great thing, and all those big thoughts swept from Flanery's mind, gushed out of it like floodwater down a storm drain and he blinked at everyone around him, almost wincing at the barrage of noise.

He checked. No one had noticed how he had sagged. They were all busy carrying out his instructions. He tried to remember what they were, but they floated away from him like a dream he couldn't quite keep a hold of. There were a few seconds when he felt scared, and weak, and vulnerable, and completely unsuited to this job.

His father would have sneered at this weakness. His mother, too. She would have grabbed him by the scruff and pulled him towards her and called him stupid, called him a failure, called him all the names he'd hated to be called when he was a boy.

He scrambled for the box in his pocket, yanked it free, almost dropped it in his desperate need to get it open. He licked his finger and pressed it to the Splash. He put the Splash on his tongue, swallowed it – and breathed out, and all his weakness went with that breath.

He was Martin Flanery again. The president of the United States. He was in charge. Everyone did what he told them. Five-star generals saluted him and everyone called him *sir*.

He was strong. His muscles were like steel. He didn't need any other kind of Splash. Why the hell would he need an intelligence-booster when he was already so goddamn smart? He took that little box from his shirt pocket and crushed it between his thumb and forefinger and let it all fall to the ground. The generals started talking again and he roared at them, told them to slow the hell down, and he smashed the table in his anger and made everyone understand that he was the best and he was the smartest and he was the strongest, and they damn sure slowed the hell down after *that* display.

109

Omen walked into the Room of Prisms. The throne, for that's what it was, was empty. Sitting on the bottom step leading to it was Damocles Creed.

He looked awful. His scalp, usually kept shaven, was ridged with stubble. His eyes were rimmed with red and his skin was pale, unhealthy. His muscles were still huge, but the way he was sitting, slumped over like that, seemed to indicate a lack of energy – of strength. The Void sword hung from his waist, within easy reach of his twitching fingers. His mouth was moving. He was talking to someone without making a sound. Praying, perhaps.

"Supreme Mage?" Omen said. When Creed didn't respond, Omen repeated himself. On the third try, Creed looked up. And smiled.

"Yes, my child?" he said. "What can I help you with?"

"I was wondering if I could have a word."

"A word." He frowned. "I'm meant to be meeting with my Council of Advisors. They seem to be running late, though. It's funny, because they're never late. Grand Mage Praetor is always on time and Grand Mage Rubic always seems to be irritatingly early." Creed shook his head. "But they're not here, and you are. I know you, do I not?"

"I'm Omen Darkly, sir."

A slight hesitation. "Yes. The brother. Didn't you...? Didn't you run away?"

"I did, sir, yes."

"We sent people out to look for you, did we not?"

"You did, yes. Some serial killers."

"Your brother is Obsidian. You must be worried about him."

There was a long, long moment when Creed didn't say anything, didn't move, then his eyes began to focus, and he blinked and smiled again.

"Of course you're worried. I have a brother, and I worry about him. I have sisters, too, and I worry about them. I worry about their spiritual well-being. They strayed from the true path hundreds of years ago, you see, and try as I might to bring them home, to guide them to the Way and the Light, I have thus far been unable."

"Are you feeling OK, sir?"

"No, my child. I am racked with guilt."

"Oh," said Omen.

"I have failed in my mission, young Mr Darkly. My mission, my divine destiny, was to bring the Faceless Ones home."

"But... that's what you did."

"True," said Creed. "But once they were home I spectacularly failed to keep them alive."

"Was that your responsibility, though?"

Creed sighed. "Perhaps not. Perhaps you are right. I did everything I could – everything that could be expected of me. I succeeded where Serpine and Vengeous and Mevolent and countless other sorcerers had failed. I should be proud of myself, should I not?"

"Maybe."

The door behind Omen opened and Grand Mage Rubic hurried in, his robes brushing the floor as he walked. He frowned for a moment at Omen, then turned his attention to Creed.

"My apologies, Supreme Mage," he exclaimed. "My duties

and responsibilities have kept me busy these last few hours, and I humbly beseech your forgiveness for being late!"

Creed nodded, gesturing for Rubic to get on with it.

"And, ah, even more apologies, Supreme Mage, this time on behalf of Elder Praetor. He sends his regrets, but he simply cannot make today's meeting. Events in America demand his full attention. He hopes you understand."

Creed watched Rubic. Instead of responding to him, he stood, and turned his attention back to Omen. "I feel better already, I truly do. I still hear voices in my head telling me to do terrible things, but now they're all my voice, which is a refreshing change. It can get quite unsettling to have your head filled with other people's voices, let me tell you."

Omen didn't know how to respond to that.

"Now then," said Creed, "tell me why you are here. Do you seek information about your brother, the terrifying being who wiped my gods from existence with a wave of his hand? Not all of them, of course. Those whom Obsidian didn't erase from reality, those whom Valkyrie Cain didn't murder inside her, reduced themselves to a single spark. A single, useless spark. My gods, the almighty beings I have spent my life worshipping, ran from adversity and shucked everything that made them who they were like a snake shedding its skin. What would you call such beings, my child?"

"I wouldn't like to say, Supreme Mage."

"I insist."

Omen swallowed. "Cowards, Supreme Mage."

Creed towered over him. "That's exactly the word I would use." He turned suddenly, pacing away and then back. "I'm at a loss, Omen. I am rarely at a loss, but at a loss is where I find myself. I am rudderless. I worship gods that don't deserve my worship and lead a church that has been revealed as a sham. So what do I do now, Omen?"

Rubic was looking even more confused than Omen was feeling. "I don't know, sir," Omen said.

"But of course you don't," said Creed, "and I don't expect you to. What would you know of these dilemmas I face? Do you know the one thing I have that is not built on a lie, Mr Darkly? This place. The High Sanctuary. My role as Supreme Mage. That's what I should focus on. It's the only healthy option. Channelling my energies into the Church of the Faceless will only lead to madness, of this I am sure, but leading the Sanctuaries around the world – that is a challenge worthy of my time and my talents."

"Then this is going to be awkward," said Crepuscular, walking in.

Creed turned to face him. "I'm sorry," he said, "am I supposed to know who you are?"

"Crepuscular Vies, at your service."

"Still not ringing any bells."

"I helped out Omen and his friends when they took down your City Guard at the school, back in June."

"*Ohhh*," said Creed, "that was you. Well, the reports I got describe you as a man with half his face missing, but I see no – oh, wait, I see it now. I was looking at the wrong half."

"You're funny," Crepuscular said. "I'd heard you weren't funny."

"I don't generally feel the need to be," Creed responded. "I've always viewed humour as a waste of time, but ever since the Faceless Ones fled from my thoughts I've changed my mind about a lot of things. What can I do for you, Mr Vies?"

"I don't know how to put this gently," said Crepuscular, "so I won't bother. We're taking over."

"Taking over what, may I ask?"

"This," said Crepuscular, pressing his wristwatch. "The whole shebang."

"You mean the High Sanctuary? Oh, no. No, I don't think you'll be doing that." Creed motioned to Grand Mage Rubic and Rubic nodded, tapped a sigil on his belt, and four members of the City Guard marched in.

"Officers," said Creed, "throw this curious gentleman into a cell, would you? If he resists, kill him." The officers didn't move, and Creed frowned at them. "Did you hear what I said?"

"I'm almost embarrassed to tell you," Crepuscular said, "but the City Guard work for me now."

Creed observed him. "And how did you manage that?"

Crepuscular shrugged. "By being really, really sneaky."

"Grand Mage Rubic—" Creed began.

"Also works for me," Crepuscular finished. "As does Praetor. As do all the other Grand Mages and Councils of Elders around the world that are run by the High Sanctuary."

Creed laughed, and then frowned, his face a mask of confliction. "You can't have done this. You can't have managed to do this."

"And yet I have."

"But you can't have done it," Creed said again loudly. "Do you understand? Do you understand me? It can't have happened. There's no way you've been able to do this without me noticing. It's just not – it's not possible. I've been planning this for years."

Crepuscular angled his head so the light caught his smile. "And I've been planning it for longer. You have five minutes to vacate the premises or I'll be forced to break my promise to Omen here, and take your life. Five minutes from one minute ago, by the way." He held up his watch. "Countdown's already started."

Omen watched Creed, trying to anticipate what he was going to do. He had three apparent choices: leave quietly, leave loudly or attack. Fury danced over his features and vanished, then danced again and retreated.

"Oh," Crepuscular said, "I'll be taking the Void sword before you go."

Creed's hand went to the hilt and the four officers drew their guns and aimed.

"Obsidian is still coming for me," Creed said. "If you take the sword, I'll be defenceless."

"Oh, well," said Crepuscular.

More seconds ticked by, and Creed unbuckled the sword belt and let the whole thing drop. He turned and walked out.

"Escort him," said Crepuscular, and the four officers went after him.

Crepuscular immediately turned to Rubic. "OK then, we need a new Supreme Mage, and I have an idea as to who should fill the position."

Rubic's hand went to his mouth. "You mean... me?"

Crepuscular laughed. "No, I don't mean you, you idiot. You're a useless waste of space who only got where you are today by being as inoffensive as possible. When you die, nobody will notice, let alone care. You've lived a life as empty as every promise you've ever made. You were a terrible teacher, a worse principal, and so far you've been an astonishingly ineffective Grand Mage. Why would anyone want someone like you running the show?" He laughed again, then said, "I don't want to be mean."

"No, don't be silly," Rubic said quietly.

"I've already spoken to Praetor about it, so he's on board, I just need you to officially agree to the nomination."

Rubic nodded quickly. "Yes, of course. You have my vote, Mr Vies."

"You're not voting for me."

Rubic gaped. "You mean...? Well, I suppose... Very well." He cleared his throat. "I vote for Omen Darkly."

Crepuscular sighed and Omen almost laughed.

"You're going to vote for Cadaver Cain," Crepuscular said.

On cue, Cadaver walked in. "I was waiting outside for ages," he said.

"Sorry about that," Crepuscular responded. "I like to be dramatic. Rubic, do you vote for Cadaver? Just say yes before you make another mistake."

"Yes," Rubic warbled.

"And so, with both members of the Council of Advisors voting for him, and with Omen Darkly as witness, I name Cadaver Cain the new Supreme Mage. Trumpets, please."

There were no trumpets.

110

Sebastian took to the rooftops to avoid the patrols. He didn't know if they were Faceless Ones fanatics, rioting because their gods had abandoned them, or Null lunatics, rioting because they didn't have anything better to do – but, either way, the streets were unsafe.

The rooftops, unfortunately, didn't seem to be any safer.

There was someone else up here, crouching by the edge of the roof, looking down on the patrols. Someone tall but powerfully built – rangy. A Black man. Bald. His head moved slightly, as if he'd sensed Sebastian's presence, and Temper Fray turned and straightened and showed his fangs.

"You're a funny-looking birdman," said Temper. "What're you dressed up like that for? How curious. How odd. I'm gonna peel that mask off you. What do you think about that? Maybe peel your skin off, too. Lot of peeling in your future, birdman."

Sebastian took a step back. "I don't want any trouble."

"Unlucky," said Temper, spreading his long arms. "I'm all trouble."

Temper sprang and Sebastian jerked sideways, feeling those claws rake across his arm. He stumbled and Temper slashed again, would have opened up his back were it not for the coat and the suit beneath.

And then Nuncle was standing between them, hands by his sides and his head tilted. "Hello, Mr Fray," he said. "I'm afraid

I must insist that you do not kill, murder, slaughter, eviscerate or otherwise harm, damage or injure my very good friend here."

Temper snarled and started for him and Nuncle held up his hand. Temper faltered, a frown passing over his face, and then he sank to his knees and toppled over, unconscious.

Sebastian hesitated. "What did you do to him?"

"I gave him back his conscience," said Nuncle. "He was a good man, and he can be so again. If he wants to be."

Sebastian hurried forward. "That's something you can do? Can you do it again?"

"To whom? Darquesse? She never had a conscience. Who else? Obsidian, maybe? To do so would be to interfere more than I am prepared to. I'm sorry, Sebastian."

"Who are you? What are you?"

"I'm dying is what I am," said Nuncle. "I don't have long left, my boy, but the time I have remaining is yours, if you want it."

"I don't understand. Will you please just give a straight answer to one of my questions?"

"You're irate," said Nuncle, smiling again.

"Yes, I'm bloody irate. I'm alone, the only person I've got to talk to speaks in riddles, and I've failed in my mission."

"Have you?"

"I was sent to do one thing, and that thing's not going to work. So yeah, I've failed."

Nuncle patted Sebastian's shoulder. "Then you're not busy right now, no? If you've failed, you've got some spare time before the end of the world."

"I suppose."

"In that case, come along with me now, boy. I've got something to show you."

111

The shelves in the grocery store were bare. It was an eerie feeling, walking through the aisles, like they were in an apocalypse movie. Which, Tyler supposed, they kind of were.

They stood in front of the kid at the till, who looked at them blankly. "Anything I can help you with?"

Tyler's dad rubbed the bristles on his chin. He hadn't shaved in a week. "Yeah," he said. "Yeah, actually, there is something you can help us with. You don't appear to have anything."

"Sorry?"

"For sale. You don't appear to have anything for sale."

"Oh," said the kid. "No, that's not true. I think there are a couple of colouring books in the back."

"I mean more in the way of food," Tyler's dad said.

"Oh. Yeah. No, we got none of that." The kid looked around, making sure they weren't going to be overheard, even though there was no one else in the store. "But I tell you what I do have. I got toilet paper."

"Toilet paper?"

The kid nodded. "Fifty bucks a roll."

"Fifty dollars for a single roll of toilet paper?"

"I snagged a bunch of it when all this started. First thing to go in an emergency, you notice that? The toilet paper. Filled the trunk of my car with the stuff. I'm running low, but I can get my hands on some, if you really want it. Fifty bucks for one, one-fifty for two."

"Why is it more expensive if you want two rolls?"

"It means you really want them, so you're desperate, so you're willing to pay. It's simple capitalism, man. Hate the game, not the player."

For a moment, Tyler was pretty sure his dad was going to reach over and drag this kid out from behind his till and beat him to death, but then Tyler was following him on to the street and towards the pickup.

The whole town was bare. Anywhere that sold food had been picked clean. Vending machines had been overturned and smashed open. The hardware store had been cleared out. People who had known each other their whole lives suddenly resented their neighbours because they might be hoarding more supplies than them. No one was sharing. No one was coming together. All of a sudden, the world had become a ruthless place.

The ground rumbled and Tyler frowned, looked at his dad, and his dad scowled, and the store window beside them cracked and dogs started barking and alarms went off – and then it all calmed down again.

"Was that an earthquake?" Tyler asked.

His dad grunted a reply, and they'd almost reached the pickup when a woman screamed and came running and a monster leaped on her.

Tyler's dad grabbed him and threw him in the pickup, ran round the other side and jumped in. The pickup lurched forward, mounted the kerb and then got back on the road. Tyler turned in his seat, watching as the monster tore through the people trying to escape.

They got home just as Tyler's mom was leaving for work, and his dad braked right in front of her hybrid.

"In," his dad said, dragging Tyler by one arm and pulling his mother by the other.

"What the hell are you doing?" Tyler's mom said. "Dammit, Cooper, let me go!"

His dad turned to her. "One of those monsters is on Main Street," he said. "It killed Harry Brockman. Killed him, Cynthia. I watched it in the rear-view."

"The... the Sheriff's Department—"

"Aren't built for this. Not this. The National Guard ain't gonna come down here, not when they're already stretched thin everywhere else. We ain't leaving this house, you get me? We ain't going nowhere."

Tyler's dad went round locking every door and Tyler's mom told Tyler to go fetch his sister.

He knocked on Mila's door. She didn't answer. He knocked again, opened it, poked his head in. Frowning, he hurried into the living room.

"Grams," he said, "do you know where Mila is?"

"Hmm?" said Grams. "Oh, she's gone off to meet that boyfriend of hers, that nice boy."

Finn, that nice boy who lived on the other side of town – on the other side of Main Street. Tyler turned to call for his dad, but his dad was right there, standing in the doorway with the gun in his hand, staring at Grams.

He looked at Tyler. "You know where Finn lives?"

Tyler nodded.

"Do you know exactly where he lives? Do you know the house? Can you lead me to the house? Can you point it out?"

"Yes," said Tyler. "I pass it all the time on my way to Paulie's."

His dad let his stare settle for a moment, and then he bolted for the basement and Tyler bolted after him, terrified of what he was about to do. But when they got down there Tyler's dad dropped the gun and clasped his hands.

"My daughter's out there and one of those monsters is loose in town," he said to Frightening. "Please help me get her back. Please."

112

Skulduggery Pleasant held the hot cup of coffee, inhaled the steam rising from it, then took a sip. He sloshed it gently in his mouth for a few moments, then his eyes widened and he spat it out.

"That is disgusting," he said, clearly appalled.

Valkyrie laughed. "You don't like it?"

"You told me coffee was delicious. You told me it was like drinking liquid heaven. Why would you lie to me?"

"I honestly thought you'd love it."

"I hate it. It's disgusting and horrible. Why won't the taste leave my mouth? Why is it stuck there?"

"It'll take a little time to fade."

He stared at her. "I have to keep this taste inside me? That's ridiculous!"

"Here," said Valkyrie, passing him her bottle of water. "Wash it away with that."

He unscrewed the cap and drank, gulping it down until the bottle was empty, and then wiping his mouth.

She waited. "Is that better?"

"Yes," he said, and hiccuped. "What was that?"

"A hiccup, dude. Relax."

He hiccuped again. "I don't like it. How do I stop?"

"I don't know. Hold your breath — sometimes that works."

Another hiccup, and Skulduggery narrowed his eyes slightly.

"Actually, maybe I'll keep doing it. It's not entirely unpleasant. It is strange, though, how the body will entirely misbehave of its own accord." *Hiccup.* "I had quite forgotten what it's like to do this. What else have I forgotten about? Oh, sneezing! I used to adore sneezing! How does one sneeze, Valkyrie? I need something, don't I? Maybe this body is allergic to dust, or cat hair. Is there a cat nearby?"

"I don't think so."

Hiccup. "Perhaps we could find one. I'll sniff it, hopefully have an allergic reaction, and I'll be reminded what it is to sneeze."

"Or we could focus on the job."

"I'll be able to focus and sneeze at the same time."

"Skulduggery, look at me. If you sneeze before we reunite you with your skeleton, great, but let's not make it a priority, OK?"

"Yes. You're right. Of course."

"How's the other guy," she asked, "the one you hijacked?"

"He's sleeping," Skulduggery replied. "Every time he wakes, I just put him under again – it's easier than you'd think. His will-power isn't all that strong, to be perfectly honest with you. Hey, where have my hiccups gone?"

"They just go away."

"Can I get them back?"

"Not on purpose."

"How incredibly odd." He frowned. "I think I'm hungry."

Tanith walked by, slowing to a stop as she eyed Skulduggery's security uniform. "We have a prisoner?"

"Actually, no," said Valkyrie. "Tanith, I'd like you to meet Skulduggery's temporary home."

Skulduggery smiled stupidly wide. "Hello, Tanith."

Tanith blinked. "No way."

"Crepuscular Vies and Cadaver Cain absconded with my bones, so I've commandeered a meatsuit in the meantime. You are very attractive." He suddenly frowned. "I'm... sorry. I don't know why I said that."

"You've found yourself in a flesh-and-blood body after a few hundred years," said Valkyrie, unable to stop the smirk. "I'd imagine it's like waking up one day and realising you're a teenager."

"Good Lord," Skulduggery said. "I'm having all kinds of thoughts."

Tanith grinned. "Oh, yeah?"

Valkyrie gave Tanith's shoulder a light punch. "Leave him alone, you."

She laughed. "I'm not doing anything except standing here, being attractive."

"Go be attractive somewhere else."

Tanith winked at Skulduggery and walked off, hips swaying.

"Stop it!" Valkyrie shouted after her.

"We need to focus on business," Skulduggery said quietly. "Focus on the job. Find me something to get aggravated about and then get me out of this meatsuit. I've changed my mind about it. It's uncomfortable and I don't like it."

Valkyrie glanced over his shoulder. "You're in luck. Here's something to aggravate you."

"So it's true," Nefarian Serpine said as he walked up. "You've actually possessed someone else's body. I don't know if you've done it purely to antagonise me after what I've been through, but it's in very poor taste, regardless."

Skulduggery glared at him, then glanced at Valkyrie.

She shrugged. "I was told about this while you were in the bathroom – because you were taking ages. He got back here this morning, and he's been scanned, and all of our Sensitives confirm that this is the Nefarian from Dimension X – and he's alone in there."

"And I'm very, very angry," said Nefarian. "The other me barged into my head without warning. I didn't have time to mount any kind of defence. One moment I was talking to Valkyrie in the bar, and the next I'm waking up on the floor of my safehouse and watching my spare body towel itself dry. Then he dresses and laughs and walks out."

A muscle twitched in his jaw. "We have to track him down. You can't very well have him running around, can you? Skulduggery, this is your arch-enemy we're talking about, in a body that is identical to mine. The most dangerous man in the world. You need to catch him, and I need that spare body back."

"Having evil-Serpine out there is a major problem," Valkyrie conceded, "but we've got other things to think about right now."

Nefarian seemed oddly offended. "I'm evil."

"Ah, not really."

"No, really. I'm just as evil as he is."

"You're not, though, are you?"

"I'm a dangerous man," he insisted.

"You're very dangerous, and you've done really evil things in the past, but I feel like you're kind of redeeming yourself now, in a way? And I know you don't want to hear this, but you should probably say goodbye to the spare body."

"What? No. I need it."

"You're not even sick. You don't need a spare."

"But one of these days I might."

"Nefarian—"

"Fine," he said irritably. "Then can you grow me another?"

"I mean... no. The first one was an accident. I have no idea how I did that and no idea how to do it again."

"Well, this is fantastic," Nefarian muttered. "Not only have I joined the resistance – something I swore I would never do again – but I don't even have a spare body in case something goes wrong with this one. What's that phrase you use? Everything sucks? Well, everything does indeed suck."

"While we all sympathise with the inconveniences you're currently suffering," Skulduggery said, "at the same time, we really don't care, and you're a very attractive man."

Serpine hesitated. "I'm sorry, what?"

"Oh, dear," Skulduggery said.

Valkyrie hooked her arm through Skulduggery's and started leading him away. "Good talking to you, Nefarian. We have a lot of work to do so we'd best get to it."

When they were out of earshot, she leaned closer. "Will you please keep it together?"

"I don't like this at all," Skulduggery muttered. "How can you exist like this? How can you exist in a shell that dictates to you how you're feeling?" He shook his head. "It all makes so much more sense now – the flawed logic of the living. You've been dragged away from the pure light of reason by biological impulses. It's a wonder you get anything done."

"Tell me about it."

"Oh," he said – more gasped, really – as China walked towards them.

"Valkyrie," she said. "Skulduggery. How are you both?"

"I'm good," said Valkyrie.

"I'm a meat puppet controlled by strange biological impulses," said Skulduggery.

"Aren't we all, dear?" China replied. "I feel it best to move swiftly past the expected conversations regarding your appearance and focus on the crux of our current problem – namely that Crepuscular Vies and Cadaver Cain have proven to be entirely untrustworthy."

"Yeah," Valkyrie growled.

"This is quite unfortunate for a number of reasons, but primarily because I have done something very logical and practical that now seems to have backfired."

"China," Skulduggery said sternly, "you..."

"Yes?"

While Skulduggery continued to falter, Valkyrie sighed. "Ignore him. He's about to tell you how attractive you are. What did you do, China?"

"You will remember, of course, Abyssinia's plan to detonate a life-force bomb beneath the White House. You will also remember that she had two such bombs constructed."

Valkyrie nodded. "One went off in the High Sanctuary but you contained the blast, and you dismantled the one under the White House."

"Indeed," said China.

"You did dismantle it, didn't you?"

"I did not. I reached it, disabled the first of its triggers, and then constructed a shield around it. I foresaw a time – an emergency – when such a device might be needed, as part of a last-ditch effort to stop some murderous fiend and save the world. As I said, a purely practical and logical precaution to take."

Skulduggery didn't seem confident of his ability to converse while looking at China, so he frowned at the wall. "You disabled the first of its triggers? There was a second?"

"The bomb was linked to Abyssinia herself – it was set to detonate upon her death, once her own life-force left her body."

"But Abyssinia died," said Valkyrie, "and the bomb didn't go off."

China didn't respond. She just stood there, poised, while Skulduggery focused on the floor.

"You had her remains teleported to the High Sanctuary moments after her death," he said. "You had her cremated. We saw her ashes the next day."

"You saw ashes," said China. "I had the High Sanctuary's top scientists come up with a way to keep Abyssinia's life force contained within her physical form."

"You've been keeping her on a life-support machine?" Valkyrie asked.

"No," said China. "Her life force is merely contained within her shell."

"I'm not sure what that means."

"Her body is dead. There's no pulse or brain activity. No life at all. It would already have decomposed, in fact, were the device in which it's being kept not maintaining its, shall we say, freshness."

"And her soul is trapped inside?"

"Trapped? I wouldn't say trapped. I would say contained. Confined. Restricted. Trapped, if you will."

"You can't just... You can't trap her soul," said Valkyrie. "That's cruel. It's barbaric."

"And yet necessary. Her soul, as you call it, leaving her body is what triggers the life-force bomb. As it was, we barely contained it in time."

"And you kept this from us?" Skulduggery asked, talking to the wall again.

"I had an inkling that you wouldn't have approved."

"I agree with Valkyrie."

"I'm shocked."

"This is cruel."

"*Necessarily* cruel. Why do you two keep skipping over that word?"

"OK, hold on," said Valkyrie. "So you have the bomb, and you have Abyssinia's remains, so you can set off the bomb at any time?"

"No," China said. "The bomb was too unstable to move from underneath the White House so it's still there, though I *did have* Abyssinia's remains, so I *could have* set the bomb off at any time. But now Cadaver Cain has the remains, and he plans to detonate the bomb, killing Martin Flanery and as many of his fellow politicians as possible."

"But assassinating the president of the United States – even *this* president of the United States – would be an act of war. That would be sorcerers declaring war on mortals. There's no coming back from that."

"Yes," said China.

"And you know about Cadaver's plot how, exactly?" asked Skulduggery.

"People tell me things."

"People?"

"Cadaver."

Valkyrie groaned. "You were in on this?"

"Before I was betrayed, I was a co-conspirator, yes."

"Why is it, China, that whenever there's *any* kind of plot or scheme or conspiracy, you're involved?"

She shrugged. "People have always involved me in things – clubs, organisations, coups, attempts at world domination. But I have since seen the error of my ways and changed my mind regarding this particular plot, so, if you would like to help me stop the bomb from going off, I will consider allowing it."

"Wow," said Valkyrie. "Thanks."

"Think nothing of it, my sweet girl. Disarming the bomb will be down to me. Abyssinia is being kept in the High Sanctuary – ensuring that Cadaver doesn't kill her before I secure the bomb will be down to you."

"Wait," said Valkyrie. "I've seen this. In my vision, I've seen this. The first time, you were lying on a field of broken glass, but it changed. I saw you lying on concrete, and your... You were drained. It was the life-force bomb. It kills you, China. I've seen it."

China took a moment. "That's disheartening."

"It doesn't work. You don't disarm it."

"That might not necessarily be so," said Skulduggery.

"I know, I know, knowledge of the future changes the future, but this is too much to risk. China can't be the one to dismantle the bomb."

"I'm afraid I'm the only one who can," China said. "But, if it is destined to go off before I'm finished, I can compensate for that with a few more protective barriers, just to be safe. I contained the blast of the bomb in the High Sanctuary and, even though this one sounds considerably more powerful, I'm fairly certain I'll be OK with this one, too."

"Fairly certain doesn't sound too certain."

"Nonsense. Fairly certain is an entirely adequate amount of certainty."

"The only thing to remember," Skulduggery said, looking at China.

"Yes?" she responded when he didn't continue.

He blinked. "Sorry?"

Valkyrie sighed. "Any idea when Cadaver's going to detonate it?"

"He'll want to dismantle the entirety of the American government in one go, which means taking out the White House and the US Congress – who will be meeting in less than half an hour."

Valkyrie shook her head. "It gets worse! I can't believe that you were a part of this. You were actually part of a plan to commit mass murder."

"No," said China. "I was part of a plan to kill Flanery before he tipped the world into a war that would trigger the Doomsday Protocol and unleash the Twenty. I'm still in favour of that, by the way. The agreement I reached with Cadaver was that the bomb should be detonated when there would be a minimal loss of innocent life. Obviously, he has reneged, and so I'll go straight to the bomb. You'll need to go straight to Abyssinia – which means you'll need to get into the High Sanctuary. I can arrange access for you through one of my secret entrances, but we'll need a distraction."

"Pull together everyone here, everyone available," said Valkyrie. "The resistance is going to have to stage an attack on Roarhaven in the next fifteen minutes."

"I do love issuing orders to Tanith Low," China said, and strode out of the room.

Valkyrie looked at Skulduggery. "What do you think?"

"They'll know we're coming," he said.

"I don't like it, either, but while we're there we might be able to pick up your skeleton and get you out of that meatsuit."

"Then let's do it. Let's walk into a trap."

"That," she said, pointing at him, "that right there. That should be our new motto."

113

Sebastian wasn't sure how it happened, but slowly he became aware that he wasn't in the world any more.

He wasn't in anything, actually. He made an effort to examine their surroundings but it was difficult to focus on anything except Nuncle standing beside him, so he gave up.

"Your mind won't be able to process a lot of this," Nuncle was saying. "I wouldn't worry about it, if I were you."

"Where are we?" Sebastian asked. "What did you do? Did we shunt? Are you a Shunter?"

"We're not in your universe, if that's what you're asking. I was brought here, back when I was your age. I think I was anyway. Some days I remember things happening one way, other days some other way. It's hard for this brain to keep track of it all, you know? It's what you'd call a design flaw in the human being."

"Who brought you here?"

"I did."

"Well, that clears that up."

"A part of me brought me here. Or, to be more precise, I was a part of the me that brought me here. There's a subtle difference there. It's important to get it right."

They moved now – walking except not walking – and something in the distance was all of a sudden right in front of them: a swirling mass of darkness with tiny pinpricks of light.

540

Sebastian resisted the urge to reach out and touch it. "What is this?"

"Don't you recognise it?" said Nuncle. "It's your universe, so it is."

Amazingly, Sebastian didn't freak out. "Huh. Smaller than I remember."

Nuncle chuckled. "'Tis, aye – although that might just be a matter of perspective."

"And how are we managing to see our universe from this perspective?"

"*Your* universe," Nuncle corrected. "And we've just been able to step back a bit in order to see it in all its grandeur. It's a beautiful thing, is it not? All of that creation whirling and twirling and fizzing with matter and ideas and potential. Really makes you think, doesn't it? Makes you take stock of your life."

"So this is *my* universe," said Sebastian, "but not yours?"

"That's right."

"So that means you're from another dimension?" When Nuncle made a face, Sebastian guessed again. "You're *not* from another dimension?"

"Not as such, no."

"Nuncle, I think you should tell me who you are."

A wave of an old, wrinkled hand. "There'll be time enough for that at the end, most likely. Though maybe not. I don't know. I brought you here to look at your universe, boy. I was hoping you'd come away with a greater understanding of the forces at work."

"Are you God?"

Nuncle laughed. "God's a Kerryman, is that what you're saying?"

"I really don't know."

"I'm not God, lad, no. I'm pretty far from that."

"Are you the Devil?"

"I'm pretty far from that, too."

"Nuncle, please. You've brought me here to show me a new perspective, but you won't give me any straight answers."

"Giving straight answers is not my job."

"What is your job?"

Nuncle looked at him, and smiled. "I've a question for you."

"You're not answering any of mine so why should I answer any of yours?"

"Because you said you would. Back in the dungeon, where we met."

Omen sighed. "You're annoying. You know what? Fine. Ask."

"Why do you think you've failed in your mission?"

"Because the world is about to end and nothing I've done matters. I was sent to do a job. I was sent to bring Darquesse back so she could save us all. But she can't save us. So, yeah, I've failed."

"But your mission wasn't to save the world, was it?"

"That's why I was sent."

"But your mission," said Nuncle, "was to get Darquesse back into your dimension, isn't that right? And that's what you did. You went looking, you found her, you convinced her to come back. Sounds to me like the mission was a success, but the idea behind the mission was the failure."

"Yeah," said Sebastian, "maybe. It's all the same, though, so who cares?"

"You do."

"Why amn't I panicking right now? I should be having, like, an anxiety attack or something."

"Do you suffer from anxiety attacks?"

"No, but... But I'm really confused and I don't understand why I'm not terrified."

Nuncle shrugged. "It's this perspective. It changes you. Take a look at your universe, boy. See it for what it is. Energy in all its forms."

"I've heard this before," Sebastian said. "I've had arguments with Darquesse about whether people are any different from rocks. Please don't make me go through that again."

"I won't, don't be worrying yourself," Nuncle said with a smile. "But she's quite right. From this perspective, the people down there in your universe don't really feature, do they? They're so small. So insignificant. They don't even affect their own reality. Nothing they do matters. But if nothing has meaning, if nothing has value in the great, grand scheme of things, then the only value anything has is the value you place upon it, wouldn't you say?"

"I... suppose."

"So then, from this perspective, it isn't simply energy we're looking at, is it? This is energy that has had its value decided by the beings that make up its consciousness. The universe assessing its own worth."

"You've lost me."

"Look at it this way. Up close, the people matter. Take a step back, the energy matters. Take another step back, the people are the energy, and so the people matter."

"Right. What does this have to do with anything?"

Nuncle shrugged. "Not a whole lot, I'll be honest. I just want you to realise that the things you say and do in your life are the only things worth anything, and the people you surround yourself with are a big part of that."

"And why do you want me to realise this?"

"Because you're the first in a long time, Sebastian."

"The first what?"

"The first," said Nuncle, laughing. "The *first*! Things like that, they ought to be celebrated! Their value ought to be recognised."

"Right, fine, whatever. Can we go home now?"

"Home? My dear boy, we never left."

"I meant, like, back to Roarhaven."

"Oh, there," said Nuncle, and shrugged again. "Sure, no problem."

114

Roarhaven sang with the wails of City Guard sirens, the song propelled by the drumbeat of gunshots and explosions. Valkyrie and Skulduggery hurried out from cover and crossed the street. Flying would be quicker, but Skulduggery was having trouble accessing his magic in his current state.

"This is so awkward," he muttered.

"What is?"

"This," he said.

They moved away from the street, got to the rear of the High Sanctuary and searched for China's secret entrance.

"What, walking?" Valkyrie asked.

"Walking, yes. And running. It's very hard to co-ordinate. I'd forgotten that people are sixty per cent water. When you have that amount of fluid sloshing about whenever you move, no wonder you all fall over so much."

"It *is* a struggle being us."

"Although it's a small price to pay for a sense of smell," he said, adjusting the bag on his back. "Smell is such an important part of detective work. When I was alive, I could detect the faintest traces of poison that still lingered in the air. I could identify killers from the perfumes they wore. I once saved a king's life because of the aroma of a spice that shouldn't have been anywhere near the palace. I'm going to miss this sense of smell."

"And is that the only thing you're going to miss about having a body?"

"I'll also miss the sense of touch, I imagine. I experience varying levels of sensation as a skeleton, but it's all a crude substitute for the real thing. Except for pain, of course. The pain I feel as a skeleton is exquisite. But with flesh and blood, you experience the feel of clothes. The way the skin reacts to a breeze." His head tilted. "Human contact."

"What about it?"

"It's different when you have flesh and blood. It's better. It's the difference between witnessing the third-ever performance of Vivaldi's *The Four Seasons* and then listening to it again playing on a cheap stereo from the 1980s."

"Did you?"

"Did I what?"

"Witness the third-ever performance of Vivaldi's *The Four Seasons?*"

"Yes," he said.

"That must have been special."

"It was almost transcendent."

"Only almost?"

"I was not, as they say, in a good place at the time. Even so, that concerto, what he was able to do, the sheer conception at the heart of it all... It proved that you don't have to be a sorcerer to perform magic. Funnily enough, when I listened to it playing on a cheap stereo in the 1980s, I was in a much better mood and that experience *was* transcendent, so it goes to show that you never can tell, as Chuck Berry used to say."

"Vivaldi to Chuck Berry. You are a man of many tastes."

"And all of them good. Ah, here we go." Skulduggery pressed his hand to a slight groove in the wall and a section of the wall slid open, and Valkyrie led the way into a dark, narrow tunnel.

Cerise the Administrator stepped out ahead of them, beckoning them to move quickly. They reached her and she ushered them towards a set of stone steps.

"Take these up until you reach a door marked with chalk. Do not even *touch* any other door – they're all booby-trapped and they'll kill you. You'll emerge on Level Three, and you'll have to make your own way to the Research Wing from there. I'll try to divert as many City Guard officers out of your path as possible, but I can't promise anything."

"Thank you," said Valkyrie, and started to move off.

"Don't hurt anyone," Cerise blurted out. "I mean, hurt whoever tries hurting you, and hurt all the City Guard officers you want, but the sorcerers aren't the bad guys here. Give them a chance, and I think they'll be on your side."

Valkyrie nodded, and Skulduggery followed her up the dark, winding staircase. They got to the door marked with chalk and Valkyrie tapped the amulet. Her necronaut suit flowed over her clothes and she pulled up the hood. At Skulduggery's nod, she opened the door.

"I'll go first," Skulduggery said. "I'm the one wearing the clever disguise."

She followed him into an empty corridor and they moved quickly towards the elevators. They met two Sanctuary operatives coming the other way, but neither paid them any attention. They got in the elevator and jabbed the button for the Research and Development floor. Right before the doors closed, an operative hopped in. She saw Valkyrie's face and froze. The elevator started moving.

No one said anything. The elevator chimed and the doors opened and the operative stepped to one side, allowing them to pass. When they stepped out, they turned. The operative looked at Valkyrie, and smiled.

"I'm a big fan," she said as the doors closed.

Keeping their heads down and away from the cameras, they strolled as casually as they could manage to the Research Wing. Once there, they found Professor Regatta's office and knocked.

"Enter."

Skulduggery stepped in first. Regatta raised his eyebrows in anticipation of a question, but then he saw Valkyrie and the colour drained from his face.

"Hi, Reggie," she said.

He shook his head. "You can't be here. You can't. We were told if we saw you, we have to report you. That went out to everyone. Cadaver Cain is looking for you."

"We don't want to be an imposition," Skulduggery said. "We just need a little information from you. We're looking for Abyssinia's body."

"I don't even know who you are."

"He's a friend," said Valkyrie. "Don't worry about him. We have to find Abyssinia, Reggie. Where is she?"

Regatta glared. "The last time I helped you, I gave you the Sceptre of the Ancients and you... you destroyed it."

"It destroyed itself, actually," Valkyrie said. "I tried to fire it, but the whole thing exploded. I don't want to blame you, I'm sure you did the best you could, but— Anyway, that's not the point. The fate of the world hangs in the balance, Reggie. Once Abyssinia flatlines, a bomb goes off that will kill thousands and send the world down a dark path it'll never recover from."

Regatta blinked. "Her body's connected to life-support machines in a small room behind the Biology Department."

"Can you take us there?"

"Yes. Yes, of course. I'll take you there immediately."

"And what about Skulduggery Pleasant's skeleton?" Skulduggery asked as they headed for the door. "Would that be on the premises?"

Regatta frowned. "Yes, actually. Cadaver Cain gave instructions that it be held in a secure location in case he ever needs some spare parts. How did you know?"

Skulduggery ignored the question and gave the professor an unsettling smile. "We need those bones, Professor. The world needs those bones."

115

Tyler's mom took the long way round to Mila's boyfriend's place. She had to go north and then cut through a load of back roads, then do a loop to approach the town from the opposite direction. It was going to take her over an hour – but she was the backup. She was in case they didn't make it that far.

Tyler sat in the pickup between his dad and Frightening Jones. Once they passed Mason's Garage, they slowed, the pickup crawling closer to the first cluster of buildings that signalled the start of Main Street. They pulled over and got out.

Tyler's dad stuffed the handgun into his belt and loaded a round into the rifle. "You stay behind us," he said to Tyler. "If we see the monster and we tell you to run, you run, you understand me? You leave it to Mr Jones and me. You run all the way back home and you do not stop and you do not argue. We can't focus on getting to Finn's and getting your sister back if we have to worry about you."

Tyler nodded. "I'll run, I promise."

Tyler's dad looked at him, and hugged him, kissing the top of his head. "I love you, kid."

"I love you, too, Dad."

Frightening led the way onwards. They moved from cover to cover, from abandoned car to abandoned car, from the corner of the mayor's office to the corner of the laundromat. Blood stained the ground. They stepped over broken glass and torn-up scraps of clothing. They could have gone the long way round, could have added another ten minutes on to their journey, but Tyler's dad would never have accepted that. His little girl was in danger and it was taking all his self-control not to just run down the middle of the street.

Frightening motioned them both to duck behind a car about a stone's throw from the first intersection. They waited there for at least thirty seconds. When Tyler's dad went to whisper something, Frightening shook his head, and they waited some more.

The monster came scuttling out, dragging a body behind it. Tyler recognised its meal – it was Mr Gracy, a nice old guy who did odd jobs for people around town. The monster stopped in the dead centre of the intersection and settled on to its haunches.

At Frightening's instruction, they moved back the way they'd come, getting round the corner of the grocery store before straightening up.

"It's still eating," Tyler's dad whispered.

"The Shalgoth have spent their lives in caves below the Earth," said Frightening, "living off whatever they can find. I'm not surprised that they're gorging themselves."

"Maybe it'll be so busy eating that it won't notice us," Tyler said.

"That's what I'm hoping," said Frightening.

They cut through the grocery store, emerging out of the side entrance, down a bit from where the monster sat, its back to them. Frightening pointed to the two cars that had collided in the middle of the street. Tyler's dad ran quietly, ducking behind the crumpled hood of the Honda. Frightening put his hand on Tyler's shoulder, held it... and then gave a little push, and now it was Tyler's turn to run.

Halfway there, the monster looked round.

Tyler dived, scrambling behind the rear wheel of the Ford and freezing in place. Through the reflection in the hardware-store window, he could see the monster rising up slowly and coming forward to investigate. It left its meal where it was.

Tyler's dad wiped the palms of his hands on his shirt, and gripped the rifle. Tyler looked back at Frightening, who gestured for everyone to stay calm.

The monster stopped at the Ford's bumper. One more step and it would see Tyler. He kept his eyes on its massive, terrifying shadow.

The shadow moved as the monster bent over, and now Tyler could see the top of its head.

Tyler's dad reached out, pulled Tyler to him, pressing his back against his chest so tightly that Tyler could feel his dad's rapidly beating heart. When the monster decided there was no one there and went back to poor Mr Gracy, Frightening joined them, and together they ran to the other side of the street.

They picked up speed now that they knew the monster was behind them, and Tyler led them into the residential areas where people stared at them from behind twitching curtains. They got to Finn's house and Tyler's dad knocked quietly but insistently until the door opened.

Mila came rushing out, crashing into her dad with her arms wrapped around him, the tears streaming. "I was so worried."

"It's OK," Tyler's dad said, keeping his voice down. "It's OK, sweetie. I got you. You're OK."

Mila saw Tyler and pulled him into the hug. In the house behind her, Finn stood awkwardly with his parents and little brother.

"The creature is still on Main Street," Frightening told them. "If you want to leave town, I suggest now would be the best time to do it."

"What about you?" Tyler's dad asked.

"I have to try to stop it."

"It'll kill you."

"It can try."

"Mr Jones, you can't just... Listen, come with us. We're gonna meet up with Cynthia, take the long way back to our place. We can wait it out there."

Frightening smiled. "That's a good plan. You should do that.

You have a family to protect. But I have a responsibility to kill monsters, and that's what I'm going to do."

Tyler's dad looked at him. "I'm sorry," he said. "For everything."

"You nursed me back to health," Frightening said. "I think we're even."

Tyler's dad pulled the handgun from his waistband and passed it over.

Frightening took it and nodded. "You stay safe," he said. "You, too, Tyler."

Tyler nodded, and Mila took in a sharp breath of air, and Frightening turned. The monster came round the side of the house across the street, its black eyes fixed on them.

Frightening ran at it without hesitation and Tyler's dad shoved Tyler and his sister into the house and Tyler tripped on the welcome mat, fell over, as the world became a place of gunshots and shouting and panic. Tyler scrambled up as Finn's father slammed the door and locked it. He ran to the window, saw his dad walking towards the monster, rifle held to his shoulder, firing with each step. He saw Frightening empty the handgun into the monster's face and then drop it. While his dad reloaded, Frightening's eye-blasts made the creature stagger back, and when Frightening stumbled away, blind, Tyler's dad resumed shooting.

But the creature lashed out, lifting Tyler's dad off his feet. Mila yelled and Tyler ran for the door, unlocked it and slipped out before Finn's parents could grab him.

Frightening had somehow clambered on to the creature's back and his eye-blasts were burrowing through its skull, but Tyler didn't care about that. He slid to his knees beside his dad, but his dad didn't say anything, didn't move, didn't even blink.

The creature collapsed and Frightening tumbled off, breathing hard, unable to see. Mila came running out and she screamed when she saw what the creature's claws had done to their dad's chest.

Tyler didn't cry until his mom got there.

116

The bomb sat on the ground. It didn't perch, or coil, or lurk – it merely sat as an object sits, boringly and without drama. It didn't need drama. Its existence was dramatic enough.

It was a black box, the same kind of black box that had housed the bomb she'd contained the night Abyssinia had sent an army of convicts to attack the High Sanctuary. But this was bigger. This was much, much bigger.

After making sure there were no traps to set off on her approach, China circled the bomb slowly, acclimatising to the chill of the concrete tunnel. Above her, beyond the tons of earth and rock and the bunker that would offer no protection against this particular weapon, people went about their business in the White House, people drove by on the road, people walked their dogs and sat in their offices and watched television and prepared food, their lives glorious and full and vibrant. That this bomb, this contraption, could drain them of this life was at once a wonder and a horror of magic and science.

It was also, China reflected, the device that she would fail to defuse, if Valkyrie's vision came true. The device that would kill her.

The first sigils she carved in the walls and the floor, therefore, were designed to contain the blast. She made a circle around the bomb and filled that circle with ancient writing, and, when she estimated that it might just be enough, she made another circle. Just in case.

And then she got to work.

117

Hoc shoved open the door and strode to the bank of monitors. "What the hell is happening?"

The officer on duty, Malyk, shot up out of his chair. "Commander, sir! Approximately three minutes ago, I recognised Valkyrie Cain on my screen, sir! She's here with an unknown male, in the Research Wing, sir!"

"I know all that," Hoc snarled. "It's the message you sent me to get me here. What has happened since then, you idiot?"

Malyk pointed at two screens. "They seem to have coerced one of the scientists into helping them, sir, and then they split up. Cain and the doctor are headed for the Biology Department and the unknown male seems to be headed for... well, actually, I don't know where he's going. He keeps changing direction. Almost like he's lost."

"It's a ruse," said Hoc. "If he's here with Valkyrie Cain, then he knows exactly where he's going, but he also knows we're watching him."

"He had a bag on his back, sir. It could contain explosives. He gave it to her before they split up."

"Have you dispatched response teams?"

"You, uh, you said to wait until you—"

"Dispatch response teams, dammit! Take some initiative!"

"Yes, sir. Sorry, sir."

While Malyk did what he was told and no doubt contemplated his imminent future guarding the latrines, Hoc took out his phone, flicked and tapped and then froze, his thumb hovering over Damocles Creed's name. Glowering, and then snarling, he scrolled up, and stabbed at the screen.

"Commander Hoc," Supreme Mage Cadaver Cain said when he answered, "what a lovely surprise! Haven't I fired you yet?"

"No, Supreme Mage, you haven't," Hoc responded, struggling to unclench his jaw. "Sir, you may be aware that we have intruders."

"Intruders!" the Supreme Mage repeated, sounding appalled. "Well, that's dreadful, Commander! Absolutely dreadful! Is one of the intruders, dare I venture, Valkyrie Cain?"

"It is, sir. She's here with an unknown male."

"An unknown male, you say? So not one of her usual acquaintances? That is interesting. That is very interesting. Where are they going?"

"Valkyrie Cain is headed for the Biology Department and the unknown male is disguising his destination. Teams have been dispatched to intercept."

"Biology Department, eh?"

"Commander Hoc," said Malyk, "the response teams are about to make contact."

Hoc hurried closer, watching as Valkyrie Cain took on five City Guard officers and kicked the living daylights out of them.

"How's it going, Commander?" Supreme Mage Cain asked.

Hoc forced down his fury. "Valkyrie Cain seems to have bested the first response team, sir."

"Well, I for one did not see that coming. How about the unidentified man?"

Hoc watched the other monitor as the second team descended on the male intruder, who had his hands up in surrender. They bludgeoned him to the floor with their batons and kept him down there with their batons and generally hit him with their batons an awful lot. Hoc smiled grimly. "He is in our custody, Supreme Mage."

The Supreme Mage didn't respond for a moment. "Is he?"

"Yes, sir, he is."

"He went down easily, did he?"

"Quite easily, sir. He tried surrendering first, though."

"But our brave City Watch officers overcame his offer to surrender and proceeded to beat him, yes?"

Hoc didn't appreciate the Supreme Mage's tone. "Yes, sir."

"I see. Congratulate your people on a job well done, Commander."

"Thank you, sir, I will."

"And ask them if he managed to say anything before they attacked him. Something along the lines of *no, wait*, or *you're making a mistake*, or even, *I don't know what's happening, you idiots.* Something like that."

Hoc paled. "Supreme Mage?"

"I believe that Skulduggery Pleasant is still alive, after a fashion, and his consciousness was possessing that unknown male."

"Then we have him, sir!"

"Please note that I was using the past tense in that sentence. Send everyone after Valkyrie, there's a good man. And remind me to fire you later, yes?"

"Yes, sir."

"Excellent. I'll be down presently."

118

Regatta entered the room first and froze so suddenly Valkyrie actually walked into him.

"They must have moved her," he said.

The room was empty – just a few cables lying around and a bed without a mattress. Regatta snatched up a clipboard and turned the page.

"They came last night," he said. "The City Guard. They moved her, but it doesn't say where."

"Cadaver knew we'd be coming," Valkyrie muttered.

Regatta looked at her, nervous. "How does this affect, you know, the bomb?"

"If we can't protect Abyssinia, we have no chance of delaying the detonation." She pulled her phone out, tried calling China. There was no answer. "Damn. Oh, damn. Professor, we need to find that body."

"They could have put it anywhere," Regatta said. "They've taken the life-support equipment, too, so all they'd need is a room with electrical sockets. But we have no way of knowing if it's even in the High Sanctuary. I'm sorry, Detective."

Valkyrie stared at him, trying to come up with a solution, but then she just shook her head. "You'd better get out of here, Professor. I'm sure the City Guard are already on their way."

He hesitated, then nodded, moved to the door. "Oh," he said,

"Skulduggery Pleasant's bones. Three rooms down that way." Then he hurried out.

Valkyrie tried China again as she strode to a large laboratory with five clean tables and one table, at the back, with a load of bones piled on to it. No one had yet had time to arrange the skeleton properly, so it was all one big clacking, clattering jumble. She dropped the bag on the ground.

"Um," she said, and put the skull and the jawbone at the top, the ribcage somewhere beneath that, and the femurs down near the end. The rest she pushed into some sort of shape. "I'm really sorry," she said. "I know the hip bone's connected to the leg bone, but that's about it."

She arched her back and gritted her teeth as Skulduggery's essence flowed out of her. His remains moved slightly, and then the jawbone clacked into place and it opened and Skulduggery screamed.

Wincing, Valkyrie darted forward, found the spine, brought it closer to the base of the skull and then it jerked from her hand like a magnet leaping to a fridge. The ribcage attached itself next, and she found the clavicle and the scapula and then she ran out of bone names. But after a few seconds Skulduggery's right arm was attached, minus a few fingers. He'd stopped screaming by this stage.

"My other arm," he said, his voice strained. "Assemble my other arm."

Valkyrie moved round the table, searching for the correct pieces. "This is like doing a puzzle," she informed him. "I'm quite enjoying myself, actually."

"Oh, me too," Skulduggery muttered, obviously still in an extraordinary amount of pain. He managed to sit up, then raised and bent his arm. "It's on backwards," he said.

The door behind her burst open and four City Guard officers ran into the lab, guns out.

"You're gonna have to reassemble yourself," she muttered, and stepped towards the cops with her hands up. "Do not shoot," she said, smiling. "I mean you no harm."

The cops looked at her like she was an approaching tank. They were as nervous as hell and their fingers were on the triggers.

"You folks need to calm down," she said. "That's poor gun discipline you're displaying right now. You never put your finger on the trigger until you mean to pull it."

"That's right," one of them said.

Valkyrie smiled. "You don't want to pull those triggers, fellas."

Someone fired and the bullet hit her chest and Valkyrie hissed in pain and turned, pulled her mask over her face. Gunfire filled the room and bullets slammed into her back and a wall of air lifted her, threw her over the tables. She twisted and landed and tumbled backwards to one knee, letting loose with white lightning from both hands. She got one of the cops and put him down, but missed the others.

They kept firing at her and Valkyrie feinted right and then left as she sprinted at them. One of the cops dropped his gun and went for his sword, and she rolled under his swing, slamming into the officer behind him, hand on his throat, giving his system a jolt. His knees buckled and he fell and a stream of energy skimmed by her head.

The cop with the sword went for her neck and she swerved out of the way, caught his arm on the backswing and used him as a shield as the last cop fired another stream. It hit his buddy and Valkyrie let him drop. The final cop lunged and she hit him three times and then whacked his head into the same table that Skulduggery was sitting up on. Skulduggery fixed his foot on to his ankle and did a few rotations.

"You doing OK?" she asked him, breathing a little hard.

He got off the table and picked up the bag, opening it. "Don't look at me, please. I'm naked."

"Mind hurrying up? We've got to find Abyssinia."

He took out his suit. "I won't be but a moment."

119

Abyssinia's body lay on a hospital bed, hooked up to five different machines that all beeped and looked very important.

Omen stayed at the door, and frowned. "I really don't get what's going on. Isn't she meant to be dead?"

"She is dead," said Crepuscular, walking in. "We're just here to finally allow her soul to leave her body."

Reluctantly, Omen joined him. It was a small, dark room in a small, dark part of the High Sanctuary. "Why have you been keeping her like this?"

"You think I'm responsible for this? No, no. This is all the work of China Sorrows. Creed didn't feel the need to change anything, but Cadaver understands. I think it's time we let Abyssinia rest, don't you?"

"Why now?"

"You think she should stay like this for longer?"

"No. I just mean why are you doing this now? With everything that's going on, with all the emergencies, why are you switching off a life-support machine at this exact moment? Something else is going on here. Tell me what it is."

Crepuscular watched him. "OK," he said. "You deserve an explanation so you can walk through this metaphorical door with me. When Abyssinia's soul leaves her body, that will trigger an event that will strike a blow for sorcerers everywhere."

"What will it do?"

"It will eliminate Martin Flanery."

Omen stared. "You're going to kill him?"

"It's an unfortunate necessity."

"What are you talking about? Why do you need to kill *anyone*? I agree that the world would be better off without him as president, so just send a Teleporter to grab him and throw him in a cell."

"That won't be enough," Crepuscular said, sounding sad.

"When you say an event – do you mean a bomb?"

"A life-force bomb, yes. When it goes off, there will be no damage to physical structures, I promise you that."

"I don't care about physical structures, Crepuscular! I'd much rather a building gets destroyed than the people who live in it! You're talking about taking a life!"

"Sometimes these things are necessary."

"We had a deal," Omen said, anger swelling. "We said we wouldn't kill."

"And we're not killing. I'm killing."

Omen shook his head. "I don't get it. Why am I even here if nothing I say matters? You told me, you convinced me, that we'd do things the right way. That's why I'm here. It's the only reason I'm here."

"You're upset. I apologise."

"That's it? That's all you're going to say? You're going to apologise and then kill Flanery anyway?"

"I have to."

"No, you don't."

"Someday, hopefully, you'll understand." Crepuscular reached for a switch on the wall.

"Just answer me this," Omen said quickly. "Why am I here? Why did you need me here?"

Crepuscular hesitated. "Because you're my friend, Omen."

"Clearly, I'm not. People listen to their friends."

"Not when they're misguided."

Omen hurried over and Crepuscular watched him, and Omen stood between him and the switch. "I'm not going to let you do this."

A moment went by. "Please stand aside."

"No. I can't."

"You'd fight me? You would physically attack me, would you?"

"To save a life, I would."

"To save an innocent life," Crepuscular said, "I could appreciate. But Martin Flanery? The man was a threat to the world even before magic got involved. He's corrupt, he's dangerous, and he's getting people killed even now."

"But killing him is wrong."

"Please don't be so naive."

Omen shrugged. "There's always another way, if you want it badly enough. But you don't, do you? Whatever plan you have, it starts here, right? With Flanery's death?"

"It doesn't start here," Crepuscular said. "It started years ago – but his death is a part of it, yes. I don't want to fight you, Omen, and you certainly don't want to fight me. But I need to trigger that bomb in the next few moments and unless you get out of my way, I'll have to hurt you to do it."

Omen clenched his fists and he tried his very best to look big and strong and threatening, but he couldn't maintain the act. He felt his body betray him and he sagged, no longer able to meet Crepuscular's gaze.

"Thank you," Crepuscular said softly, putting his hand on Omen's shoulder as he passed.

Omen twisted, his hands snapping and the air rippling, and Crepuscular grunted as he spun sideways, went crashing into the wall.

Before he could recover, Omen was upon him, fists searching for the hinge of his jaw, seeking out that instant end to the fight, but Crepuscular covered up and Omen's punches bounced harmlessly off his arms and then Crepuscular had him in a stranglehold.

Omen clicked his fingers and burned Crepuscular's arm and he cursed and let go. Omen stomped on his foot and Crepuscular grabbed him and flipped him and the ground crashed into the base of his spine and Omen cried out. All he could do was writhe in pain and curse as Crepuscular walked over to the switch.

He flicked it and the machines went quiet.

"It's done," said Crepuscular.

120

No. Too soon.

The life-force bomb continued to hum and China back-pedalled. The shield wouldn't hold. She needed ten more minutes – that was all. Just ten. But she didn't have ten more minutes. It was going to go off and there wasn't anything she could do about it.

She glanced at the tunnel behind her. There was no way she could outrun it, either. It was going to envelop her just like it was going to envelop the White House above, and drain away all her dreams and triumphs and regrets as it drained her life, and it would be over in an instant and she would be no more, having sacrificed everything in a futile attempt to save a few thousand selfish, stupid, pathetic mortals.

How pointless. How frivolous. How unlike her.

"Right then," she muttered.

She slammed her fist on to the sigil she'd just carved into the wall and it lit up and, one by one, all the other sigils lit up after it. The sigil she had yet to carve, the bridge that would have connected the disparate elements of her shield, she dismissed from her mind. There was no time left to think about opportunities missed.

The bomb went off.

It flashed, and the sigils formed a shield around it, a single column of bright blue energy that sizzled in its doomed efforts to contain the blast. China tapped her palms and stepped forward. Just as the shield was about to falter, she pressed her hands to it.

Her body locked suddenly into position. Her teeth clenched. Her lips pulled back. Her eyes went wide and started streaming water. The energy played with her hair like electricity. All the sigils on her body faded up on her skin until she was covered in beautiful, gentle, lethal tattoos.

The energy from the blast sucked at the shield and China did her best to reinforce it, to hold it together with her own magic. Despite her efforts, the blast continued to creep outwards.

It latched on to her.

There was a sound, like a wounded animal, and China realised she was screaming.

Drawing on the very last dregs of her strength, she focused on narrowing the column. The blast energy thrashed. She felt it pulling her life away from her. She watched her hands – her perfect, long-fingered hands – start to wrinkle. Start to shrivel. She listened to her bones weaken and creak. Her strength washed from her like a wave retreating from the beach.

The column narrowed again, and again, and it contained the blast energy and then extinguished it, and the sigils stopped glowing and China fell to her knees.

121

"I'm an idiot," said Omen, his back to the wall, his knees drawn up to his chest.

"You're not an idiot," said Crepuscular.

"I believed you when you said we were friends. I believed you when you said you weren't doing this to prove a point. I was on your side. I helped you. What an absolute idiot I was."

"Omen – I am sorry that I manipulated you. I needed you onside, but I didn't enjoy that aspect of it. You're a good kid. You're smart and capable. You're—"

"Don't tell me what I am," Omen said, getting to his feet. "I'm tired of people telling me what I am. They don't know. Skulduggery and Valkyrie don't know, the teachers at school don't know, and you don't know. You know who else doesn't have a clue who I am? My parents. You all think you know me, but you just know this." He jabbed his own chest. "You know this person. This Omen Darkly. But Omen Darkly's an idiot and he lets everyone lie to him and manipulate him and he's never in charge. He never gets to decide what the best thing to do is."

Crepuscular watched him. "It sounds like you're approaching a turning point in your life."

"Oh, I'm past it," Omen said. "I passed it a while ago. I just didn't realise."

"Then there may be hope for you yet."

"Drop dead, Crepuscular."

Omen walked over to the door. Before he reached it, he heard Crepuscular curse softly, and turned in time to see him looking at his phone before he vanished.

Frowning, Omen took out his own phone. He hesitated for a moment, then checked the news sites. Everyone was talking about more Shalgoth attacks and the various military responses. No one was talking about an assassination.

He hurried back over to Abyssinia's body. He felt for a pulse and couldn't find one. She wasn't breathing, either. She certainly looked dead and, without the machine to keep her soul trapped in her body, that life-force bomb should have killed Flanery by now. Omen tried to figure out what could have gone wrong, but quickly abandoned the attempt. He hadn't a clue, and he wouldn't know where to even begin.

Cadaver Cain walked in, accompanied by a City Guard officer.

"You knew about this, didn't you?" Omen said. "This was all part of your plan, right? Kill Abyssinia, set off the bomb, kill Flanery."

"That was the plan," the Supreme Mage conceded, "but I don't think things have run smoothly. Abyssinia's dead, but Flanery isn't – which makes me wonder if someone got to the bomb before it detonated."

Omen smiled. "Skulduggery and Valkyrie."

"Actually, no," said Cadaver. "They're both here, in the Research Wing. You're a helpful lad, aren't you, Omen? Would you mind fetching them for me, maybe bringing them to the main chamber downstairs? That's where all this is going to end, you see. You're welcome to come, too, if you'd like."

"You can fetch them yourself," said Omen. "I'm not doing anyone else's dirty work. Not any more."

"I'm not all bad, though, Omen. I brought Sergeant Yonder with me, did I not? Sergeant, if you wouldn't mind?"

The cop came forward, shoving Omen out of the way. He

pulled the tubes and wires away from Abyssinia's body and placed a seven-sided metal star on her chest. Omen had never seen one before now, but he knew what a Sunburst looked like, and he knew what it did.

"You want to revive her?" he asked, confused.

"I've always had a soft spot for Abyssinia," Cadaver said.

The cop grunted. "It won't work. Sunbursts can revive the recently deceased – but this lady's been dead for a while."

"Abyssinia is an exception," Cadaver said, his voice friendly and most pleasant, "so do what I ordered you to do, there's a good sergeant."

Yonder muttered something under his breath and tapped the Sunburst. The sigils carved into it lit up, and then flashed red and Abyssinia's eyes snapped open.

She gasped and sat up and grabbed Yonder as he yelled, her hands on either side of his head. Omen stumbled back as he watched her suck the life force out of the cop, then left his wrinkled, dried husk of a body to collapse while she rolled her neck in the most luxurious of stretches. Her skin shone with health. Her silver hair was glorious. Her lips reddened and her eyes sparkled.

"Welcome back," said Cadaver, and then nodded to Omen. "Skulduggery and Valkyrie – could you tell them where I'll be? There's a good lad."

He walked out.

Abyssinia turned her head to Omen, and smiled. "I know you."

122

Skulduggery's suit was black, matched by his tie and hat. His shirt was white.

"My bones need a deep clean," he said as they stepped out of the elevator.

"They look fine to me," Valkyrie responded, blasting a City Guard officer who happened to be passing at precisely the wrong time.

They strode across the foyer. "People have been handling them," Skulduggery said. "I can feel their dirty, smudgy fingerprints all over my ribs."

"How long will it take? Cleaning the whole thing?"

"I'll clean one bone every evening. Barring incident, or skipped evenings, that will take me two hundred and six days."

"That seems a ridiculously long time. Couldn't you just have a shower?"

"There are some stains a shower can't remove."

They opened the main doors. A cool breeze toyed with Valkyrie's hair. Roarhaven was quiet. No sirens, no shooting, no explosions. They didn't step out.

"What are you thinking?" she asked.

"We're here now," Skulduggery said. "We take the opportunity to end this. We might not be able to stop the Twenty being unleashed, we might already be too late, but we can stop whatever plans Crepuscular and Cadaver have for them once they're free. We go back in; we hunt them down. Arrest them if we can. Kill them if we have to."

"They're probably saying the same thing about us."

He shrugged. "Let them try."

They turned, and another set of elevator doors opened and Omen and Abyssinia emerged.

"What?" said Valkyrie.

"She came back to life," Omen said helpfully.

"What?" said Valkyrie.

"Hi there," said Abyssinia.

"What?" said Valkyrie.

"The bomb," Skulduggery said.

"I don't know what happened," Omen told him. "Crepuscular turned off the life-support for –" he nodded to Abyssinia – "and she died. It should have gone off right then, right? But I don't think it did."

"And then a nice man revived me," Abyssinia said with a big smile, "and provided me with a nutritious meal to get me up and about again. Omen has been giving me a quick rundown on what's been happening since I've been gone. You have been busy, haven't you? Alternate dimensions, wars, a future version of Skulduggery, the Chosen One turning bad... and this Crepuscular individual. Now him I am quite eager to see again, sit down and talk with, maybe kill him a little bit."

"Cadaver Cain's waiting for you," Omen said to them. "He asked me to bring you to the main hall. That's where it's going to end, he said. It's just, it really sounds like we'd be walking into an obvious trap – that's the only thing."

"Probably," said Abyssinia.

"Definitely," said Valkyrie.

Skulduggery straightened his tie. "Walking into traps is what we do, Omen."

"Oh," Omen said miserably, "good."

"But just in case this goes hilariously wrong," Valkyrie said to him, "if it looks like we're in trouble, let Fletcher know, would you? You have his number, right? He's waiting for a message."

Omen nodded, and fell into step beside them. It was weird walking through a building that was usually teeming with people. Their footsteps echoed in the emptiness. The doors to the main hall were open wide, where an old woman was waiting.

For a moment, Valkyrie thought it was Solace, but then the woman's knees buckled and she stumbled, and Valkyrie ran forward, catching her as she fell. Now that she was up close, she frowned at the stylish grey hair, frowned at the wonderfully understated but loose-fitting clothes, frowned at the once-beautiful face that was now lined and sunken, the skin mottled. The eyes, at least, were still a startling blue.

"Oh, China," Skulduggery said, moving up and kneeling by her, "what did they do to you?"

Valkyrie froze and her thoughts jammed.

"I did this to myself," China answered, smiling. "Trying to be a hero. Trying to save lives. You're a bad influence on me – you always have been."

Valkyrie broke out of her frozen state and together they helped China stand. The arm Valkyrie gripped was thin and frail.

"When Crepuscular came to check on what had happened," China said, "he asked me if it was worth it, exchanging my youth and beauty for the life of Martin Flanery. I'm relying on you to make sure I don't regret that decision."

"It wasn't just Flanery you saved," said Valkyrie. "It was thousands of others. Thousands of innocent lives."

Abyssinia came forward, looked China dead in the eye. "There's definitely something different about you," she said, "but I can't quite put my finger on what."

China glanced at Valkyrie. "Abyssinia's alive, then?"

"Apparently."

"Typical."

Helping China, they walked through the doors, into the gloom. In the centre of the hall was a wide patch of light. Cadaver Cain stood in the middle of it, his skull gleaming, the shadows in his eye sockets pitch-black. Solace stood beside him.

"Abyssinia," Cadaver said, "it's so good to see you again. Did they fill you in on what happened after you, for want of a better word, died? Did they tell you what happened to Caisson?"

"I know what happened to Caisson," Abyssinia responded. "He was murdered by an assassin sent by Serafina Dey, and he died in my arms."

"And then he came back to life."

"No. Then his body came back to life, but my son was dead. It was my father inhabiting Caisson's body from that moment on. Omen told me all about it."

"He told you how his brother stabbed your father with the Obsidian Blade and wiped him from existence?"

Abyssinia smiled. "Do you think that will upset me, Cadaver? Do you think I should kill Omen Darkly out of some misguided sense of revenge?"

"Oh, that's not what I'm trying to do here," Cadaver said, amusement in his voice. "But it's all connected, you see. You're all connected. Bound by the decisions you've made in the past. Mevolent killed your family and fatally injured your father with the Obsidian Blade. To exact your revenge, you joined his army centuries later – you and Lord Vile. You got close to your enemy. Too close, as it turned out."

Abyssinia looked at Omen. "I had an affair with Mevolent. I'm not proud of it, but it's what happened. I hope you don't think less of me."

"I just think of you as someone who murders people," said Omen.

"Thank you," Abyssinia responded.

"And because of that affair," Cadaver continued, "you fell pregnant. And then you fell out of a window."

"I was thrown," Abyssinia said, sparing a quick glare for Skulduggery.

"Indeed you were. But you survived, and your baby survived, and you gave birth to Caisson, the apple of your eye."

"We know all this," said Valkyrie.

"I don't," said Omen.

Valkyrie sighed. "Abyssinia gave Caisson to China to raise as her ward in exchange for Abyssinia's surrender. Abyssinia was executed, China raised Caisson, Caisson tried to kill Skulduggery—"

"Wait," Omen said, "why did he do that?"

"Because I'm the one who executed Abyssinia," Skulduggery said.

Omen nodded. "OK. That's fair enough."

"Caisson barely survived that encounter," Cadaver said, "and China's daughter, Solace – who had escaped from her position as Serafina's handmaiden and fled Mevolent's castle – nursed him back to health."

Everyone looked at Solace to continue the story. "I'm not doing this," she said.

They all looked back at Cadaver. "And they fell in love," he continued. "And they married. And they started a family."

With a flourish, he swept his arm behind him and the back of the hall lit up, illuminating the men and women standing there in complete stillness. They were dressed in black bodysuits and their faces were blank, impassive, their eyes closed. They each had an identical sigil burned into the sides of their necks. The sigils glowed, pulsing with darkness.

"And they trained their children to be killers and saboteurs," said Cadaver. "Trained them to be the Hosts' last-resort weapon against the mortal world. The Twenty."

"And I'm the middle child," Crepuscular said, drifting down from above. "The spare. The one to fill in the gap if one of them fell." He landed beside Cadaver, who nodded appreciatively.

"Very nicely done."

"Thank you."

"That's a very well-timed entrance. You have a gift for the theatrical."

"Theatre is life."

"But you left us," Solace said.

Crepuscular sniffed, and brushed lint from his sleeve. "Mother, I thought you weren't going to involve yourself in the storytelling part of today's festivities."

"You abandoned us," Solace said.

"You say nothing about this for the last few days and *now* you admonish me? When we have an audience? Apparently, I didn't lick my theatricality from a stone." He sighed. "Fine. I did. I did abandon you. I grew tired of it all: the training, the preparation, the Hosts' interference. I grew tired of the fact that my brothers and sisters were being raised to be nothing more than robots. Look at them. Look at them standing there. This is what you wanted for them? Drained of all individuality? You said you loved us, but all you did was programme us."

"Your brothers and sisters understand," Solace said.

"No, they don't," Crepuscular responded. "They were taught to never question their orders. To never question if their lives could be different, or better. They had their roles and I had mine and you wouldn't let us break free of them, would you? You never even gave us the chance."

"And yet," said Solace, "you still managed to abandon us."

Crepuscular took a breath. "I did. I didn't want to spend my entire life being a spare part. I didn't even know who I was when I left. I had no one to help me, no one to guide me. I had to make up who I was as I went along."

"You betrayed us."

Crepuscular laughed. "No, Solace. *You're* the ones who betrayed *us*. You and our father. You and Caisson betrayed your own children. My brothers and sisters deserve more than what you gave them. You used to tell us that China Sorrows was the worst mother who'd ever lived – but, in her own small way, she loved you. She gave Caisson to Serafina Dey – gave away her ward, the boy she'd raised – instead of you."

"And then she locked me in a tower."

"I wish she'd done that a lot earlier," Crepuscular said. "It might have spared us the grief of being your children."

A moment of silence passed.

"I'd just like to point out," said Abyssinia, "that, out of everyone here, I am *by far* the best mother in this room."

Cadaver held up his hands like he expected to stave off conflict, but no one argued the point, so he shrugged. "Be that as it may, we find ourselves here, gathered together to witness the fruits of Crepuscular's masterful orchestrations of world events, ensuring that the Hosts' Doomsday Protocol has been activated. The Twenty have been unleashed. Hurrah!"

"They're not doing much," said Valkyrie.

"That's true," Cadaver said, glancing back at them. "I wonder why that is. Crepuscular, do you know why your siblings aren't running around, destabilising the mortal world?" Crepuscular didn't answer, so Cadaver turned to Skulduggery. "What about you, young man? Do you know?"

"Those sigils on their necks," Skulduggery said, "the pulses are getting quicker. Why is that?"

"All will be revealed in mere minutes, I promise."

Crepuscular tilted his head at Cadaver. "You know something you're not telling me about my siblings?"

"Patience, Crepuscular."

Cadaver went to pat Crepuscular's shoulder, but Crepuscular grabbed his wrist, twisted it into a lock, and Cadaver countered and whirled and flipped Crepuscular over his hip, pressing a gun into his cheek when he hit the ground. "I wouldn't try that again, if I were you."

Crepuscular didn't move.

"I didn't like very many members of the Hosts," Cadaver said, "but I understood them. Dismantling mortal power structures in a case of absolute emergency is something I can appreciate. Would I have done it if I'd been in charge back then? No. I was too concerned with maintaining the status quo. That is, after all, the entire purpose of the Sanctuary system, is it not? *We are here to protect the mortals from magical threats. We are here to guarantee that sorcerers do not influence the evolution of human society.*

"These days, however, I take a different view. My current outlook on life has been coloured by centuries of being able to see the future. Now that this ability has been denied me, I find myself positively revelling in the idea of uncertainty. Let's do it, I say. Let's dismantle those power structures. Let's see what happens. At the very least, it'll be interesting."

"I have a counter-proposal," said Skulduggery, taking his revolver from its holster. "Let's not."

"Shooting me won't do you any good," Cadaver said. "Even if you manage to disperse my life force and actually kill me, what's going to happen will happen. The only thing you could possibly do to prevent the end of mortal civilisation as we know it is to kill the Twenty." Cadaver took his gun away from Crepuscular's cheek and backed off.

Crepuscular got up slowly. "No one is killing my family," he said. "Let me rephrase that: no one is killing my siblings. Anyone can kill my mother if they feel like it."

Cadaver put his gun away. "Skulduggery, it's up to you."

"How very magnanimous," Skulduggery murmured.

"I firmly believe that we each should choose our own destinies. It helps, of course, to be furnished with all the relevant details – as such, the only thing that might affect your decision one way or the other is the one tiny, almost insignificant little fact that only four people in this room are privy to – myself included."

Valkyrie sighed, and sent her magic into her hand, where it crackled. "Cadaver, just spit it out, for Christ's sake."

But Cadaver was having far too much fun. "It's a question no one has asked. I'm surprised, actually, that it hasn't occurred to the rest of you. Or... maybe it has. Has it, Skulduggery?"

Skulduggery said nothing, but his head tilted very, very slowly.

"Finally," Cadaver said, "after all this time."

Valkyrie frowned. "What's he talking about? Skulduggery? What's he talking about?"

"When Serpine killed my wife and child," Cadaver said, "he took away my love, my happiness, my reason to be. I wouldn't work out that my father was Gog Magog until much later, so I didn't know why I was plagued by these violent, violent thoughts – but, even so, my love for my family provided me with an oasis of calm in a turbulent world. Serpine, of course, took that away from me, and led me to become the man I am – and the man Skulduggery is. But *what if?*, I wonder now. *What if I'd had someone else to love?* Would that have steered the course of my life in a different, better direction? If only I had another child. A daughter, perhaps."

"I'm sorry," said China beside them, her eyes on Skulduggery. "I never told you. I should have. I wanted to – but by then you'd met... you'd met *her*... and you looked so happy, and I knew if I told you then you'd stay with us and you'd resent me forever. I'm sorry, Skulduggery."

The energy faded from Valkyrie's hand. "What?"

"I understand this is a big moment for you," Crepuscular said, ignoring Valkyrie and looking straight at Skulduggery, "but, if I even get a hint that you're going to try and kill my brothers and sisters, I'll smash every bone in your body."

He tilted his head. "Granddad."

123

The attention switched to Solace, who bristled. "Why are you looking at me? You're expecting an extravagant reaction? I didn't need a father back then, and I certainly don't need one now."

"She talked about you, though," Crepuscular said, looking at her out of the corner of his eye. "Ranted might be more accurate. My father hated you for executing Abyssinia and my mother hated you for simply existing. Is it any wonder I grew up to be obsessed with you, Skulduggery? You were both the hero and the villain in all my revenge fantasies. In a lot of ways, I modelled myself on you, and fighting by your side was an indescribable honour. And then, after all my work, all my efforts... I finally became your partner. I finally gained your acceptance. Your approval. I had defied my parents' wishes, overcome the hatred they had tried to instil in me, and made an ally of my childhood hero. And you promptly left me for dead."

Skulduggery remained silent, and Crepuscular turned to Omen.

"That's why I selected you. It wasn't because of your brother – it was because of your parents. People like us, Omen, we've got to prove ourselves over and over again – not for their sakes, but for ours. Your parents used you as a training aid for Auger – mine used me as an understudy. They never loved us; they never valued us; they never bothered to see us for who we were."

"You wanted to replace Skulduggery," Omen said.

"Supplant him," Crepuscular corrected. "After growing up the way I did, can you blame me? I worshipped him and then I hated him, and then I realised that by supplanting him, by proving myself to be his equal, I could then prove to be his superior. And I think I have done that. We've proven that. Together."

"And now what?"

"Now this," Crepuscular said, indicating the Twenty. "Now I get to lead my brothers and sisters out of the darkness."

"You might want to check those sigils," Skulduggery told him. They were pulsing rapidly now, and speeding up every few seconds. "Or maybe Cadaver could just get to the point and save us all some time."

"Everyone's blaming me," Cadaver responded, "when this has nothing to do with me. If it were my choice, Crepuscular could walk into the sunset with his siblings and spend the next fifty years rehabilitating them back into normal life. But it's not up to me. The Hosts didn't really give them a chance."

Crepuscular frowned. "What are you talking about?"

"The Hosts sought me out," said Solace. "They knew my heritage – they knew about Abrogate Raze – and they told me exactly what was required of me. I was to have children: special children who would change the world. All I had to do was find a mate with a heritage as rich as my own. An impossible task, we all thought, until they learned that Mevolent had had a son with the daughter of the Unnamed – and this son had been raised by my own mother while I had been away, spying for them.

"They got me out of Mevolent's castle, got me away from Serafina Dey, and brought me back to my mother. I didn't expect to actually develop feelings for Caisson – I didn't expect to actually fall in love with him – but that made it easier to bear children solely for the mission. The risk, of course, was that I would grow to love these children – but I had Caisson, and my heart was his, and his alone.

"Our task was to produce twenty mages, masters of twenty

disciplines, each discipline designed to work in conjunction with the others. Twenty children were required, and one more who would be trained in as wide a variety of disciplines as possible. Reynard isn't the only omnidextrous sorcerer in the family, but he was the most promising."

"My name isn't Reynard," said Crepuscular.

"No," said Solace, "you've had quite a few names since the one we gave you, haven't you?"

"You've spent your whole life wondering why you don't fit in, my boy," Cadaver said. "And the answer is you were never meant to. You were never meant to be anything but a vessel waiting to be filled. That's what your mother was doing, Crepuscular. That's why she raised your brothers and sisters the way she did. You're not the spare. You're the engine of mortal destruction, and they're the fuel."

The sigils on their necks pulsed one last time and then each member of the Twenty snapped their heads back and screamed, and Valkyrie's aura-vision kicked in and she watched as their souls were wrenched from their bodies and pulled into Crepuscular. The souls roiled and coiled and squirmed until they melted together in one confused jumble that inhabited every last millimetre of his body, as twenty empty husks crumpled to the floor behind him.

Nobody moved.

And then Crepuscular straightened, and breathed out.

"Hi," said Cadaver, giving a little wave. "I'm not sure how to refer to you. Are you my grandchild, or my grandchildren? Crepuscular, or something else? I don't suppose it matters, actually. I was wondering what your policy is concerning the whole concept of reducing mortal civilisation to rubble. Are you for or against?"

"It has already begun," Crepuscular said, his voice soft. "We have destroyed the financial systems around the world. We have shut down communications, overloaded power plants, and disrupted the support structures that the mortals fall back on."

Cadaver tilted his head. "You did all that from standing here?"

"Our reach is vast," said Crepuscular.

Skulduggery approached, gun in one hand, shackles in the other. "Then you're going to stop reaching," he said, "and get on your knees."

Valkyrie frowned at Omen as he took out his phone. "Are you messaging Fletcher?"

"I think you might need help."

She smiled. "We've got this covered."

"Crepuscular doesn't look worried."

"Omen, trust me, OK? We can handle it."

Crepuscular's eyes flashed orange and a blast of energy threw Skulduggery back. Valkyrie cursed and left Omen to his texting, and launched herself forward. She covered the distance between them in a heartbeat, but Crepuscular plucked her from the air, the collar of her suit bunched in his fist, and he stepped back and slammed her into the ground. Before she could react, he picked her up with inhuman strength and flung her like he was shooting her from a cannon. She crashed into the wall and dropped, gasping.

Skulduggery got up as Fletcher teleported in with Tanith and the Monster Hunters and Dexter.

"All right, then," said Gracious, "which one is the bad guy, and who do we punch first?"

Skulduggery picked up his hat, put it back on. "Everybody, meet Crepuscular Vies. He's who we hit."

Dexter Vex and Donegan Bane released energy streams that forced Crepuscular back a few steps, giving Gracious O'Callahan time to charge. The streams cut off and Crepuscular looked up and Gracious hit him, a thundering right cross that – normally – would have turned his skull to powder. In this moment, however, Crepuscular merely reeled, shaking his head to clear it, as Gracious followed up with hooks to the body.

With every punch Gracious threw, he gave a shout. "Why! Won't! You! Go! Down?"

Crepuscular shook his head again and Gracious redoubled his efforts.

"For! God's! Sake! This! Is! Getting! Embarrassing!"

Crepuscular dodged the next punch, gripped Gracious by the throat, and then Tanith dropped from the darkness, her sword slicing Crepuscular's hand off.

Or that's what Valkyrie thought would happen. Instead, the blade dug into the meat of Crepuscular's forearm and stuck there, as if the sword wasn't the sharpest bit of woven steel this side of a Cleaver's scythe.

Crepuscular swung Gracious into Tanith, sending them both stumbling away, and pulled the sword from his arm as Fletcher grabbed his shoulder and they disappeared.

A moment of sudden stillness, and then they arrived right back in the same place and Fletcher didn't even have time to look surprised before Crepuscular smacked him.

Skulduggery hurled a fireball and Valkyrie got up, beginning to suspect that this wasn't going to be easy. Pulling her hood over her head and the mask over her face, she turned to Omen just as Never appeared beside him. Omen looked like he had a plan, and they teleported away before she could speak.

Fair enough.

As Skulduggery collided with Dexter and Donegan, Valkyrie strode forward, white lightning catching Crepuscular in the chest and sending him, spinning, to the floor.

"Stay down," she called, keeping the lightning flowing. "I don't want to kill you, but I will turn you to dust before I let you out of here. Enough mortals have been hurt without you rampaging through what's left of them."

Solace laughed. "Oh, sweet child, do you really think he needs to be out there among them to do them damage? *His reach is vast.*"

Valkyrie cut off the lightning. "Meaning what?"

Cadaver stood beside Solace as he flicked through the screen on his phone. "Roarhaven is protected," he said, not looking up, "but an unknown number of electromagnetic pulses have been triggered throughout the world. Power grids are no more. Technology is no more. Cars have stopped working and hospitals have gone dark and planes are falling from the sky. Phones, computers, engines, machines... They've all just stopped."

"Mortal civilisation has come to an end," said Solace.

Crepuscular stood. Valkyrie raised her hand and black energy crackled. "Turn it back on."

"We have altered this planet's electrical fields," Crepuscular said. "We have set these pulses to naturally reoccur every forty-three seconds. We will not be reversing our decision."

"Reverse it or I kill you."

"Then kill us," said Crepuscular.

"We don't want to do that," Skulduggery said, advancing slowly with Dexter and Donegan beside him. "We want to help you. Crepuscular, you're still in there. You, as an individual, as the person I once knew as Fregoli Cleft. My grandson. We can help you. Work with us; separate yourself from your siblings. Let them return to their bodies. That's what you want. That's why you've done all this."

"It's too late," said Solace.

"Your mother betrayed you," Skulduggery said. "She never wanted her children to be free – she just wanted the Doomsday Protocol to go ahead. She wanted all this to happen."

Omen and Never teleported back with Ragner and Eraddin Tomb.

"He's not going to listen to you," Cadaver said. "He isn't even a *he* any more. He's a *they*."

"That's a good point," said Skulduggery. "Crepuscular, how are you going to prove yourself superior to me if you have to cheat?"

Crepuscular tilted his head.

"We're going to beat you," Skulduggery told him, "and then we're going to fix the world."

He launched himself forward and Crepuscular's hands lit up.

Valkyrie released a fistful of white lightning, but Crepuscular used his own energy to deflect it, and Skulduggery stomped on his knee. The others ran in, firing energy streams and throwing punches, and Ragner charged. Crepuscular unleashed a rippling wave of purple energy that threw everyone back except Tomb, who walked straight through it. Crepuscular met him with a headbutt and then Cadaver dived on him, taking the God of Death to the ground.

Fletcher stepped out of thin air in front of Crepuscular and hit him with a sledgehammer. He swung again, teleporting round behind him to land the blow. When Crepuscular knocked the hammer from his hands, he vanished for a split second and reappeared with an axe. Then Never was with him, each of them taking a turn to swing a weapon and then teleport away to grab another. They tag-teamed, striking with everything from swords to cudgels to cricket bats to maces to halberds to pitchforks to pool cues to frying pans, each one clattering to the ground once used. Crepuscular, beaten and bloodied, looked to be one more strike from defeat when his hands went out, catching Never's crowbar and Fletcher's shovel, and both Teleporters shot backwards off their feet like they'd been electrocuted.

"Right," Valkyrie muttered, getting to her feet yet again. At her nod, the resistance moved in, grimly determined to end this, but then the space behind Crepuscular opened and Obsidian stepped through.

The resistance froze and Cadaver and Solace backed off immediately. Crepuscular merely tilted his head. Obsidian watched him.

Crepuscular's eyes burned orange, but Obsidian gestured and swept him from existence.

Valkyrie pulled her mask and hood away from her face and focused her thoughts, sending them straight out without giving Obsidian a chance to assess the situation. But instead of staggering him they found nothing she could identify, nothing she could attack, and he looked at her and she tried to pull those thoughts back, but he'd latched on to them. Her knees buckled and then he released his grip, and Skulduggery caught her.

"He's done it," she said, her eyes wide, trying to sort through the images in her head.

"Done what?"

"Ended it all."

While they had turned their attention to Crepuscular and the Hosts' plan, Obsidian had ended the universe. He'd started at the edges, working from the outside in. He'd wiped away the stars and the planets and the space between them, wiped away galaxies and black holes and cosmic clusters and civilisations both ancient and burgeoning. The light that had escaped those stars – the light that became the only thing left of those stars – had also been wiped away.

It was all gone. The universe was over. The only thing left was the Earth and its solar system, and Obsidian was taking his time with that. A throwback, perhaps, to when he had been human.

Sentimental reasons.

Cadaver pulled the Void sword from his coat and Obsidian turned away from him, his dark eyes on Omen, and that movement was all he needed to wipe Cadaver Cain and the resistance from reality.

"No!" Valkyrie screamed, and she grabbed Omen's hand and Skulduggery grabbed Valkyrie's.

"Run," Skulduggery said.

124

They burst through the doors of the High Sanctuary, and the wind tore at Valkyrie's hair and she looked up to see roiling storm clouds. Then the sun disappeared and the Earth was plunged into a darkness so complete that Valkyrie thought for a moment that she was already dead.

But then the world trembled.

The ground shook beneath their feet and all around Roarhaven Elementals clicked their fingers, summoning flame into their hands.

"Come on," said Skulduggery, grabbing Omen, and she felt them both lift into the air.

Valkyrie released her magic and lit up with crackling white as she shot into the sky, barely keeping them in view. When Skulduggery changed direction and vanished into the dark, Omen summoned a fireball as a guide and she flew after it, a streak of lightning in the dark, skimming low over rooftops. Lights flicked on beneath her and streetlamps lit up.

All she could do was move. If she paused, if she hesitated, she'd freeze. She'd start thinking about her parents, about Alice, about Militsa, and she'd want to rush to them, to be with them, to comfort and protect them.

But, of course, that was not protecting them. The universe was ending and there was nothing left to do.

She screamed Skulduggery's name and he slowed, but not by much. They landed and Skulduggery led the way, fire in his hand. Valkyrie didn't know what part of Roarhaven they were in. It didn't matter, she supposed. It was all going to disappear in a matter of minutes.

"Stop!" she cried. "Skulduggery, just stop!"

He spun to her, flames flickering off his skull. Omen looked terrified.

"Dear me," Skulduggery said, "why? Why would we possibly stop now?"

"Because it's over! It's done!"

He pointed at her. "Not yet."

He hurried on and she followed, Omen by her side. "What do you mean? There's a chance?"

"A chance at what?"

"At surviving?"

"Of course."

"But the universe is gone."

"It's not a particularly good chance, but it's definitely a chance."

The world rumbled so violently they all went staggering.

They got to a house, got to a door, and the air rippled and it blasted open.

"The end is nigh!" a man screamed, tottering up behind them. "Obsidian has come to wipe away the sins of humanity!"

He was one of those lunatics, those Nulls. He clutched at Valkyrie and she shoved him away. "Not if we can help it."

"You'll never stop him!" the lunatic screeched.

They ignored him and Skulduggery led the way up narrow, winding stairs. Valkyrie gathered a ball of energy in her hand and let it float above them, lighting their way.

"I hope he's in," Skulduggery said.

"Who's in? Where are we?"

They reached a door at the top of the steps and Skulduggery kicked it open and marched into a brightly lit apartment that had been converted, in a haphazard fashion, into a laboratory. Destrier watched them enter, a sandwich in his hand.

"I'm having lunch," he said. "Why is it night-time?"

"World's ending," Skulduggery responded.

"Oh," said Destrier.

The panic rose in Valkyrie's belly, went straight to her chest where it tightened its grip around her lungs. It was hard to breathe, hard to draw in enough oxygen. She could feel it around her heart, as well, squeezing too tightly, squeezing too fast, as if her heart was going to pop, like it was going to burst as she was standing here, trying to form coherent thoughts, trying to do anything but scream for her parents and her sister and—

Omen made a sound, just a tiny sound, and she looked over and saw that his eyes were wide. She moved to him, hands on his shoulders.

"Omen," she said, her voice gentle. "Omen, look at me, buddy. Look into my eyes, Omen. I need you to be calm. Can you do that for me? Panicking won't help. Panicking won't solve this. We need you calm."

"The world's ending," he whispered.

Everything's ending! she wanted to scream at him. *We've failed! We've lost! It's all over!*

Instead, she smiled. "Skulduggery has a plan. I have faith in him, and I need you to have faith in me. Can you do that?"

He nodded, tears brimming.

"Good man," she said, and wrapped one arm round his shoulders as she turned to Skulduggery and Destrier.

"It's not advisable," Destrier was saying. "It's not advisable. The consequences could be catastrophic."

"Catastrophic is where we're starting from," Skulduggery responded. "Anything other than that will be a step up. Valkyrie, what do you think?"

"I have to be honest," she said, "I wasn't listening."

"We can't stop what's coming," he said. "No matter what we

do, it's too late. The only person who could possibly stand a chance against Obsidian is Darquesse."

"And since she's not here, what's our alternative?"

"Well, that's the thing, isn't it? There is no alternative. Darquesse is our only chance."

Valkyrie waited for the logic to hit her. When it didn't, she shook her head. "I'm not getting it."

"Me neither," said Omen.

"We need Darquesse's help," Skulduggery said.

Valkyrie gave him a quick, brittle smile. "I get that bit. That bit's fine. My issue comes from the fact that we chased her out of this dimension eight years ago. My issue comes from the fact that we don't know where she is or if she's still alive or – and this is a pretty big one – if she'd help us even if we found her and asked. She did seem pretty intent on killing the universe *herself*, remember?"

"I don't see how she'd be an improvement on Obsidian," said Omen.

"Darquesse sprang from Valkyrie," Skulduggery said, "and, no matter how much she may have changed, she still has that core. She wants to do the right thing. She wants to be a good person. I think she can be persuaded."

"But we don't know where she is and we don't have time to go searching," said Valkyrie.

Skulduggery nodded. "That's true. We do not. But finding Darquesse is our only chance."

She blinked at him. "Are you trying to annoy me on purpose? Is that how you want me to die? Annoyed at you?"

"Finding Darquesse is our only chance, but you're absolutely right: we don't have time to do that. So what's the logical course of action?"

"I'm assuming there is one?"

"Yes."

"And it's why we're here, in this particular place?"

"Yes."

"I really don't understand what it is you think we can do."

"I worked it out."

"You worked what out?"

"How Serpine did it. How he killed Robert Scure *and* attacked me at the same time. How he was in two places at once."

Valkyrie stared at him. "I don't care! I don't care how he did it! The universe is ending! Why are you even thinking about this?"

"Serpine killed Scure because Scure was about to figure out that there were two Serpines sharing one body. Serpine knew there were witnesses to the murder, and he knew you were one of them. As Creed's favourite, no one would even question your version of events. Serpine would be found and executed."

"I swear to Jesus, Skulduggery, there had better be a point to this."

"He knew the only chance he had at avoiding execution long enough to transfer his soul into the spare body was to make you doubt yourself – or to at least entertain the possibility that something else was going on."

"So?"

"So the only way you would ever question yourself is if I came out and told you that you were wrong – which is exactly what I did."

"And?"

"And *I* was wrong," Skulduggery said. "Serpine needed me to be his alibi so he found me and attacked me. But, before he *physically* attacked me, he attacked me the way he attacked the other Serpine."

"For God's sake, just call him Nefarian."

"Nefarian, fine. He overwhelmed Nefarian's consciousness, blasted it into submission. He did the same to me. He implanted suggestions to fill in the blanks – techniques that wouldn't ordinarily work on me because I'm immune to psychic attacks. But this wasn't a psychic attack – this was an assault on my soul."

Valkyrie frowned.

"He stunned me. You see? I dismissed the very possibility because I didn't think it could happen and also because I refused to entertain the idea that I could be beaten like that. My own ego worked against me and allowed him to play with my perception of time and events. He robbed me of four hours. Between those hours, he *did* physically attack me and those events unfolded exactly how I remember them – but they are cushioned, on either side, by lies."

"OK," said Valkyrie. "So he fooled you into thinking he attacked you at the same time that he was killing Scure, even though he actually attacked you, like, two hours later."

"Yes. Precisely."

Valkyrie nodded. "And what the *hell* does that have to do with anything?"

"There are problems that have only one solution," said Skulduggery, "and that solution sometimes passes you by before you know what you're looking for. The solution had passed Serpine by – he needed to establish me as an alibi, but this was impossible to set up as killing Scure was a spur-of-the-moment act. But here's the thing, Valkyrie: he refused to accept it. He decided to cheat, to *retroactively* provide himself with the alibi he needed. We can cheat, too, by retroactively providing ourselves with a solution."

"And how do we do that?"

"Look around."

She did so. They were in a mad scientist's laboratory, a variation on the dozens she'd visited since she started on her journey through magic. The tables were piled high with scrap and junk and wires and machines that beeped and chirped and potions that bubbled and gadgets that hummed. The only thing that marked this place out as even remotely unique was the particular mad scientist at the centre of it all.

Valkyrie looked at Destrier, the temporal manipulator, and frowned. "Wait."

"Yes," said Skulduggery.

"No."

"Yes."

"No way."

"I don't understand what you're talking about," said Omen.

Valkyrie hesitated. "Skulduggery wants to send Destrier back in time," she said. "Am I right?"

"Yes, you are," Skulduggery said, a smile in his voice.

"Destrier, can you do that?"

Destrier paused before answering.

Valkyrie's eyes widened. "You *can* do that."

"I *think* I can do it," Destrier said, eyes locked on to his fidgeting hands. "I think I can go back in time. I've been building my engine. My time machine, as they say. I need to go back, you see, to wade through this moving image of eternity." He looked up. "I need to go back three hundred and three years. I need to go back three hundred and three years, four months, two days, eight minutes. Then I can save her."

"Save who?" Omen asked.

"My fiancée. She fell from a horse. She fell from a horse and hit her head, but I can save her. I can go back. I can take her to a healer. That's all she needs. That's all she ever needed. But... but I didn't know. I didn't know she'd fallen. I called on her, waited for her to come to the front door. I didn't go round the back because that's not what you did, not back in those days. Not if you had manners. I didn't know she'd fallen from the horse. I didn't know she was lying there, just round the corner. When I found her, it was... I was too late."

"Destrier, I am so sorry that happened," said Valkyrie. "That's absolutely awful and terrible and I'm really sorry we can't console you right now, but the universe is going to end at any moment. The thing is, we don't need you to go back three hundred and three years. We just need you to go back... Skulduggery, how far do we need him to go back? Do we need him to stop us from sending Darquesse away?"

"Can't do that," Destrier said immediately. "I can't interfere with anything you've done or I've done – or else we run the risk of this moment never happening."

"So you go back to a point *after* we've sent Darquesse away," said Valkyrie, "and maybe after she's had some time to calm down and move on from wanting to kill us all. How long will that take? A few years? Two years?"

"How's he going to find her?" Omen asked.

"You'll need help when you're back there," Skulduggery said, "but you're right: you can't go to us."

Omen snapped his fingers. "The weirdos." They looked at him. "You know the weirdos? The people who worship Darquesse? They'll help."

"That's right," said Skulduggery. "Omen, that's brilliant."

"My friend's dad is one of them – or Auger's friend's dad. Kåse's dad. I know Kase a bit, but, like, not very well. I know him better than I know Mahala, but that's not saying a lot."

"You have five minutes to come up with as many details about your friend's father as you can."

Omen nodded, started tapping his phone. He put it to his ear and turned away to talk. "Kase," he said, "I know the world is ending, but I need to ask you questions about your dad."

"I'm going to need a date to go back to," said Destrier.

"I don't think it really matters the *exact* date you arrive," Valkyrie responded. "Here, make it February the eighth – that's the day Skulduggery dragged me back to Roarhaven. Why not start on the same day? So you know what you have to do?"

Destrier nodded. "Travel back two years and nine months, to February the eighth. Talk to the Darquesse worshippers. Get them to help me search for Darquesse. I can do it. I know I can. The suit's ready to go."

"Suit?" said Skulduggery.

"My time machine," Destrier said. "It's not a machine *per se*. It's a suit that I've poured my magic into. I'd done similar work with Lethe."

Valkyrie frowned. "That black rubber thing he wore?"

"Abyssinia needed Smoke's corrupting influence to keep Lethe corrupted, so I adapted a necronaut suit, like yours, and filled it with Smoke's magic. I did the same thing with my own."

"So your time machine is a black rubber suit?"

"Not quite," said Destrier, leading them into the bedroom. He opened the wardrobe. Hanging within was a black necronaut suit with a long heavy coat, a wide-brimmed hat and a plague doctor's mask.

"Hey," said Valkyrie, "I know this guy."

125

Destrier turned to her. "What do you mean?"

"I've spoken to him," Valkyrie said, growing more excited. "Mr Beakface! It works! This means it works! You go back in time!"

"I spoke to you?" Destrier asked.

"Yeah," she said. "Not for long, though. I was jumped one afternoon. A few nice people wanted to remind me how much they didn't like my face, and you came to assist me in fighting them off. Well, kinda. You were pretty useless, all things considered."

Destrier nodded. "That does sound like me."

"You said you were a friend. You said you were here to help."

"I shouldn't have done that. I don't know why I did that, but I shouldn't have. I need to stay away from you – to stay away from everyone I know." His frown deepened. "But what do I do now? Now I *have* to talk to you. If I don't, my future and your past will be changed. If your past changes, your future changes, and this moment will never happen."

He looked around. Skulduggery and Valkyrie looked around, too.

Omen walked in. "What are you all doing?" he asked.

"Checking that I haven't disrupted the space-time continuum," said Destrier.

"Cool," said Omen. "Kase's father's name is Bennet Troth. I've got his address and everything. That's a funny-looking outfit. Why is the mask so weird?"

"The plague doctor suit is my time machine," said Destrier, taking it from the cupboard and laying it on the bed. "It's lost some of its necronaut qualities as I've worked on it – it's a relatively-fixed size now – but it's still armoured. It will still feed me, keep me hydrated, take care of my waste – it will still sustain me."

Valkyrie watched the magic move within it, watched it curl back on itself in an endless loop.

"What if you're shackled? What if your magic is bound?"

"I won't be able to use my magic anyway, not while I'm wearing that," Destrier answered. He held the mask in his hands and closed his eyes. "But I won't need to. The suit itself possesses all the magic it needs. The only thing I can't do is take it off. If it comes off, I'll probably return to this time period."

"Probably?"

"I'll either return to this time period or my body, mind and soul will be torn apart by forces I cannot even begin to comprehend."

"Cool," said Valkyrie. "Cool, cool, cool. So let's hope that doesn't happen."

"Yes, let's." Destrier opened his eyes, and put the mask on the bed. "OK, the date is locked in."

"You'll never stop him," said a man from behind them and they turned – it was the Null, the lunatic from downstairs – and he held a gun and he fired just as Skulduggery swiped at the air. The gun flew from his grip and Valkyrie ran at him. He was a small man, and thin, and she picked him up off his feet and propelled him out of the bedroom, crunching his head into the wall before hurling him back down the stairs. She watched him tumble to the bottom and sprawl, unconscious, out of the door.

"We'll have to hurry," Skulduggery said as she rejoined him. "He may have called his friends."

"Guys," said Omen.

He was kneeling by Destrier, whose shirt was drenched with

blood that leaked from the bullet hole in the exact centre of his chest.

Valkyrie rushed over, but Destrier's aura was already dissipating. He was dead, and there was no bringing him back.

"You're kidding," she said, her voice numb. "You have got to be kidding. You can't just…" She looked at Skulduggery. "This can't be how it happens. We had a way out! We had a chance! This was our chance!"

"It still is our chance," he said. "We don't need Destrier's magic to go back in time – we just need the suit." He took off his hat, started taking off his jacket.

"It won't fit you," Valkyrie said. "I'm closer to his height than you are."

"You're still too tall," said Omen, his voice quiet. They looked at him. "I'm the only one it'll even come close to fitting. It has to be me."

"Omen, no."

"We don't have much choice, do we? And we could stand around arguing about this and wait for more of those Nulls to come running in, or even for Obsidian to just end everything, or I could put the suit on and… and try."

Valkyrie looked at Skulduggery, who put his hat back on.

"You can't tell anyone who you are," he said.

She nodded. "Names are power. Remember that. If anyone knows that Omen Darkly is the one in that—"

"That's not my name."

"I'm sorry?"

Omen swallowed. "Auger was going to change his name before he became Obsidian. I didn't really get it at first, but I do now. I don't want anything to do with my parents. I took my name to honour them, because I thought it was important to be a Legacy family, but they don't love me. They never have."

"So you're not Omen Darkly any more," Skulduggery said. "Very well. Have you taken a new name?"

"I... I've been thinking about this, and I always liked the name Sebastian. And I wanted to forge my own path, you know? Make my own way. So – Tao. Sebastian Tao."

Skulduggery nodded, and Valkyrie smiled.

"I like it," she said.

126

Sebastian watched three sorcerers sprint up to Obsidian, who didn't even turn to look at them before they were wiped away. Three more lives lost.

Two more came running into the glow of the streetlights, but Sebastian couldn't bear to see his brother erase more souls from existence and he started running for Destrier's laboratory, but stopped before he'd picked up any speed.

There was a moment, and it hung there, and in that moment he was still and everything was still, and the voices he heard were simply voices, abstract sounds that had the potential to mean nothing at all. And then the moment ended, it landed, and the weight of reality came crashing down upon his shoulders as he turned and watched his parents approach Obsidian.

"Auger," his mother said, "please listen to me. Please look at me."

"It's us," said his father, as Obsidian watched them. "We're here. Auger, do you know us? Do you recognise us?"

Sebastian couldn't move. He wanted to lunge forward, push them into the shadows, get them away from the danger. He couldn't speak. He wanted to shout out, to warn them, to tell them Obsidian wasn't their son, not any more.

"Sweetheart," said Emmeline, "I want you to listen to me. Please, just listen to me. You have to stop this."

"You're killing people," Caddock said. "Innocent people. We know you don't want to hurt anyone; we know this isn't your fault. But please stop."

Emmeline was crying now. Sebastian didn't think he'd ever seen his mother cry. "This is our fault, Auger. We drove you away. We're so sorry."

"We love you," said Caddock. "We failed you."

"We failed you and Omen. We were selfish, and self-centred, and obsessed with all the wrong things. And we lost you both."

"We don't deserve another chance," Caddock said. "We understand that. From either of you. But you're our children. We have to try. Auger, please. Let us try."

"I remember you," said Obsidian, and wiped Caddock Darkly from existence.

Emmeline screamed and Sebastian screamed and he was on his knees now, his mask absorbing the tears he was shedding. He watched his mother stagger back, both hands covering her mouth, staring at the space where her husband had been a moment ago.

"He felt no pain," Obsidian said.

Emmeline sobbed again, doubled over and roared, and then straightened and did her best to compose herself. "Please stop," she said. "Auger, please stop killing people."

"You won't feel any pain, either."

"Please don't kill Omen."

Obsidian hesitated.

"Kill me," said Emmeline. "I've lived a long life. But your brother is too good a person, Auger. You know he is. He's too kind and too decent and too nice – you can't kill him. Please. Kill me but spare your brother."

"It's not death," Obsidian said. "It's just the end."

Emmeline's head dropped. "I love you both so, so much," she said, and then Obsidian wiped her away.

He turned his head, looking through the darkness, straight at Sebastian, and his posture changed slightly. "You were the best part of being a Darkly," he said, and he sounded like his old self, like Auger, and then he straightened up and Sebastian knew his brother was gone.

He got up, and he ran.

127

The necronaut suit was a pretty good fit, all in all, and Sebastian looked at himself in the mirror and blushed. "I don't even want to say what I look like."

"You look grand," said Valkyrie. "Once you put on the coat and the hat and the mask, you'll look awesome."

"I'll look worse."

"But at least no one will be able to see your face."

Sebastian sighed. "How do I find Darquesse?"

"You'll need to go looking for the Faceless Ones," said Skulduggery. "If Darquesse is still fighting them, that's how you'll find her. You'll need to track their energy signatures."

"How do I do that?"

"My blood," said Valkyrie. "If you can get some of my blood, you'll be able to get the energy signature you need."

"I don't suppose you'd just hand a vial over if I asked?"

"Probably not," said Valkyrie. "And you can't ask, either. You can't ask me anything. We can have no contact. None at all."

"OK."

Valkyrie looked around, found a pair of scissors that looked clean. She rolled up her sleeve, pressed the point of the scissors into her forearm and drew it across her skin, wincing as she did so.

"Ow," she said, and handed the scissors to Sebastian. "My

blood's on that. Keep it safe and, when you've made friends with the weirdos, give this to someone who knows what they're doing."

Sebastian nodded. He found a clear plastic bag on a table, and slipped the scissors into it.

"Eight months after you get there," Skulduggery said, "the refugees will start arriving from the Leibniz Universe. They'll have technology that a Shunter can use to open a portal."

Sebastian hesitated. "So I'll just... I'll wait around for eight months? How long will I be gone?"

Valkyrie glanced at Skulduggery, then looked at Sebastian. "When you find Darquesse, you'll have to keep her hidden. We can't know if you've succeeded or failed. You get that, right?"

Sebastian paled. "I'll have to keep her hidden from you the whole time? The whole two years and nine months?"

"I'm afraid so," Skulduggery said. "And I'd like to give you the option to back out, I really would, but I'm afraid we're past that point."

Sebastian swallowed, and nodded.

"You're going to be gone a long time," Skulduggery said, "but you can't get distracted. You can't involve yourself in anything but this. The mission is all that matters."

"Don't get distracted," Sebastian said. "OK."

"And don't interfere, no matter what you see," said Valkyrie.

"Don't get distracted and don't interfere."

"And even though it's brand-new," Skulduggery said, "don't tell anyone your name. We can't hear the name Sebastian Tao until tonight. If we hear it, you might hear it, and if you hear it before you take it, you won't take it, and so your past will change, and if your past changes, your future changes, and this moment might not exist."

They all looked around. When nothing happened, they nodded to each other.

"Don't get distracted," said Sebastian. "Don't interfere. Don't tell anyone my name."

Valkyrie helped him into his coat, then looked him in the eye. "You can do this. We wouldn't be sending you if we didn't think you could."

"You're sending me because I'm the only one the suit fits."

"No," she said. "We're sending you because we trust you. The big question is, do you trust yourself?"

"I can do it," Sebastian said, his voice cracking just a little.

The house rattled with thunder that wasn't thunder and then they poured in from the stairs, the Nulls, their faces warped by madness and rage and ecstasy. Skulduggery used the air to swat the first few away, but the rest of them charged into him, took him down.

"Him!" the Null from earlier screeched, the one who'd killed Destrier. "The one in the mask! He's going to stop Obsidian!"

Valkyrie blasted them and when they got too close to blast she grabbed them, hit them, swung them into the path of their friends, got them all tangled up. "Omen," she cried. "Go!"

They got by her, knives in their hands, and Omen spun and ran for the window and he leaped through and Valkyrie glimpsed him falling to the rooftop and then the suit rippled and he was gone.

The Nulls whirled, seething with fury, and Valkyrie threw a chair and they scattered. She broke a Null's kneecap and punched another's throat and fried another's nervous system and broke her hand on another's jaw. Wincing, hissing, she backed off, and Skulduggery stepped in to finish the fight.

"Dammit," she snarled. "*Ohhh*, this bloody hurts."

Cradling her hand to her chest, she looked round at the Nulls. Some were unconscious. Some were moaning in pain. A few were sobbing.

Skulduggery went to the window, looked out into the darkness. "Omen jumped?"

"And vanished," Valkyrie said, trying to dampen the pain. "No lights, no flashes, no cool, swirly tunnel. He just disappeared. But at least we know it works. I mean, the time-travelling part. He arrives in the past and talks to me and then... ah, dammit." She picked up the plastic bag containing the scissors with her good hand. "He left without my blood."

"I'm sure he'll manage."

She dropped the bag on the table. "Do you think he'll find her?"

Skulduggery shrugged. "He's had a little over two and a half years."

Valkyrie managed to reduce her pain to a manageable level, and was grateful for it. "Two and a half years to search for one person in an infinite number of alternate universes isn't a whole lot of time."

"No, it isn't. I suppose we just have to hope. And wait."

"Waiting sucks. How long do we have to wait for?"

More footsteps thundered up the stairs and Sebastian ran in. They stared at him. He stared at them.

"Am I gone?" he asked.

"You're gone," said Skulduggery.

Sebastian flung off his hat and his hands went to the buckles on the mask. "Help me with this. Help me get it off. Oh, God, help me get it off."

Valkyrie stayed back, careful of her injury, while Skulduggery rushed forward, batted Sebastian's hands out of the way and went to work.

"Did you find her?" he asked, undoing the first buckle.

"I found her," said Sebastian. "I brought her back. I told her what we needed her for."

"And?"

The last buckle opened and Sebastian grabbed the mask by the beak and ripped it off his head, hurled it into the corner. He roared, scratching at his hair, at his face, rubbing his nose, rubbing his eyes.

"Oh my God!" he cried. "Oh, thank you! Thank you! I hate this stupid suit! I hate it! Never want to see it again!"

He dropped his coat, pulled off his gloves, went back to scratching his face, leaving long red marks on his waxy, sun-deprived skin. He needed a haircut and he needed a shave and he needed some pimple cream, and he was suddenly two years older than he'd been a few minutes ago. He also looked like he'd been crying. He started kicking off his boots.

"Sebastian," said Valkyrie, "where is Darquesse?"

He turned to them. "I don't know. We've been through an awful lot. Like, an awful, awful lot." Sebastian's voice had changed, too. It was deeper. "I found her and she was a giant, and she was fighting the Faceless Ones. She came back with me and I asked her to help us, but she didn't know if she wanted to. Then she sent out all these other aspects and it got really confusing."

"Other aspects?"

"Other Darquesses. She's been sending them all over the universe, as part of her research into whether or not she'll help."

"How many?"

"I actually don't know," said Sebastian. "I'm thinking trillions."

Valkyrie blinked. "She can do that?"

"Yep. And each Darquesse is as powerful as she is. I don't know how it works. She thought that'd be enough, you know, to make a decision, but then she said she needed to experience what it was like to be a person. She needed to have her own childhood."

"And what does that mean?" Valkyrie asked.

"She, uh, she got pregnant – immaculate conception, don't worry – and she gave birth... to herself. And I raised her."

"You what?"

He smiled, and Valkyrie saw that same uncertain boy who had just jumped out of the window. "I raised her," he said. "She aged, you know, quickly, and she's, I'd say, your age now. She needed to do it. Needed to form her own opinion on whether we're worth saving."

Valkyrie looked at him, and nodded. "Seems fair."

"Are my clothes still in the bedroom?"

"Yeah, of course. Hey, Sebastian – well done. No matter what happens – you did it."

"Ah, it was nothing much," he responded, blushing again. Halfway to the bedroom, he stopped, and turned. "And I think I've changed my mind. About the name thing. My parents... they were flawed, and mean, and selfish – but I think, if we're all going to die, I think I want to be a Darkly again."

"So back to Omen?"

"If that won't be too confusing for anyone."

"You've been Sebastian Tao for two years," said Skulduggery. "For us, it's been ten minutes."

Omen smiled sadly, then disappeared into the bedroom.

"If Darquesse is going to help us," Valkyrie said to Skulduggery, "she's cutting it fine."

"A flair for the dramatic is a requirement for saving the world – you know that."

"So you think she'll do it?"

Instead of answering, he went over to a Null who was clambering awkwardly to his feet and knocked him out with a single rap on the chin. As he turned back, he passed the apartment door, and froze. Valkyrie didn't have to ask. She knew.

Obsidian was coming up the stairs.

Omen emerged from the bedroom. His jeans were a little too short – they stopped at his ankles. "I'm lucky that necronaut suit was stretchy," he said, managing a smile.

One of the injured Nulls, she'd found the fallen gun as she lay there on the floor, and she screamed something stupid and pulled the trigger and three bullets burrowed into Omen's torso. He jerked back, went crashing against a table. Bits of machinery clattered. Valkyrie stomped on the woman's wrist before she could fire again, her ears ringing, not even hearing the snap of bone. Skulduggery darted over, caught Omen in his arms as he fell.

Obsidian walked into the apartment.

He waved his hand gently and the Nulls went away, wiped from the universe.

"Roof," said Skulduggery.

Valkyrie released a handful of black lightning that turned the ceiling to dust, and they flew upwards.

128

Roarhaven was gone. The Earth was gone. Around them was only emptiness. Nothingness. Valkyrie's eyes hurt and her brain screamed when she glimpsed that nothingness so she kept looking at Skulduggery as he laid Omen on the roof and straightened as Obsidian stepped out of thin air ahead of them.

Valkyrie released another ball of energy that hovered over her right shoulder, casting what remained of the universe in a white, crackling light. She was crying, she realised. She was crying and she couldn't comprehend what was going on around her. She felt her mind teeter on the edge of sanity.

Obsidian looked at Omen, and Skulduggery took Valkyrie's good hand and squeezed it. She focused on that pressure. That pressure was one of the last things left in this reality.

"Don't let go," she said.

"I won't," he said.

Omen coughed blood, cried out, and Obsidian eased his pain by wiping him from existence.

That was it. It was over now. Obsidian had erased the last thing that made him human.

"Interesting," said Darquesse.

Valkyrie snapped her head towards her, her eyes locking on to the nothingness that lay over Darquesse's shoulder, and her thoughts were cut down the middle, and then Darquesse was putting her hand on Valkyrie's forehead and her mind came back and Valkyrie gasped.

"Not yet," said Darquesse.

Valkyrie's legs went and Skulduggery held her up, and they watched Darquesse approach Obsidian.

"You are interesting," she said. "I was brought here to stop you, but I don't know if I can. I'm... plugged in. You know? I've visited every corner of the universe. I've seen what makes up life, and what makes up matter, and what makes up the things between and beyond. I've seen everything. I am everything. But you... you're nothing. And I don't know if everything can beat nothing. I don't even know if I want to." She put her hand on Obsidian's cheek. "You're beautiful."

"Help us," said Valkyrie.

Darquesse looked back at her. "I'm sorry, Valkyrie. I don't want to fight anyone any more. I don't want to hurt, or kill, or destroy. We each have our paths, and we go where they take us. Auger's path took him to Obsidian, and Obsidian's takes him to the end."

"And us with it," Skulduggery said.

"Nothing lasts forever." Darquesse smiled sadly. "I'm sorry I can't stop him," she said, and disappeared, and Obsidian held out his fist. Valkyrie could see the power that churned within. When that hand opened, the last piece of the universe would blink out of existence.

Skulduggery hugged Valkyrie tight. "Until the end," he said.

Tears ran down her face and she smiled because there was nothing left to do but smile, but before she could answer, Obsidian started to open his hand and that wiped Skulduggery away. Valkyrie fell to her knees.

She laughed, because now there was nothing left to do but laugh, and she answered him, and she said, "Until the

In the nothing before the beginning, there was a thought. And the thought became the beginning.

And from the nothing came the everything.

And from the everything came the universe, which grew and spread and took its place beside the others.

And life grew, and spread.

And all was memory.

The memory of gods and people. The memory of monsters.

And she looked upon this universe and smiled.

"Welcome," she said.

"Welcome to where?" Skulduggery asked.

The roof was hard under Valkyrie's knees. She felt its roughness through her jeans. She felt her boots round her feet and the tightness of her T-shirt across her back. She felt the air travel down her throat, felt her tongue against her lower teeth.

Slowly, she saw what she was looking at, as the information finally reached her brain. A shoe – black and polished, though recently scuffed. A shoe that had seen action. A shoe that had kicked and stomped and run. Skulduggery's shoe.

Valkyrie took a breath, filled her lungs with air, and let it out. Skulduggery's gloved hand moved into view. She took it with the hand that she'd broken, with the hand that wasn't broken any more, and he helped her stand.

It was a nice day, but Roarhaven was unusually quiet. Valkyrie looked out over the streets. Not a car, not a person, not a bird in the sky. Darquesse hovered before them.

"Where are we?" Skulduggery asked her.

"Exactly where you were a moment ago," Darquesse said. "More or less."

"More or less what?"

"That all depends on your interpretation of the words *where* and *moment*. Also the words *more* and *less*."

"Am I dead?" Valkyrie asked.

"No," said Darquesse.

"Is everyone else dead?"

"No."

"Where are they?"

Darquesse smiled. "I thought I'd give you two a preview. Everyone else will be joining you soon."

Skulduggery tilted his head. "Everyone?"

"Absolutely everyone."

"I don't understand," Valkyrie said. "Obsidian wiped away the universe."

"Yes, he did."

"So what happened then?"

"I restarted it."

Valkyrie frowned. "You restarted the universe?"

"That's what your aspects were doing," Skulduggery said. "Omen said you'd sent them out across the universe to judge whether it was worth saving, but that's not all."

"What else were they doing, Skulduggery?" Darquesse asked.

"They were recording everything."

"They were recording *absolutely* everything," she corrected. "Memorising every piece of history, noting the placement of every last atom. A lot of work went into it – I hope you appreciate that."

"You took a snapshot of reality."

Darquesse held up a finger for silence and closed her eyes, then opened them. "Sorry. That was a tricky one."

"You're still working?"

"Of course. But don't worry, I'm almost at the edges." She went quiet for a few seconds, then nodded. "There. The universe has been restored."

"You actually restarted the whole, entire universe?" Valkyrie said.

"Having trouble with that concept, are you?"

"But that makes you... that makes you..."

"It's OK," said Darquesse, "you don't have to say it if you don't want to. I didn't plan on doing any of this – not at first. Not when Omen sought me out. And it's not that I didn't think humankind was worth preserving – I didn't think *life* was worth preserving. There were still other universes that I could explore – the end of this one, I thought, wouldn't mean that much to me. But then I started looking around – really looking around – and I saw the little bits of beauty in the way atoms danced and molecules arranged themselves... And then, finally, there was you. Beings of sentience. People, with all your flaws. For the longest time, I thought that your *stuff*, your *peopleness*, your *personalities* meant nothing. I was far more interested in who you were as *energy*.

"But after spending that time with Sebastian, with Omen, and then merging with the aspect that you called Kes, Valkyrie... it reminded me that your inner lives are worth something, too. That each and every one of you is worth something. That you all matter. That you contribute to the universe just by being in it. There is evil in the world and evil in the universe, and there is hatred, but there is also love and kindness and understanding. And loneliness. Oh, so much loneliness. That's the thread that connects all sentient beings. That's what I'll be bringing back. Loneliness connects you – it means you're not alone."

"You're bringing back the people?" Valkyrie said. "Mum and Dad and Alice? Militsa? Tanith?"

"I'm bringing them all back," said Darquesse. "A few modifications, though. A few tweaks. You can call it cheating if you want – I don't mind – but I'd prefer that this world did not destroy itself the moment after I remake it. So the mortals get an adjustment."

"You're taking away their knowledge of magic," Skulduggery said.

"I'm resetting reality to my specifications," Darquesse said. "And this won't affect all mortals – just the ones who didn't know about magic until recently. I'm allowed to do that, you know."

Darquesse closed her eyes, breathed in, held that breath, and when she breathed out there were people in Roarhaven and there were birds in the sky and dogs barking and cars, and the world shook its head and woke up.

"There. The rifts to the Source of all Magic have been reset to their usual size, so that should cut down on the number of sorcerers losing control of their power." She smiled at Skulduggery. "Oh," she said. "And I brought back the Bentley."

Someone moved behind them and Valkyrie turned as Omen sat up.

"Wait," he said. "I'd been shot."

Skulduggery pulled him to standing. "Long story short, Obsidian ended the universe and Darquesse restarted it. She also gave me back my Bentley, but I'm trying not to focus too much on that right now."

"Where is he?" Omen asked, eyes widening. "Where's Obsidian? What happened to him?"

Darquesse faded slightly.

"Are you OK?" Valkyrie said, stepping forward.

"I'm fine," Darquesse answered. "I'm... I won't be able to maintain this for much longer."

"Maintain your body?"

"My being," said Darquesse. "I'm a universe now, Valkyrie. Things take... precedence."

"Darquesse," Omen said, "where is Obsidian? Is he still alive?"

A tiny smile flickered. "I cheated. Again. I had a... I made a recording of your brother before he used that blade, before he... was infected by nothingness. I merged the two and brought him back."

"You brought Auger back?"

"He's on the bottom step, outside the High Sanctuary – talking with your parents."

Omen stared at her, bolted for the hole in the floor, then spun. "You're going away, aren't you?"

"I am."

"Will I see you again?"

"Of course." Darquesse smiled. "I'm all around you."

Omen lunged, hugging her. "I'm so proud of you," he said softly, then dropped through the hole and was gone.

"You know," Valkyrie said, "since you're remaking the universe, I have some ideas on how to make things a little better for people."

"I'm afraid all the changes that I was able to make have been made," Darquesse responded, "but I've done you one last favour. This box is called the Cage. I put the Faceless Ones in there, the little spark that they became. They won't bother you again if you never let them out." She gave the box to Valkyrie and thought for a moment. "I should probably say something wise at this point, but I'm afraid I'm a little... stretched..." She laughed softly. "Oh. Oh, dear. I'm losing so much of who I am. I get it now. The stuff that's important is the stuff you can't measure. It's the who, not the what. And now I'm losing it. That's a shame. I worked really hard on that."

"Is there anything we can do?" Skulduggery asked. "Any way we can help?"

"Absolutely none," she said, her voice floating. Her smile faded and her features lost all expression. "*Ohhh*, this is weird..."

"Thank you," said Valkyrie quickly. "Darquesse, can you hear me? Thank you for doing this. Thank you for saving us."

Darquesse's body faded until Valkyrie could see through her, and it started to gently drift apart.

"Be good, you crazy kids," said Darquesse, and her form evaporated on the breeze.

Seven months later.

129

It was good to get out of the house.

Tyler's folks had been arguing lately, mostly about the election. His dad – he was a Flanery man – had the bumper sticker on the back of his pickup and a sign on the front lawn that he refused to pull up. He claimed that the election was rigged, that the presidency had been stolen, but Tyler suspected that he didn't believe it.

When they weren't arguing about politics, his folks argued about other stuff, smaller stuff, everyday stuff. It was just a way for them to get out their frustrations and fears, though – even Tyler knew that. They didn't care about the small stuff, the little problems, and they weren't really arguing about Flanery, either. This was all about the bank and its threats to take the farm. Everyone had their own way of dealing. His dad would snipe and complain. His mom would lose herself in her work. His sister would play her music too loud and waste her time with her boyfriend. And Tyler would ride his bike around town, enjoying the sun on his face.

But he couldn't ride his bike forever, so he steered towards home and pedalled lazily, and when he got back there was a rental car parked beside the pickup and the hybrid. He rested his bike against the side of the house and walked to the front door just as it opened.

A tall, broad-shouldered man in a suit with no tie emerged.

"You must be Tyler," he said, smiling. Tyler would have guessed him to be African-American, but there was no American in that accent. African then. They shook hands.

Tyler's parents came out of the house. They were both smiling. His mom looked dazed.

"This is Mr Jones," said Tyler's dad. "He's from the bank. He just came by with some good news. Great news, actually."

Mr Jones chuckled. "I came by with an admission of a mistake, Tyler. Due to unforced human error, your family's account has been unfairly penalised with rates your parents never signed up to. I took a look at what could be done to alleviate the problem, and I've convinced my superiors to wipe the slate clean."

Tyler blinked. "Does that mean... we get to keep the farm?"

"We do," said his mom. "Isn't that amazing?"

Tyler gaped. "Thank you!" he said to Mr Jones. "Thank you so much!"

"It is the very least I could do," Mr Jones replied, and nodded to them all. "I wish you nothing but health and happiness."

"Same to you," said Tyler's dad, hugging his wife.

Mr Jones got in the car, reversed out, then drove back towards town.

130

Omen lined up beside his brother and watched the younger students scurry into their rows, the afternoon air crackling with delight and good humour. The last day of school was – generally – a cause for celebration, but for Omen and the rest of Sixth Year that excitement was tinged with sadness. There was a vague sense that what lay ahead would be empty and hollow without the people they'd grown up with.

"It's the people we meet along the way," said Auger.

Omen smiled. "Sorry? What's that?"

"It's what you're thinking, isn't it? The school experience? What it all means? I'm just saying, maybe it's not the journey that matters; maybe it's the friends we meet along the way."

"That's very wise of you."

Auger shrugged. "You may be two years older than me, but I've been around, you know? I've seen things."

Omen smiled, and glanced back to where the families and loved ones of the graduating class were sitting. The Elementals among them circulated cool air to stave off the heat, which had a tendency to build in the courtyard. Emmeline and Caddock Darkly were sitting in the front row, because of course they were, and they were conversing too intently to realise he was looking at them. Gretchen, however, seated beside them, gave a little wave and blew him a kiss. He grinned, winked at her, and turned his gaze to the stage in front as Principal Sorrows slowly approached the podium, her cane flashing silver in the sunlight.

"Children," she said into the microphone, and the students went immediately quiet. Her voice was soft, and at times it trembled, but there was still an authority there that nobody dared defy. She looked at them without smiling. "Most of you gathered here will return in September to continue your education. To you I say take the summer to ready yourself for the work that lies ahead. Corrival Academy exists to prepare you for the future – we will not accomplish this by mollycoddling you. In this school, you will be respected as strong, resourceful individuals. Some of you are even passably intelligent. Those of you who are not passably intelligent have other qualities that will stand you in good stead. We'll just have to work harder to find them."

The assorted parents and families chuckled.

"Stop laughing," said Principal Sorrows, and they did. "But there are, among you, students who will not be returning next term," she continued. "Our current Sixth Years have been through a lot – you all have, everyone gathered here – and, with notable exceptions, they have conducted themselves admirably. Life as a mage *can* be boring – it *is* possible to be a magic-user and lead an uneventful life – but such a life demands a tragic lack of curiosity. I would hope none of you count yourselves among the uncurious. In my opinion, there is nothing worse.

"More likely, as a mage, you will live through interesting times. You will be witness to dangers that threaten existence itself – as we have done. As our Sixth Years have done. And once this threat passes, and once the next threat passes and the threat after that, you will need to refocus on matters too mundane to quantify. You will have to study, and make notes, and sit your exams, so that you are fully armed as you enter the next phase of your life.

"It won't surprise anyone to know that students of Corrival Academy, no matter their age, regularly find themselves in situations of great peril, where they battle sorcerers with wicked intent, and more often than not need to count on their friends to save them. Judging by the expressions on their parents' faces, I see I was wrong about it not being a surprise. Children, I apologise. Parents, what did you expect?

"I can point to fourteen students in the first three rows alone who have plunged recklessly into so-called *adventures*, and four more who have almost died after being unwittingly dragged after them. Spare me your complaints and outrage – they are young sorcerers. They will have to deal with their own stupidity at some point – I would much rather it be here, where we can at least reattach their limbs. If we're lucky. I feel we should take a moment to think of poor Sarah McLaren, whose head detached itself a week before Christmas and grew legs to scuttle away. There are those who claim that if you listen really carefully, you can sometimes hear her plaintive cries, even now."

In the eerily quiet hall, there came a faint, "No, you can't," from somewhere in the rafters.

"The world ended," China continued. "The people we were... ended. They were wiped away – erased from reality. We are the copies. The world, the universe, is a copy – a memory. What do we do with that knowledge? How do we reconcile the facts with who we think we are? Who we remember ourselves to be? That will be the defining question of our time, and we will come to rely on the new generation to find the answer."

She nodded. "That's all. You may disperse."

The students cheered and China rolled her eyes. Omen hugged Auger and Never and Axelia, and, as he tried making his way over to his parents and his girlfriend, he was mobbed by his fellow pupils who all wanted to shake his hand and pat him on the back and make him promise to keep in touch, no matter where life took him and what it had in store.

He paused a moment, watching Kase hug his mother while Conrad, her Hollow Man boyfriend, stood by. Bennet went over, hugged his son, said some words to his ex-wife and they both laughed. Kase's mum put her phone in Conrad's hands and she posed for a photograph with her son, and Bennet stepped away.

Omen went over. "Excuse me," he said, "Bennet?"

Bennet turned to him, smiling. "Yes? Oh, you're that Darkly boy. How are you? Very good to meet you." They shook hands.

"Yeah," said Omen. "Hi. Uh, I was actually hoping to talk to you, just for a minute. On the day – you know, the day it all restarted – when everything was going wrong and it was all ending, I actually spoke to someone you know. Sebastian Tao?"

The smile froze on Bennet's face and he stepped closer. "Is he OK? Is he alive? Where is he?"

"I don't know," Omen said quickly. "All he said to me was that, if I could, I had to tell you goodbye. He said his mission was complete and it was because of you, and all the members of the Darquesse Society. He said he couldn't have done it without you and that this, all this, it's because of you and your support and your friendship."

Bennet looked at him, his eyes filling with tears. "He's gone?"

"I think so, yes."

"Did he say where?"

"He didn't."

"Do you know where? Do you know anything about him?"

"I'm afraid not," Omen lied. "I just met him that one time and he, he just wanted me to, he needed me to make you understand how much your friendship meant to him." Omen's voice cracked a little when he said that.

Bennet watched him, and then he smiled slowly. "You're older than you're supposed to be, aren't you?"

"I am, yeah. I've heard of a few other people having the same issue. I think Darquesse got some details wrong, and there are a bunch of us who are a little older."

"That's interesting," said Bennet. "I hadn't heard that."

"Yeah. It's a thing."

"I'll take your word for it. You're, what, a little under three years older than you should be? That's definitely interesting. See, I only knew Sebastian for a little under three years. Never saw his face, of course, or heard his voice without that mask. So, hey, I know that a lot can happen in a little under three years. A lot of important things."

"I suppose so."

"If he were here, you know what I'd say to him? I'd tell him that his friendship meant a lot to me, too. It got me through a very rough patch. Just when everything was falling apart around me, he arrived and not only gave me purpose, but... he made my life better. I totally understand if he has to leave. I get that he had a mission and it must have been so secret and important, but I would just need him to understand how much of a good friend he was to me."

Omen nodded, and tried not to cry, and Bennet stuck out his hand and they shook again.

"Have a good life, Omen."

"You too, Bennet."

Omen turned, walked over to his family and his girlfriend. As he walked, he looked up and waved, and Skulduggery and Valkyrie, hovering high in the air above the school, waved back.

131

Focused as it was on its feeding, the vampire didn't notice as Temper dropped into the alley behind it. Minutes ago, the corpse beneath its claws had been a person, a being, a living thing bursting with thoughts and feelings and vitality. Now its vitality leaked across the dirty ground.

The vampire turned, its eyes narrowing. It saw Temper standing there and a growl rose in its throat. It didn't know what to make of him, but it treated everything as either prey or a potential meal – usually both.

Temper snarled back, showing it his teeth.

The vampire came for him and Temper's palm opened and what Razzia had liked to call the Parasitic Murder Tentacle shot out, plunged through the vampire's shoulder before retracting. The vampire shrieked and stumbled, then dived at him, but Temper could move even faster than a vampire. The creature crashed against the side of a dumpster and lashed out, finding nothing but air.

Then Temper was beside it, crouching next to it, whispering into its ear as his own claws went to work. He gripped it as it thrashed, feeling the struggles gradually grow weaker. When it was dead, he lifted it and threw it in the dumpster.

"I want you to come home," Kierre of the Unveiled said behind him.

He turned slowly. Not many people could sneak up on him these days. Kierre was one of the very few. She stood there in the dark, though his new eyes could see her clearly. Not many things could take his breath away these days. She was one of the very few.

"I am home," he said.

"New York is not home." Kierre stepped forward. "Your home is with me."

"The old Temper, the human, yes, his home was with you. But I ain't human. Not any more."

"You're in control."

He smiled. "Barely."

"I love you. I can help you."

"No one can help me. I'm the worst parts of the man you knew."

"The worst parts of Temper Fray are still the best parts of anybody else."

He raised his arms and both tentacles shot out of his hands, gripping the walls high above. "Let me go," he said, and lifted into the air.

Kierre watched him go, and followed.

132

They got to their knees on the mat, and Valkyrie hooked one hand round the back of her sister's neck and the other in the crook of her elbow. "You ready?"

"Yes," said Alice, her hands in the same position.

"You sure?"

"Yes."

"You absolutely sure?"

Alice grinned. "Yes."

"You absolutely, positively, resolutely sure?"

Alice giggled, went to answer, and Valkyrie pulled her down into a guillotine choke.

"I thought you said you were ready?" she teased. "*I thought you said you were ready?*"

She felt Alice move and knew what she was going to do to escape and she let it happen, but when her sister tried to scramble away Valkyrie dived on her. Immediately, Alice wrapped her legs around Valkyrie's waist, her legs long enough to cross at the ankles. She was no longer grinning. Now her mouth was a straight line of determination and her eyes were narrowed.

Valkyrie started throwing slaps into her sides, hard enough to be felt, but not so hard to actually hurt. Alice used her elbows to cover up and then suddenly moved, wrapping her arm around Valkyrie's neck and pulling her in tight. She snapped at Valkyrie's ear, growling, and Valkyrie recoiled like she'd been bitten. Alice used the momentum to flip the fight and Valkyrie rolled on to her back with Alice on top and Alice went for an arm-bar. It would have worked against an opponent who didn't know how to capitalise on tiny mistakes, and now Valkyrie was on top again, hands closing round Alice's throat. She tightened her grip and loomed over her.

Raising her hips, Alice tried pushing her back and Valkyrie let it happen. She didn't give it to her easily – Alice had to work for every move, every grip and transition. Suddenly her own shoulder was pressing into her neck and Alice's legs were around her head and the hips came up again and the pressure came on. Against someone her own size, this triangle choke would have been the end of the fight, so after seeking out any weaknesses in the application of technique, Valkyrie let it come on. Blood pounded in her head and she made a weird gurgling sound, and tapped out.

Alice released her immediately and scooted back into a seated position. "Made you gurgle," she said, the grin once again on her face.

Valkyrie smiled and shook her hair out of its ponytail. "Yes, you did. That was good. That was really good."

"Am I the champ?"

After taking a moment to pretend to consider it, Valkyrie got up, took the cheap, battered trophy from the folding table that held their stuff, and presented it to her sister. "I'm winning this back next time."

"Nuh-uh," said Alice, waving the trophy above her head like she was standing on a podium. "I'm getting better every day. I'm the forever champ. All shall bow down before me!"

Valkyrie laughed. "And where on earth did you hear that phrase?"

"She heard it from you," Militsa said, standing in the doorway. "You have a habit of shouting it out whenever you win."

"Which isn't very often," said Alice.

They laughed, and Valkyrie scowled. "I don't like this. You shouldn't be ganging up against me. It isn't fair."

Militsa winked at Alice. "Sore loser, that's what she is. OK, the pair of you hit the shower. We're leaving in fifteen minutes."

They showered and dressed and went downstairs, where Xena was lying on her back, tail wagging, and tongue hanging out of her goofy mouth.

"You're so weird," Valkyrie said to her as she passed, but Alice couldn't resist dropping down for a cuddle. That made the dog go nuts, and within seconds Alice was lying on the floor, laughing uncontrollably with her arms covering her head while Xena bounded round her, licking her ears and trying to get at her face.

"I should just let you grapple with the dog," Valkyrie called as she walked to the kitchen, where Militsa was finishing off a cup of coffee.

"Ooh," said Valkyrie, "did you make me one?"

"I did not," Militsa responded. "You have enough adventure in your life without adding unexpected jolts of caffeine to your system." She ran the empty cup under the tap, watching Valkyrie as she put on her jacket. "Have your folks made a decision?"

"I don't know. Didn't get a chance to speak to them."

"What do you think they should do?"

Valkyrie took a few steps and turned, leaning one shoulder against the doorframe. "I don't know," she said. "A few years ago, I would have been against it. Let her have a normal life, you know? That's why I was doing what I was doing, after all – to make sure the people I love were protected. But I don't know any more. I don't know if that's the smartest thing for Alice. Not in the long run."

"What's the smartest thing for me?" Alice asked, following Xena past Valkyrie.

Militsa smiled at her. "We're just talking about your training. How's the magic coming along?"

Alice clicked her fingers an[d]
She poured more energy into
and then she covered her hai
them both over her head. She c
either side, forming a brief arc
attached to the fridge by magn[e]

"Oops," she said.

"Stop showing off," Valkyrie
extinguishing the fire.

"Sorry. Was it important?"

"The postcard?" said Militsa, t
off the fridge. "No, not really. It 〈 ... 〉 ιαsτ postcard that
my parents sent to me before they died."

Alice gasped.

"Sorry," Militsa said, "did I say died? I meant had lunch.
They're on holiday in Bermuda."

Alice put both hands over her heart and laughed. "I felt so bad!"

"Aw!" cried Militsa, hurrying forward to hug her. "I'm sorry,
sweetie! It was a mean joke!"

While they hugged, Valkyrie made sure there was water in the
dog bowl, and then she locked up and they got in the car. When
they arrived in Haggard, her mother was bringing the groceries
in from the car. Militsa waved and Valkyrie got out with Alice.

"How was it?" Melissa asked, and Alice brandished the trophy.
"Ah! The champion, once again!" She handed her a bag. "Here,
bring this inside."

Alice whirled, gave Valkyrie a hug. "Thanks for training me!"
she said, then hurried into the house with the bag.

Melissa waited till she was out of earshot. "I know you're
expecting an answer."

Valkyrie smiled. "Don't worry about it. There's really no rush.
She has another two years of primary school and there'll always
be a place for her at Corrival Academy – China will make sure
of it."

s the best thing for her."

don't know, either. Now I know how you
d out. All I want to do is wrap her in cotton
ct her. At the same time, hey, look what I'm doing.
g her to fight and use magic."

that's necessary," Melissa said. "She'll probably need to
how to defend herself sooner or later. She's already been
rough so much. I'd love if her life was quiet and normal from
this moment on, but I highly doubt that'll happen. But even so
– having you train her is different from sending her to a school
of magic. I might be wrong, but I'm of the opinion that once
you send your child to a school of magic, you're basically signing
them up to a lifetime of adventure. Right?"

"I can't argue with that."

"And adventure means danger. And danger means trauma."

"They do tend to go hand in hand."

"I just don't know."

"You don't have to make any kind of decision yet. If she
goes to a regular secondary school and you decide, when she's,
like, fifteen, that she should be in Corrival, China will take her
in without hesitation. By then, there'll be day pupils, too, if you
don't want her to board. Corrival is changing."

Melissa closed the boot of the car. "Have you asked Alice what
she thinks?"

"No," said Valkyrie. "I'm almost scared to. She'll say that she
wants to go, because she loves magic and she loves combat and
she's, I have to say, really good at both."

Desmond came out of the house. "What are you two talking
about?" he asked. "Planning my fiftieth birthday party, are you?"

Valkyrie frowned. "No."

"Ah, but that's exactly what you would say if you were going to
make it a surprise party, so forgive me if I don't quite believe you."

"We're talking about Corrival. I was just pointing out to Mum
that you don't have to rush into a decision."

"Right," he said. "Yeah. Good. But she has to go, though, doesn't she?"

"Why does she have to go?" Melissa asked, frowning.

"Because of friends," he said. "You meet people and make friends in school and if you're lucky some of them will stay with you your whole life. She's learning magic, and she's going to be using magic, even if she decides to live a perfectly normal existence. Let's face it, you're not going to *be* magic and *know* magic and not *use* magic, right? So she'll be this otherwise normal person living in this normal, mortal world, but she's not going to age. And her friends will age, and her husband or wife will age, and her kids will age, and she'll be left alone." He shrugged. "So she'll have to surround herself with people like her. Magic people."

"Surrounding herself with magic people will automatically put her life in danger," said Melissa.

He nodded. "And that's why Steph is training her, right? To give her the best possible chance to come out on top?"

"I mean," said Valkyrie, "I suppose..."

"Then I don't get what there is to discuss."

"I thought we were thinking it over," Melissa said. "Is that not what we've been doing for the past few days?"

"I thought we were taking the time to get used to the idea."

Valkyrie's mum blinked at him. "I suppose we were, actually."

She seemed suddenly sad about it, and Desmond smiled and hugged her.

"Hey," he said softly, "she's going to be OK. We want to protect her and keep her safe, but in this crazy world – and I do mean crazy world – that doesn't mean what it used to. It doesn't mean keeping our child away from danger – it means preparing her for it. She has the best big sister, who will train her, who will give her every tool and weapon she's going to need. She'll be going to the best magical school in all the land, where they'll teach her stuff that you and I could never even dream about. Steph, what are some of the classes they teach in that place?"

"English," Valkyrie said.

"Apart from English."

"Maths. Geography."

"Apart from normal stuff, Stephanie."

"Oh. Combat. Teleportation. Energy Throwing. Invisibility. They teach you how to forge mortal documents."

"They do?"

"It's kind of a necessity for people who have to reinvent themselves every few decades."

"That's so cool," said Desmond. "Do they do adult classes?"

"No."

He took a moment to reflect on how unfair life was, and then returned his attention to Melissa.

"This is the world we live in. We have to give Alice the best chance to be the best version of who she can be. My God, Melissa, think about the life she's got ahead of her. Think about the mysteries that are going to unfold purely because she's going to live for so long. Think of what she'll learn about herself, about humanity. All the things she'll discover. She's going to be so happy. She'll be sad, as well, absolutely, and I'm not pretending it's all going to be fun and exciting. But think about it from her point of view. Think about what she's got in store."

He shook his head. "I envy our daughter so much right now, and I am thrilled that she's going to embark on a life we'll never fully understand. It's not our place to understand it, sweetheart."

"Stop," Melissa said, wiping her eyes. "You're making me cry."

He smiled, and kissed her forehead. "I can be pretty wise when I have to be."

"Yes," she said, "you can. If only you were wearing trousers."

He looked down at his Y-fronts and made a dismayed sound, and hurried back inside.

"I have to go," Valkyrie said, and gave her mum a hug. "Please don't let him out of the house unsupervised."

"Oh, God," Melissa responded, "those are the exact words his mother told me the day we got married."

Valkyrie and Militsa drove to Roarhaven. Evening prayers were about to start in the Dark Cathedral and a steady stream of worshippers was filing in. The Plague Doctors shook their hands as they passed, bestowing the blessings of Darquesse upon them. Some of the worshippers saw Valkyrie's car and waved. She pretended not to notice.

School was done for the summer, but Militsa's research work continued, so Valkyrie dropped her off at Corrival and drove back towards the High Sanctuary, taking the ramp down to where Skulduggery was running a cloth over the bonnet of the Bentley. She parked beside him and they rode the tiles up into the foyer.

Tanith saw them, indicated that they wait, and when she'd finished issuing orders to a pair of Cleavers she came over. She'd altered her uniform yet again, moving it closer to a grey version of the brown leather she used to wear.

"Is that allowed?" Valkyrie asked, casting a glance at the ensemble.

"It is if I say it is," Tanith answered, walking beside them. "I heard about Ottman. What was he – Order of the Ancients? Soldiers of Magic?"

"Something new," Skulduggery said. "Something potentially worrying."

Tanith nodded. "I'll have my people look into his background, see who he spent his time with. Thanks, by the way. This could have been a bad one. You sure I can't tempt you to come back full time?"

Valkyrie smiled. "We're happy being Arbiters, thank you very much. It means we can keep an eye on everyone who needs keeping an eye on."

"Whoa – was that a not-subtle-at-all warning? We're your friends, remember?"

"And, so long as you don't step out of line, our friends you'll remain."

Tanith raised an eyebrow. "Valkyrie Cain – I'm almost offended. As if we'd step out of line. As if we'd be allowed, even if we wanted to. Are you forgetting who our Grand Mage is? Are you forgetting that he handed power back to the Sanctuaries? We're the good guys here."

Valkyrie smiled wider. "I'm not forgetting any of that, don't you worry – but people in power need to be checked. Even the good guys."

Tanith grunted, but did so in an amused fashion. "When did sweet little Valkyrie Cain get so cynical, eh? Your suspect's in holding cell eight. The Sensitives are waiting for you to talk to him before they have a go. Oh. Have you heard?"

"Have we heard what?" Skulduggery asked.

"Crepuscular's escaped. He got out sometime last night."

Valkyrie frowned. "How did he manage that? The guards check on him every hour."

"And every hour they confirmed that he was in his cell, sleeping or reading, his head down. Only it wasn't him. He'd managed to sneak in one of the kitchen staff to take his place."

"He could be anywhere by now," said Valkyrie. "Doing anything. See, this is why he should be in Coldheart. He wouldn't escape from Coldheart."

"We're not keeping Crepuscular Vies and Cadaver Cain in the same prison," said Skulduggery. "Besides, we know where he'll be."

"He's not going to go back."

"Of course he is. His siblings are being rehabilitated. He won't be able to stay away for long."

"The Cleavers have already been alerted," Tanith said. "When he turns up, we'll know about it." Then Cerise was beside her, demanding her attention, and Tanith barely had time to wave before she was gone.

Valkyrie walked on beside Skulduggery. "You seem awfully relaxed about an extraordinarily dangerous man – who hates you with an unending passion – being on the loose. Maybe feeling a little proud, are we, that your talented grandson has escaped prison yet again?"

Skulduggery shrugged. "He can't help it if genius runs in the family."

133

Palomino Ottman sat in holding cell eight, his wrists in shackles. He looked pale, his left eye was almost swollen shut, and his shoulders were slumped in defeat, though he tried to square them when Valkyrie and Skulduggery walked in. They sat on the other side of the table.

"How's the eye?" Valkyrie asked.

He didn't answer.

"You may as well co-operate," said Skulduggery. "We checked up on you, Palomino. You're not strong enough to withstand our Sensitives."

"The least I can do is try," he said, his voice quiet.

"You don't want to do that," said Valkyrie. "You don't want the headache that follows, or the nosebleeds. Talk to us, instead. Just fill in the gaps in what we know, give us some names, and we'll see what we can do about reducing your sentence. You're facing a long time in prison, Palomino. An attempted terrorist attack, on mortals? A bomb that would have taken, what, half a dozen lives? We're talking decades in a cell. We can halve that right now, right here, if you co-operate."

"You think I care what happens to me?" asked Ottman. "This isn't right. You shouldn't even be trying to stop us – you should be working with us. We know what the mortals will do if they ever find out about magic – we've seen it. We've lived it. You think it makes the slightest bit of difference that Martin Flanery is no longer president? You think the new president's gonna be different? If they find out we exist, we know what they'll do."

"Key word here being *if*," said Valkyrie. "Right now, you're trying to take revenge for something that hasn't even happened."

"But it will," Ottman said. "One of these days, one of them will put it all together. The sightings, the stories, the unexplained occurrences – it's already out there, just waiting to be linked. Or one of those videos that the Sanctuaries always manage to find and get rid of just in time... They'll miss one, and it'll be all over social media, all over the internet, all over the news... then what will you do?"

"We'll deal with it," Skulduggery said.

"No," said Ottman, almost laughing. "No. We can't wait for you to deal with it. We have to be pre-emptive. Our survival is at stake."

"We're not going to let your friends kill innocent mortals," Valkyrie said.

"They're not innocent. Not one of them is innocent. You saw what they did. You saw the hatred in their eyes. They killed sorcerers. They hanged them. They burned them alive."

"None of that happened."

"It did, though!" Ottman shouted. "It did! Just because Darquesse reset reality doesn't mean we don't remember! She altered the mortals' memories and repaired the damage and brought back the dead, and she did some other stuff, too, right? I heard you got your car back. How nice for you. How lovely. But you know what she didn't do? She didn't erase *our* memories. My daughter was one of the mages they burned at the stake. She remembers that. She remembers how it felt, to die like that."

He shook his head. "We're not going to let that happen again. We don't have another Darquesse to click her fingers and make everything all right. The next time they burn my daughter to death, she'll stay burnt to death. Unless we act now."

Skulduggery glanced at Valkyrie, and they stood. "We're on our way to see the Grand Mage, where we'll be recommending a sentence. If you won't co-operate, we can't be lenient."

"It doesn't matter what happens to me," Ottman said. "I'm part of something bigger. You think we came back happy? No. We came back angry and afraid, and there are more like me out there. There are so many of us out there. You have no idea."

They left the holding cell and Skulduggery spoke to the Sensitives. Valkyrie kept walking, eager to leave the area before they started work. Being in the vicinity of a psychic interrogation always gave her a headache.

Skulduggery joined her and they rode the elevator up.

"Are you feeling OK?" he asked.

Valkyrie hesitated. "What if he's right? We now know exactly how the mortal world will react if they ever find out about us. It's no longer a theoretical exercise. We've seen what they'll do."

"Are you saying the Hosts had the right idea? That we should dismantle mortal civilisation?"

She laughed. "No. No, I'm not. At all. I much prefer mortals running the world to sorcerers running it, and I don't want to see that change. But the focus of the Sanctuaries has always been *protect the mortals from the sorcerers*. Maybe we should expand it. Maybe the focus should now also be *protect the sorcerers from the mortals*."

"That's a dangerous path."

"Is it? It probably is. I don't know."

"It's a dangerous path for the Sanctuaries to go down," Skulduggery said, "but I think you're right. I think it's something we should keep an eye on." He looked at his reflection in the elevator doors, and adjusted his tie. "I notice you haven't complimented me on my suit yet."

Valkyrie had to smile. "It's new, is it? It's really nice."

"Nice?"

"Exquisite."

"That's better."

The doors opened and they stepped out. Cerise walked by, saw them, indicated that they go into the Grand Mage's office.

"She's everywhere at once, that girl," Valkyrie said.

"It's a busy time," Skulduggery responded. "Lots done. Lots more to do."

The doors opened. When they walked in, the Grand Mage looked up from the report he was reading, and Valkyrie smiled.

"Hi, Ghastly," she said.

SKULDUGGERY PLEASANT
WILL RETURN